Praise for *What Casanova Told Me*

"Utterly seductive. . . . In its inventive range, its playful engagement and tantalizing mystery, *What Casanova Told Me* is breathtaking, a tour de force." —*The Globe and Mail*

"Swan invites the reader to become a surrogate traveller. She has a marvellous ability to take ordinary characters out of their ordinary places. There's a dream-like quality to the prose. Her depiction of a troubled young woman on the cusp of self-hood is powerful."
—*The Gazette* (Montreal)

"Swan is no miniaturist. She wants to write stories that are like sprawling castles in which every room is different. Her novels adamantly celebrate the epic, her canvas the wide world's sweep. Her characters embark on odysseys, voyages of discovery that lead to dramatic adventures."
—*Calgary Herald*

"The beauty and elegance of [Casanova's] language, written and spoken—or rather of Swan's rendering of his correspondence and their conversations—is striking. . . . Swan . . . [demonstrates] how matters of the heart may be considerably altered in the process of making journeys." —*Books In Canada*

"Part travelogue, part bodice-ripper, there is something both titillating and fantastical about this type of historical fiction, and Swan is adept at spinning facts into vividly imagined scenes and characters." —*Quill & Quire*

"Susan Swan gets all romantic on us in her new novel, *What Casanova Told Me*. But with its historical base and crafty parallel structure, it turns out to be a winner. . . . One of Swan's best."
—*Now* (Toronto)

# What Casanova Told Me

~ *A Novel* ~

# SUSAN SWAN

VINTAGE CANADA

*For Louise Dennys, beloved editor and friend*

VINTAGE CANADA EDITION, 2005

Published in Canada by Vintage Canada, a division of Random House of
Canada Limited, Toronto, in 2005. Originally published in hardcover in Canada
by Alfred A. Knopf Canada, a division of Random House of Canada Limited,
Toronto, in 2004. Distributed by Random House of Canada Limited, Toronto.

Vintage Canada and colophon are registered trademarks of
Random House of Canada Limited.

www.randomhouse.ca

Library and Archives Canada Cataloguing in Publication

Swan, Susan
What Casanova told me : a novel / Susan Swan.

ISBN 0-676-97577-1

I. Title.

PS8587.W345W43 2005     C813'.54     C2004-906981-0

The quotation on page 206 is from *Sheep's Vigil by a Fervent Person*
by Erin Moure, published by the House of Anansi Press.

Text design and map: CS Richardson

Printed and bound in Canada

2  4  6  8  9  7  5  3  1

When a writer calls his work a Romance, it need hardly be observed that he wishes to claim a certain latitude, both as to its fashion and material, which he would not have felt himself entitled to assume, had he professed to be writing a Novel. The latter form of composition is presumed to aim at a very minute fidelity, not merely to the possible, but to the probable and ordinary course of man's experience. The former—while as a work of art, it must rigidly subject itself to laws, and while it sins unpardonably so far as it may swerve aside from the truth of the human heart—has fairly a right to present that truth under circumstances, to a great extent, of the writer's own choosing or creation. . . . The point of view in which this tale comes under the Romantic definition lies in the attempt to connect a bygone time with the very present that is flitting away from us.

NATHANIEL HAWTHORNE
Preface to *The House of the Seven Gables*

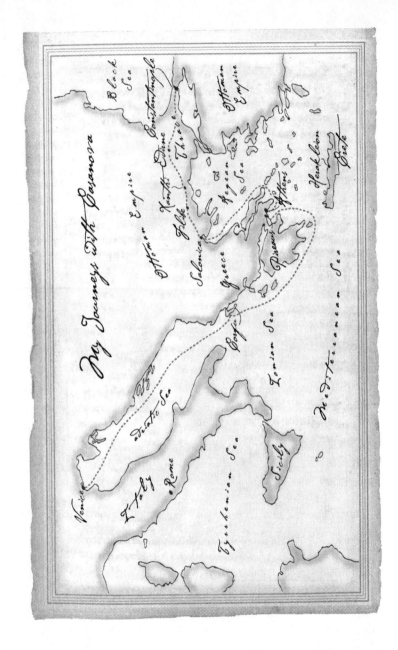

My Journeys with Casanova

Black Sea

Constantinople

Ottoman Empire

Ottoman Empire

Youths Drine

Three

Aegean Sea

Heraklion

Crete

Salonica

Athens

Greece

Piraeus

Corfu

Ionian Sea

Adriatic Sea

Mediterranean Sea

Venice

Italy

Rome

Tyrrhenian Sea

Sicily

Pusey Library, Harvard Yard
Cambridge, MA 02138

April 29, 2000

Luce Adams,
291 Brunswick Avenue,
Toronto, Ontario, M5S 2M2

Dear Miss Adams:

As instructed by your aunt, Beatrice Adams, I am returning the family documents found in the St. Lawrence cottage, along with my comments on their authenticity.

The journal of Asked For Adams, with its lined pages and red-ribbed trim, displays features commonly found in late eighteenth-century diaries. Its most notable characteristic is the title embossed in gold leaf, which mentions your ancestor's travels with Casanova. In the absence of a watermark it is difficult to confirm a date, but the journal looks to be a colonial product, perhaps manufactured in an East Coast American paper mill before the cheaper method of using acid to break down wood pulp was discovered.

I'm afraid I wasn't able to decode the Arabic manuscript with the interesting designs incised on its leather cover, nor do I have any idea why something so curious was found in the same box with your family documents. Perhaps some linking documents were misplaced or destroyed. However, I can say with some certainty that the paper used in the manuscript with Arabic writing has been treated with *aher*, a sizing material made from egg white and rice flour.

I had better luck with the letters found with the eighteenth-century journal. The 1795 Fabriano watermark and the signature, Giacomo Casanova de Seingalt, appear to be authentic. In addition, the frequent slips in syntax suggest that the letter writer was someone who used French and Italian as promiscuously as Casanova is known to have done.

Remarkably, most of his letters are in fairly good condition and eminently readable. Eighteenth-century letter writers wrote in a prose more akin to modern English than the fussy, over-descriptive language used by the Victorians. The Sansovinian Library in Venice will be delighted to have them on loan.

In closing, please note that I have included a photocopy of the old documents so that your family can read them without fear of damaging the paper.

I suspect your ancestor's journal will be of general historical interest but it is the letters by Casanova that considerably increase the financial value of these documents.

Sincerely,
Charles Smith

*what Casanova told me*

PART ONE

*The City of Longings*

W rapped tightly in a pink plastic raincoat, the box of old documents lay snug in the bow of the *motoscafo*. Luce Adams sat huddled nearby, peering out the window of the cabin at the domes of San Marco rising up through the fine, slanting rain. In the next seat, an older woman in a dove-grey Borsalino was snoring, her head rolling with the swells. A young man sat in the stern, fiddling with an enormous telephoto lens.

As the *motoscafo* pulled up alongside the Molo, the boatman spoke rapidly in Italian, pointing at the square where hundreds of empty benches stood waiting, as if in preparation for a celebration.

"*Scusa*, signora."

The young man entered the cabin and bent to touch the shoulder of the middle-aged woman. She recoiled, pushing back the brim of her hat to see who had disturbed her sleep.

"The boatman wants to be paid."

He rubbed together his thumb and forefinger, his eyes turning to Luce as she stooped to retrieve the box near her feet. Glancing at the rain outside, Luce opened her travel pack and carefully placed the box inside and fastened the clasp. The older woman left the cabin and gave the boatman his lire, and, smiling and gesturing, he began to heave their suitcases onto the dock.

Just as the two women stepped onto the Piazzetta, where a cat was chasing pigeons across the stones, the sun rose in the east, lighting the sky of rainclouds beyond San Giorgio Maggiore a muddy pink. They stood staring at the sea streaming like grey-green banners beneath the medieval churches and *palazzos*. The misty rain still fell and from the faraway Lido came the faint, doleful boom of waves. Across the Piazzetta, Luce noticed the young photographer pointing his camera at the Basin of San Marco. She turned and saw half a dozen small boats slipping like water bugs out of the fog: in the light skiffs, rowers in sleeveless jerseys bent over their oars.

"This way!" Lee Pronski called, and Luce followed her companion across the square that Napoleon had once called the largest living room in Europe. Luce walked with a slight forward stoop, pulling the cart stacked from stem to gudgeon with their luggage.

After several minutes of walking down side streets, Lee stopped by a small Venetian bridge and stared into the window of an antiquarian bookstore. Its door stood open even though it was early for Venice, and the *vaporetti* chugging by on the canal looked largely empty. With a yelp of excitement, Lee disappeared inside. Dragging the luggage cart behind her, Luce walked over to see what had claimed her interest. The window of the shop was draped with a regatta poster proclaiming *Vogalonga, Venezia 14 maggio*. Below the poster, Catholic reliquaries were displayed alongside a pile of ancient books in Italian whose titles she couldn't understand. Next to the books stood several diminutive figurines.

She peered closer. The Venus of Willendorf. There was no mistaking the huge, swollen stomach bulging over a tiny pubis, or the featureless face hidden beneath a bumpy top-knot. But she had never seen the ugly figure with two beaky faces standing next to the Venus. From inside the shop, she heard her name being called. She parked the cart by the door and stepped inside just as the woman shopkeeper was explaining to Lee that these figures were thousands of years old.

"Well, no. These are only copies of prehistoric artifacts." Lee picked up the double-headed icon and licked it, causing the shopkeeper and Luce to exchange startled glances. "Pure sandstone," Lee nodded.

"Another fertility goddess," Luce sighed.

"They're much more than that!" Lee paid the clerk. "Here, Luce. I'd like you to have it. See the wavy bands across its chest? The chevrons indicate her metaphysical powers."

"Your mother is knowledgeable," the clerk said, smiling at Luce.

She's not my mother, Luce wanted to reply. My mother is dead. She stuffed Lee's gift into her enormous knapsack and they set off again through the narrow streets.

At the Hotel Flora, the bellhop greeted the women with a sympathetic smile, his eyes resting on Luce in her rain-soaked jacket.

"A bit of weather never hurt anyone." Lee waved at the terrace where a waiter was setting the tables with bowls of croissants. "Luce, why don't you change out of your wet things and meet me for breakfast?"

"I'm not hungry," Luce mumbled.

"What did you say?"

"I think I'll go to bed." Luce bowed her head and started up the stairs after the bellhop, now bent double under the weight of her travel pack.

"I see. Well, sleep all day if you like," Lee called out after her. "I'll leave instructions at the desk on where to meet for dinner."

Luce offered her mother's lover a barely perceptible nod.

As she stepped through the door, the light in her hotel room seemed to dim. She heard the beating of wings.

"*Piccioni!*" The bellhop mimed the gesture of eating and pointed at the dozens of puffy grey birds settling back along the eaves. "They saved Venice in the plagues."

As the door closed behind him, Luce peeled off her wet sweater. Then she opened her travel pack and removed her raincoat from around the box to see if any moisture had leaked through. The box was made of translucent plastic with the cloudy sheen of a shower curtain. She was impressed by the care Charles Smith had taken with the documents. The box was the latest thing in archival materials, only two and a half inches thick, or "slim size," the best for hand-carrying documents. As an extra precaution, he had wrapped it in twine in case the tabs came unfastened.

Luce snipped the twine with her nail scissors and nervously stripped away the layering of acid-free tissue, exposing a photocopy of the documents, an old red-ribbed journal, an ornate leatherbound Arabic manuscript and a sheaf of letters.

It's all dry, she thought. Thank goodness. Casanova's letters lay next to the old journal, bound with a faded rose-coloured ribbon. She examined the letters first, untying the ribbon with her long skilful fingers. The staff at the Sansovinian would be pleased: not a drop of twenty-first-century moisture marred the paper bearing the Fabriano watermark.

There had been a great deal of disbelief and amusement in Luce's family after the letters were authenticated by Harvard's eighteenth-century-manuscript expert, Charles Smith. Holding the letters under the light on the bedside table, she saw that the pages glittered slightly, and she realized sand had been sprinkled across the paper—perhaps to dry the gold ink. Casanova had used a darker ink in his later letters and some of their pages were frail and lacy, as if the ink had eaten through the paper. No doubt this was what Charles Smith had meant when he said Casanova's letters were in "fairly good condition." She longed to read the letters, but their fragile condition made her hesitate. What if she tore one by mistake and lessened its value? Better to read the photocopy that Charles Smith had provided, though it didn't hold the same glamour.

The family documents made up a *fonds d'archives*—the archival term for an assortment of papers generated by one person in a lifetime. Although most people would be satisfied with calling the documents a collection, Luce's training as an archivist had taught her to use the proper term, and she still enjoyed rolling the words around in her mouth.

The *fonds* appeared to belong to Asked For Adams, who bore a Puritan name of the sort usually bestowed on boys. She was Luce's great-great-great-great-great aunt to be precise, and so not, strictly speaking, her "ancestor," but that was how Luce always thought of her. After all, they were both Adamses. According to the Adams family Bible, Asked For Adams had vanished in Venice one spring evening during the eighteenth century and was presumed dead, possibly the victim of Napoleon's soldiers.

No one knew how Asked For's papers had come to be in the attic of the old Adams cottage on the south shore of the St. Lawrence. After the death of Luce's mother two years before, her aunt Beatrice had found the papers buried under other old documents, mostly letters from forgotten family members. The attic itself was a mess of detritus from generations of Adamses—Japanese temple bronzes, prints, embroidered oriental hangings, Turkey carpets (as they were then called) and military swords. It was assumed the documents had been brought to Canada over a hundred and fifty years before by Aaron Adams, a temperance reformer who lost touch with the Boston branch of his family after he walked north by foot from Albany, New York, looking for a wilderness where the poor weren't ruined by drink.

As the pigeons fluttered outside her window, she put Casanova's letters back in the archival box and removed the thick, red-ribbed journal, smiling at its title: *What Casanova Told Me: My Wanderings with Jacob Casanova through the Mediterranean's Ancient Kingdoms.* The name Asked For Adams appeared on the title page along with a list of places seen, things done—a precursor to the tendency of modern tourists to chalk up destinations like golf scores. The date read 1797.

It wasn't just the wonderful title that made her catch her breath. She noticed a small sketch of a woman in Turkish trousers inserted between the back pages of the journal, and on the frontispiece was a hand-drawn map with a tiny black dotted line marking a journey from Venice to Constantinople. Opposite the frontispiece was an inscription by Asked For Adams and a declaration of her ancestor's travel principles. Flushed with excitement, Luce held the journal so its red-ribbed sides rested evenly on the hotel desk. The documents had arrived only the day before their flight, and she hadn't had the chance to do more than scan a few pages. She began to read.

In my lifetime, I have done many things for a woman born a Yankee in Quincy, Massachusetts. I have saved the life of a Sultan and travelled with Jacob Casanova who taught me there is only one lesson worth learning: Never try to realize the ideal, but find the ideal in the real.

Find the ideal in the real? Now what on earth did her ancestor mean by that, Luce wondered. She turned back to the opening page.

Our longings give rise to faiths (of which there are many) but the best faiths are five and they are also pleasures: (1) the Faith of our Forebears; (2) Love and Sexual Congress, which Jacob Casanova never separated; (3) Literature; (4) Beauty; and (5) Travel. No matter which faith we choose of the thousands that await us, we must practise it with as much reverence, compassion and exuberance as we poor beings possess, because the words of all doctrines will pall in time.

In 1797, when I met Jacob, I did not know I was about to take up Travel, the Fifth Faith, whose principles Jacob so wittily invented and whose precepts I have translated freely from the French to suit my purposes. I was also ignorant enough then to think that Travel stood on its own, not understanding it depends on the other four faiths to be complete.

## JACOB CASANOVA'S TEN PRIMARY
## PRINCIPLES OF TRAVEL:

1. Do not set out in a spirit of acquisition, but go forth in the utmost humility, experiencing the same fervour you feel when choosing a lover, knowing a world of possibilities awaits you.

2. Write down what it is you desire and tear your wish into a dozen pieces. Then fling the scraps into a large body of water. (Any ocean will do.)

3. Travelling is like breathing, so exhale the old, inhale the new and allow your heartbreak to fall away behind you.

4. What you desire always awaits you if you are brave enough to recognize it.

5. Go only where your fancies take you. The path of pleasure and freedom is the best path for the traveller.

6. Arrange easy entrances and exits. Refresh yourself at comfortable lodgings. Then move on to other quarters, and forgive yourself the indulgence of necessary luxuries.

7. If you find a place that suits you, by all means stay. But you will not know the soul of its people until you can speak to them in their own language.

8. Accept others as you do yourself, but see them for who they are.

9. Your journey is not over until you bestow a gift on the lands you have visited, knowing full well that you will never be able to repay half the riches they bestow on you.

10. Go now and at once, taking Jacob Casanova's words to heart: *Un altro mondo è possibile!*

How whimsical of Casanova, she thought wryly. And his tenth principle, from what little she knew of Italian, suggested that Casanova believed he could change his reality like a suit of clothes. She didn't like to travel herself and anyway, she couldn't afford holidays, not on her salary at the Miller Archives and Rare Books. Given the choice, she would rather collapse into a book and let the world come to her. Because no matter what her ancestor said, travel was dangerous. Death lurks in the unknown—the unwanted surprise no traveller is capable of turning to their advantage. Better to burrow in at home and avoid a disaster like the one that had claimed her mother in Greece. If it hadn't been for the nagging worry that she owed it to her mother *and* herself to see the island where Kitty had died, she would never have let Lee pay her way to the memorial service in Crete. And, of course, she had been intrigued when her aunt asked her to deliver the documents to the Sansovinian Library in Venice. It was the first time Aunt Beatrice had taken Luce's archival work seriously, and she was flattered to be offered the role of custodian of the family papers.

She carefully placed the journal back in its archival box, along with the photocopies and the Arabic manuscript. Outside the window, rows of terra cotta roofs steamed in the morning sunlight. It was going to be a sunny day, after all. She could see Lee in the courtyard below helping herself to a breakfast roll.

She closed the curtains and began to unpack the knapsack she'd bought at a local camping store. First: the pendulum kit her mother had given her several Christmases before. Then her cache of books. Along with *The Stones of Venice* and her *Rough Guide to Venice*, she had brought with her some essays on

Casanova, a hardback text, *Casanova: The Man Who Really Loved Women* by Lydia Flem, and a well-thumbed paperback of the first volume of *History of My Life* by Jacob Casanova, describing his Venetian childhood. She'd had to leave the other volumes of his memoirs at home as well as a prized copy of his only novel, *Icosameion*, a surprisingly modern science fiction fantasy about a new human race that lived in the bowels of the earth. Next: the small cloth bag with her mother's makeup, which still retained the scent of her mother's perfume. She stacked her books on the windowsill and started in on her new clothes. Not her usual style, but she had wanted something livelier to buoy her spirits. She hung up the three semi-transparent chiffon blouses and three clingy dresses, and neatly repacked her low-cut spandex tops and the pretty white Malibu pants she'd bought for Greece. On Lee's advice, she'd thrown in a woollen scarf and her favourite jacket with the patchwork of Chinese-coloured silks sewn into its shoulders because Venice was cold in the spring.

Unexpectedly, her fingers closed over the little figure Lee had given her that morning, and she pushed it deeper into her knapsack.

Luce didn't know how long she'd been asleep. She threw on a pair of beaded jeans and her favourite jacket and then lifted her ancestor's travel diary out of its box again. Should she take it with her? Reading the user copy provided by Charles Smith wouldn't feel as personal. Its loose, photocopied pages did not bear the original ink, the impress of a writer's hand. Even though she knew she shouldn't, she couldn't resist. She wrapped the diary up in acid-free tissue from the archival box and placed it inside a small knapsack. At the hotel desk, she picked up the directions Lee had left for her and walked out into the streets of Venice, carrying her ancestor's journal.

It was a little late in the day for her sunglasses but she was near-sighted and needed their prescription lenses to see at a distance. In the square beyond, she noticed a celebration. A figure in red robes and lace was swaying into the basilica, carrying a gold cross the length of a body. The scarlet figure was followed by a large throng of men and women and children singing a Latin hymn. She felt slightly awed, as if she was observing a mysterious anthropological rite. Her aunt Beatrice was the last member of the family to believe in a formal Christian doctrine. She had insisted on taking Luce to Anglican services when Luce was small and proudly shown her the family's ancient copy of *The Optimist's Good Night*. Held together with Scotch tape, her aunt's well-handled little book of cheerful axioms listed over 230 selections, including Lord Byron's recommendation that "to do a man's best is the way to be blest."

There was her mother, of course—but her mother's brand of religion was not what anyone would call Christian. And anyway she suspected that a wilful self-deception lurked inside all religious conviction—a deliberate setting aside of what is true in favour of what the believer needs to be true, like the suspension of disbelief during a film or a play. Still, it's lonely work to be a postmodern skeptic.

Turning her back on the basilica, she followed Lee's directions and found herself at the restaurant Da Raffaele. She walked out to the terrace where tables had been set up along the canal, and saw the young photographer from the water taxi drinking a cappuccino. He was dressed in what looked to Luce like a magician's outfit: an ill-fitting black jacket with flaring lapels and a slight shine to the shoulder seams. His bulky camera rested on the chair beside him. He stood up, grinning, and she shyly turned away, pretending not to see him. "Miss!" he shouted, and as she turned back, flattered by his persistence, a burst of lights flowered behind his head like miniature strokes of lightning—several simultaneous flashes that illuminated his handsome wolfish face. Then a gondola glided by, crowded with Japanese tourists in the act of lowering their cameras. At the bow stood an accordion player and a middle-aged singer dressed in white sneakers and a homely windbreaker. The singer began his version of *"Arrivederci, Roma"* and the tourists clapped like schoolchildren. At the rear of the craft, the gondolier poled on glumly, a red ribbon dangling from his straw hat.

The young photographer wagged his head at her, as if sharing his contempt for mass tourism. Luce nodded gravely and stepped inside the Da Raffaele to find a table away from the sea air. She had at least an hour of reading time before Lee arrived for dinner. She felt slightly ashamed of herself for bringing the old journal to this public place—especially to a restaurant with the possibility of food and wine stains. However, her ancestor's travel journal was in better condition than Casanova's letters and she felt a little freer with some-thing written by a family member. She would make amends by treating it with extra caution.

Cradling its handsome spine, she supported the diary on her lap and opened it to the first entry. Asked For Adams' consistently rounded letters were as economical as the bold italic script of Jacob Casanova was extravagant. Here were no mannered dashes or sweeping flourishes. This was the hand of a Puritan descendant, after all. Broad strokes would be too sensual. She smiled, marvelling at its owner, who had defied her Boston upbringing to travel with a man like Casanova.

She had first read his memoirs for an undergraduate course in eighteenth-century literature. And she hadn't forgotten her professor's description of Casanova as a master of deception. In his lifetime, he'd been a spy, a man of letters, a preacher, a novelist, an alchemist, even the director of a state lottery. There were other professions that she couldn't recall now. Casanova could be counted upon to invent any role for himself that the situation warranted, her professor had said.

What role did he invent for Asked For Adams, she wondered.

April 12, 1797

God Bless our journey! And bring us the boon of good weather!

Last night Father and I came into Venice at sunset in strange company. Father's secretary, Mr. Francis Gooch, accompanied us. Our companions on the public boat, a group of young dandies from Trieste whom Father calls Macaronis, tinkled as they moved, their tight-fitting breeches and damask coats hung with glittering fob chains from which dangled watches, rings and eyeglasses, the source of the delightful little noises. On their heads, the dandies wore powdered wigs in the fashion of the old French court and these full-blown headpieces gave off a stench of pomade oil and starch as they paraded up and down in front of us, demanding that we look at them and not at the beautiful orangeries on the shores of the Brenta.

These human music boxes laughed and whispered to one another each time they gazed at me. I knew it was my great height that had provoked their sniggering smiles but I did my best not to feel put upon.

What I found far more unsettling than the silly Macaronis, what riveted me to such a degree that I could not take my eyes off her, was an enormous old woman in a towering, beribboned wig, garnished with every likeness imaginable from the natural world—strawberries and butterflies, small, stuffed birds—even little wire-framed portraits of what may have been sons or husbands woven into her hair. She sat on a bench a few feet away moaning softly and holding her jaw.

The young man sitting next to her—a chubby, excitable-looking fellow whose ponytail was encased in a silk wig bag—was teasing the old woman, pulling ornaments out of her hair and holding them up for the passengers standing nearby to see. First, a small locket, next an artificial rose-bud, and now a miniature portrait of a sweetly smiling fair-haired girl. The old woman seemed unaware, holding her head and groaning, when suddenly, with a happy cry, the young man plucked something from the curls close to the great dame's ear. Turning to me, he mouthed a foreign word—German, I believe, so I could not understand the joke he was trying to share. Then he thrust the thing he wanted me to see under the old woman's petticoat.

"You beast! Leave Finette alone!" The old dame spoke French in a low, gravelly voice. She began to fuss about her crinoline, and a fuzzy grey snout poked through the lace of its hem. A small, excited fox terrier bounded towards me and pressed itself against my skirt. I patted the little dog and it gazed up at me lovingly. I picked it up and brought it to the old woman and she bent over the dog, smiling: "Ah, she likes you, *ma pauvre!*"

As the old woman caressed her dog the sunlight caught the ornaments on her wig and I saw that it was crawling with beetles. Their veined wings glistened as if the bugs were part of the stupendous adornment she had contrived on her person. I had no time to feel shocked, for at that moment the barge rounded a marshy curve in the Brenta and for the first time Father and I saw the city of Venice, perched like a fairy-tale kingdom on the arc of the horizon. Holding up her little dog so it could see the legendary city, the old dame exhaled such a sigh of longing that I too felt my breathing cease. Then the Brenta curved back on itself, shutting out Venice and leaving us with the silvery glints of river water flowing to the sea.

I excused myself and went off to take my guidebook out of my valise. Before we left Paris, Father had bought me the latest edition of *The Grand Tourist's Guide to the Picturesque Landscapes of Europe* by Sir Thomas Peabody, and *Exile: The Royal Education*, a travel panegyric by an anonymous author who claimed that the exile of Charles II was an unexpected boon for England's young monarch. I preferred Peabody. I turned to the section on the Brenta and was pleased to find the name for the pretty barges on the canal, done up like little houses. On the roofs of these *burchielli*, men and women sat or stood, drinking and chatting, the women carrying little fans and parasols. I overheard one of the Macaronis tell Father the passengers were Venetian nobles sailing to their summer houses to escape General Bonaparte. The French army has invaded Northern Italy and is encouraging peasants and nobles alike to rebel against the Republic of Venice, Father says. But he claims the French are our allies, so we have nothing to fear.

When the public barge stopped for more passengers, Father and I disembarked to stretch our legs, leaving Francis on board. Moments later, near a small palace in the Palladio style, we met the old woman and her young companion. They were sitting on a bench with a group of pilgrims in capes and round hats. One of the pilgrims was mending his clothes. As we approached, the old woman and her friend rose, and I saw she stood almost a head higher than the young man. She looked sleepy now, almost happily so. She held out a large blunt-fingered hand, which I thought odd to see at the end of a lady's wrist, and offered me a quadrant of fruit.

I shook my head, not daring to look at her for fear of the horrible bugs.

"I am Joseph Karl Emmanuel von Waldstein—Count Waldstein," the young man said, bowing. "And this is my aunt, Countess Flora Waldstein. She is feeling much better because the boatman gave her something for her toothache."

"Theriaca." The old dame smiled, uncapping the topper on a small glass vial and taking a lusty swig. "In Venice, we believe in friendly poisons."

They spoke in French and I answered them in that language as they seemed not to know a word of English, and Father speaks French with the slow, clam-chowder tones of a Quincy person.

"Do not apologize, monsieur. It is French, not English that is the universal language," I said, explaining that Father and I were travelling to Venice because my parent was on a trade mission.

"According to my cousin, the President of the United States, my work will profit the Republic of Venice," Father said. "Unless, good sirs, Napoleon gives us a war." Father is a handsome man with a ruddy countenance, a legacy of his life farming apples. But I am afraid he talks loudly so that people will overlook his twisted mouth, the unhappy result of a physical seizure.

"That Corsican bandit!" the old woman exclaimed in her strange, gravelly voice.

"I'm pleased to say, madam, that your Corsican bandit is now fighting valiantly on your northern border and he will crush the medieval tyranny of Austria as easily as I might squash a bug!" Father bayed.

The old woman's lips quivered as if she wished to argue. Count Waldstein shook his head and the Countess stared down at her gold-buckled shoes. They must once have been handsome, but the red leather was now badly worn and the toes unfashionably square.

"Like Venice, our cousin, the President," I spoke the words reprovingly for Father's benefit, ". . . also favours a neutral stance. That is why we are here."

Father glowered at me; he has become an admirer of the young Napoleon whose military success was the talk of Paris.

"So you are here on a trade mission, Monsieur Adams?" Count Waldstein asked, flapping his wrist at the young Macaronis who were strolling our way and staring at our small group with amusement! One of the dandies bowed; the other lifted off his small chapeau with a walking stick and twirled it saucily. I believe the more people stared at us, and the more discomfited we all became, the more Count Waldstein enjoyed himself, because he was now laughing quietly.

"Gentlemen, my daughter speaks up freely," Father replied. "It is because I have allowed her a son's liberties. But yes,

I am here on business matters. My cousin, the President—
ah, look now, Asked For. Here comes your young groom."

Francis came towards us along the river path, lumbering
and gap-toothed and wearing his own hair. He refuses to
powder it and clothes himself in the same dark amber
breeches and wide-brimmed hat as my parent.

"May I introduce my secretary, Mr. Francis Gooch of
Massachusetts. My sturdy country heifer will soon be joined
to this young bull in a bond which no man can put asunder."
Father bowed towards me to show there was no mistake.

"A sturdy heifer, sir?" Countess Waldstein said. "Surely,
that is no way to speak of a woman who is an adornment
to her sex?"

"Are you talking about Asked For?" Father asked.

"Monsieur, will you look at your daughter's eyes?" the
old woman replied. "Are they not as green as the Adriatic
glistening before us? I believe the loveliness of her eyes was
bestowed upon her by Venus, while her lofty stature
ensures no man will dare condescend to a being of such
beauty." The Countess took my hand and squeezed it, and
I was grateful to her for her kindness.

"Aunt Flora—let us say goodbye to these pleasant folk
and return to the boat," Count Waldstein said. "Will you
sup with us in Venice, Monsieur Adams? I have an important personage I would like you to meet."

"I would be honoured, Count Waldstein," Father replied.

Count Waldstein returned his bow, and off they went, his
aunt holding the small glass vial carefully. She had hardly
gone a step when the little fox terrier darted out from under
her skirts and ran yipping down the path. I began to laugh.

Francis scratched his armpit. "Is that a man or a
woman?" he said as we started back towards the boat.

"A woman surely, by all accounts." Father smiled. "I reckon Asked For has met a Brobdingnagian as big as herself."

The old woman was half right about my green eyes. They are plainly my best feature: neither my size (I am too tall by half) nor the shape of My Poor Friend (which is the name I give my physical being) are up to my eyes, although Aunt Abigail once told me I have "an intelligent plainness" as opposed to "a dull-eyed beauty." Aunt Abigail said my intelligence is sure to win the heart of the man who will see me as I am. She told me this was my dead mother's notion of love: the person who truly sees and cherishes you is the person who loves you best.

As for myself, I have no opinion on love. My only experience is with gap-toothed Francis, who does not *see* me or anything else except the size of the livestock on the farms our coach passes and the fields of corn growing here, which he boasts came from the New World's Indians. The Gooch family has been very good to Father and me since Mother passed on, leaving only myself and two brothers who live in Vermont. It was Mother who wanted me named Asked For because she so dearly wanted a female child. After he married, Father asked God for forgiveness, believing his love for Mother overshadowed his reverence for the Lord. "God, teach me to leave behind the affliction which stands in the way of thy Divine love," Father prayed. "I have grown proud and am secretly full of sensuality, delighting more in my dear wife than in loving You." The day I was born Mother died— despite Father's best efforts not to prefer her to his Creator.

Towards sunset we entered the Adriatic Sea and gondoliers swarmed around our barge, calling out offers of rides and lodgings in Venice. The pilgrims pushed past us onto

the cheapest boats, leaving us the costly gondolas with
wood-covered cabins. Father went with Count Waldstein
while Francis and I followed his aunt off the barge into a
sturdy black craft manned by two gondoliers. I noticed the
elderly lady studying me as they poled us towards the distant domes of Venice. I smiled politely, as if Francis were
not pushing his heavy thigh against me, and tried to make
lively conversation about the beauty of the soft rose light
spilling across the lagoon.

When we docked by San Marco, Father, who does not
favour sea journeys, walked dizzily from his gondola.
Politely ignoring Father's distress, Count Waldstein indicated the Ducal Palace and asked, laughing, whether I had
heard of the infamous rake and lover of women, Jacob
Casanova de Seingalt, who was once imprisoned there.
When I said no, the Count explained that this man
Casanova, as he called him, had made a daring escape
from its gaol in 1759, using a piece of granite to break
through the lead roof. Casanova, the Count said, had
managed to persuade another prisoner, a priest, to go with
him. Twenty years later, Count Waldstein added,
Casanova came back to Venice, only to be banished again.
And now Casanova was obliged to make a living entertaining European society with the tale of his escape.

His aunt gave the Count a forbidding stare, which
made me curious to learn more about this adventurer.

"Why was Monsieur Casanova put in prison?" I asked.

"The Inquisitors considered him a threat to the
Republic," Count Waldstein said.

Meanwhile, Father had recovered his equilibrium and was
announcing to anyone who would listen that the Basilica
of San Marco was an example of "the barbarous Gothick."

As I turned towards him, Father bellowed at me, "Asked For, Venice is a stinking sewer, fit only for beavers!"

I looked away in mortification, and the Countess took my hand and whispered, "Miss Adams, you, like me, are a prisoner of your circumstances. We must do what we can—unbeknownst to the others—to set each other free."

I stood like a silly gawnicus and let the old woman crush me to her flat-bosomed body. She gave off the delicate scent of rosewater and soap, unlike the gamey smell of Francis. I glanced at Father to see if he had overheard but even he, by now, was absorbed in the sights of Venice.

First Inquiry of the Day: Why did the Creator permit Father's face to be frozen on the left side? I know Father suffered a blow to the heart last autumn. But it seems to me there is a second reason. Since Mother's death, Father has been half a man with a half face and I am his daughter, whole and entire in her large parts.

Second Inquiry of the Day: Why do I have to marry Francis who is five years younger than I and ignorant of everything beautiful and grand? Who reads practical books like *The Farmer's Almanac* and shuns anything lively and bold such as Voltaire's *Candide*? Who deplores the French and the happy months I spent in Paris as Father's hostess? And why should Father tell one and all that Venice is a filthy place, suitable for beavers?

Lesson Learned: It is my task to cherish my aging parent even though Father is not the source of bountiful love my soul wishes him to be. He is a Human Creature who must be cherished.

Luce felt touched by Asked For's desire to cherish her aggravating father as a "Human Creature." From the west came the harmonies of string quartets, and somewhere closer to the Da Raffaele, the tolling of a bell. It struck Luce that these sounds had been heard in Venice for hundreds of years. Perhaps string quartets were playing when Asked For Adams had landed at the Molo with her father and Francis Gooch.

She turned back to the passage with Count Waldstein's description of Casanova's escape from the Leads. She was sure he had escaped in 1756, not 1759, and returned in 1774 to Venice, eighteen years later, not twenty years later as Count Waldstein had told Asked For Adams. But she would double-check his dates; no account should be wholly trusted. When her aunt had told her about the journal, Luce had made it her business to research the man and his times.

Proud to be chosen as the guardian of Casanova's letters, she had spent hours at the Miller poring over old texts about Casanova that she had retrieved through the interlibrary loan service. She had also joined an Internet group called the Society of Casanovistes and attended a talk about eighteenth-century Venice. She had liked the French psychologist Lydia Flem who had told the smirking audience that Casanova believed that the women he loved had the same rights to sexual enjoyment, public accomplishment and respect for their intelligence as he enjoyed himself.

At Flem's talk, she had also discovered that Casanova had been imprisoned for the offence of owning books written by Freemasons. The Republic had charged him on the pretext that these books proved he dabbled in the occult when the truth was the independent views of the Freemasons were believed to threaten the Catholic religion.

Luce noticed the restaurant filling with customers and wondered if the young photographer was still on the terrace. She put on her sunglasses and, yes, there he was four tables away, taking a picture of a woman with a child. As he looked up, he saw Luce watching him and gave her an ironic smile. She quickly took off her sunglasses. Flustered, she lowered her eyes back to the journal.


Good Friday, April 17, 1797

May I be forgiven my unkind words about Father.

Tonight I met Philippe de la Haye, the brother of Countess Waldstein, in the Cafe Florian, situated on the great Piazza San Marco. He is tall like his sister, and like her he wears clothes long out of fashion: striped gold-and-white stockings and a faded jacket of corn-coloured satin. I saw patches on his breeches, the seams of which are cleverly hidden beneath ivory-coloured braiding. Monsieur de la Haye also sported a chestnut tie wig, and in the crook of his arm he carried a bamboo walking stick with tassels that jiggled as he moved. Several café-goers stared curiously in his direction, but most of the crowd at the Florian was too engrossed in talk about General Bonaparte to notice him. Father learned this morning that General Junot, a French officer, is in Venice to see the Doge, demanding money to finance General Bonaparte's war against Austria.

Monsieur de la Haye arrived with Count Waldstein and a man named Guido Pozzo, who wants to sell Father sketches from a collection called the Paper Museum. Bowing deeply in the style of the old French court, Monsieur de la Haye asked if I liked Venice.

"Very much," I replied. "Despite the fear of an invasion by General Bonaparte, I nevertheless feel enveloped in an atmosphere of safety."

Father and Monsieur Pozzo turned to listen.

"You feel safe in Venice?" Monsieur de la Haye asked.

"Even from the perils of time." I paused, pretending not to see Father wiggling his eyebrows at me. "In Venice, one does not age, one floats."

The two gentlemen brayed with pleasure, and Father grunted. "Thank you, child. Now Mr. Pozzo and I have important matters to discuss."

From a small leather bag, Monsieur Pozzo produced a sketch entitled "The Artist moved by the grandeur of ancient ruins." Drawn by a man named Fuseli, it portrayed a melancholy young nobleman sitting by the pedestal of a shattered colossus. Nothing remained of the statue except a gigantic foot and a single hand with a beckoning finger. The young nobleman's arm was stretched across the foot's monster arch, his head bowed as if receiving inspiration from the gigantic antiquity.

"Fuseli's sketch shows the impact of our great Roman heritage on the European traveller," Monsieur Pozzo said. "In the more peaceful days of this century, no English-speaking visitor"—and here Monsieur Pozzo bowed to Father—"could see Rome without visiting the Paper Museum."

"What Grand Tourist goes abroad with General Bonaparte on the march?" Father nodded.

As the men talked, the brother of Countess Waldstein pulled a portable writing box from his satchel. He set it on his lap and began scribbling in a journal. His concentrated expression suggested he was absorbed in his writing, and

I thought of my own journal in which I am recording my travel adventures. In the style of French novels, I reproduce dialogue and other literary devices. I carry a new edition of *Les Liaisons dangereuses* in my trunk. Father says the French novels I admire are an immoral influence on young people like myself. So I have not told him about my method of journal keeping. I am afraid Father cannot think hypothetically. If I say, Imagine this, he will say I am taking liberties with truth. My parent prefers empirical facts, such as the number of Quincy apples he sold to the army during our revolutionary war.

Like my parent, I, too, must check, test and verify, and in that sense at least, I am my father's daughter.

"Are you willing to sell me what is left of the Paper Museum?" Father asked Monsieur Pozzo. "My cousin would be pleased to display this drawing and others like it in our White House."

"Please approach me, sir," Monsieur Pozzo whispered. And in a low, agitated voice, he asked my parent to adjourn to our hotel. It was then I noticed the French soldier in a tricorne hat calling out for free champagne. We overheard the man say the liberators of Venice were on their way and a few café-goers hurried out of the Florian, fear engraved on their faces. Father went off with his companions and I set out to find the Listone, the promenade in the Piazza San Marco that Venetians like to frequent. I wanted to avoid Francis, who would be returning from an inspection of Burano's lacemaking industry. Fortunately, Father often sends Francis off on research tasks, sparing me his company.

It was early evening as I threaded my way through the throngs who had come out for Good Friday mass at the Basilica of San Marco. I ignored the beggars in silk who accost foreigners like myself and hurried past the pitiful coops of chickens and pigeons waiting to be auctioned for Easter dinners; I sidestepped a battalion of sturdy peasant women from Friuli selling water from buckets that hang in ox-like yokes across their shoulders, and tried to ignore a small dwarf who brought the blood to my face when he called out to me to suckle him.

Seeking fresh sea breezes, I went and stood between the two granite pillars on the Molo. Venetians avoid this place because executions once took place there but I am not concerned by superstition. I gazed about me, imagining myself a kind of executioner's victim, and the hand holding the noose that of my own father. Slowly, I became aware of a man by the landing where the gondolas are tied for the night, his face and body hidden in the shadows cast by the Ducal Palace. I looked to see if he was someone I knew but I couldn't make him out. I felt rather than saw him, felt his gaze, curious and compelling. I moved away a little, taking a few steps towards the north, and he did the same. I took a few steps backwards into the Piazza and he too took a few steps backwards. I could see that he was wearing a coat and large hat shaped like a black fan. Its width marked it as a Kevenhuller.

I am not used to exciting interest in a man, since my height lets me see over the heads of most, but this evening I felt something stir in My Poor Friend, whose misfortune it is to house the spirit of Asked For Adams. I turned away from him and headed towards the Campanile. I did not stop and look over my shoulder. I knew, that is to say,

I *felt* that he was following me and I was not certain whether this was what I wanted. The Campanile has no stairs. I made my way up the wooden incline, a gently sloping floor that goes round and round inside the tower.

At every pillar, I stopped and looked out of one of the small portholes cut into the brick. I was beginning to enjoy myself. I was alone in the Campanile and the sun was setting. This fact registered on me, nevertheless I felt neither fear nor excitement—only a sure, steady calm when I heard his footsteps echoing behind me.

After a long climb, I reached the platform with the bells where red and green marble columns support the four arches that hold up each side of the tower. The platform above the bells offers a vantage point that allows the eye to wander over the whole of Venice and the horizon beyond. Too fatigued to climb higher, I stopped and took out Peabody's guide and found I was looking down at the Sansovinian Library. On its roof, I saw the large white statues representing Venus and Neptune and other allegorical figures. The sudden appearance of these figures moved me greatly. Here on the rooftops, a city of white, silenced beings, created and now forgotten by the people below, were marching with steadfast expressions in the air above Venice.

I knew he was there before he spoke. I turned. He took off his Kevenhuller and Philippe de la Haye, the brother of Countess Waldstein, stood before me.

I did not speak and neither did he. As we studied each other, I was surprised to see signs of strength in his aged body, the huge bull neck and large aggressive nose, the sunburnt face, almost African in complexion. He was still handsome to look upon and he moved with the grace of a much younger person, confident of his physical strength when he no longer had a right to be so.

Then he groaned and sat down on a little bench by one of the arches and I realized he was short of breath. With some effort, he took off his greatcoat and put it on the bench beside him, next to a leather satchel.

I could smell urine and other bodily wastes left by Venetians who visit the watchtower, and I was glad Father was not there to disturb the moment with his righteous fastidiousness.

"I am not who you think I am," he said in a low voice. "Please forgive me, but it is dangerous in Venice for me to have my identity known and at this moment, even, I am being watched."

"Who are you?" I said.

"I am known as the Chevalier de Seingalt."

"Monsieur, do you have a Christian name? I am the child of a revolutionary people, and we do not put stock in titles."

He smiled slightly. "I am delighted to offer you the truth, mademoiselle. You were kind to Finette on the public barge. My true name is Giacomo—or Jacob, as you would say in English."

"And your surname, monsieur?"

"Casanova."

"You are the man who escaped from the prison in the Ducal Palace? The lover of women described by Count Waldstein?"

He nodded.

"I do not believe you," I said.

He bowed his head. Then he reached into a pocket in his greatcoat and pulled out Countess Waldstein's great wig. He settled it on his head, causing a cloud of powder to rise slowly skyward like dust on a country road.

From the square far below rose the noise of orchestras and people laughing. I inspected the mountainous wig whose curls had been sprinkled with *poudre à maréchale*. There was no sign of the shiny beetles and I found myself disappointed.

"Mademoiselle, my disguises have been sadly necessary. I left Venice in disgrace over twenty years ago after publishing a satire of the playwright Abbé Chiaria. It was the year the Abbé's friend headed our inquisition . . . There were often false charges, too." He lowered his voice. "And since the revolution in France, Napoleon Bonaparte's spies have been hard at work, gathering evidence against anyone suspected of sympathizing with their king. I admire neither the revolution nor Napoleon. But it makes no difference to the fools who run Venice."

"Surely, those fools will have no time to persecute you now that Napoleon is in Italy?" I said, seating myself on the bench across from him.

He shrugged. "One should not expect reason from the Republic, Puritan girl. In Paris, some years ago, I met Benjamin Franklin and he told me the story of your brave young country." He removed the wig and placed it next to his satchel, which I realized was moving with little bursts of energy.

"Thank you for your good words about my country, but it was not I but my forebears who were Puritans," I said, my eyes on the convulsing sack. "I was brought up in the Congregational Church and taught to value the republican virtue of simplicity."

"Ah, simplicity! And yet you seem to manage so well in a city like Venice!" He leaned over and opened his satchel.

"Please forgive me for following you. I came to ask you a favour . . ."

"Monsieur?"

"It is said the spies know I am fond of fox terriers. Will you keep Finette while I am in Venice?"

His fox terrier wriggled out of the satchel's mouth and ran towards me, yapping happily as if to demonstrate how willingly she would accept her master's suggestion. She stopped at my feet, wagging the stump of her abbreviated tail. She was cat size, with a sad grey face. I picked her up and she panted up at me with the same adoring look she had given me on the public barge.

"Who could resist such a loving creature?"

He consulted a gold watch and I saw him kiss a small miniature hanging from its chain.

"It is a portrait of my great love—Aimée Dubucq de Rivery," he said when he noticed my curious look. "Would you like to see?" Without waiting for my reply, he unhooked the miniature from the watch chain and gave it to me. Inside the dainty gold frame was a portrait of a woman sitting by a window. She looked younger than my age of twenty-five, and her clothing was in the formal style of the old French court.

"Is she French?"

"She was born in the West Indies. And now she rules all of Turkey. Her husband, the Sultan, recently departed from this world."

"She lives in a harem?"

The shock in my voice amused him. For the first time, he laughed and his broad, sunburnt face relaxed.

"Yes, she was a favoured wife. But she loves me still. My greatest wish is to see her once more before I die."

"Oh," I said, thinking, *You are far too old for her, although perhaps she has also aged, like you.* He must have divined something of this in my face because he groaned wearily.

"Again, you do not believe me?"

"I would like to believe you." I hesitated. "Is your friend unhappy in the land of the Turks?"

"One day, I will tell you our story, if you would permit me the honour. In the meantime, let me entrust you with my journal. If I have not been apprehended, I will reclaim it from you tomorrow morning at the Florian."

"And I will keep your dog for you," I said, surprising myself. "We stay in Venice two months more."

"I am in your debt then. You saw how Count Waldstein taunts Finette. She was once a circus dog and savagely beaten by her owner." When he saw my scandalized face, he nodded. "Count Waldstein has his faults. As do most benefactors. He likes to amuse himself with cruel jokes. The day we left Dux, his valet placed my clothes in a nest of flying ants. Even now I am not sure I am rid of the pests."

"You must tell him to improve his manners."

"Ah, Miss Adams, how you please me!" He threw back his head and laughed loudly. "There is no hope for Count Waldstein, while you are kind and pleasing to look upon." He beckoned me close. "Can I trust you? I see that I can," he said, as I took a nervous step forward. "Count Waldstein brought me to Venice for the purpose of a money-making venture. Out of gratitude, I have been obliged to help him. But the Pozzo drawings are fakes—worthless copies done by a talentless fraud. No great Roman or Venetian artist made those sketches. You must warn your father."

"I will. Thank you," I said softly.

"Without proof, your father may not believe you. But at least you will have done your republican duty."

"I must go now," I said. "Father will be looking for me."

Carrying Finette in my arms, I made to leave the platform, but he continued to sit on the bench and I understood he was exhausted.

"Are you all right, monsieur? Can I have someone in the square fetch you water?"

"I am grateful to you. But the climb was hard on bones no longer young. Forgive me for not getting to my feet."

"I wish you a pleasant evening, monsieur." He must have noticed my hesitation over using his name because he called after me as I began my descent:

"My inscription is still in the prison at the Ducal Palace. No one but myself knows where it is. The seventh cell, under the third plank to the left of the door. A tiny inscription. 'I love. Jacob Casanova, 1756.' If I were only a few years younger, I would prove it to you surely."

This last comment made my heart flutter. What a foolish, frivolous expression—a fluttering heart, as if the organ were not the sturdy blood pumper that fuels us all. Yet that is how I felt in the presence of the courtly Venetian gentleman. As I left, I saw him pull out the miniature portrait and his lips moved as if he was murmuring an endearment to the woman under the little glass casing. I suddenly felt very sorry for him.

I quickened my step, going round and down as fast as I could into the darkness, the noise and the lights of the Good Friday evening in Venice.

A shadow fell across the page.

Luce noticed the pair of brogues squarely placed by her chair. She had a weakness for men's shoes, especially brogues, the only shoes she could remember her father wearing. These were worn and rubber-soled, and the sight of their scuffed toes sent a shudder of longing through Luce.

"May I join you?" His voice emptied into the air over her head. "I am not dangerous." And now a card appeared on the page of the old journal—"Dino Fabbiani," it read, "Photo-journalist, *The European*."

"I'm here on assignment," he said, speaking English with a slight, musical accent. "It's always nice to see Americans coming out for the regatta."

"I'm Canadian." Luce was startled to notice how breathless she sounded.

He slid his lean body into the empty chair. "North American then. You know—you have a very unusual voice . . ." He cocked his head, as if listening to far-off music. "What is the expression in English? My lady's dulcet tones . . . ?"

Luce felt her cheeks pinking up. It was a nuisance that she blushed easily; people often suspected her of lying. As a child, she'd learned there was no remedy for pale-skinned people; the harder you struggled, the deeper and more incriminating the blush. He pointed to the old journal.

"Is that yours?"

"It belonged to my ancestor . . . she travelled with Casanova." Why had she blurted out the truth? Some girlish compulsion to please? She carefully placed the journal out of sight on her lap.

He closed his eyes, nodding portentously. "This is remarkable. You don't understand how remarkable." He opened his eyes again, his expression good-natured and alert. "I admire

Casanova greatly. Did you know he broke out of a prison in the Ducal Palace? There are guides at the palace who say he was allowed to escape, you realize, because he was a spy for the Venetian Republic."

"That can't be true. The bill for the damages he did to the roof of the Ducal Palace was found in the Venetian archives."

"So you know Casanova's story. Would you like to see his prison cell? I have a friend who could show it to us this evening—after hours."

Across the canal, a heavy-set woman in a Borsalino fedora was trudging slowly towards the small footbridge. Luce gave Lee a faint-hearted wave. "I have to meet someone," she said.

"Tomorrow then. You will come to the Piazza San Marco. At one p.m. By the café with the loudest orchestra," he added. He stood up and bowed, his slimness apparent in his black jacket and jeans, and she half expected him to click his heels like a dancing master. He went back to his table outside. Then he paused and gave her a tentative smile as if he expected her to disappoint him.

"I'll see," Luce nodded.

Dinner did not go well. As they finished their first course, Lee Pronski seemed distracted and glum, and Luce didn't know how to talk to her mother's scholarly lover who wore her jaunty Borsalino throughout supper, its wide brim shadowing her fine Roman nose and wide, down-turned mouth.

"Is that a friend of yours? He seems to think so." Lee nodded towards Dino Fabbiani who was now standing at the door of the restaurant. He waved then in their direction before turning and walking off. Aware she was using a faux, singsongy tone, Luce explained that he was the photographer they had met on the *motoscafo*.

"If you ask me, he looks like the kind of local who preys on tourist women."

"Maybe they prey on him?" Luce suggested in her whispery voice.

"Speak up, Luce. I can't hear you."

"I was just wondering if some of the tourists are looking for love?"

"Oh, love." Lee stared gloomily around her. "After your mother's death, I don't have the stamina. I'll leave that to you, although—as I recall—Kitty used to worry that you were lacking in the romance department. She tried to encourage you to be more outgoing, didn't she? Of course, gregarious women like Kitty don't understand introverts."

Her cheeks reddening, Luce thought she'd heard wrong, but Lee ventured on, making small talk about Venice and their hotel, Lee's eyes brightening over the arrival of their desserts, an apple dumpling with toasted almonds for Luce and a large tiramisù for Lee.

"Now, Luce, shall we get down to business?" Lee asked, spooning up the last of her dessert. As Luce watched meekly, she delved into her capacious handbag and brought out a bundle of papers that included a map of Greece and a large booklet. Lee handed the booklet over to her.

"Have you seen this?"

Luce shook her head. The booklet was a newsletter for the Association of Canadian Archaeologists. On its first page, there was an article about her mother's memorial service in Crete:

## A Group of Scholars And Friends To Pay Tribute To Dr. K.A. Adams, The Well-Known Canadian Archaeologist, In Northern Crete

An unusual memorial tribute will take place this June in Crete when friends and colleagues gather to celebrate Dr. K.A. Adams, who was killed in a car accident there eighteen months ago.

The tribute is being held in an island cave believed to have been a shrine of the ancient Minoans. Most of the participants met Dr. Adams in Crete where she took part in tours of Minoan sites run by the tour guide Christine Harmon.

The most recent of Dr. Adams' ten books was *The Minoan Way*, a collection of essays about life in early Crete. Her bestseller, *An Archaeologist Looks at Prehistory*, has been translated into 26 languages.

Dr. Adams began her career studying the pottery of the Iroquoian-speakers of Southern Ontario. In 1982, she was made full professor at the University of Toronto. Her monograph *What they Wrought*, about female potters in North America's Neolithic communities, was strongly influenced by the late Lithuanian archaeologist Marija Gimbutas, who believed early Europeans worshipped an earth mother known as the Great Goddess of Regeneration.

Rejecting the statistical approach usual in her profession, Dr. Adams became a controversial figure when she wrote about women playing an important role in Neolithic religion.

Her books and articles expressed the belief that prehistory provides cultural models that show humans can create peaceful, industrious societies without wars or class distinctions.

"It's a nice write-up, isn't it?" Lee asked.

"Yes."

"When I think of how some of your mother's colleagues ostracized her . . . I suppose we should be grateful they can acknowledge her now." With a sigh, Lee unfolded the map of Greece.

"We'll meet the group in Athens," she said, pointing to the city. "And I'll give my talk at the consulate. It's on the controversy about the Minoan sacrifice—one of your mother's subjects. I'm sure you know about it."

"Not really."

"I can't hear you, Luce."

"I'm looking forward to your talk."

"Thank you. Then we'll spend six days with Christine in Herakleion." Lee ran her finger along some unreadable place name in northern Crete.

"Is that where she died?"

"No, it was Zaros."

"I was hoping to see Zaros."

"Well, we will have to see what Christine has planned for us. Don't you fancy it?" she asked, pointing at Luce's untouched dessert. Luce had done her best with the risotto Lee had ordered for her, but the tiramisù was too rich, even for someone who could eat whatever she liked and stay slim. She handed over her dessert and politely hid her surprise as Lee made short work of it. There was no more talk about what Kitty thought of Luce, or the memorial service in Crete, and Luce herself was loath to continue the conversation. It upset her to think of her mother discussing her deficiencies with Lee.

Lee paid the bill and then she and Luce set off for the Hotel Flora, going slowly to accommodate the older woman who walked with a magisterial bounce. The moon was full over

Venice, and in the narrow streets gaggles of sightseers moved between the pockets of silver and mauve shadows, enjoying its giddy influence. As they entered the Piazza San Marco, Lee pointed at the large watchtower.

"Did you know Venetians hoisted criminals in a cage up the Campanile? The inquisitors had spies everywhere. You could get your neighbour arrested just by sending them a letter."

"Wasn't Venice the first modern police state?"

"Speak up, Luce. I can't hear when you whisper."

"I think Venice is lovely."

"It is, isn't it?" Lee nodded as they passed the Quadri where a string quartet was playing "Yesterday."

"Oh, Lordy! The Beatles. I find nostalgia a bore." Luce saw Lee frown, as if daring her to disagree, and she found herself nodding obligingly. As they passed by an arcade, Luce noticed a man watching her from under one of its arches. He looked familiar, but she couldn't see his face without her sunglasses, and it was too dark for them now. Could it be Dino Fabbiani? Or was she just alarmed by the density of Venice, where everyone appeared to be watching everyone else? She turned to stare at him and the man stepped back into the shadows.

As they walked on, Luce felt sure the man was following them. Yet when she turned around to look, no one was there. She must be imagining things, influenced perversely by the play of moonlit shadows on the old buildings. A moment later, she turned again.

"I think someone is following us," she said.

"Well, I wouldn't worry about it. Venice has the lowest crime rate in Europe."

"I don't like being stared at."

"Hang on for a minute, will you?" Lee stopped to catch her

breath in a lane outside the square. "You know, Luce, you tilt your head just like Kitty."

Not certain she had understood Lee properly, Luce bent her head down to hear the shorter woman.

"You remind me of your mother, Luce. The way you listen."

"I'm nothing like her." Luce shook her head in a fierce, embarrassed little gesture.

Lee's smile wavered but she composed herself and pointed down a side street. "The Flora is that way."

A few minutes later Lee admitted she had overlooked the little lane, hardly wider than a pair of shoulders, that led to the Hotel Flora. They had to retrace their steps three times before they saw the hotel's discreet sign, with the symbol of a tree in white on a black background.

Alone in her room, Lee Pronski exchanged her leisure suit for a black kimono sprinkled with tiny yellow tigers, and reflected on the evening. Despite Luce's ridiculous clothes——what was that fringe of lace peeking above the girl's jeans, anyway? Her underpants? Probably. The jeans were cut so low you could see her belly button. Still, despite the girl's clothing and her boyishly cropped chestnut hair, there was an old-fashioned air of naivety about her lover's grave, soft-spoken daughter. She saw it in the girl's large, trusting grey eyes, the beautiful, myopic eyes of someone prone to introspection. A pity Luce tried to hide her short-sightedness behind those round sunglasses. And then the incongruous combination of her height with that whispery voice, a frustrating susurration of apology mixed with resentment. What, she wondered, did Luce feel resentful about? She had led a life of ease in the bosom of Kitty's well-to-do family.

Lee wanted to feel protective towards her lover's child, but it had made her sad to see the solemn way Luce tilted her head when she concentrated. The mannerism induced a slight double chin, out of place on someone her age though it had seemed so endearing in Kitty. Otherwise, Luce was right: she was cut from a different cloth than her petite, energetic mother whose skin and hair were so fair she seemed to have been hewn from pine.

At dinner, she had put her foot in her mouth, she knew that, telling Luce how Kitty felt about her daughter's shyness. But she had been trying to convey that she, too, had sometimes felt like an introvert with Kitty, whose chatty, outgoing manner disarmed everyone she met. Time was, Lee thought, when I would have handled the situation with more finesse. She wasn't unkind by nature, although her blunt manner had often been misconstrued by her students. She had grown up in Brooklyn and she struggled with the reserve of Canadians like Luce who didn't come out and say what they meant. You had to guess with Torontonians, and if you failed to get it right, you were judged silently. Nevertheless, she had enjoyed passing on her knowledge about women's role in Neolithic cultures, even though many students were bored by the subject now. Young women dismissed her generation of feminists. It wasn't as if women, like men, had a solid tradition to fall back on. Who read Susan Griffin now or studied Daly or Christ? Only Kitty had seen through her carapace and knew the pride she took in her teaching.

Smiling wistfully, she removed the small photograph she had tucked inside the pages of her guidebook and stroked it sadly. "Kitty, I'll do better with your girl next time," she whispered.

She put away the photograph. It was time to run through the little chores she had planned for herself that evening.

First, from the innards of her overstuffed purse, she extracted a manuscript titled "The Minoan World: A Peace-Loving Matrilineal Society or a Culture Based on Blood Rituals and Human Sacrifice?" Lee's face softened at the sight of the large, generous *o*'s and *a*'s. Kitty had written her essays out in long-hand first; it was a superstition of hers, that thoughts come more easily using a pen than a keyboard. Lee had misplaced the published version, but she had wanted to consult Kitty's text for her talk on the bogus Minoan sacrifice: she'd need all the ammunition she could muster for her audience in Athens.

She set the manuscript aside and took out a postcard of the Piazza San Marco that showed pigeons sprinkled in the air like flashing coins flung by a beneficent Doge. The brightly lit scene did nothing to convey the vortex of perpetual motion in the square, where tourists walked through flying birds. In slow, deliberate strokes, she wrote to her old colleague Martin Wells:

Dear Marty,

Arrived this morning with Luce on the early plane. I am fine if a little low. To be expected in the aftermath of the last eighteen months. I trust Luce will be able to look after herself. Today we found a mother-daughter pair in an old bookshop. A Bronze Age copy, Caynkenar type, provenance unknown. Luce pleased by my token. Consoling myself with gourmand fare.

Lee

P.S. The chair of our division sent me your course description with a note, urging me to come out of retire-ment. Thanks for thinking of me, old friend. I haven't for-gotten the good times we had teaching together.

She stuffed the card into her purse and withdrew a well-worn black-ringed notebook. A syllabus had been Scotch-taped to its inside page:

Humanities 6491. 02: Special Topics: The Journey of Aphrodite, the Greek goddess of love and beauty, from a multi-faceted Neolithic deity to one limited primarily to sexual functions. The course will emphasize the cultures of prehistoric Europe and Minoan Crete whose people worshipped an all-powerful goddess of regeneration.

It wasn't good to think of work when she felt disoriented by memories of Kitty. Yawning, Lee put away her notebook and went to her window overlooking the moonlit domes of San Marco. She had meant what she said to Luce about Venice. Aside from the occasional pickpocket, there was nothing to fear. The residue of an atavistic loss lingered beneath its legendary suspension of time—perhaps a futile longing for the mainland the Venetians had abandoned over a thousand years before. To escape Attila and his army of Huns, they'd cut their ties with what remained of the Roman Empire and built homes on the swampy islands a few miles from shore. Like me, Lee thought. I, too, have chosen isolation, but the price of isolation is the pain of feeling abandoned and forgotten. Was that why she had asked Luce to come with her to Crete and offered to pay the girl's fare?

Her gesture had surprised her friends—and herself. She had prided herself on avoiding faux intimacies with her students and yet, she thought ruefully, here she was trying to shepherd her dead lover's daughter through the Mediterranean. Now that Kitty was gone, she felt like just another middle-aged woman with a past receding like an ancient shoreline.

With a groan, Lee threw herself down on her bed. I will not feel sorry for myself like those sad English women I read about in Anita Brookner novels, she thought. I must choose and know that I chose my circumstances.

Luce awoke, trembling, from a dream. Already she could barely remember it, but it brought back a memory of waiting for her mother who was working on a dig near the Wye River in Ontario.

On that long-ago day, Luce had been waiting bravely by herself in the marsh by the old Jesuit ruins. All morning, she'd played in the bulrushes whose roots intertwined into a spongy carpet under the surface of the water, imagining she was one of the Jesuits from medieval France who left behind old axes and gun casings and did not renounce their faith even when the Iroquois scooped out their sizzling flesh with clam shells.

She had spent hours watching sturgeons flash their yellow bellies and fishermen chug up the river in aluminium outboards, their lines trailing through clouds of algae, listening in vain for her mother's voice above the muffled sound of traffic beyond the trestle bridge.

Now her mother was dead, and in her place she'd left the Polish Pumpkin, who insulted her intelligence with patronizing speeches about her mother's worries over her retiring nature. As if shyness was a fault. She's punishing me for being alive when Kitty is dead, Luce thought. Well, she wouldn't stoop so low as to take out her own grief on someone else.

She turned on the bedside light and sat up. She longed for her comfortable room at home. Her mother had told her it was easy to feel sad after a cross-Atlantic flight, that jet lag trails in its wake little tendrils of woe, like the start of a depression. And her mother would know. After all, Kitty had spent the last years of her life visiting hot, happy, faraway places, leaving Luce to look after herself at home.

She thought of their century-old Victorian house in Toronto. It was their first Christmas with Lee and they were celebrating by the fireplace. Lee sat in an armchair eating Belgian chocolates and watching as Luce opened a present from Kitty, the oracle kit with its handsome tasselled pouch. "I know you don't usually like this sort of thing. But I thought you might find it fun," her mother had murmured, smiling over Luce's shoulder at Lee. Luce had thanked Kitty and then angrily taken the kit upstairs. That evening, her mother had followed Luce to her bedroom.

"I've upset you, haven't I?"

Luce had turned away so she wouldn't see the lines of strain on her mother's face. *You dyke*, she had wanted to shout, though such a word had never rolled off her tongue. *You think you can appease your guilt about having an affair by giving me presents.*

"I know you think I've been a bad mother." She heard Kitty sigh. "And I'm sorry. But Luce, you're twenty-one. And I shouldn't have to feel guilty for loving someone."

Her mother had sounded so sad and despairing that she had relented and told her she wasn't upset.

Packing for her trip with Lee, she had come across the oracle kit again. Half-jokingly, she had put it in her suitcase, secretly hoping it held a magical connection to her mother.

Sleep wasn't going to come now. What was she going to do with herself? She found the stack of essays tucked inside her knapsack and turned to one by the Englishman Arthur Symons who had visited Count Waldstein's castle in Dux one hundred years after Casanova had died. It was just as she had thought. Symons confirmed that he'd seen the bill for Casanova's damages to the roof of the Ducal Palace in the Venetian archives. And here, too, was the date of Casanova's arrest, July 26, 1755. On the night of October 31–November 1, 1756, Casanova escaped from the Piombi—or the Leads—as the prison was called under the lead roof of the Ducal Palace. He was thirty-one at the time and he would live in exile for eighteen years, according to Symons who said that most of Casanova's 122 love affairs and experiences with historical personages could be verified.

Luce admired Casanova for keeping to the facts. She relied on facts supported by historical research and distrusted theories. Master narratives usually disappointed those who espoused them, while facts, with their specific, limited nature, were built to last. Her mother's profession of archaeology had consisted of interpreting worlds from small artifacts, but the nature of her own archival work was more dependable. For instance, the laundry bill of John Macdonald would always stay the laundry bill of Canada's first prime minister, no matter what anyone said. But the fat Venuses of prehistoric times might be any-thing—symbols of an ancient deity who represented the great creative power of the universe, as Lee had reminded her that morning in the Venetian shop, or a pornographic icon. Once you moved as far back as prehistory, Luce thought, the past was just a story someone made up. Not that she tried now to under-stand her mother's views. After her mother had met Lee in Crete, Luce had given up.

Her thoughts still on Kitty, she started her iBook and opened her old e-mails, pausing at one whose address said, "katherine.adams@sympatico.ca." How often had she placed her finger on delete, only to stop herself? It made her feel calmer to keep the e-mails in her system, as if she and her mother were still communicating. It was hard to believe that someone as vital as Kitty could just vanish. But it wasn't only that: she hated to think of the valuable correspondence that people deleted every day when they sent their mails to the trash. The future will lack the historical records of past generations, she reflected. Nothing online remained. The Internet was like a beach churned up with footprints that waves washed away on a daily basis.

Reluctantly, she bypassed her mother's e-mail and opened a new message from Aunt Beatrice.

Dear Luce,

I am delighted that Lee agreed to stop in Venice so you can give the family papers to the Sansovinian Library. I told Mr. Smith (of Harvard University) that I was entrusting them to a young family member who works as an archivist and he was very relieved when I said you would be delivering them personally.

I am sure you remember that your appointment is at noon with Mr. Goldoni on May 14, so please forgive anxious old me for reminding you. Mr. Smith set the whole thing in motion and he says the Sansovinian is extremely grateful to us for allowing them to exhibit our documents in their celebration of Jacob Casanova.

I know your time away will be memorable, especially since it's your first trip to the Mediterranean. So let me give you a few words of advice. Hide your passport in a little cloth bag around your neck and be sure to take along a calculator so you won't be cheated in a foreign currency. Thirdly, never invite theft by leaving a sign on the door—"Occupant out. Please clean." And lastly, dear, avoid conversations with strange men. They won't have your best interests at heart. But I realize there's really no need to say this to someone as sensible as you.

You won't let us down, will you, Luce? Mr. Smith seems to think the old papers are worth a great deal of money. So they can rest in the Sansovinian for a while until we decide what to do with them. Venice is where they started out from, after all!

Love,<br/>Aunt Bea

P.S. I am so sorry I can't join you for the tribute to Kitty, but the restaurant gets very busy this time of year and I just can't manage it. And I hope you'll understand when I say this, Luce, but your mother's New Age thinking was never something I was very comfortable with.

Luce noted the time of her appointment with Goldoni at the Sansovinian and logged off. She closed her iBook and turned to look for Asked For Adams' journal. It was right where she'd left it, in its box on the bedside table. She lifted it out, and this time she also took out the Arabic manuscript. She peered at it curiously. Inside its tea-brown leather cover, dense flawless symbols spilled across its margin-free pages. She would look at it more carefully later. She opened the journal to the next entry.

April 18, 1797

The day is dank and cool and the lagoon tide has overflowed, wetting the feet of peevish Venetians obliged to cross the Piazza San Marco on raised planking.

Early this morning, I went to the Florian to meet Monsieur Casanova and give him back his journal. Father had taken Francis and me to dinner yesterday evening after his meeting with Monsieur Pozzo so I had no time to read it. Using hand gestures, I conveyed to the proprietor of the café that I wanted a fried doughnut. I seated myself, and without the slightest hesitation began to read the diary he had loaned me. On the first page, in large, sprawling handwriting, its author began by claiming that he was the cause of all his own misfortunes, as well as his fortunes. I was so taken by his candour that I conveyed his words immediately to my own journal.

"My vices never burdened anyone but me, and seduction was never characteristic of my behaviour because I never seduced anyone except unconsciously, always being seduced myself first."

No American man would make such a boast, I thought, although I myself know nothing of seduction. On the next page, I found the author's philosophy of travel under "Casanova's Advice to Travellers":

"The traveller must start his journey with the same fervour he feels when choosing a lover, knowing that a world of possibilities awaits him. And if his choice goes awry, he must quickly select a fresh destination. Just as the best remedy for heartbreak is a new lover, so it is with travel."

I grew aware of someone watching me. The journal's owner stood beside my table in his thin jacket of corn-coloured satin, though the dampness that spring morning was extreme. I noticed a fresh patch on his sleeve and wondered what industrious female hands had worked to make his careworn suit last out another season.

"I believe you have something of mine." His voice was deep and lively, and I felt a stir of excitement although he is too old to be a suitor for someone like myself. "May I join you?" he asked. "The rains are inescapable." He lifted his foot so I could see the mud encrusted on its buckle, and smiled. "Please excuse my shoes, Miss Adams."

"Think nothing of it, monsieur," I said. They were the same shoes he had worn as "Aunt Flora" on the public boat, an old square-toed pair with clogs fastened to their soles so that the wearer's feet could rest evenly on the cobbles.

"Did you read it?" he asked, pointing at the journal.

"Sir, I read only the opening page with your comparison of travel to lovemaking."

"Do you think my comparison is a mistake, Puritan girl?"

I knew he used the word Puritan to tease me. "Please do not address me so. I am no more a Puritan than yourself." He widened his eyes, but I resolved not to falter. "I was raised on the writings of the Roman stoics. Cicero was my uncle's favourite and Seneca is the philosopher whose ethics I learned from my aunt. Perhaps you know him?"

He shrugged. "I find Seneca's philosophy too severe, Miss Adams. Why should I maintain a contrived indifference to pain, or for that matter—pleasure?"

"The virtuous man should be indifferent to both and so learn to master suffering." I had a copy of Seneca's *De Beneficiis* in my travelling satchel. I pulled it out and placed it on the table. "This is my Bible, monsieur."

"You do not pray in your Congregational church, Miss Adams?"

"I prefer rational inquiry to religious speculation."

"Ah, so I am conversing with a *philosophe*?"

"How else can we know the truth if we do not question what we see? But I am exceedingly interested in your views on travel, monsieur. I was taught that the Grand Tourist travels to get an education."

"Then you have read too many guides, Miss Adams. Travel is a faith, like love. And a faith involves pleasure as well as the challenge of pain or hardship. So for the utmost success, a traveller must follow the same methods as love—selection, satisfaction, seduction and separation."

When he saw my doubtful look, he added, "My travel principles are empirically sound—worthy, I hope, of a great *philosophe* like Voltaire."

"Please tell me one, monsieur."

"What you desire is always waiting for you, but you must tell the Fates what you are searching for. First, you should write down your wish on a scrap of paper and then throw it to the winds. It will scatter best if you tear it into a dozen pieces, Miss Adams."

"How strange. And another?"

"We must not follow the dictate of our will but go only where pleasure leads. And we should grant ourselves the comfort of graceful entrances and exits. Although I am not as skilful with my exits as I would like . . ."

"Only your entrances, monsieur." I laughed, thinking of him in his strange wig on the public barge.

"Ah, so you make fun of me, Miss Adams! And I so dearly enjoy talking to you!" He was smiling broadly now, and for the first time I felt the youthfulness of his spirit.

"I, too, enjoy our conversations," I said. "And I am eager to hear about the woman in the locket."

"I did promise, did I not?" He glanced at his watch, where the dainty miniature hung from his fob. But this time, he quickly tucked it away.

"That will have to wait. Forgive me, Miss Adams. I must go to an appointment. May I reclaim my journal?" He took it, and without another word he bowed, and melted into the crowd.

I sat for a while, watching the spot where he had vanished, my soul disturbed by longings.


April 25, 1797

We are soon to be at war. General Bonaparte is in Austria while his army remains in northern Italy. But the situation has become critical. I saw this with my own eyes. I was standing with Father on the shore of the Giudecca near the Convent of the Capuchins. On Easter Monday there was an uprising against the French army in Verona and yesterday we witnessed a foolish gun battle—Venetian soldiers firing on French sailors from a fortress by the harbour. Father says the Venetians have brought war upon us sooner than he would like. Who knows now what will happen to Father's trade mission? He had hoped the army would bypass Venice in its hurry to crush the Austrians.

Poor Father. He was feeling poorly, and he became seasick on the gondola taking us to the Convent. Afterwards, I held his head on my lap and massaged his scalp while the gondolier studied us with cunning eyes. Francis had gone to Murano to talk to the glass merchants, and I think the gondolier assumed Father was my aged husband. I stared coldly back and continued massaging my poor father's scalp.

I do not hold this marriage plan against Father. I understand that he is doing what is best for me before he dies, and that he does not want me to make my way in the world without a husband, whereas I would be content to live alone in a city like Paris, far from the world of the Gooch farm with its views of the great Atlantic and the humpbacked islands near Boston. Aunt Abigail brought me up to know Greek and Latin, and I could make a modest living teaching the Classics to French school-children. Father dismisses these plans and jokes that it is better for me to wed a dullard who will be too slow witted to mind my bookworm habits than choose a learned man who will assume a wife should obey her husband. There is little point trying to tell Father I am not reassured by this advice.

So I was thinking, as I massaged his head, that I forgive Father for wanting me to do and be things I do not wish to do and be. And perhaps it was the tenderness in my face that the gondolier misinterpreted. As for my betrothed, I feel only boredom. Each night, he comes to dinner and grumbles on about the lace industry in Burano, or the glass furnaces in Murano—both are sadly in decline, he claims. And despite his own lack of cleanliness, Francis has taken up Father's practice of searching for bodily wastes in the streets as proof of Venetian sloth and depravity. Father had thought we might be married in Venice if his trade mission prospered. But yesterday Francis announced he will not be married in a Papist soap bubble—he means the Basilica of San Marco—because he found human excrement in the vestry.

My parent and I made our way up from the landing to the little Convent of the Capuchins near San

Redentore. The Abbess was waiting for us at the door, dressed in a white robe that left the tops of her round shoulders as naked as those of the French actresses we saw one night in Paris. Perhaps Father, too, was thinking of those daring thespians because I caught him gazing admiringly at the curve of her neck as she let us into an elegant hall.

Aside from a tall grilled wall rising up like the bars of a cage at the end of the room we could have been in a count's banqueting hall in Paris. On one side of the barrier, dozens of young novices in pretty white dresses smiled and dipped like goldfish in a water bowl. On the other, young male visitors stood gossiping with them through the holes in the grille, designed for that purpose.

The Abbess, who spoke a pretty French, explained that young girls enter her convent to receive an education because Venetian schools are very poor, and Venetian girls among the most untutored in Europe. Most of the novices, she told us, will marry the young men visiting them there that afternoon.

Although I envied the novices their small bodies and flirtatious ways that so easily elicited the suitors' attention, they appeared trapped in their pretty cage, and their suitors were a weedy, pale-faced lot, less imposing even than Francis who, like Father, at least looks ruddy from farm work. Our arrival disrupted the flirting, and a few of the suitors turned to listen as Father described the simple wedding ceremony he has planned for Francis and myself. He told the Abbess he wanted a minister of our own denomination and that the ceremony should be done before war is declared.

"You think there will be a war in Venice?" the Abbess said, smiling at the notion.

Father brought out a little box of powders he'd bought at a local apothecary shop. He took some up his nostrils.

"I pray I am wrong, Mother," he said. "But I believe Napoleon will avenge the Verona uprising against his army. He is encouraged by the weakness of Venice. Already, your Senate has given in to his request to punish Venetians who resist the French." The Abbess sat very still, as if she didn't believe a word Father said, and then she broke into a tinkly, sly laugh.

"You Americans are a deadly serious race," she said. "A month from now when your daughter is married, you and I will laugh at your foreboding."

Our discussion over, the Abbess took us down a long hall and into another grilled room and then another until we found ourselves in a library. She produced a journal and quill-pen and proceeded to make notes about the cost of posting the banns while Father waited fretfully, twirling the curls on his bob wig between his fingers. I guessed that he was brooding about the fate of his mission.

I resolved not to worry about politics that afternoon and wandered over to enjoy the view from the library window. It overlooked a pretty hedged courtyard, and I was startled to see Monsieur Casanova sunning himself there in his body corset; nearby, a young nun stood washing clothes in a water trough. On a hedge behind him a long white garment was heaped like a snowdrift. Other pieces of clothing hung off little bushes and shrubs. Although I cannot help feeling the old Countess and Monsieur Casanova are two beings, I saw below me only one: a handsome old gentleman sitting amid the bean-poles in his white undergarments while the laundress cleaned his clothes.

Then, suddenly, in the distance, I saw a great flash of light and heard several loud cracking booms, one after another. At first, I imagined it was the sound of a storm breaking over the Lido beaches. A nun rushed into the courtyard shrieking, and now an army of them came pounding down the hall outside the library, calling to one another in Italian, their voices frightened and awestruck.

Father and I hurried with the Abbess down to the main door where a large crowd stood staring at two warships by the harbour entrance. Fortunately, it was some distance away.

"Our soldiers are attacking a French gunboat." The Abbess no longer sounded girlish and merry, and the three of us stood in mute apprehension. I could not help thinking that if war comes to the Republic of Venice, there will be no time for weddings in Venetian churches.


May 3, 1797

There will be a war and a marriage.

The incident at the Lido that I witnessed the other day with Father and the Abbess has determined the fate of Venice, just as Father prophesied. Napoleon has been waiting for such an opportunity. Shots from Venetian soldiers at the fortress of St. Andrea near the harbour entrance killed four French sailors and their captain, Jean-Baptiste Laugier. The French captain was killed even though he shouted again and again through his trumpet, "I surrender!" Privately, Father told Francis and me that Venetians do not understand the vengeful determination of General Bonaparte.

There is little anyone can do. The Senate has apologized for the incident but my parent says this will not appease Napoleon, who needs the money chests of Venice to pay for his Austrian invasion. I am certain Father is right; when we were in Paris, the new martial pride of the French was a wonder.

Father told me yesterday that my wedding will take place on June 4, Whitsunday, at the Convent of the Capuchins. My distress over his announcement is severe, and my only joy is the comfort I find in Finette, Monsieur Casanova's fox terrier, who always jumps up to meet me with affection.

Towards sunset I took her for a walk in the Piazza San Marco. Without realizing what I was doing, I began to climb the Campanile, the dog leading the way. I believe she was hoping, as I was, that Monsieur Casanova would be waiting in the shadows of its bell tower, but not a soul showed his face except for two French soldiers in Phrygian caps lurking by the entrance. As I passed by them with the dog, they made mocking comments about my size, not knowing I understood. I began to feed a flock of pigeons, shouting "*Cochon! Cochon!*" to the greedy birds scrabbling for my crumbs. The word "pig" was not meant for the birds but the soldiers. And behind me, to my satisfaction, I heard their laughter cease.

Inquiry of the Day: Why do I admire those who can escape their circumstances?

Fruitful Thought for the Day: It is because I come from a people who dared the Atlantic for a new life.

~

The next morning, Lee Pronski awoke late. It was already ten. She knocked softly on Luce's door. No answer. Slowly, feeling parental and foolish, Lee opened the door and peered inside. The girl lay asleep on the bed in her bra and panties, her lovely young face half buried beneath a pillow. An old manuscript sat open on the bedside table, no doubt one of the family documents Luce was bringing to the library in Venice.

Lee softly closed the door, thinking uneasily of appetites that could be stirred by the sight of a young woman in her underwear. She'd always rejected the notion that middle-aged women like herself envied girls like Luce, that envy of the young was part of growing old. No, it was pity she felt looking at Luce's vulnerable, long-limbed body. Pity and a great weariness. She left Luce a note at the reception desk and set out to find the old waterfront apartment she'd lived in with Luce's mother on the Riva degli Schiavoni during their last winter together; Kitty Adams had been teaching at the university, and she had tagged along on a research grant.

Despite the crowds, she made her way there quickly and stood gazing up at the huge, blank windows overlooking the Basin of San Marco. Who was enjoying its splendid view of San Giorgio now? And its huge, light-filled rooms with the breeze from the Adriatic always fresh through its hallway? The stay in Venice had been their last happy time together, despite the exhibitionist who had singled Kitty out at the university. For two weeks, the man had stood buck naked in the window of an apartment across from Kitty's classroom, as chubby as a Ducal Palace cupid. It was soon apparent he was visible only to Kitty lecturing on her dais; the students couldn't see him. One morning, when her class was on break, Kitty leaned out her window and lifted up her shirt to reveal her bare breasts. The man retreated into the shadows, wearing, Kitty told her later, a look of immense sorrow. He didn't reappear. "I have 'breasted' a man," Kitty told Lee. "The way explorers breast a river."

How like Kitty to tread wittily through unpleasant situations, she thought. Kitty had joked that the exhibitionist was lucky he could satisfy his longings so simply.

Lee turned her back on the apartment and set off down the boardwalk, her face mournful. Did anyone understand the depth of love she had felt for Kitty? Sometimes she found herself wondering if Kitty herself had understood. If Kitty had known how to handle her moods, perhaps she wouldn't have driven off without her and died. But that was rubbish. She, Lee, was the guilty party.

She supposed Luce, too, was still finding things hard. Beatrice, Kitty's sister, had told her that Luce had been obliged to rent out rooms to students in her mother's old house to defray costs. The money coming to Luce in the form of a trust wasn't hers until she turned thirty-five. How old was Luce, anyway? She'd forgotten. Almost twenty-eight? When Lee was the same age she had already secured a tenure track position and was teaching students who stumbled about campus wearing the same glassy, distracted look as Luce.

Of course, she didn't really know Luce. Kitty had been protective and secretive about her relationship with her daughter, but Lee knew a deep love had existed between them. Then she and Kitty had left Luce behind when they set out on their travels, going back to Toronto only occasionally when Kitty wanted some time with her daughter. The last occasion she had seen Luce had been at Kitty's funeral.

A year after Kitty's death, an archivist at the Miller Archives and Rare Books had telephoned Lee and explained that she was worried about Luce who had become withdrawn since her mother's death. The archivist, a friend of Kitty's, had asked for

Lee's help, and Lee had replied brusquely: "Not my business." What could she possibly do for a young woman she barely knew? When Kitty died, Lee had taken early retirement and gone to live in Brooklyn. She had no idea what Luce was thinking or feeling.

And she knew even less about being motherly. Nor was it easy to learn at this stage, she told herself as she left the board-walk, heading for the Piazza San Marco. She'd considered herself too much of a solo operator to put up with a family—even Kitty's family. Still, she had decided to try for Kitty's sake.

Looking across the square, she spotted Luce reading at a café near the basilica. Luce was what used to be called a strapping girl, Lee thought. And yet despite the boyish crop cut and broad shoulders, nearly everything about Luce was shapely and soft. Yes, she was pleasing to look at and luminous with health, Lee decided grudgingly, from her full-lipped mouth with the striking white teeth to the long, milky white neck lightly ringed with lines like the markings on a statue. But it irritated her to see Luce avidly reading her family documents when, in the same breath, the girl dismissed the truth of her mother's views. How often had Lee lectured her students not to trust the "I" narrator? And how often had she watched them ignore her cautionary advice? If the text said I, they embraced it unthinkingly. And why was Luce wearing that transparent blouse unbuttoned to the breastbone with nothing under-neath? Didn't she have the sense, in this very male culture, to bring a jacket?

Luce had just opened the journal when she noticed Lee com-ing towards her across the square. How frustrating to have company at breakfast when she wanted to read. She was still tired from their flight and she felt slightly achy, as if she was coming down with the flu. At least the regatta would relieve her of the burden of making conversation. Hundreds of boats were already jockeying for a starting place in the Basin of San Marco. The hotel clerk had told her the regatta was late this year, postponed because of high winds and unexpected cold weather.

"Ah, you're looking at the family documents. Is this one of Casanova's letters?" Lee pointed at the journal as she sat down.

"No. It's my ancestor's travel journal. I have to deliver it to the Sansovinian at noon, along with the other documents."

"May I see it?" Lee picked it up in her plump fingers and peered inside. "The writing's so quaint."

"You shouldn't touch it without gloves," Luce said.

"What's that?"

"I shouldn't even be looking at it in the open air," Luce said. She took the journal back and put it in her archival box, resting her hand possessively on its lid.

"I wouldn't worry about the journal—it's Casanova's letters everyone will be interested in. Too bad. He was a reflection of a patriarchal age."

"Casanova's reputation is unfair. He wrote novels and operas and saw women as his equals."

"It sounds like you've been taken in by Flem and her defence of Casanova."

"You've read Lydia Flem?"

"Only a review of her book in *The Times*," Lee said, reaching for the menu. "Interesting idea, that Casanova saw desire as an expression of a mother's omnipotence. But the man was a predator, who, even from his own account, deliberately misled women. I can tell by your frown that you don't agree. Here—let me order for you. The menu is in Italian."

Ignoring Luce's frown, Lee placed the order for their costly breakfast: eggs Benedict with Bellinis, the Venetian concoction of champagne and peach juice served in a flute. When the food arrived, they ate in an uncomfortable silence. The only sound was the flapping of their tablecloth in the damp spring wind and the noise of the crowd, some in gaudy medieval costumes, gathering in the bleachers to watch the start of the thirty-kilometre Vogalonga. Out on the Basin of San Marco, thousands of boats with rowers the size of stick figures now swarmed across the milky green waters of the lagoon. Beyond the Basin glistened the domes and church spires of San Giorgio Maggiore and Il Redentore.

"Luce, are you feeling all right? You've hardly touched your breakfast," Lee asked.

Luce nodded vaguely. A tourist at a nearby table was photographing a birchbark canoe gliding past a cluster of rowing skiffs. "I was just thinking about—about Casanova. His birthplace is somewhere near here, isn't it?"

"Maybe so," Lee replied. "We could try to find it. After that we can drop off your family papers at the library and visit a museum."

"I guess." Luce rose and followed Lee out of the café. It was warm now and she felt slightly light-headed in the heat. She thought of Dino Fabbiani and wondered if he would be waiting for her in the Piazza San Marco at one o'clock. She wanted to tell him he was mistaken about Casanova faking his escape from the Ducal Palace. If he would listen. There was a good-natured confidence about Dino that suggested he wasn't used to women disagreeing with his views.

Ten minutes later, the two women were walking up the narrow lane by the Peggy Guggenheim Museum. Their waiter had said Casanova's house was near the Salute Cathedral on the Giudecca, but he had been vague about the street address. Following his instructions, they veered first left, then right, and ended up in a jewellery store. A salesgirl said the waiter was wrong—Casanova had been born near the San Samuele Cathedral. Starting over, Lee paid for tickets on the *vaporetto* to San Samuele and the two women found themselves in a lane where glassblowers sat working at the open windows of their studios. Each glassblower pointed them further down the lane past the stores whose windows were jammed with glass polychrome flowers and carnival masks.

At the end of the lane, Lee and Luce found a house with a plaque declaring it to be the birthplace of the artist Giorgio Vasari, who had lived two centuries before Casanova.

"I feel dizzy," Luce murmured.

"What did you say?" Turning towards Luce, Lee dropped the guidebook, and without thinking, Luce bent quickly to pick it up—too quickly. She saw the curious little square with its empty water fountain and then, of all things, stars. Such a cliché, she thought afterwards. Moments later, she heard a woman's voice calling her, and she saw a little oval window in the shape of an eye. Lee's face appeared in this aperture of light, tiny and frightened and Luce heard Lee's voice ask if she was all right.

Luce struggled to her feet as her vision cleared.

"Sometimes an overnight flight does this," Lee said.

She grasped Luce's arm and guided her through the crowd who turned to stare at the sight they made: the short, fierce middle-aged tourist in a dove-coloured fedora and the tall, bewildered young woman in a pretty chiffon blouse and bright turquoise jeans.

At a water taxi stand, Lee found a young gondolier who said he was glad to help and called them an ambulance boat.

"Better now?" As the launch sped along the Grand Canal, Lee rested her hand lightly on the girl's shoulder.

"I'm sorry to be a burden," Luce whispered.

"Oh, balls!" Lee said, and removed her hand from Luce's shoulder. They sat in silence while the ambulance boat roared down a canal whose edges were lined with peculiar blue-tipped barge poles; in the distance lay the ghostly island of San Michele, with the famous cemetery created by Napoleon. Their launch swerved under a small bridge and came to a stop inside the hospital buildings, next to a door marked with a red cross. They disembarked and found themselves in the emergency room where a doctor in baby blue clogs confirmed that the disorientation caused by jet lag sometimes led to dizziness and fainting.

"The rule of thumb for jet lag is one day for every time zone you cross."

He gave Luce a Valium and told Lee to go off and watch the regatta.

"Thanks, but I'm staying with her," Lee said.

"No, please! I'm fine." Luce stared imploringly at the doctor.

"She needs rest," the doctor said.

"All right, Luce. I'll come back for you later—we'll make plans for dinner then."

Closing her eyes, Luce waited for Lee's footsteps to die away in the hall. When she was sure Lee and the doctor were gone, she brought out the old journal and settled down to read on the hospital cot.

May 4, 1797

I look for evidence of Jacob Casanova.

I took Finette with me when I accompanied Father to the Ducal Palace today. Father met with General Junot,

Napoleon's aide-de-camp last night, and the General asked him to make a report on the prisoners in Venetian gaols to assure our government of the good intentions of the French. It was a lucky coincidence because I was eager to see the gaol where the man Jacob Casanova was imprisoned. My parent knows nothing of my tête-à-tête in the Campanile with the old Venetian. Nor had I ever told him who had given me the dog. I had said I found Finette in the street, and Father was too preoccupied to bother with a stray.

The old justice building hides beneath its frilly Gothic façade three prisons: the Wells, a horrible sewer beneath the edifice of Istrian marble, where prisoners float in sea water; the Fours, which Father refused to describe to me; and the Leads, built directly under the lead roof of the Ducal Palace. Because the lead heats up in the summer sun, the cells are deadly during the warmer months.

We entered the Palace of the Doge by an old door called the Porta della Carta, ornamented with slender pillars, statues and the inevitable winged lion of San Marco. Father puffed and sighed as we made our way through a series of rooms—too beautiful to be properly described—rooms such as the Sala dell'Anticollegio, the waiting room of the ambassadors, and the Sala del Maggior Consiglio, the banquet hall where the Doge gives state dinners. The walls of the banquet hall were hung with portraits by Tintoretto and Bassano. Father noticed only the rills of stinking water on the stairs. He looks poorly. There are dark rings under his eyes and from time to time I glimpse an empty look in his eyes.

The news of war has upset my parent who hoped the sea air in Venice would do him good. Instead, he claims his constitution is bothered by the filth of its stopped-up gutters and the slops the Venetians empty onto the roofs of their neighbours' houses. And he misses the Boston newsrooms where men gather to talk politics.

"Venice is the Grave of Virtue," Father said as we made our way into the Great Council Hall, his eyes alert for human offal.

"Oh, Father!" I cried, hoping to distract him. "Look at Tintoretto's portrait of Heaven! Is it not beautiful?"

As we stopped by the painting, the Doge's minion, Marino Faliero, introduced himself. He told us he was a descendant of the first Doge who had built the Ducal Palace.

Monsieur Faliero led us first to the cells in the east overlooking the canal, the Rio di Palazzo, and the famous Bridge of Sighs where for centuries prisoners have taken their last look at Venice before descending into the watery quarters of the Wells. The little arched bridge was picturesque but I was interested in the Leads, where Finette's owner had been kept prisoner, and was relieved when Monsieur Faliero took us there directly afterwards, Father wheezing beside me. As we peered into these empty rooms, I tried to caution myself about accepting the old Venetian's tale. You see, I possess a gullible nature and am only too eager to believe whatever marvellous things I am told— simply because they are marvellous.

I told Father I did not see how any prisoner could escape from the Ducal Palace. He laughed and asked why any prisoner would wish to escape. With their easy chairs and pillow beds, and despite the low ceilings— both Father and I had to stoop as we entered the rooms— the gaol is more comfortable than the parlours of many farms in Quincy.

I asked Monsieur Faliero if he knew Jacob Casanova and he said that many years ago he'd seen the Chevalier de Seingalt taking a hot chocolate drink at the Florian.

"What did Monsieur Casanova look like?" I asked.

"A dandy of the first order! Very tall, with a strange, sunburnt complexion."

"Why are you interested in this man?" Father asked me.

"It is part of the lore of the Palace," I said, pleased Monsieur Faliero had described someone resembling Monsieur Casanova. I spoke not a word more in case Father noticed my excitable state. I wanted to see the inscription under the plank in the seventh cell that Monsieur Casanova described. But the little dog trotting ahead of me began to pull and strain at her leash, sniffing the floor. She led me past the small airless passage where former prisoners like my new friend had taken their exercise, and into a large room heaped with dusty furniture. Finette began to whine and pull me towards some household goods piled in the corner. Among the pieces of furniture, I saw a warming pan, a kettle, brass tongs, old candlesticks, a chest and a pile of papers sewn into a large manuscript. I picked up the old papers that looked to be records of legal trials dating back several centuries. Finette would not let me read, sniffing and bumping the trunk with her nose, and when I opened it, she leapt inside. A moment later, she leapt back out, and I was obliged to retrieve an old bone from her mouth. In the corridor outside, Father was calling my name.

"Our inspection is over!" He poked his head under the door frame. "There is only one prisoner left up here."

A Greek, very old and stooped, was locked up in the seventh cell—the one Casanova claimed had been his.

THE CITY OF LONGINGS

Moaning in fear, the poor creature withdrew into a corner and put his head on his knees. Father said the bewildered fellow must think we had come to lead him to his execution so we made our excuses to Monsieur Faliero and departed. My spirits fell when I realized I would not be able to search for the inscription under the plank.

"General Junot will not be pleased," Father said. "There are few prisoners here for him to liberate."

"Perhaps there are more down in the Fours."

"There are only two. I heard that from the Doge himself." Outside the Palace we met Francis, who had spent the morning in Torcello talking with lobster fishermen. My betrothed took my arm, and we strolled together as if we were the loving couple my parent wishes us to be. Meanwhile, Father lectured us on the advantages of married life—the delightful business of acting as gardeners to small children, the wifely safety for a plain female like myself, and a husband's need for a female companion who will nurse him in his old age—an earthly blessing denied Father. Francis nodded while I said not a word, staring past the Doge's Palace to the sea, thinking of the wonders of the Levant awaiting the traveller who dares to go.

A Fruitful Question to Be Considered: Is Jacob Casanova who he says he is? And why does this matter to me?

Undertaking Left Undone: I am chagrined that I could not peer under the plank to see if Jacob Casanova told the truth about his inscription: *I love, Jacob Casanova, 1756.* And yet I feel relief. Why? Is it because I do not care to find out if my new friend is a liar? On our way out of the Leads, Father and I passed a tavern in the

Ducal Palace. It was a tavern for the prisoners, and a much pleasanter one, Father said, stopping to inspect it, than the taverns he used to frequent in Quincy before the death of my mother when he became an abstainer. If Mother no longer experienced the joys of existence, he had reasoned, then neither should he indulge in habits that gave him pleasure.

From her hospital cot, Luce saw nurses in light blue clogs hurrying up and down the corridor. They glanced at Luce and she stared back at them over the top of the journal. It was so cool and peaceful in the hospital, and she still had a few minutes to spare. Her appointment at the Sansovinian was more than an hour away. Why not read on for a few more pages?

May 5, 1797

Today I was witness to the fall of an empire.

I walked back to my hotel this morning through a vast, sorrowing crowd who watched in silence as the three Inquisitors of Venice were led in chains through the Piazza San Marco. They were taken to a gaol on San Giorgio Maggiore on General Bonaparte's orders; Father told me it was the Doge himself who issued the command, as most of the French army is still camped far away on the western edge of the lagoons.

At least this means there will not be battles with the French in Venice. The Doge and his Grand Council have surrendered their city. Prisoners, including the old Greek whom Father and I saw yesterday, stood with the silent crowd. The French have thrown open all the gaols and these fortunate wretches can hardly stand upright.

When I arrived back at our hotel, Monsieur Casanova was waiting in my room. How he persuaded the concierge to let him in, I do not know. I found him sitting at my desk, Finette asleep by his feet. I thought of what people would say about the impropriety of entertaining a man in my bedroom, but a sly voice whispered: Asked For, do not fear. Although he is a few inches taller, you have the advantage of youth and can easily outwrestle him. This is a trustworthy feature of My Poor Friend: my muscles are as strong as a boy's from cutting pond ice in Massachusetts.

"Ah, Miss Adams." My visitor rose from his seat, and I caught the scent of rosewater as he bowed to kiss my hand.

"Such formality is out of fashion, monsieur," I said, shaking his hand firmly. Like titles and court wigs, I thought.

"I do my best to uphold the standards of polite society," he smiled. "Please forgive me for intruding. I hoped in the privacy of your quarters I could tell you the story of the woman in the portrait."

After a moment's hesitation, I nodded, and we seated ourselves. I was aware of his scrutiny as I removed the cape Father had bought for me in Paris. It was made of blue silk with brilliant quilted thread in the modern style.

"I admire your *zenda*. And the Grecian banding on your gown."

I thanked him, surprised that a gentleman who still uses dress wigs would care for my republican taste.

"Where is your friend from?" I hid my nervousness by asking a question, an old childhood habit.

"Aimée was born on the island of Martinique into the noble French family of the Dubucqs."

"Ah, so she was affected by the Terror!"

"Her convent in Nantes was closed early, because of political agitation in the countryside. She was on her way back to Martinique when she disappeared, travelling with her childhood nurse, Da. May I?"

He pointed at the water pitcher. I nodded and Monsieur Casanova poured us each a glass of water. It had become very warm in my little room.

"First, will you grant an old gentleman a simple courtesy? I long to hear a female voice speaking the words of my beloved."

With a theatrical shake of his lace-trimmed wrist, he unfolded several wrinkled sheets of writing-paper and handed them to me.

The letter was in French and the penmanship delicate. There was neither date nor address but I did not think much about it because my visitor was talking again in his gravelly voice.

"We met only once, in 1784, five years before the Revolution. Nantes, like many cities on the French coast, was feeling the anger of the peasants." He gave me a sweet smile. "But I cannot complain about the turmoil of those times, Miss Adams, since the Revolution which I abhor made it possible for Aimée and me to find one another. Will you begin?"

"My French is not good enough to read your letter out loud, monsieur. "My father and I speak a Boston twaddle."

He turned on me one of his heavy-lidded glances. "And I speak French like a Venetian. Does my accent mean that I should censor myself?"

I shook my head. It was true, the old gentleman spoke French with an odd, lilting accent, emphasizing the second-last syllable of his words. I had noticed his peculiar tic when we met on the public barge.

"Will you grant me this favour, Miss Adams?"

Slightly breathless, I began:

*My beloved Giacomo,*

*I write to you no longer as Mademoiselle Aimée Dubucq de Rivery but as Nakshidil Sultan, wife of Abd-ul-Hamid I, the Sultan of all Turkey. The arrangements for smuggling this letter out of the Seraglio have been made with the greatest difficulty, although luckily I have made a friend in the harem, born a Christian like myself. She is a Georgian and the mother of Selim, who stands next in line to the throne. When I told her my story, she took pity on me and agreed to send this letter with a Jewish doctor who visits the harem to help the women with their pregnancies. I am well, despite the way my life has changed since you and I met. I was travelling to Martinique and the arranged marriage that had been prepared for me after the death of my parents, bringing such sorrow to both of us. How could I know the remorseless Fates were negotiating an arrangement more powerful than anything my relatives could devise?*

*Our ship crashed into a sea gale as we passed the Strait of Gibraltar and its seams began to open. As Da and I spoke our Hail Marys, a Spanish ship rescued us. You can imagine what rejoicing followed, although Da and I stayed below deck to avoid unpleasantness. But stranger events were to come. As we neared the Palma di Majorca, our Spanish vessel was attacked by Algerian pirates. Da and I were taken aboard as prisoners to be sold into slavery. A change of circumstance that by now may have killed Da—I have not seen my old nurse since Algiers where we* were sold to different bidders. I was bought by Baba Mohammed Ben Osman, the King of the Barbary Corsairs, a terrible old man who Da thought was sure to ravish me and indeed when he took me to his quarters, he made a great show before his servants of leading me into his bedroom. But once there, the old pirate poured me heavily sugared tea and announced he was going to make me the Empress of all Turkey—and himself a fortune.

Dearest love, you may imagine my bewilderment over such a suggestion. What fools these Barbary men are over fair hair! The flaxen locks of my Viking forebears saved my life. And I cannot help thinking, Giacomo, that because their blood thunders in my veins, I have been able to meet my terrible fate with courage.

The old pirate outfitted me with clothes and jewels and sent me in a magnificent ship as a present to the Sultan of the Ottoman Empire. I was received there by the chief of eunuchs in the Seraglio, and shortly thereafter brought before Sultan Abdul. He seemed delighted by my appearance, although he spoke no French. He sent me off for a hot bath in the palace and when I was washed and oiled and refreshed, a servant took me into a large room where veiled women sat on floor sofas eating a meal of quails and rice. I was greeted by Selim's mother, the kindly grey-haired lady who has become my friend. She had recently lost a child and was dressed in the plain jacket and pantaloons of a commoner to show she was in mourning.

We ate pilaf with a flavoured dish of minced meat rolled up in vine leaves and served in tomato sauce. Then came little birds toasted on a skewer and lastly, candied and dried fruits. My new friend presented me with two handsome bracelets. Before I could thank her, a servant appeared and led me along a passage called the Golden Path.

How did I survive that night? The answer is simple. I looked at this old Turk, my husband, whose breath smells like musty *clothing left in attics, whose skin is as papery as parchment, this soft, puffed-up creature who, the women whispered to me, has been weakened by lazing about the harem—and then I closed my eyes and imagined he was you.*

I heard a gentle moan and looked over at my guest. I have never seen a man give way to tears, at least not a man of his stature and age, and I found myself deeply saddened.

"I am very sorry," I whispered. "Should I stop?"

"It does my heart good to hear you. It is like hearing Aimée herself. Please don't stop, Miss Adams."

*Oh my darling, several weeks before I encountered the Sultan, I realized that I am pregnant with your child. If only you could rescue me—you who escaped from the worst prison in the Venetian republic. I am miserable in the world of the Turks. The Seraglio despite its beauty and luxury—its grilled rooms, its aviaries and incomprehensible Arabic libraries, its lovely baths, its kitchen with the great ice pits made from snow that was wrapped in flannel and brought on muleback from Mount Olympus for the making of sherbet and other cooling delicacies— the Seraglio is as much a prison to me as your Venetian Leads.*

*The Sultan's wife has promised to help me escape. For the moment, do not write. It is too dangerous. One of the odalisques who was "in his eye," as the women say, disappeared last week. Some of the wives whisper that she was put in a sack and thrown into the Bosphorus because she was having an affair with a French trader. I cannot afford to be careless with my affections, as she was. I intend to live, dearest one, to return to you.*

*Your Aimée*

*Postscript*

*It is months since I began this letter to you. The birth of our son was a strange affair, Giacomo. They placed me in the royal birthing chair—made of walnut and shaped like a horseshoe with a plank seat, while the midwife chanted "Allah is most great." When all was over and our son, Mahmud, had arrived, these superstitious women placed three sesame seeds on his navel to protect him from the evil eye, put me to bed under gold shawls, and set the Koran wrapped in a silk bag on my stomach. To celebrate Mahmud's birth, my husband, the Sultan, believing your son is his, ordered cages of nightingales to be hung in the groves of lilacs. On his command, lights were set near enormous glass globes of coloured water in order to reflect the gushing fountains of the palaces. If I hadn't been miserable, I might have enjoyed all this beauty, but the truth is, my soul, that I thought only of you. No one knows of my bewildered, angry feelings. The child is sitting in the lap of his taya who is feeding him marzipan water to keep him calm. He is smiling at me as I write.*

"She gave birth to your son! He will be a young boy by now. You must find them both," I said, thinking of the loneliness of growing old without the one you love. Father says I wish to deny the nature of the universe because I want to keep those dear to me from experiencing sorrow. He is fond of quoting Ecclesiastes: "to everything there is a season . . . a time to be born and a time to die . . ." But Father became an Atheist after Mother's death and has no right to quote the Bible to make his arguments. "I could help you."

"You would help me?" he asked softly.

"Gladly. You should rescue her from that terrible world."

"Perhaps that world is no more terrible than ours." He

turned so that I could not see his expression. When he faced me again, I extended my hand and shook his firmly.

"Your French is good for an American," he said, smiling. "May I come another time? I have a second letter I would like you to read for me."

I hesitated, thinking of what Father would say about the impropriety of meeting in my rooms.

"Perhaps we should meet in a café."

I thought a look of disappointment crossed his face but it was gone so quickly that I could not be sure.

"A café will be noisy. But I understand how our friendship could cause problems for you and a man in your father's position. So let us meet by the Florian at sunrise, while Venice sleeps."

Luce paused. At dinner with Lee she had thought she recognized the young photographer at the door of the Florian, although she hadn't been able to see the man's face. It pleased her to think the café had been in existence during the time of Casanova and Asked For Adams.

"It will be an adventure," he continued. "At that hour, the cats are on the prowl and it is a marvel to watch them chase the pigeons who fly off in great clouds of feathers." I agreed since I was eager to see the grandeur of the great square empty of all souls except the four-footed citizens of Venice. And, after loaning me Aimée's letter so I could enter it here, he bowed to me and left. Finette began to yelp for her master. I put the dog on my lap and brushed her coat with the implement he had left for that purpose. It was touching to see the melancholy in the small creature's face, ordinarily so alert, and I thought of the love its owner has for his pet and of the hopeless circumstances surrounding the mother of his child. If only I *could* help him.

Ah, I have begun to believe my new friend is who he says he is. Am I too trusting a soul?

A Fruitful Thought for the Day: Trust must sometimes be rewarded, or it wouldn't be cherished by the human heart.

May 6, 1797

Finette is gone and I am bereft.

This morning, I went to the Piazza San Marco at dawn and he was not there. I saw two French soldiers on a ladder, changing the hands on the clock to French time, whose day starts at midnight as it does in America. Before the arrival of the French, the day began here at dusk. The sight of their soldiers moving the hands of the old Venetian clock distressed me, and for the first time I understood I am in a conquered city. As the faint light increased, small, dark feline forms began flitting like smoky wisps through the columns of the arcade, but there was no sign of Monsieur Casanova. So at least he had not lied to me about the cats. I was filled with a longing I do not understand. It seemed to me my emotion was connected to Monsieur Casanova. I sensed his presence in the piazza, just as I did that first evening when he followed me up the tower, and I had the notion he was directing my thoughts and feelings.

I set out for home in the murky early light. Small boats had begun to crowd the docks by the Molo and fishwives with brightly painted shoes hurried past me carrying their baskets. When I reached my lodgings, Finette was gone.

The concierge told me he had seen a tall man in a frock coat leave the hotel, carrying a bundle under his arm. Bewildered, I went upstairs and found his note:

*I came for Finette, as the spies here have taken note of our friendship. Do not try to find me. When I can, I will notify you of my whereabouts. Thank you for all your kindnesses.*

*Your servant, Jacob*

*Postscript*
   *I have enclosed Aimée's first letter—the first I ever received. I know you will treasure it, as I do, and return it to me when you can.*

   I looked around the room and saw that he had taken the dog's toys. I became dispirited, thinking I might not see Jacob Casanova again. Venice is in the hands of the French, putting an end to Father's trade mission, and the wedding is fast approaching. Soon we will be on our way home to America. I sank down on the chaise to read Aimée's letter, hoping her words would comfort me, and when they did not do so, I tried to amuse myself by copying a translation of her letter onto these pages so I will not forget the sentiments she expressed to Monsieur Casanova:

*Darling Giacomo:*
   *Do you know, my soul, how much I wanted you, from the moment you stepped out of the small wood near the Château d'If and helped me rescue my pet from the swan—that vicious, deceptive bird which pretends to be so serene. I am no longer a*

girl—as you know—and it amuses me now when men see seduction as an act they inflict on us, the weaker sex. From you, I learned that a true attraction moves naturally and at once in both directions. When I felt this mutual recognition between us the world blurred into a kind of ether and I saw nothing except you. Why does this recognition occur between two people in the first place? If I understood the reason, I would be the wisest woman in the world. I know myself a little—I am fiercely proud and a good Catholic, while you, Giacomo, are forced to disguise your abhorrence for Europe's snobbery to make your way in life. Your capacity to appreciate is a gift for me and all of us who know you.

I suppose someone more skeptical than I would not have returned with you to the Château, where you were writing Icosameion—your delightful phantasy of the world beneath the earth. Remember? You spied me from the windows of your bedroom on the grounds below, chasing Charlotte. As I write, I see you—a tall, chestnut-haired man, vigorous, rushing towards the swan waving your hands and making such a commotion that the bird stopped pecking at my dog and hissed at you instead.

In a moment, you had Charlotte in your arms—barking furiously because she did not know you—but the great bird no longer had its prey. It plunged back into the lake and swam off to join its fellows and the two of us laughed because it was clear that Charlotte longed to go after them, pawing your chest so eager was she to renew the chase.

I did return to the Château and I knew when I went up to your room and watched you dip biscuits into your rather vinegary wine—I am sorry, Giacomo, it was vinegary—that I would let you make love to me. As you ate the wine-soaked biscuit, I found myself wondering how your fingers would taste in my mouth. And when you played the old lute you found in the *closet, and Charlotte began to snore on your canopy bed, how natural it was for me to lie down beside her, the wine warm in my veins. That day, it seemed as if all the time in the world lay before us.*

*You undressed me, your eyes grateful. I imagined the swans floating below us, and when you made your connection, I too was a swan floating on a nameless lake. Strange, fragmented visions appeared before me—of myself submerged in water as white feathers drifted above my head. I lost sight of you completely and thought only of myself. Afterwards, you told me that what I felt is how all lovers feel as the moment of* jouissance *approaches, that we use each other well in order to please ourselves. You begged me to stay and said you would find a pastor to marry us. Is it not odd the way life surprises us? Perhaps if I were not an orphan, I would have had the courage to tell Da to go home without me.*

*Your loving Aimée*

*Postscript*

*Do not fear that your age will lessen my desire for you. My love will make you young, Giacomo, and stop the ticking of the clocks. Love is the force that stares down the face of time itself.*

My hands were trembling when I finished copying Aimée's letter. I know nothing of the physical truth of men's bodies, and I found myself wishing I had been the young woman at Château d'If. This thought made me restless and I stepped out onto my balcony overlooking the Grand Canal. Venice was coming to life; the streets echoed with the voices of shopkeepers and gamblers returning from a night in a local casino. In the lane below my balcony, three German men in capes and high boots were

singing a high-spirited round. Their exuberant male noise
made my spirits sink still further. What can Venice—
which has not a single museum or gallery of art—offer a
traveller like myself?

First Inquiry of the Day: Will I find a love such as
Aimée speaks of in her letter? No sooner do I ask this of
myself than a dreadful answer comes: Not in this lifetime,
Asked For Adams, not in this unkind universe is there a
man who will see your value.

Lesson Learned: It is better for a woman like me not to
think about love. Are we not all monsters spawned by
other well-meaning monsters?


What a bleak outlook her ancestor had on love, Luce
thought as she lay on the hospital cot. Of course, at twenty-
five, Asked For would have been considered a spinster and
lucky to have found Francis. Luce was twenty-eight and,
despite her mother's anxieties, her single state did not
inspire that kind of reaction—the very opposite, truth be
told. But she had a secret she hadn't admitted to anyone.
She longed to fall passionately in love, in shameless retro
fashion, one glorious windy spring evening when the tides
were high and the moon golden above her lover's head.
Except that her longing was suffused with a sensation of
futility. Her earlier sampling of love affairs had been
disappointing. Luce knew that Kitty meant well, but she
sometimes thought her experiences had been influenced by
her mother's proactive views on sex, left over from the
1960s. When she was sixteen, Kitty insisted she go on the
birth control pill. Then one night Kitty had invited over a
neighbourhood boy Luce liked and dimmed the lights,

calling over her shoulder, "Enjoy yourselves. I won't be back for three hours." Luce had felt dizzy from fear and nothing much had happened—not then or since.

In the days when they had talked together about such things, her mother warned her not to expect sex to be like the glorified Hollywood depictions. But she stopped trusting her mother's insights on love after Kitty fell for Lee Pronski.

Meanwhile, there were too many nagging questions about love. She longed to be swept away but how could she fall in love without losing all sense of herself? She didn't want to suffer the fate of lovers in Greek myths or romantic novels. It was cheesy and grim to die in a cave like Katherine, the adulterous wife in *The English Patient* and it smacked of self-indulgence. And how do you tell a frog from a prince, or recognize a frog is a prince? He wasn't going to show up in satin tights and slippers that turn up at the toes, now was he? There was no simple answer. And, just as she was convinced that she needed to keep on searching, she was equally sure she would never find anyone who would make it worth her while to surrender to the transporting love she craved.

She supposed her yearning was the sort of thing Lee used to deconstruct in her women's studies courses. She could imagine what the Polish Pumpkin might say: the signifier is looking for a non-existent object to signify. She smiled wistfully. Is that what she was up to? The perfect lover with the perfect nose, and a row of perfect toes? Well, love was the ultimate floating signifier as far as she could tell. The word referred to something no scholar could define or concretize. Anyway, her feelings about love were convoluted, and their complexity left her bewildered. Too bad she couldn't follow the example of Asked For Adams and seek refuge in axioms that glorified paradox, like, say, telling oneself that without doubt hope wouldn't live. If one found paradoxes comforting, that is. Personally, she found them sickening.

May 20, 1797

I have suffered a grave misfortune.

Earlier this evening, Father and I stood together on the balcony outside the salon belonging to Madame Gritti. We were waiting for the guests to arrive in her small apartment (called a *casino*), which overlooks the Piazza San Marco. Father admires Madame Gritti. He wags his head sheepishly when I tease him that the independent ways of Venetian women should help him forgive me mine. In their *casini*, upper-class wives entertain their *cicisbeos*—the escorts who act like second husbands. I notice that Father is pleased if Madame Gritti icily ignores her *cicisbeo* and he winces whenever this fellow appears a few steps behind her, bowing to her one minute and the next running to fetch a hot choco-late drink.

She, at least, found Father interesting enough to offer him her apartment and he has invited some of the élite of Venice to see the sketches from Monsieur Pozzo. Despite my warning, Father had insisted on going ahead with his purchase, saying I had acquired my knowledge of art from Peabody's guidebook. His lack of suspicion is out of char-acter, and I fear the effect this city is having on him. He was no longer in good humour by the time we found our-selves on the balcony watching the angry mob in the square. They were smashing the doors of anyone sympa-thetic to the French because they believe the Doge and his council betrayed them by surrendering their city. At one end of the square, we heard boys yelling, "*Viva San Marco!*" And by the Molo, brigades of French soldiers rushed into the melee, shouting, "*Viva la libertá!*"

"They are not bringing freedom to Venice, Father. This is tyranny. Do we need to have the French consul to our party?"

"He declined, child. And I worry the others will not come. Let us check to see if Monsieur Pozzo has brought the sketches."

Together we walked back into the *casino*. It was nearly midnight and, to Father's relief, our Venetian guests began to arrive. They were a mix of rich merchants and poor members of the aristocracy, though many of these *barnabotti* have already fled Venice. I could hear the chatter of the women, dressed in long black silk coats and the mannish hats that spout a single white feather. The men wore frock coats and perukes and appeared untroubled by the sounds of the violence in the square. As we greeted them, the chalky smell of hair powder floated in the air around us, mingled with the vinegary scent of the cologne that is the fashion here.

Bestowing his gap-toothed grin upon our guests, Francis emerged from the thicket of perfumed bodies and whispered that he and our guests had come through the back entrance to avoid the mob of angry citizens. For once, I felt glad to see him. I took his arm and we went in to our late dinner of champagne and risotto served with platters of local artichokes. After the meal, while Madame Gritti translated his awkward French into Italian, my parent spoke about his mission. He told our guests that Uncle John, together with Thomas Jefferson and Benjamin

Franklin, had sent a letter to the Venetian ambassador in 1789, expressing interest in trade with Venice.

"And I am here to extend our invitation. We in America will trade our cattle and wheat for your Venetian glass and lace."

"You're setting up shop in the midst of a civil war!" someone called out in French.

"Is there a better time?" Madame Gritti replied. "What is more conducive to money-making than a war?"

Our guests clapped and laughed. I stared shyly at their powdered Venetian faces, alight with excitement. A few of our guests wore silver masks and I admit I found their faces strange and alarming. Outside, the noise of the crowd had grown louder, and Father had to shout to be heard.

"Welcome guests, today we from America will show you Rome's finest art and you will see how greatly our republic admires yours."

Once again, our guests clapped, but they had begun whispering to each other, their eyes wandering, and I realized they were only feigning interest in Father. I told him that we should get on to the exhibit and he responded with, "My friends, let us proceed now to the Paper Museum."

The guests stood aside as Madame Gritti put the key in the lock of a door leading to an adjoining room. The door swung open and they pressed in ahead of us. We heard laughter and angry exclamations. The walls of the little chamber were bare. Except, alas, for the single sketch Monsieur Pozzo had shown us that day in the Café Florian. The sketch lay on a small table, held down by stones. There was no sign of Monsieur Pozzo. Madame Gritti removed the stones and inspected the drawing with her lorgnette.

"Monsieur Adams, this is a forgery." She beckoned Father over and pointed to the corner of the drawing. The tiny watermark read 1795. Father staggered backwards, and Francis had to catch him by the arm so he would not fall. Madame Gritti dismissed our guests and they filed out, neither thanking Father nor looking at us. It was a humiliating occasion.

Madame Gritti left quickly with her *cicisbeo*, leaving only Father, Francis and myself. My betrothed at least had the good grace not to pester Father with questions. We hurried down to the square where some Venetian men were setting little fires. Fearful, we rushed by them, but they did not harm us. Outside our *pensione*, a large group had gathered in the *campo* around a tall beggar in a Harlequin mask standing with another beggar in a sleeveless coat. A covered basket sat nearby, guarded by a small, rough-haired dog. The tall beggar growled some words in Italian and the dog bounced over to the basket and raised one of the sides with its teeth. It hopped inside and out again, holding in its mouth a small piece of folded paper. It placed this at the feet of the old man. He called out in Italian, and some of the audience shrieked and waved their slips of paper at him. Others walked away, their heads down.

I knew Venice is fond of gambling. No one can miss the colourful windows in lottery offices which display the winning numbers on placards decorated with fantastic figures in blue and red and gold. At night, these windows are well lit with lamps and candles so the Venetians can check their ticket with the winning numbers predicted by the city's successful gamblers.

Still, I had never seen two wretched beggars and a half-starved dog holding a lottery in the midst of a civil war.

What kept these unfortunates from taking the money for themselves, I wondered.

Suddenly, the little dog stopped its jack-in-the-box performance and turned a pair of familiar golden eyes on me, wagging its tail. The tall beggar man looked at me warningly. Then he whistled and the little dog trotted to his side, its head down. And I realized I knew the beggar man.

Francis and I have put Father to bed. I have retired to my room and have brought out my new quill.

First Inquiry of the Day: Why did Jacob Casanova dress up as a beggar? To avoid Count Waldstein? And why did Father, a suspicious judge of character, believe a man like Monsieur Pozzo, a person he would not have invited to our home in America?

Lesson Learned: When in a strange country, trust no one, not even your own travelling companions who may be altered by their experiences in new lands.

Newest Thought I Am Entertaining: I am wiser than my own parent, and this is a melancholy prospect.

Postscript

A few hours ago, I heard Father shout my name from his bedchamber. I hurried to his side and found him, his bed-clothes a-tumble, his cotton nightcap still on, vomiting into his chamber pot. When I rushed over, he raised his eyes up to me like a frightened child and pointed at his heart.

"Father, please don't talk!" I began to wipe his face with a cloth I dipped in the washing bowl. His forehead felt feverish and he was struggling to catch his breath.

"I must talk, child," he whispered as he tried to sit up. "Before the pain makes it impossible to speak."

"Father, be still!" I pushed him gently back on to the
bed and for a moment I thought he might strike me,
although he was as feeble as I have ever seen him.

"You must marry Francis if anything happens to me.
Promise me that," Father said as I pulled the coverlet
across his chest.

"Nothing will happen to you, Father."

"Do you trust me, child?"

I nodded.

"Then say you will marry Francis if I do not live to see it."

I took a quick breath. "Father, I trust you," I said. "But
I do not trust myself."

"Is that your answer, little one? If so, it does me no good."

"I do not wish you unhappiness, Father," I said.

"Then say it—say it, Asked For!"

"No." I was shocked by the firmness of my answer.

A shattered hopeless roar rose out of Father's throat
and he threw himself out of the bed linen. The noise
struck me like a hammer blow. He raised both fists,
I thought to strike me, but instead he hit his fists with
singular force against the front of his chest, and fell backwards on the bed. I knew, before bending to check his
pulse, that he was dead.

When dawn came, I was still lying across his chest.
From the street came the cries of vendors selling their
fresh melons and strawberries to the late night gamblers.
Father, there is nothing you can do for me now, I thought
sadly. I am alone in the world. As the sun grew brighter, I
washed myself and set out to find Francis.

On such a day there are no new thoughts or lessons learned.
There is only life, as absolute and as unbiddable as death.

Luce realized that her appointment with Signor Goldoni at the Sansovinian was in half an hour. Where was Lee? Why hadn't she returned? She put the journal back in its box and checked out of the hospital. Reading about the death of Asked For's father had distressed her and she longed to be reassured by the companionable bulk of regatta crowds. Ignoring the sign that said USCITA, she found herself in a shady arcade where patients with drawn faces sat talking to one another. Luce remembered seeing the cemetery of San Michele on the way to the hospital, so conveniently close to its customers, and grew frightened she wouldn't be able to find the exit. She asked a family for directions, and the mother and father began to argue in Italian over the best way out. To her relief, the son walked with her to the front door and pointed her towards the square of Santi Giovanni e Paolo. Two minutes later, she was lost in a new square that looked exactly like the one by the hospital. She hadn't realized how confusing Venice could be, despite the ubiquitous plaques with little yellow arrows pointing in the direction of Piazza San Marco. At a café, she pleaded with a waiter who drew her a map but in minutes she found herself lost again. She felt dehydrated from the heat of the still May afternoon, and in the next *campo* she made herself stop and take off her jacket.

She stood by a news kiosk, a striking figure with her height and bright clothes. A few of the young men in the crowd stared her way, with sly looks of appreciation. The exertion of walking had made her cheeks ruddy and her cropped brown hair was windblown and standing slightly on end. Out on the canal, gondolas with straw-hatted rowers scudded past the *palazzos* that rose up in the water-dappled sunlight like country houses fringed by narrow green lawns. Except that the green borders under the houses were not lawns but algae exposed by the tide.

She realized she had stumbled into the midst of the regatta whose start she and Lee had witnessed earlier in the morning. A skiff with an all-female crew in long pleated skirts rowed by. As they passed, the cox stopped talking on her megaphone and lifted her hand to Luce in a woman-to-woman salute. The men on the embankment cheered noisily.

Farther up the canal, gondolas were pulling in at a refreshment booth to accept their cans of Gatorade and oranges. As the rowers and regatta officials milled together and chatted, she thought of Casanova and his leisurely approach to travel. What was his advice about going only where your whims take you? She relaxed and began walking at a thinking pace. A few minutes later, without trying, she arrived at the Piazza San Marco, where she was supposed to meet Dino in an hour. At the San Marco station, a *vaporetto* was discharging sightseers who had been packed in the low, squat ferry like refugees. They swarmed onto the crowded wharf, while out on the lagoon, she saw the flotilla of regatta boats jostling and bobbing towards the finish line at the mouth of the Grand Canal. It was Sunday, and the door to the Sansovinian Library stood open; tourists were pouring through its doors.

Inside the library, a guard said Signor Goldoni was waiting for her. A guide led Luce upstairs and into a crowded room where families stood by a tall window watching the regatta. She felt touched by the sight of the mothers and small children waving at the milling boats on the green shimmer of the Basin.

"You like our regatta?" A man emerged from the group and introduced himself as Signor Goldoni. Luce noticed that his loafers were made of beautiful copper-coloured leather. Nodding politely, she followed him to his office.

"The boat race always takes place on a Sunday, and the library opens this office for all of us who work here so we can come and watch it with our families." He seated himself at a desk.

"How kind," Luce murmured.

"Yes, yes, very quiet," he replied, mishearing her. "Do you realize it's the only day in Venice when you can't hear a motorboat? They are forbidden today. Will you show me your documents? I am eager to see the letters, of course."

Signor Goldoni removed the documents from their plastic case. He examined Casanova's letters, reverently drawing on white gloves to avoid leaving a fingerprint, and holding them by the edge of the page.

"It looks authentic," he said, excitement rising up in his voice. "What an extraordinary contribution for our exhibit!"

To Luce's disappointment, he barely glanced at Asked For's journal. He only scanned the flyleaf, smiling and nodding. Then he placed it back in its archival box.

"Is this all?"

"Yes," she whispered, aware that a fiery heat was spreading from her neck to her face. She realized she had left the Arabic manuscript in her hotel room. How could she have overlooked it? She saw it in her mind's eye—on the bedside table.

"Well, if anything else about Casanova turns up in your family's attic, please be sure to let us know." He gave Luce a release form and handed her box to a young assistant to lock safely away.

"Yes, we will," she said, signing the document granting the library the loan of their family documents.

"Do you like Casanova? Most women do." He glanced inquiringly at Luce. "He belonged to all of us, you understand? Some historians say the chapters in his memoir describing his love for men have been lost or suppressed."

"I didn't know that." Luce handed him back the release form. "Everyone has their interpretation of Casanova, it seems."

Signor Goldoni gave Luce the smile of a comrade-in-arms. "We archivists don't know everything, do we? Yes, Charles Smith told me we are in the same business," he added. "That is why I was not worried for the safety of the documents. I knew you would take good care of Casanova's letters."

Overcome with embarrassment, she said goodbye and hurried out into the square. She was upset with herself for botching the delivery, but tomorrow she would make her apologies and bring the Arabic manuscript to the Sansovinian. She looked around for Dino Fabbiani. Had he waited for her? He'd said 1 p.m. It was already one-thirty, and the young photographer was nowhere to be seen. She considered returning to the hotel to get the manuscript and find Lee, but on impulse bought a ticket to see the prison that had housed Casanova in the Ducal Palace.

As she walked through the courtyard and up the Staircase of the Giants, she thought of Asked For Adams visiting the waiting room of the ambassadors with her father. Dust and nostalgia. The universal smell of ancient buildings. When she was in her late teens, she and her mother had toured Somerset, England, and seen the bronze plaque in the medieval church of St. Mary the Virgin, honouring the ploughman and maltster Henry Adams. In 1638 he had set sail to the New World at the age of fifty-eight. He had taken with him his wife and their eight sons.

"You see, Luce, we have inherited optimistic genes," her mother had laughed. That was their last trip together before Kitty met Lee.

On the first floor of the Ducal Palace, Luce joined a group on the "Secret Tour" through the Leads under the palace's lead roof. Outside the first cell in which Casanova had been imprisoned, their guide told them that because Casanova stood two metres tall, he'd been allowed to leave the room with its low ceiling and exercise in the attic. The cell lay directly over the room where the three State Inquisitors had voted to arrest Casanova. She peeked into the box-shaped room with its tiny, barred windows and a ceiling barely higher than her head. She asked the guide if she could go in. With a little bow, the guide opened the door. The third plank to the left of the door of the seventh cell, she told herself, thinking of Casanova's instructions to Asked For Adams. She bent down, feeling the guide's eyes on her back, and ran her hand over the floorboards by the door. They appeared to be nailed firmly in place. She rose to her feet and caught the guide smiling indulgently, as if she was one of thousands of Casanova fans who made the pilgrimage to this dusty room.

She sheepishly followed the other tourists into the attic of a large tower where this man who had known her ancestor had been given permission to stretch his legs. The attic resembled the hull of an old galley, the guide said, because it was built by the workers at the Arsenal, who worked so quickly and skilfully they could finish a ship in an afternoon. Its walls of birch, larch and oak had been treated with salt water to turn the wood as hard as stone. As she stood on the walkway strewn over the floor beams, thought she heard Casanova whisper, *Watch out—I am still here, a cat among pigeons!*

Staring up at the beams in the attic, she was amazed by his persistence. How could anyone cut through that roof with a hunk of granite? But he had not given up, no matter how many setbacks he suffered. No wonder Asked For Adams fell under his influence, she thought. He was a man who could talk you out of yourself.

She felt disappointed when the tour was over. As the others hurried out of the palace, she stopped to gaze down through a high, grilled window onto the Sansovinian Library. There, marching across its roof, she saw the forgotten stone people with the steadfast expressions that had moved Asked For Adams. She brought out Lee's guidebook to find the names of the lonely figures, and something fell out onto the stone floor. It was a photograph of a petite, fair-haired woman with a youthful face. The photo was dated the year her mother met Lee, when Luce was twenty. In the photo, her mother's lips were curled in a spirited smile, as if she was saying to the photographer, "I don't like the way you are bossing me around, but I still wish you well." Luce remembered the same look of sunny determination on her mother's face.

Slowly, she bent her head until her cheek was resting against the cool stone of the palace wall. She heard herself weeping and she was amazed at the sound of her anguish.

~

In Luce's childhood there had been one great sorrow: the loss of her father when she was six. He was a young medical intern who had left her mother and gone off to Australia. He had written to them once and then they heard nothing after that. Kitty had been too proud to search for him. As a child, Luce used to look for her father under the bedsheets and her bewildered face would make her mother cry. In a rage, her mother had given away his clothes to the Salvation Army, but Luce had smuggled a pair of his oxblood brogues to the back of her closet along with his huge rubber stethoscope, which she used for testing the heartbeat of her dolls. She would bring out her father's shoes when she felt sad, and stroke their perforated toes. Then, when her mother inherited the hundred-year-old house that had belonged to Luce's grandfather, her father's things were lost in the move.

As she grew older, she thought of him less. She adopted her mother's name and discovered that she liked living in the old house, whose foundations had been put in place by the grandson of Aaron Adams. A portrait of its pretty, pale blue board-and-batten façade had been painted by a member of the Group of Seven and curators sometimes included the painting in their retrospectives. Luce did her schoolwork and ran the household while her mother worked long hours at the university. In the early years, her mother had researched pottery-making by Iroquoian-speaking tribes, a term that included the Hurons and the Iroquois who lived in Eastern Canada. In monographs with truly boring academic titles like *Southern Ontario Pottery: Art among the Iroquoian-Speakers*, K.A. Adams argued that pottery-making in these Neolithic tribes was practised by women who taught the craft to their daughters. Luce sometimes helped her mother with the research and for that she would be included in the credits.

It was her mother's interest in the goddess movement—so derided in archaeological circles—that undermined the bond between them. Luce felt skeptical about her mother's theory that the peoples of prehistory worshipped a deity called the Great Earth Mother. She didn't understand how her mother had gone from pointing out the possibility that women in some Woodland tribes might have been potters to the grandiose claim that most prehistoric relics were sacred objects used in the worship of a goddess. When her mother became a follower of the late archaeologist Marija Gimbutas, Kitty began to attract older female academics and women interested in the goddess movement. And being the daughter of the well-known Dr. K.A. Adams started to feel like waiting her turn in a crowded hall of strange women, each one claiming her mother's attention. As if her mother's fans didn't have mothers of their own.

After public appearances, Kitty would seize her hand and exclaim: "Luce! My stalwart! I am so tired of all this!" She liked the strange little glassy look of exhaustion in her mother's eyes. It made her feel needed. And she would be overcome with a rush of protective love and pride because she was the one her mother leaned on. Then her mother would go back to her work, and Luce would start plotting how to get her attention again.

Luce hadn't realized how far her mother's views had pulled them apart until she encountered one of Kitty's fans in the reading room at the Miller. That afternoon, she came back from lunch to find that a schoolgirl with a nose ring was reading an old essay Luce had helped her mother write about Aataentsic, the woman in the origin myth of the Hurons.

In that instant it seemed as if she saw her life go by; how she had helped her mother with her work and run the household; and then, how her mother had left her behind and gone away with Lee Pronski. No matter what her mother said, she knew she wasn't stalwart or patient. She felt only hurt and jealous.

Downstairs, she walked listlessly past the room where, more than two hundred years before, the Inquisitors had voted on Casanova's case. She entered the Great Hall and saw before her the same famous painting, *The Coronation of the Virgin* by Tintoretto, that Asked For had shown her father. It covered the eastern wall—a vast, sombre canvas in which hundreds of little human bodies, likely saints and popes, floated in a mud-coloured sky, their lifted arms and straining bodies turned towards the numinous circles of light around Christ and the Virgin Mary.

In the crowd of tourists around the painting, she noticed a woman wearing a long red scarf. The woman was talking to a man carrying a camera.

"Dino!" Luce cried happily.

Startled, he stopped talking to the woman and ambled over.

"Were you waiting for me?" she asked. "I'm sorry I was late."

"Of course, *bella*." He bowed, snapping together the heels of his brogues.

After her lapse into sadness upstairs, she felt relieved to have his company, and they walked out across the arcade around the Ducal Palace and into the square. He pointed at the Campanile, explaining that Galileo had demonstrated his telescope to the Doge in the tower in 1609. The tower had fallen down in 1902, but no one had been hurt, Dino said, except for a cat named after Casanova's dog, Melampyge.

"He had another dog called Finette," Luce said, and Dino shrugged absent-mindedly. She told him then about the passage in the old journal in which Asked For Adams described meeting Casanova in the tower, and he began to listen thoughtfully. Overhead in the Campanile, a bell was tolling again.

At the other end of the piazza, a small crowd had gathered at the base of a second tower. The people were staring up at the richly ornamented clock face. Following their gaze, Luce saw three little kings and an angel trundling out of the doors on either side of the tower—the angel raising its trumpet to its lips and the kings bowing as they bobbed past the Virgin and the Christ Child in the niche above the clock.

"The three Magi always draw an audience," Dino said, bringing out his Mayima and aiming it at the clock. "Would you like to go inside and see its mechanism? My friend Alberto lives there."

He lowered his camera and without waiting for her answer, he took her by the hand and drew her towards the archway under the clock tower. He knocked on a door partly hidden by the scaffolding.

"Dino!" A young man with a receding hairline stood before them.

"Alberto!" Dino kissed the young man on both cheeks and they proceeded up a set of stairs and into a kitchen.

The room pulsed with a sound like the beat of a giant heart. The muffled bang was broken every few minutes by a frenzy of whirling and crashing flywheels and ratchets. Loops of chains and ropes ran through the wooden ceiling and floor. Sleeping on a table in the midst of this immense mechanical toy lay a three-legged cat.

"She's missing a foreleg so I named her Venus," Alberto said. "I think she is what you English call Siamese."

"Ciao, Venus!" Dino made a mock bow towards the cat, who sat up and yawned at the sound of their voices.

Looking closer, she saw that the cat's right eye was the opalescent blue of a Siamese, but its left was shut tight. A yellow ooze ran from the corner of the eye. "You poor thing!" she said.

"Alas, I can't take her to Milano."

"You are going on holiday, Alberto?" Dino smiled.

"I'm staying with my sister while they repair my big baby." Alberto waved grandly at the clock. "My sister is allergic to cats. If you know anyone who would like Venus, be my guest, as you say in English."

The cat leapt off the table and hopped in a funny little lop-sided motion over towards Luce. She could hear the rattle of its purr as it rubbed itself against her pant leg.

"It likes your voice, *bella*." Dino smiled as he took a

photograph of Luce crouching down to stroke the cat's battered-looking head.

"I wish I could take her," Luce said. "But we leave tomorrow."

"Ah, well, think it over." Alberto nodded at Dino. "If you change your mind, Dino will bring it to your hotel. I hope you will remember seeing the greatest wonder of Venice. If it is true as they say, that time is money—then I am the richest man in the world."

"Oh, time is much more complex than that," Dino said, winking at Luce, and she smiled shyly. It was true: she could feel the arrow of time bending mysteriously. It seemed to her that time was thundering backwards, like a river returning to its source.

A few minutes later, she was walking with Dino through the great Piazza San Marco, where tourists moved among the pigeons like currents of sea air from the Adriatic, their cameras bobbing on their chests, the side veils of their Tilley hats fluttering. One of the larger groups, judging from their boisterous, drawling voices, came from the American South. They called out to one another as they pushed their way into a crowded pizzeria on the edge of the square.

"Are the pigeons a metaphor for the tourists?" Dino asked sarcastically. "Or are the tourists a metaphor for the birds?"

Luce smiled obligingly. Near the middle of the square, she noticed the guide who had been talking to Dino in the Ducal Palace. As she watched, the woman lifted up a huge scarlet umbrella and the tourists scurried in her direction.

"The tourists can't be a metaphor for the birds," Dino said. "They are too badly dressed."

Luce laughed, her usually solemn round face as unguarded as a schoolgirl's, and Dino bowed like a performer accepting applause. Then he pivoted on the heel of his brogue and waved at a figure in a frock coat who was calling out to him in Italian. The man's head sprouted a mountainous plumage of yellow curls, and his high-heeled pumps shone bright pink against the cobblestones.

Luce felt a surprised little thrill. Could it be Donald Sutherland under the curls? She recalled that the actor had played Casanova in an old movie by Fellini. Or was it a Sutherland look-alike? The man had caught Sutherland's lugubrious style—the long, horsey face with the bulging eyes.

"You know him?" she asked.

"Leopardo's been hired to dress up for the regatta," Dino said. "It's over two hundred years since the death of the great Venetian, you know."

The lanky actor strolled across the square and kissed Dino on both cheeks. He beamed toothily as Dino focused his Mayima on him.

"My friend is interested in Casanova," Dino said, from behind his camera.

"Were you in Fellini's movie?" Luce asked.

"Leopardo is too young to claim that honour." Dino laughed.

Someone was shouting Casanova's name. The trio turned towards the wharf, where an enormous golden gondola was being landed by five men, all of them dressed in the same style of frock coat as Leopardo and wearing the same golden wigs. Once ashore, they began to tumble and somersault on the dock while the tourists clapped. They bowed, acknowledging the applause, and sprang into a human pyramid; Leopardo strode whistling over to join them. Despite his size, the others hoisted him up to the shoulders of the two men on the top of the pyramid, as the crowd around them clapped and yelled. Out of the corner of her eye, Luce noticed the guide with the red scarf looking their way. When Luce met her gaze, the young guide turned her back and began talking to one of the American tourists, paddling the air with her hands as if she was irritated.

On the Molo, the six Casanovas had begun declaiming in English to the audience. The smallest of the six knelt before the crowd and began to describe the childhood of Casanova. The actor switched to Italian, and what he said made the crowd laugh.

"He's telling us how Casanova amused his mother's dinner guests!" Dino said, sliding his arm around Luce's waist. "He was only eleven, *bella*, and he did it by answering an adult riddle. Why is the Latin noun for the female genitals masculine, and feminine for the male?"

Dino paused, and Luce said softly, "Because the servant takes his name from the master."

"Ah, *bella*, you are clever."

"Do you think Casanova's mother loved him, Dino?" she asked, thinking of Lee's comment about Casanova seeing a mother's omnipotence in desire.

"An excellent question! She delighted in his wit, naturally. But she left him with his grandmother to go on the stage."

"Poor Casanova," Luce murmured. Over by the *vaporetto* station, a woman in a large Borsalino stood watching the performers. "Let's get out of here," Luce whispered.

They hurried away across the Molo. She kept her head down, and when they were out of sight, she let Dino take her hand and leaned into him, grateful for his warmth in the cool spring afternoon.

Lee waved to Luce, but she couldn't seem to catch the girl's eye. Or Luce didn't want to be seen with that wolfish-looking young man. Who would have guessed that someone as timid as Luce could be sly? She had been slow returning to the hospital, and when she returned, Luce had left for her appointment at the Sansovinian.

She had hoped to take Luce to the island of Torcello for dinner at the trattoria that specialized in *carciofi*, the lovely, plump artichokes that were first boiled and steamed, then coated in the thickest olive oil and served cold, their long stems trailing wistfully across the crockery. In the midst of her concern at the hospital, it hadn't occurred to her to let Luce in on her plan. She had wanted to tell her, in a quiet moment, that the island of Torcello, with its clogged canals and deserted piazza, had been Kitty's favourite spot in Venice. She was sure Luce would want to hear how she and Kitty had photographed its sad stone Madonna and eaten picnics of tasty artichokes by a muddy stream behind the old cathedral.

Now what was she supposed to do, go back to the hotel and wait? Lordy, it was a nuisance dealing with the needs of a young person. Perhaps Luce didn't want to be with her. She had overheard Kitty once reprimanding Luce for calling her the Polish Pumpkin. She had been called worse things by her students. Still, it had stung her at the time.

Well, she would forget about Luce and work on her lecture notes at the Cantonine Istorica, another small restaurant she and Kitty had enjoyed. She'd eat their artichokes and toast Kitty with a glass of *prosecco*. Her mind made up, she strode off. But when she arrived, she found the restaurant closed. She peered through the window, looking for signs of waiters in their formal white jackets and saw the menu posted in the glass. Yes, there were the *carciofi* and the other dishes they had enjoyed together: *frittura mista*, a mixed fish fry; *capesante alla veneziana*, Venetian scallops cooked with garlic, parsley and lemon juice; and *ragno di mare*, the spider crabs that Kitty had loved so much.

She started her walk back, alone, to the Flora.

Dino took Luce to Harry's Bar, once the watering hole of Ernest Hemingway. They huddled together at the bar, looking at his shots from the previous day. He shook his head apologetically over some of the photographs and she realized that the rowing skiffs were slightly out of focus. She made sympathetic little noises when he said he'd had a day of bad luck. She found his droll, old-world manner touching.

"Do you want to go back to the square and take some more?" she asked.

Shaking his head, he offered her the last of the long-stemmed bitters in the silver bowl on the bar. "Come, *bella*. I have something to show you."

He led her down a maze of streets lined with high stone walls that concealed private gardens. A fresh sea breeze was rustling the tops of the half-hidden trees, and overhead, a newly risen moon cast its watery light, changing them into silvery creatures. In one instant, Dino became Punchinello, with a long, comic nose, and next the plague doctor of Venice in a beaky mask and flowing white gown. They crossed into a well-lit alleyway, and Dino became a man again. She sighed in relief, and he tugged her close to him, staring into her eyes with an unsettling intensity. She realized he was standing on his toes so his face could be level with hers.

"You must like tall women." She smiled at him.

"You are very beautiful, *bella*," he whispered. "Your great big eyes—*bellissima!*" She could feel his longing for her in his touch, and the sensation made her giddy. She pulled back, giggling nervously, and they started off again, their arms around each other's waists. And now, unexpectedly, they stood on the Zattere wharf. Under the pink glow of street lamps, she noticed Dino's friend, the tour guide, with her group of Americans sitting at one of the cafés. She pointed them out to Dino and he nodded dismissively. It was extraordinary, she thought, how small Venice was. Lee had told her the city was in an area no bigger than Central Park.

He took her arm and tugged her in the direction of a water-stained building.

"Luce, come. My flat is here. Look." He pointed at a plaque on the wall.

"'Beauty is religion if human virtue conjures it up and the reverence of the people holds it to its heart,'" she read. Half turning, she stared in the direction of the tour group and noticed that Dino's friend was on her feet now, gazing at them.

"Did you know John Ruskin refused to make love to his bride?" Dino asked.

"Yes." Luce decided to ignore the guide. "He expected her to have no pubic hair, like a statue."

"So you know Ruskin too?" Dino sighed as if she had disappointed him and inserted his key in the door of the *pensione*. His flat turned out to be just two rooms—perhaps the very rooms, Luce thought, in which Ruskin had composed *The Stones of Venice*. She felt shy again, glancing nervously about the shabby space. To calm her nerves, she began to examine some black-and-white photographs scattered on the bed. Now that she'd come this far he would expect her to have sex with him. She knew she either had to sleep with him or explain why she had led him on. Thank goodness she had a moment to think. He had disappeared into a room off the entrance hallway. Rifling through his photographs, she stopped at one with a letter clipped to it and read it without thinking. It appeared to be a cover letter from Dino, offering the sale of his photographs to an English paper:

To whom it may concern,

Would you like to buy my photographs of the Vogalonga in Venice? This year, the amateur regatta will draw over four thousand contestants from all over the globe for the rowing race that covers thirty kilometres and some of the most picturesque parts of the Lagoon.

The Vogalonga was started in 1974 by a Venetian family, the Rosa Salvas, owners of a bakery and catering service near Piazza San Marco. The family patriarch wanted a day of peace, without the wash of motorboats which erodes the foundations of the old palaces. There is no corporate sponsor of the regatta, nor are there traditional winners. Every contestant who passes the finish line is given a Venetian medallion and a small diploma in the form of a poster.

Sincerely,
Dino Fabbiani

So he really was a photojournalist. She felt slightly ashamed of herself for doubting him. Then she noticed the scribbled memo attached beneath: *Dear Dino, I am afraid your photographs are not up to the professional standards of* The European.

She hid the memo quickly beneath a pile of photographs as Dino emerged from the other room, holding up a blow-up of an eighteenth-century painting of a man in a wig and frock coat. The head was in profile, showing a youthful male face whose single, bulging eye seemed to express astonishment at something just outside the frame of the picture. Luce knew from her research that it was a painting of Casanova at twenty-six, by his brother, Francesco Casanova.

"For you, *bella*. Do you recognize him?" he asked, setting the photograph down on the cluttered table.

"Casanova?"

"Who else? I am very proud of it. The matte finish works well, don't you think?"

"Yes, and it's so clear, especially compared to your other photos."

He looked downcast, and she felt a sisterly tenderness for him.

"There is a fungus on the lens of my camera. It happens sometimes in Venice. Our humidity is bad for my equipment. When I have more money I will fix it."

"I didn't know about that. It must be expensive to replace a lens."

He nodded morosely. "Yes, the tourists make everything expensive in Venice, *bella*. They are like cows, mooing in our faces. If I could leave, I would." He gave her a sweet, ironic smile that she realized was characteristic of him. His bleakness disturbed her; she wanted to correct his fatalistic interpretation.

"Maybe you could leave and start over somewhere else?"

She became aware of voices below the window speaking English. She found herself straining to hear what they were saying, but Dino was suddenly standing in front of her, as if he wanted to block out the distraction on the street.

"*Bella*, your skin is white and fine—like Istrian marble," he murmured.

"But my complexion won't last forever, Dino."

He laughed. "What a thing to say! Great beauty is the hallmark of the immortals!" He pulled her into his arms, and she let him turn her face to his so he could kiss her.

"You are sweet and good, *bella*," he whispered. The musk of his cologne tickled her nose; she felt faintly aroused.

"Do you have a condom?" she whispered.

"There is no need. I can tell you aren't sick."

"How do I know you're not sick?"

"What did you say, *bella*?"

"You need to wear a condom, Dino."

"No, I can see who is healthy and who is not. And you, *bella*, have the face of a virgin."

She stiffened. Behind Dino's shoulder the doorknob was turning, just as it did in the old movies, and now the door opened and Dino's friend, the tour guide, stood on the threshold. She began to scream in Italian. "You must go, *bella*. My friend is here," Dino whispered. Dumbfounded, she let him take her hand and lead her quickly to the room off the hall. It was a photographer's darkroom. He opened the window and pointed to a fire escape.

Before she could protest, he hurried her towards the window, one hand pressing on her neck as if he was already pushing her through the window. Humiliated, she ducked down and climbed onto the fire escape. Once she reached the ground, she began to run through the side streets behind Dino's *pensione* until she came to the Hotel Flora. She realized he lived close by, and it seemed as if she had known her way back from another life. She leaned, panting, against its stone entrance and was assailed by a familiar lethargic sensation—indifference, or something worse: a disappointment past bearing. She thought of finding Lee. But what would be the point? She straightened herself up and walked with her little forward stoop into the lobby.

According to the clerk, there was no note from Lee. Relieved, she went up to her room and pulled out the user copy of Asked For Adams' journal. She had given the original to Signor Goldoni but she would make herself feel better by reading the rest of her ancestor's account on Charles Smith's photocopy. Trying to put Dino out of her thoughts, she took the time to insert the copies of Casanova's letters into Asked For's entries so she could read Asked For's story in chronological order. Feeling slightly consoled, she opened the user copy where she had left off. No one who saw the sheaf of Xeroxed pages would guess its importance. Only the words in red ink, "Harvard Library and Special Collections Reproduction Services," stamped on the back of the pages hinted at their history.

May 23, 1797

I pray the weather stays temperate so that Father will not spoil.

I went early to a chapel by the Arsenal and prayed for Father's soul. When I returned, the hotelkeeper told me he is keeping my parent in an old gondola on the bottom floor of his *pensione*. He has filled the gondola with ice, and to preserve Father's body we must buy daily supplies from fruit vendors who bring it from the island of Murano. Francis says the price is highway robbery, and for once I find myself agreeing with him—fifty American dollars! I will not let Father be pickled in alcohol. I intend to bathe my parent in aromatic vinegar and wrap him in linens soaked in aloes.

Poor Father. How he would dislike his resting place.

Alas, no funerals are being conducted since the French came. This morning an undertaker on the Rialto refused

our request because he had been ordered by General
Junot to accept only military commissions. The undertaker
was anxious to get us out of his shop and he hinted that
the French will kill any Venetian undertakers who fail
to comply.

Francis and I took a gondola to the convent run by the
Capuchins and met with the Abbess. She was sad to hear
about Father. He was the only supplicant, she told us, who
had ever given her a present, and she was clearly disappointed when Francis explained that in New England,
parents of engaged couples always give presents to their
pastors. I believe she had taken Father's gift for an
expression of romantic interest.

The Abbess took us out into the garden and I found
myself looking for Monsieur Casanova. She showed us a
plot of pumpkins with hopeful pride and Francis pointed
out that pumpkins, like corn, are from America.

"Is that so, Monsieur Gooch?" she said, winking at me
as if she wished to share her amusement over his stolid
manner. "Well, I cannot hold your wedding now. Perhaps
late in June—when things have settled again. None of us
know what to expect from the French."

"Let us settle on a date, then," Francis said imperiously.
"I will marry Asked For on the third Sunday in June."

"A very romantic time for a wedding." The Abbess
smiled. "If the French permit it."

"The third Sunday, then. I will ask their permission."
My gap-toothed Francis seized my arm and steered me
out the garden, muttering that our Indians at home know
more about growing vegetables.

In our gondola, I asked why he fixed the date without
consulting me.

"Asked For, you are under my charge now," he said.

"But I am in mourning. I cannot be married so soon after Father's death."

"It was your father's wish that we be married at once. Venice is at war and you and I lack a chaperon. We shall marry as soon as we can and depart soon after for Massachusetts."

I hid my angry face in a handkerchief of Father's. It smelled of him and gave me comfort. Francis has no right to tell me what to do. I do not love him. And I will not return to America as his bride. I would rather be shut up in the convent with the silly, stunted pumpkin garden than go back to Massachusetts as the wife of Francis Gooch.

I am omitting my catechism of questions. Until Father's body is properly buried, I can think of nothing else.

May 24, 1797

Showers have staunched the sun's heat so Father can rest safely in his wooden ship.

This morning a note arrived, slipped under the door of my hotel room. I recognized the hand. It was from him. From Jacob Casanova. He uses a gold writing ink, which he sprinkles with sand. "A friend is waiting for you at Rio ————. He is trustworthy and will take care of the precious cargo you are keeping on ice."

I did not show Francis the note, nor did I ask him to accompany me to the undertaker. I set out on my own, somewhat afraid as I walked quickly through the half-deserted city. Small bands of French troops patrolled the streets but there was no sign of Venetians. They have retreated behind the curtains of their tall, narrow houses, waiting to see if Napoleon will inflict the same bloodshed the Jacobins brought to Paris. I feel a kinship with these frightened people forced to host their gaolers in their own homes.

I was carrying an English guidebook bought for me by Francis. It was written for Grand Tourists by a Mr. Gilbert Burnet and it is stuffed with attacks on Popish icons and religious orders, which the author argues manifest luxury, vanity, superstition and misery. I soon became weary of Mr. Burnet, but I relied on his small hand-drawn map of Venice for my compass.

Walking through a labyrinth of lanes and across several small bridges, I found myself in a section I had never seen before. I was in the north part of the Cannaregio, moving through deserted squares and half-empty streets where clothes hung drying upon cords and dirty children were throwing stones at one another.

I came suddenly upon a shipwright caulking a boat amid an evil-smelling cloud of smoke. Down another lane, wretched-looking mattresses stood on end against the houses—as if the Venetian sunshine could do anything for the ugly stains I saw upon them. I noted the absence of religious signs or images. I saw no chapels, no Madonnas, no carved crosses in the squares, no effigies of saints used in the display of religious devotion one finds in other quarters of the city. Nor did the faces of the occupants of this section look Venetian. The men wore black jackets and small caps from which coiled long, straggly curls.

Turning a corner in a narrow little laneway, I bumped headlong into Francis, who cried out in surprise when he saw me.

"What are you doing here?" he asked.

"I was told an undertaker lives in this part of Venice. And you?"

"I came in search of a moneylender," he said sheepishly.

Francis said we were in the Jewish ghetto, and together we set out to find the establishment on Rio ———. I was relieved to have him by my side although he eyed each passerby, from the smallest child to the eldest beggar, as if they were responsible for our sorrows.

At last we came to the street address on Monsieur Casanova's note. It was set off by two ruinous bridges at either end of a filthy canal. Dead cats and excrement floated on its surface. I held Father's hanky over my nose and knocked on the door. From inside, I heard footsteps; the door opened a crack, and I said my name loudly.

A hand seized my wrist and drew me in, leaving Francis on the doorstep. I found myself in the reception hall of a modest *palazzo*. My host wore breeches and a simple coat, his long grey curls quelled by a skullcap.

I considered calling for Francis but the stranger's hand remained firmly on my arm, preventing me.

"My name is Isaac Bey, and I will not harm you," he said. "We have no time to waste. Your father can be buried in our cemetery by sunset, if you are willing."

" 'Our' cemetery?" I asked.

"The Hebrew cemetery at the Lido. The humble spot has given sanctuary to my ancestors."

"Why should I believe you?" I asked. "Perhaps you will take my money and throw Father's bones into the canal."

"I need no payment. It's a favour for my friend Giacomo." He put a finger to his lips and opened a small stained-glass window in the wall behind us, motioning for me to look. "You see him, in his *vestimenti di confidenza?* These hard times require many disguises."

In the next room, I saw a tall Venetian lady in a grand court wig playing dice with two men in nightcaps and undershirts. I did not know the gentlemen, but I recognized Monsieur Casanova. He wore a petticoat and smock sleeves with pretty trailing ribbons. As my host closed the panel, Monsieur Casanova turned our way and smiled.

"Handsome, isn't it?" my host said. "His mother wore the wig on the Vienna stage."

"She was an actress?"

"One of the most beautiful in Europe."

Father or Francis would be humiliated to be seen in such a costume, while Monsieur Casanova appears delighted to garb himself in the clothes of my sex. As for me, my size often leads people to mistake me for a man. "What is it you desire, sir?" shopkeepers call out before they notice my skirts. Then they stammer apologies. I should be accustomed to these blunders. But I still feel a great shame when it happens.

"Miss Adams, let us return to the business at hand." My host was purposeful now, his voice low and serious. "We will say the funeral Kaddish for your father as if he were one of us. You understand?"

"I would like to see Father buried," I said.

"It is better if you do not know how I am able to arrange this. But I will do this for you as a good Christian woman because the Chevalier tells us you have been kind to him. Look for the red gondola by the San Marco wharf at seven o'clock this evening." Isaac Bey led me to the door. "All will be taken care of. You need only appear."

He nudged me outside, where I found myself face to face again with Francis.

"Why did you leave me out here, drumming my fists on the door!" Francis cried.

Before I could shush him, two men in skullcaps leaned out the window above us and screamed in Italian.

"Shut your mouths, you foreign swine!" Francis yelled.

Somewhere higher up, another window creaked open, and the next thing I knew, Francis was standing before me, spluttering and shaking like a bedraggled rooster, his homespun suit covered in yellow slop.

~

The next morning Luce was startled to find Lee waiting in a chair outside her bedroom. A large plastic box punched with air holes sat on the floor next to her feet.

"Are you better today? You didn't wait for me at the hospital," Lee said.

"I had my appointment. I had to leave."

"But you didn't come back to the hotel, Luce. If you and I are going to get along, I have to know your plans. Is that too much to ask?"

"I'm not used to being accountable to anyone. Not since Mother left."

"Louder, Luce. I can't hear you."

"I am used to taking care of myself."

Lee cocked her head, as if puzzled. "I'm not angry, Luce. I was only worried."

"Oh." Luce hesitated. "I didn't mean to make you worry."

"Well, that's a start. But we have another problem." Lee pointed to the box. "A man called Alberto left this down at the reception desk. He told the clerk you promised to take the cat off his hands."

Luce crouched down and peered inside. The sight of the small brown nose pressed against an air hole aroused in her a surge of protective feelings.

"I don't think you should get too close to it." Lee heaved herself out of the chair. "It looks diseased."

"Her name is Venus."

"Well, someone should look again. The little sacs under its tail say differently."

"Where are you going?" Luce asked.

"To pay our bill. We have to catch the boat. You can tell me what you want to do about it later."

"I guess so."

"Let's hope today will go smoothly," Lee said over her shoulder. "I'm not in the mood for more problems."

From the deck of the Ancona ferry, Luce watched the flat, sandbar-strewn coast of eastern Italy dwindle into the Adriatic. By her feet sat the carrying case. She had checked the cat out before breakfast and found Lee was right: Venus was male. In a shop near San Marco, she had bought beautiful Venetian notepaper with swirling, feather-like designs, as well as antibiotic drops for babies, to use on the cat's infected eye.

She was sad she had missed seeing Casanova's birthplace. But Lee had booked them on the morning train to Brindisi and hurried their leave-taking. There had been no time to take the manuscript with the Arabic writing to the Sansovinian, and she had been too embarrassed to admit to Lee that she had forgotten to give it to Signor Goldoni the day before.

As they were leaving the hotel, the clerk had handed Luce a message from Alberto. She took it out now and reread it.

Dear Luce: You look very kind so I know you will take
good care of Venus. Forgive me, Alberto.

Along with the note, Alberto had sent a slightly overex-
posed photograph of Luce stroking the cat's head in his
kitchen. A token from Dino, she thought with chagrin. After
she refused to leave the cat in Venice, Lee had said they could
take it to Greece on the ferry and try their luck with customs.
But how would she manage with an animal in Athens?

"What are you reading?" Lee asked.

"Alberto's note." Luce stuffed it back into her travel pack.

"Oh, about the cat. Have you thought about what you're
going to do with it in Athens?"

"Not yet," Luce said, stroking Venus's nose through an
air hole.

"It's a sorry-looking thing, isn't it?"

"He has one beautiful blue eye."

"Your mother always took in strays," Lee said.

"You don't like cats?"

"I am not a cat person, Luce. I think people overwhelm pets
with emotions they can't express to their friends. I'm sure
most animals would prefer to be left alone. Shall we find the
snack bar?"

Lee began to jostle her way through an obdurate group of
backpackers. Luce hesitated and then, with a muffled groan
of protest, she picked up her bag and Venus's carrying case
and followed the older woman down the stairs to the ferry's
lounge. She felt the same old watery sadness she often experienced when she left a place. It was as if she had been abandoned by someone. But who was there to abandon her now?

In the lounge, a smiling lounge singer was struggling
through an Elvis Presley hit. Two beats behind, a music box

played the same tune. Four Scandinavian girls were singing along, whether in mockery or admiration she couldn't tell. Lee glowered in his direction and then headed off to the sandwich bar, her grey fedora dipping with the rolling deck.

Luce sat down and opened the user copy of the old journal. What was it Asked For Adams had said about starting a journey?

> Write down what it is you desire and tear your wish into a dozen pieces. Then fling the scraps into a large body of water. (Any ocean will do.)

Luce took a piece of her new Venetian notepaper and scribbled: "I want to meet someone like Casanova." She reread her sentence. Now what did she mean by that exactly? Was she putting herself at risk of meeting another poseur like Dino Fabbiani? She scratched out the sentence and wrote instead: "I want to meet someone who can show me that love doesn't mean disappointment." Folding the notepaper carefully, she put it in her pocket. Then, as the singer moved tunelessly into a rendition of "Blue Suede Shoes," she brought out the pendulum kit, her mother's old Christmas present. She examined the small brass pendulum attached to a long velvet ribbon. The fob of the pendulum looked like a miniature top of the kind children spin, she decided.

She skimmed the booklet with the pendulum kit's folkloric instructions: avoid red-haired lovers in months with *r* in the name, and seek blond-haired admirers when the moon is full but dark-haired adventurers when the tide is high and the moon is new. Glancing around the lounge, she checked to see if anyone was watching. No one was. At the far end of the room, Lee stood in a long line of passengers placing orders at the snackbar. A look of hopeful concentration on her face, she delicately lifted up the pendulum and held its string between her thumb and index finger so the fob swung slowly back and forth. When it seemed to her that the pendulum was motionless, she whispered, "Will I know love?" Very, very slightly, the pendulum started to swing in what looked to her like a tiny clockwise circle over Asked For's clear, rounded letters.

May 25, 1797

Father is gone.

I said goodbye to him in the cellar of the hotel last night. I lit twelve candles and placed them on the floor nearby. He no longer looked like himself but seemed to have shrunk into the packing ice, as if he, too, were melting. I anointed him with lavender to dispel the unpleasant, sweetish odour.

"Father, forgive me for what I am doing."

I meant by that his burial in the Hebrew cemetery. But those words clanged over and over in my head, as if they had another meaning I could faintly grasp.

We were poled to the Lido in one of the red gondolas the Venetians use to carry the dead. Isaac Bey sat with Francis and me in the *felz*, and Father lay in the stern in a box of cypress wood. It was alarmingly hot and raining a strange dry rain, like a mist. I was glad the burial had been arranged, because it would be difficult now to keep Father preserved.

At the Lido, a rabbi met us at the wharf. He stood aside scowling, as if the task of burying Father was being done at great cost to him—and perhaps it was. Francis hired a cart from a nearby merchant and we put Father in it and then sat around him like small animals at the foot of a fallen tree.

A few families on the streets by the wharf stopped to watch us go by. A man cried, "*Il povero*," and the woman beside him crossed herself.

In no time, we reached the cemetery. I would have missed it because most of its tombstones were crumbling, and their inscriptions hidden by ivy vines. The entire site was made of sand. I asked my companion if the sea was a threat to the graves. Isaac Bey would not answer, and I realized he was praying. At least Father will look east and south at the Adriatic, I whispered to Francis, and he nodded sadly.

The cart driver produced shovels, and Francis and the men began to dig. It did not take long, as the sand was loose, but soon the evening light started to fade. I watched the watery horizon, praying the sun would go down slowly so we could get this ordeal over and done. The cart driver's wife offered us olives and a flask of wine that had been much watered. We drank and ate without speaking. The men, whose faces were oily with sweat, took her refreshments silently.

At last the hole was dug, and Francis and the others slid Father's coffin into it. It landed with a shocking thump and I let out a cry. Meanwhile, the rabbi had begun to recite a low, wailing dirge. Isaac Bey whispered that this was the Kaddish, the prayer for the dead which his people say as a pledge of renewed commitment to life, and he joined him in the ritual answers.

I wanted to fall into the hole myself and lie with my parent, so terrible was the rending of our bond. I put my hands on my ears to shut out the hollow thumps as spade-fuls of wet sand landed on Father's coffin.

Francis tightened his grip on my elbow. I was grateful for his human touch. He is not all bad, my Francis, only rigid and slow—far too slow in most instances to notice the troubles of others.

I would not leave after it was done. Francis watched from the laneway as I walked among the forgotten graves, tears spilling down my face. I wanted Father to hear my footsteps, because I believe this is what we can do for our dead: tread over the ground that nourishes them so they will hear us and know life goes on.

Finally, I pulled myself away from Father and the neglected cemetery and walked with Francis back to the wharf. Isaac and the rabbi were nowhere in sight, but three French soldiers were searching for young couples in the crowd. One of the soldiers came over to Francis and myself, and, in a high, nasal voice, read out an official document ordering us to take part in General Bonaparte's victory celebration. We have been asked to be one of the young couples representing Domestic Fecundity on the fourth of June. As American revolutionaries, Francis and I are to dress in French colours and wear their red liberty bonnets. Francis bowed and accepted. I hated him at that moment. The soldiers left in a small boat, the wind ruffling their capes. We had to wait several hours before we could find another gondola that would take us back to Venice.

First Inquiry of the Day: Why should parents die before us? Should they not be like gods, watching over us always?

I said this to Francis on the gondola ride back to the hotel, and he gave me one of his idiot smiles. "The dead watch over us from Heaven. Every Christian knows that."

The wind, stronger now, blew Francis's red hair over his eyes. As it did so, I stuck out my tongue, but I think he saw me, because he sat like an angry boy, staring stonily into the water which grew black and still while the night clouds massed above our heads.

A few hours later, I awoke to the sound of someone trying my door. I flung my bed robe about my shoulders and found Francis on the threshold.

"Asked For, I will teach you how to respect a man," he said, and stepped unbidden into my room. "My sisters learned from me how to do it and so shall you."

Before I could protest, he seized me around the waist and tried to pull me close. Angered, I hurled him up against the door. How dare he do such a thing? As a girl, I had wrestled with my male cousins, so physical sport is not strange to me. After these games, I would fall asleep reciting the names of the boys I had trounced. Meanwhile, Francis came back puffing and cursing and threw me against a wall. Once again, I pushed him away from me, laughing, whether in shock or fear I do not know. As I stood, shaking with mirth, he threw me down on the bed, whose frame splintered into a dozen pieces, making a boom like thunder.

Moments later, the landlord's head in his nightcap appeared at my door and two *sbirri* entered, waving their clubs. They had come expecting thieves, and when they saw only Francis and me, they snickered and whispered among themselves. The landlord made Francis pay for the broken bed and then he showed me to a new room while a sheepish Francis retired to his quarters. Our landlord seemed to think it a good joke. As he bid me good night, he whispered that he understood that breaking beds was a custom among a frontier people like Americans, but Venetians did not engage in the sport. I did not laugh.

This morning, I spoke not a word to my betrothed who greeted me gruff and shame-faced. I do not know how I can tolerate Francis without Father to speak to him on my behalf.

First Inquiry of the Day: How many times should one overlook the erring ways of a husband-to-be?

Lesson Learned: If to err is human, and to forgive divine, then one must choose one's husband foolishly so that one can forgive endlessly and approach a state of grace befitting a saint. But I believe this is not wise. Far better to choose carefully in order to forgive less often. This is also the best way to avoid the self-congratulation that accompanies frequent acts of generosity.

May 28, 1797

Hot and miserable, with only a few weeks of freedom remaining. I have received a note. At first, I thought it was another message from Monsieur Casanova, but the letter slid under my door had been written by Francis:

*Dear Asked For,*

*Please forgive me for what I did. I know that I have not been the man I should be. As Christ is to the church, so a husband should be for his wife. But I have been sorely vexed by our circumstances. The Adams orchards are doing poorly so President Adams devised the pretext of a trade mission to help your ailing father. While you toured Venice, I was obliged to spend many hours out of your company taking useless notes. But that is behind us now. I swear I will not lay a hand on you until we are made one in God's eyes.*

*With affectionate respects,*
*Francis*

I shuddered at his phrase "lay a hand on you." Francis was trying to make amends, but how long will his fear of God keep him from forcing himself on me, as he has forced himself on his sisters? He is my sole companion in this foreign place, and if I did not know that Monsieur Casanova was close by, I would be greatly frightened. How curious I now see that older gentleman as my friend.

It is only a few days until Napoleon's Liberty celebrations, when there will be bonfires, military parades, fireworks and Trees of Liberty installed in the square. Before the bonfire is lit, Francis and I and other engaged couples will dance the *forlana*, a peasant dance from Friuli. Yesterday we went to our first practice and our instructor grew cross with Francis for stepping on the toes of his female partners, while I was whipped back and forth in a great show of tapping feet and criss-crossing of calves. It is the first vigorous exercise I have had since we arrived in Venice.

Two days after Father was buried, Isaac Bey arrived at my hotel with a printed placard. He asked one of the hotel staff to affix it to the front wall of the building. The placard stated simply: "Thomas Adams, b. 1747 Quincy, Massachusetts, d. 1797. Received sacraments like a good Christian. All those who read this are asked to pray for him."

"It is the custom of your people to do this in Venice," Isaac said gently. His gesture touched me, although my parent would have been shocked to see the placard that claimed he had received the sacraments in the Catholic fashion. In death, Father has become an emblem of all faiths—died an Atheist, buried as a Jew, memorialized as a Papist, and in the deepest part of his heart still a stern Congregationalist.

"Where is Monsieur Casanova?" I whispered. "Is he safe?"

"Yes—and he wants you to have this." Isaac handed me a note. It was addressed to the Chevalier de Seingalt.

*Beloved,*

*My heart overflows with joy over the news that you are on your way to Constantinople. Now that my husband, the Sultan, is dead, nothing can keep us apart. The new Sultan, Selim, and his mother, my grey-haired friend, have promised they will help us begin the life we were denied so many years ago.*

*Hurry to me, beloved. We will make up for everything the Fates have stolen from us. You are the man the most important of all the men.*

*your loving Aimée*

Puzzled, I reread the last sentence. It made no sense. Was Aimée suggesting that Monsieur Casanova was the most important of all her lovers? It was an odd thing for a woman in a harem to say, but perhaps it had a significance that only two lovers would understand.

"This is from Aimée Dubucq de Rivery?"

"He received word from her yesterday," Isaac said. "And he wishes you to join him on his voyage. He leaves Venice on the day of the Liberty celebrations."

"Will he go by frigate?"

Isaac Bey smiled kindly, I thought. "He leaves in the

same gondola that took your father to the Lido. It will be at San Marco by noon. Should he expect you?"

I thought of Francis. "Yes," I whispered.

Isaac told me to wear my mourning clothes. There was no time to ask for an explanation. I gave him two florins for Father's funeral and insisted that he distribute my parent's clothes to impoverished Hebrew families. To protect myself from the Liberty mobs, I will bring the flintlock pistol Father bought for my mother when he left on farm business; it is a pretty pocket model with a tiny bayonet and a brass frame engraved with the Stars and Stripes.

Today I was able to claim Father's funds from the account he had opened in a small Venetian bank. Despite their social freedoms, Venetian women are not permitted inside banks, and at first the sight of me perplexed the clerk, but in the end my status as an American citizen prevailed and I withdrew the money Father had deposited.

Thanks to Monsieur Pozzo and his sketches, the account has diminished considerably. Still, it is enough to pay my expenses here in Venice for several years. At home, this sum would support Francis and me three times over—if I were to return with him to Massachusetts.

First Inquiry of the Day: What is the truest freedom? Freedom from or freedom to?

Lesson Learned: If it is true I am alone in the world, it is also true that I am free in the world.

Second Inquiry of the Day: Do I have the courage to leave Venice with Jacob Casanova and seek a more adventurous life?

Second Lesson Learned: Jacob Casanova knows I am a woman of my word and I will not disappoint him.

On the next photocopied page was a small advertisement that must have been inserted between the pages of the original journal. From the look of the streak marks on the page, the original had been refolded many times.


BIGGE REWARD FOR BOSTON GIRL!

ANYONE KNOWING THE WHEREABOUTS OF MISS ADAMS OF BOSTON PLEASE CONTACT FRANCIS GOOCH AT THE HOTEL FENICE. SHE DISAPPEARED FROM THIS GRAVE OF VIRTUE, JUNE 4. HER FINANCE DOES NOT KNOW WHERE TO FIND HER. SHE WAS A KIND GIRL WHO LIKED TO HELP HER SICKLEE FATHER. MR. GOOCH LEAVES FOR AMERICA IN 3 DAYS.


Luce wondered if Isaac Bey had noticed the announcement and sent it to Asked For Adams as a souvenir. Did her ancestor smile over the spelling mistakes, no doubt the work of a Venetian printer with a faulty command of English? Francis Gooch had offered a reward for news of his beloved, but would not stay more than three days to wait for a response. Maybe he was in no hurry to get married himself.

Ah. At last, she had come to one of the photocopied letters from Casanova. His penmanship was unmistakable, although the user copy did not convey the dramatic glamour of his handwriting. Gone were the gold ink and the faint sparkles of sprinkled sand. And gone too was the lacy look of a few of the later letters, whose paper had been corroded by an acidic ink. At least, she had a good reading knowledge of French, although she spoke the language badly and with a nasal Toronto twang.

She felt thrilled to hold the letter in her hand and to hear his voice speaking after Asked For Adams, as if she were listening in on a secret conversation. Casanova's letter was addressed to Isaac Bey.

*June 15, 1797*

*Dear Isaac,*

*A thousand thanks for our safe departure, old friend! Our stowaway came to the Molo, looking her part in a black silk vesta. Naturally, I felt sad to leave the city of my birth to Napoleon and his pack of French wolves. But I could not risk another run-in with the Corsican. He has borne me ill will since one of his men told him falsely that I had made love to his youngest sister. How fortunate for me that you keep up with your spy work and that my old enemies on the Council will now be under his guard. The fall of Venice has that at least to be said for it.*

*Peering through a knothole in my hiding place, I heard Nino whisper that he would take Miss Adams to meet me at the crab fisherman's hut. She seated herself in the felz not far from where I lay, and I was moved by the expression of hopeful equanimity on her face. I believe Miss Adams is braver than other women. Alas, the wind rose after we set out, and I realized a June storm would soon overtake us. You know such storms, Isaac. They turn the sea cold and unfriendly and make the horizon appear a thousand miles off.*

*In no time, the gondola began to bob and quake, while Miss Adams continued to regard the lagoon with a hopeful look. She seemed pleased to see my little Finette again, who sat by her feet, staring directly at the place where I lay hidden. My pet wore the forgiving expression that says she wants to understand but, failing an explanation, she will wait loyally for a signal from me.*

*The journey through the gloomy marshes took many hours and I confess I fell into a heavy sleep. The bricoli that mark this deserted part of the lagoon are few in number, and it was twilight by the time we came to the islet of Cason dei Sette Morti. As soon as Nino saw the old stone house, he tapped the coffin lid with his oar, and I showed myself to Miss Adams. She uttered a cry, as she believed the corpse in the coffin was coming to life. When I spoke to her, she put her handkerchief to her mouth and couldn't answer. The poor child had lost her voice, so overcome was she by the strangeness of her circumstances.*

*I cursed myself for falling asleep and promised I would never again allow her to think she was alone and in danger. Then Nino, thinking to divert her with his macabre wit, told her the story of the seven dead fishermen who once lived in the stone house. I do not think you know this story, Isaac, as few go any more to the lagoon's southwestern marshes: Six fishermen and their cook, who was no more than a boy, lived in the old house. One day the fishermen found a corpse floating in the water. They took it back to the boy, telling him the corpse was deaf and dumb, and asked the boy to feed it. As they sat down to a meal of red-cheeked triglia, the dead man came to life, and greeted the fishermen. Then the hearts of all seven men stopped. In the end, the boy swam away to Venice to tell his tale.*

*As you can imagine, this story did her no good. Nino and I were obliged to lift her out of the boat and into the shallows by the shore. In the confusion she lost her copy of Seneca's De beneficiis, but the dear child said not a word of protest. Tears streaming down her face, she followed me as I ploughed on through the waves, holding my satchel and shoes above my head. Nino came after us with our belongings.*

In the kitchen of the old stone house, I found a large pile of dry kindling and built a fire. After we drank tea, she squeezed my arm gratefully. "Monsieur, I am sorry for the trouble I caused you. Today, I was too frightened to move or speak."

"Dear child," I said, "there was no need for speech in the bobbing gondola. It is my fault for not showing myself to you sooner."

"Thank you, Monsieur Casanova. It is true I am downcast because Father is dead but I am glad you are with me."

Could there be a more charming statement, Isaac? In the morning, we made a breakfast from crayfish we found on the shore, and she went about with the hopeful resolve I associate with her people. The Americans set out on an unknown ocean believing the Lord would take care of them, and in this she is true to her race. The Venetian people, may God bless us, exhibit no such willingness, and our empire lasted a thousand years because we expect the worst of everyone. And now it, too, has ended.

And so, dear friend, thank you for the ducats that secured our passage. The crab fisherman comes shortly to row us to the frigate anchored outside the Lidi. The vessel is taking a shipment of Murano glass to Corfutown. Then we will go on to Athens, where Miss Adams will be safe from her fiancé. We've spent the past ten days or so hiding in this old house and I've learned much about Miss Adams' circumstances.

Your friend always,
Jacob Casanova

PART TWO

# In the Land of the Gods

Across the table from Luce in the ferry lounge, Lee sat reading a book about Crete, occasionally stopping to make notes in a black scribbler. Luce noticed the name Yannis Sakellarakis under the title: *Digging for the Past*. Wasn't he the archaeologist whose findings her mother had challenged? She remembered her mother mentioning his name in connection with the discovery of the remains of a human sacrifice in Crete.

Human sacrifice. Luce was inclined to believe Sakellarakis: Minoan Crete hadn't exactly been the peaceful artistic culture her mother claimed it was. Pretending she was absorbed in her reading, she covertly studied Lee's face. It had been shocking at first to think of her mother as a lesbian. *You're the one who decided to love a woman, not me*, she had shouted. *Why should I have to deal with your sexual choice?* Now she was used to the idea at least. But how could her mother have left their comfortable life together for the person sitting across the table? An overweight complainer who believed in a fairy tale about a golden age for women?

Lee looked up.

"How's *your* journal?"

"I was just thinking about something."

"Well, so was I."

Lee bent again to her notes. Through the porthole above her head, a panorama of turquoise waves seeped into the sugary blue swell of the Adriatic. Soon the Aegean was unrolling ahead, mile upon mile in all directions, like a fathomless green sky.

June 21, 1797

Somewhere on the Adriatic. A new world and a new life.

I am writing this on the deck of our frigate, using Monsieur Casanova's portable writing box. He is pacing the deck near me, an arresting figure in his frock coat and Kevenhuller. Just now, when he saw me looking his way, he took off his hat and bowed joyously.

We have been almost a week at sea and I am subject to fits of homesickness, wondering if I will see Quincy again. He has apologized for the difficult start to our journey and the long wait in the lagoon marshes. It was done to fool Count Waldstein into believing my companion fell into the canal and drowned after a night of gambling. How relieved we were to see the crab fisherman who poled us to our frigate. Our ship was preparing to set sail, having given up any hope of seeing us.

Monsieur Casanova has been encouraging my journal writing, to distract me from my homesick longings. So perhaps it is only fair—if there is to be a reader of these journals—that I explain my upbringing. I was born in 1772, shortly before the Revolution, when courtesy was still revered. "Never be seated until required, ask for nothing, speak not, salt only with a clean knife, spit nowhere in the room but in the corner," was Father's dictum. As a baby, I wore a necklace of wolf fangs to keep away the pox, and my schooling began in 1778, in Quincy, Massachusetts, six years after my mother's death and my birth. My lessons were supervised by the woman I call my aunt Abigail Adams, wife to the president, known for her kindness to her female cousins. Despite the limitations of colonial life, she was able to pass on to me a devotion to the principles of honesty and self-reliance that have formed the basis of my character. I read Shakespeare and Seneca at home. Aunt Abby taught me to admire Seneca for denouncing the notion of women as frail vessels for men's seed. "Should women wish it," Seneca wrote, "they have an equal amount of vigour, an equal capacity for the performance of good deeds; they endure grief and suffering equally with men if they have been trained for it."

Aunt Abby believed women were men's equals and she was fond of saying that if she'd been born a man, she would have been a rover. But Uncle John, for all his interest in my aunt's philosophy, is more concerned with feminine skills. So like most young girls in Massachusetts, I was taught to make dresses, sing from the New England Psalm Singer in our Congregationalist church, and stand each morning against a board that braced my back so that I would grow straight and tall. In my case, it seems to have worked.

During those years, when Father ran his orchards, I learned to spear eels with my male cousins and pick cotton in the fields near Quincy, and when my aunt could not make ends meet, I helped her sell her Canton china to passing salesmen. It was sad to see her struggle because the American government paid Uncle John poorly, but Aunt

Abby showed me how to live frugally. As I grew, she taught me to leave behind my country ways and hide my muscles under my sleeves like a Boston lady.

She was glad for me when Uncle John sent Father abroad on the trade mission. For three months, I enjoyed my life as Father's hostess in Benjamin Franklin's old house in Passy outside Paris. Father was not happy there because he never trusted the French—no matter what pronouncements he made publicly about their revolution. In his heart, like some of his friends, Father remained loyal to the British crown. But he would have died sooner than admit such a heresy.

I credit Aunt Abby for my ability to accept French ways. It was she who encouraged me to see that it is possible to like the French without forgoing our republican simplicity—as she herself had learned earlier during her years in Paris with Uncle John.

As for my religious instruction, I received it in Quincy's Congregational church. We listened to the Sunday sermon from the front pew. Behind us sat the shopkeepers and the millworkers and, last of all, the two sections labelled BM and BW (Black Men and Black Women).

I admit I do not have strong religious beliefs. Perhaps this is because I am the daughter of an Atheist. After Mother died, Father said God had withdrawn from him so he would withdraw from God. My parent stopped attending church and was no longer capable of receiving visions. Father told me he had once seen God's face in Halley's Comet, warning of Doomsday. On another occasion, our founding fathers turned into the seven sins before Father's eyes. Jefferson was vanity, Franklin sloth, while Uncle John became the image of pride—an Adams failing.

A Sombre Notation: A few hours ago, I broke off writing and wept. Father is dead, and my aunt will be gravely disappointed in me for breaking the Fifth Commandment: Honour thy father and thy mother. For all her talk of being a rover, Aunt Abby is stern with family members who put aside domestic duty.

At least I am helping a friend while doing a little roving. I could not save Father or lighten his dour mind, but I can do my best to help Monsieur Casanova find Aimée Dubucq de Rivery. If Seneca speaks the truth, and I believe he does—the practice of virtue means we are obliged to perform good deeds without expecting a reward in return.

First Inquiry of the Day: Will I ever return home to America and see my Aunt Abby and my cousins John and Nabby?

Lesson Learned: Freedom is so close to exile it may well be the same word.

June 23, 1797

Moored in Corfu. Bad weather has confined us to ship in the pretty little port of Corfutown. To pass the hours, Monsieur Casanova recounts his escape from the Leads to other passengers who, like me, are spoiling for entertainment. Sparing no detail, my companion describes how he broke through the roof of the Ducal Palace only to realize that the moonlight might reveal Father Balbi and himself to the crowd below. He decided to go on after the clock in the square struck midnight. Our eyes widen as he relives the moment when he coaxed Father Balbi across the roof on his hands and knees, carefully lowering him through a window with a sheet, and finally, how he nearly fell over the parapet trying to push a ladder into the room below, knowing the priest was ready to abandon him.

Each time Monsieur Casanova comes to the point in the story when he is obliged to let Father Balbi pull him through a broken door in the Ducal Palace, his thighs bloody from the splintered wood, I gasp as if I am hearing the tale for the first time. These dramatic recitations have brought us the attention of a painter from Naples and a Mahometan merchant named Zak.

Every morning, Monsieur Casanova brings cups of frothy chocolate to Zak and asks about Zak's wife, who keeps below deck with her daughter. Zak says his wife weeps whenever the sea grows rough. So Monsieur Casanova sends her down olives and honey after he finishes "blackening paper," as he calls his writing. This morning, while I watched, he tore up a page from his journal and tossed it to the sea winds. When I asked him what wish he'd thrown to the Fates, he said, "The hope you will think well of me, Miss Adams."

His words made me laugh, and he insisted I join him for tea with Domenico Gennaro, the landscape painter, and his interpreter, Manolis Papoutsis.

Monsieur Papoutsis is from a wealthy Greek family in Venice, and like many educated Greeks, he speaks French, the universal language of Europe. He wears a cocked hat and frock coat over long pantaloons drawn up a little above the ankle. Thus, his top half resembles a French gentleman while his baggy breeches evoke a *pasha*. Monsieur Casanova says he wears a fashionable coat so he will be well treated by the Turks, the conqueror of his people.

Monsieur Papoutsis is agreeable enough but Monsieur Gennaro is a gloomy, shambling creature with a belly and spade-shaped beard. He barely spoke to me when I entered his cabin, but as soon as Monsieur Papoutsis filled our cups with wine, he relaxed and showed us his tools: the telescope for enlarging his view of the classical sculptures, and the numerous pencils and knives for cutting his canvases—some as long as eighteen feet—on which he paints his panoramas.

He has been commissioned by a wealthy merchant in Naples to do oil paintings of the Acropolis, and he expounded on the ideal of "noble simplicity and calm grandeur" in the art of the ancients. His talk reminded me of that rascal Pozzo, who cheated Father, and I soon grew weary of it. It was only a matter of time before Monsieur Casanova held out the miniature of Aimée Dubucq de Rivery.

"The long torso is in the French style," Monsieur Gennaro said. "And I admire your portrait's epic sweep. You see, Giacomo? The details of slaves picking cotton in the background?"

"The château belongs to the family of Dubucqs," Monsieur Casanova replied. "Aimée liked to describe the charm of its Atlantic views."

I hadn't noticed the slaves in the background, and I leaned forward to see what the painter meant by "epic sweep."

Monsieur Papoutsis asked for Aimée's story, and Monsieur Casanova explained that Aimée's fate had been predicted by an island soothsayer: her cousin Josephine was to marry an emperor, and Aimée to command a palace without enjoying public honours. It is many years since the prophecies were made but today Josephine is the consort of Napoleon, while Aimée is the wife of an Ottoman sultan.

"In her last letter," Monsieur Casanova said, "my darling told me we shared a star-crossed love—"

"Those are not Aimée's words," I interrupted gently. "She wrote, 'We share so much, dearest love . . . two star-crossed fates and ardent hearts who cannot be truly happy without the other to love.'"

My friend gave me a pleased look. He then placed his head in his hands and groaned sadly. "Do you think I am worthy of such a woman?" I have never known anyone whose emotions so vividly visit his brow. One moment his face rages like a summer storm, and the next it is as peaceful as early morning light. Perhaps it is a Venetian trait.

"Birth bestows the same value on each of us," I said.

To my surprise, Monsieur Casanova and the painter guffawed. "Miss Adams, your New World charm is a tonic for old vagabonds like Domenico and myself."

I did not have the courage to ask him my own question—the one that most concerns me: does he understand that Aimée, too, has aged? That she will no longer be the girl he met so many years ago? I fear my new friend makes no allowance for time and sees in his mind's eye the youthful figure in Nantes. I curse my narrow, republican heart—by that, I mean my urge to tell my friends where in their lives danger lies. And yet I admire those who act boldly and foolishly—who dash my warnings to the ground and stamp on my fears (which Father would call "trustworthy insights") and so prove me wrong.

I am too homesick for lessons learned.

June 24, 1797

I cannot fathom Greek men.

I awoke last night to loud sounds in the hall by my cabin and quickly grew alert. Over the noise of shuffling steps, I heard the deep, guttural tones that seem characteristic of Greek men, or at least of the sailors around us. Whether the Greeks are more virile than Americans I do not know, but their gruff voices sound menacing, as if being a man means they must speak from the bottom of their lungs. I was searching for Father's pistol when my door opened a crack and the baggy silhouette of Manolis Papoutsis came billowing towards me in the moonlight.

"Dear lady, I know how sad you are," he said. He arranged his features into a smile that perhaps he thought I would find pleasing. "Ouzo will help your broken heart."

"You big gilly, begone!"

He paused, swaying wildly, then he toppled forward, whether from drink or desire I do not know, and for a moment his shaggy head with its black curls rested on my breast, and he began to kiss me where I have not been kissed before. I gave him a heave, and he fell onto the floor muttering Greek oaths.

"What are you doing, Papoutsis!" The figure of Monsieur Casanova loomed in the door frame. He pointed sternly to the hall and my intruder gathered himself up and hurried from the room.

"I apologize for him, Miss Adams. When I declared my love for Aimée, he assumed you were no longer under my protection."

I was astounded that an educated Greek like Manolis Papoutsis thought I would accept his advances. When

I mentioned the foolishness of what he had said about the ouzo, Monsieur Casanova warned me not to believe anything a Greek tells me. But the Greeks gave the world democracy so one man's behaviour will not change my admiration for them.

Lesson Learned: In a strange land, there are strange surprises.

*June 25, 1797*

*Dear Isaac,*

*I am writing to remind you to send on the herbs I need to fortify my health, as I am hard pressed to keep up with my young companion.*

*We have remained in the harbour of Corfutown these few days. And today the beautiful Puritan girl came on deck, pale-faced but in a better humour. She spotted me at my writing desk and talked with pleasing honesty about her life. She is American but well versed in the ways of civilized people after her months in Paris.*

*She told me that it is common "back home" for young Yankee girls to play quoits and do farm work like field hands. Judging from what I saw today, she was overused in that regard. As we talked, we took off our jackets, glad to catch the sun. It has stormed here since we arrived, so bad weather, along with an old gambling debt, has kept me from going ashore. (There is a certain wife of a certain infantry captain I have no desire to meet again, in Heaven or Corfu.)*

*Miss Adams' proportions weren't lost on our interpreter, Manolis Papoutsis, who clearly has a weakness for large women. I was obliged to scold him for going into her room, but in truth,*

I don't blame him. Miss Adams reminds me of the beautiful girl whose portrait I keep on my watch chain. You like to scold me for loving a chimera, Isaac, but you have always been cautious about affairs of the heart. How else could you succeed for so long at your spy work?

Miss Adams speaks several European languages—a rarity for an American. When I met Benjamin Franklin in Paris, his command of the French tongue was scandalous. At any rate, our young stowaway is already showing an interest in the Greek of the common folk and speaks highly of their dubious race for giving us democracy.

"We Adamses believe in the democracy of humankind," Miss Adams announced when I told her I was born into a family of actors. As if we have not seen enough of the democracy of humankind at the Bastille! But at this moment it is not my social standing that is bothersome. I confess I'm not recovered from the last dose of love's folly although I begin each day, as you directed, with powder of rhinoceros horn in my chocolate and trust my vigour will increase. Good chemist that you are, would you ship a carton of boiled kelp from the stones of Venice to me in Athens? The best grows under the Rialto Bridge, next to the stall of the fishmongers. If this should prove difficult, I suggest packets of comfrey, lobelia and chaparral—as many as you can find in the herb market where I buy my theriaca. I am in need of an invigorating tonic so that I can enjoy my last great adventure. I intend to seek moments of jouissance wherever I can find them. Bless the French for their wit with language. Who else would invent a single verb to express joy in reading and sexual congress?

And so, once again a thousand thanks for releasing me from Waldstein's clutches. I am overjoyed to be travelling. I had begun to forget I am supposed to be a man known for bringing happiness to the fair sex. We must grow old as we see fit and not *follow society's superstitious notions—at twenty a rakehell, at thirty a paterfamilias, at sixty a corpse loved by maggots. What cowardly nonsense! I am not dead yet.*

*Yours,*
*Jacob Casanova*

*Postscript*

*Dear friend, I haven't forgotten the warning about sports that overtax a man's strength. But I see no reason not to take aphrodisiacs with my other medicines. I intend to try the nightshade plant popular with Greek ladies as an aid "for discovering treasure." An inviting phrase, is it not? I have met an interesting woman aboard ship. She and her husband Zak are sailing with us to Athens. Does the veil create the longing? Or is it the longing that creates the veil?*

In the ferry lounge, Luce stopped reading and gazed in shock out the porthole. Despite his love for Aimée, and flirtation with Asked For, it sounded as if he was set on seducing the Muslim woman.

Luce couldn't believe how innocent Asked For seemed. Innocent and decisive. It had been brave of her to leave Venice with Jacob Casanova—unchaperoned too. Surely, that was unacceptable in her society's eyes? What did this say about her ancestor's character? Had she been a foolish adventuress, or a heroine like those few European women who were world travellers in the early nineteenth century? Of course, it was difficult now to be unequivocally positive about anything, she thought, even about the value of travel. Even about courage.

June 29, 1797

We arrive at the antique land of the Gods!

Today we sailed into the port of Piraeus, Greece. It was so hot the sea shimmered before us in gauzy white strips. I perspired, wrapped in Monsieur Casanova's thick cloak, which he told me to wear so as not to draw unwanted attention to myself. He warns me that encounters with the Mussulmani, as he calls the Turks, will bring graver problems than those caused by a fop like Manolis Papoutsis. According to my companion, a Mussulmano tortures those who displease him by inserting an oiled pole through the nether parts; the pole does its cruel work slowly and exits through the mouth.

The notion was so unpleasant I suspected him of making it up to scare me, and I laughed. He laughed himself and said how good it was to see me happy, and I told him the weather has improved my spirits. I feel as if I've left Father at the bottom of a briny pool and swum up into the hot golden light. Is it so easy to find happiness? By stepping into another world, one encounters a new self? Surely not, and yet this is how I feel this sunny June morning.

From the deck, I could see no harbours or inlets in which to anchor our vessel—only solitary trees that dotted the stony cliffs like the hairs on a man's beard. I knew the great city of Athens lay a few miles beyond, yet it was impossible to imagine humans living in this lonely place. And when the wind came up, I thought the captain was delivering us to our deaths. I stood with Monsieur Casanova, who seemed amused by my fear that we would be blown off course.

At the last moment, as the cliffs grew larger and larger, the captain gave in to the prevailing winds, and our craft

swung south around a tall headland. We found ourselves
at the mouth of a narrow harbour. The wind was still
forceful, and the shore was rushing towards us.

"*Prosohi, kopela!*" Casanova motioned for me to step
behind him as the great sails were unfurled. And to my
relief, our boat nosed easily into place next to several merchant ships whose bows rose and fell in the waves. The
harbour of Piraeus must be very deep because the prow of
our ship almost touched the shore.

When the sailors threw out their ropes, Monsieur
Casanova began to strap his effects together: the collapsi-
ble writing box on which he is composing the story of his
life, a large trunk, a personal plate chest and a small crate
of books from Count Waldstein's library. I stood idly
watching as I had taken little with me to avoid arousing
the suspicions of Francis—only Father's pistol, which I
keep in my stays, my journal and some walking gowns.

Below the ship a few of the passengers were starting to
disembark. Zak, the Mahometan, was staggering under
the weight of a sack he was carrying over to a breakwater
wall. He returned to the ship for another and laid it beside
the first, then, stooping, he gathered stones from the
ground. As I watched, he threw a rock the size of his hand
at them. Monsieur Papoutsis, making his way down the
gangplank ahead of us, shouted angrily at the man.

"What is wrong?" I asked.

"There is no time to explain, Miss Adams," Monsieur
Casanova said. "Wait here."

What followed next was confusing since it was impossible to see the goings-on from the height of the deck. On
the wharf, all was noisy pandemonium. By the time I found
the courage to disregard my companion's instructions, the

crowd was going about its business again, and Monsieur Casanova and Monsieur Papoutsis were talking to a man in a long-tailed tunic and pointed shoes. I guessed he was the customs official, because he was holding their papers, though gaping rudely at Monsieur Casanova. I do not think the man had ever seen a gentleman in a tie wig before. On the wharf, Zak's sacks lay in shredded bundles, while his daughter, a girl of perhaps twelve or thirteen years, stood clinging to her mother, her look of terror heartbreaking to see.

Then came the moment I dreaded: as I walked down the gangplank to the wharf, the official raked his eyes over me as if I was a leg of mutton. I realized he was offended that I was not wearing a veil, but before I could explain he grabbed my hands and began to examine my palms. To my surprise, he flung them down disgustedly and Monsieur Casanova stepped forward, liberally dispensing silver coins into his palm. Imitating my friend, the fellow executed a sloppy bow and, through a series of hand gestures, made it clear we were to go with him to one of the whitewashed shacks along the shore.

There the customs man, along with Monsieurs Gennaro and Papoutsis, sat on its veranda floor drinking and eating what appeared to be the burnt tentacles of a dead sea-creature. I refused their food and sat huddled in my long cloak until Monsieur Casanova took pity on me and excused us, carrying his small plate chest with him. When we were out of earshot, he explained that pirates make a profitable trade out of capturing English aristo-crats disguised as commoners. The pirates recognize them by their soft hands and sell them back to their families for large sums. He said my callused palms, a legacy of Aunt

WHAT CASANOVA TOLD ME

Abby's farm, led the official to think my family was poor.

"And Zak? Why was he throwing rocks at a sack?"

"His wife and daughter were in those sacks."

"But why?" I cried.

"He imagined they had offended Allah." The irritation in his voice stopped further questions, and I guessed there was more to the incident. At last, he found us shade under a flowered tree. It was a pleasant spot on the shore of a freshwater stream. Nearby, a group of young women stood washing their clothes in this natural tub, and farther down the shore a handful of men were swimming in the sea. Their voices flew back and forth across the swollen green waves like the noise of sea birds. I thought I had never heard a happier sound.

Monsieur Casanova brought out a loaf of bread and a large chunk of homemade cheese. He unfolded a large linen cloth from his plate chest and distributed the simple fare on two china plates. Even in the thundering heat of a Greek afternoon, my new friend retains his courtly delicacy.

"What a difficult morning! Let's enjoy ourselves, Miss Adams." He held up a bottle of pale golden wine for my inspection and poured us two glasses. "This wretched retsina is an acquired taste," he said, swirling his wine. "The Greeks poisoned it with pine sap so the Romans would not drink it. Then they learned to like it this way."

He drank, twisting his lips into a sour face. I did the same, and the shock forced me to put down my glass. As I lifted my eyes, I saw Manolis Papoutsis and several Greeks emerging from the sea, their hair flattened against their necks, the water dripping from their unclothed bodies. My young cousins swam bare in the ponds near Quincy, but none of them looked like the wild, ape-like creatures before me.

"Why are you frowning?" Monsieur Casanova asked.

"I fear our bodies do not live up to the beauty of our souls." I knew I sounded earnest, like Father when he spoke of philosophical matters, and I expected my companion to laugh. Instead he smiled at me.

"Ah, Miss Adams, our bodies are how we reach divine understanding."

"The baseness of our physical natures distracts us from true friendship and love, monsieur."

"I, too, thought like this when I was young—that I should strive for some ideal not of my own making. Now I prefer to seek *jouissance*."

"*Jouissance?*"

"Do you remember what your beloved Seneca said about our physical natures?"

"That we should learn self-restraint?"

"No, dear girl. He said that God infuses all matter in the natural world, including our physical selves. Surely, if God is in nature, he is in our bodies."

"You confuse me."

"To a good end. *Jouissance* is the moment we all long for. Are you keeping yourself chaste for the marriage bed?"

Down the shore, the young women were trooping across the sand with their laundry, their long walking dresses and embroidered shawls rippling in the afternoon breeze. In Quincy, I longed for a family of my own yet no suitor except Francis had come forward. Now, sitting by the sea with Monsieur Casanova, it struck me that I was glad I was not washing clothes like these Greek women whose forebears had done the same thing for thousands of years, though no one, not even antique travel writers like Pausanias, had bothered to describe their labours.

"I would be unhappy confined to household duties in Massachusetts."

"Ah! And love? Would it make you happy?"

"Love brings domestic servitude and sometimes death. My mother died in childbirth."

"Dear girl, there is no need for that to happen to you! If you practise what I teach," he added.

"What are you speaking of?"

"You will see. You have a world of pleasure ahead of you."

I shook my head, but he had excited my curiosity.

"I swear the mode of pleasure is infallible, Miss Adams. Its power lies in this: recognize the beauty of the opposite sex, and they will recognize yours."

"Is it so simple?"

"Yes, all great truths are." He paused. "If you enjoy men's charms, they will enjoy yours. But you must accept your own beauty first."

The wine tasted less bitter on my tongue, and I found myself touched by my companion's words. Still, he does not understand the burden My Poor Friend poses.

"I fear it is not possible for a woman such as I to be so generous—with myself."

"In time, you will learn. Women, too, can enjoy their bodies. In this, you are no different from men."

"I do not believe there are such women."

"I have met them." He stared wistfully up at a cloud drifting over our heads, ensnared by a memory. Then he laughed. "But you are weary after your journey. This must wait for another time. Your are coaxing me into giving away my secrets!"

"And you?" I persisted, unable to stop myself. "Do you accept your body the way you accept the body of your lover?"

He fixed me with his hooded eyes. "I am no longer young. That is something else again."

"Surely, if what you say is true and you ask me to believe it of myself, then it extends to those who have gone beyond youth?"

He didn't answer. And for the first time I wondered if he had doubts about seeing his beloved Aimée. But when I asked my question a second time, I heard the low whistle of snores. This is how it is with Jacob Casanova. When I expect him to look old, he appears vigorous, and when I decide he is younger than he has any right to be, he looks frail, like the old gentleman asleep on the sand beside me, happily oblivious of the ant crawling over his buckled shoe.

Shivery convulsions shook the walls of the ferry as the rhythm of the engines changed and the boat began to slow. In his carrying case, Venus began to yowl as if he was being strangled. Luce slipped the cat a piece of tuna from her half-eaten sandwich and asked the waitress in the lounge to keep an eye on him. Then she hurried on deck for her first sight of Greece.

The light had changed. In Venice, the spring sun had glowed softly grey and warm, not unlike the April light in eastern North American cities. But the Greek sun shone harsh and blindingly hot. It inflamed the bright chestnut of her hair and the brilliantly coloured silks in the jacket hanging like a cape from her shoulders. She stood with the throng of passengers on the upper deck watching the ferry pull into Igoumenitsa.

The harbour nested in a bowl of limestone cliffs rising out of the sea to high, green-haired hills, a scene of wildness and simplicity, and for a moment Luce felt as if she too, like Asked For Adams, was sailing into a new beginning. Less than a day before, she'd been blown about by the spring winds of Italy, and now, here she was on the sunny threshold of the country her mother had loved.

Across the deck, she noticed a white-suited officer, perhaps the ferry captain, perched ostentatiously on the railing, pointing out landmarks to four Scandinavian girls whose tow heads had been uniformly dressed in cornrows. She was glad they weren't getting off in Igoumenitsa; they were taking the boat to Patras and going overland by bus to Athens. More hours of travelling lay ahead. She would have time to continue reading about Asked For Adams and Casanova.

She caught sight of the lounge singer standing a few feet away. Alarmed, she leaned in the other direction, pretending to be absorbed in the stream of departing cars. When she looked again, the man was gone.

Luce pulled the Venetian notepaper from her pocket and reread her wish: "I want to meet someone who can show me that love doesn't mean disappointment." Then she tore the paper into small pieces and threw the scraps over the railing, watching the wind from the wash of the departing ferry scatter them in all directions.

June 29, 1797

More about our arrival in Athens.

The customs official gave us our papers, and we started out for Athens just before sunset. Monsieur Papoutsis hired a large cart driven by a friendly Greek. His face broke into a toothless smile when he saw me. I ignored him and helped Monsieur Gennaro with his luggage, to his surprise. He was concerned the journey would damage the painter's tools. At last, the baggage was secured and we set off. Monsieurs Gennaro and Papoutsis rode in front with the driver who clasped a blunderbuss in his lap. In the back, Monsieur Casanova and I were bounced around by the road, doing our best to restrain Finette. Whenever we passed a shepherd with his sheep, the dog barked joyfully, sniffing the air as if she had never smelled anything so glorious.

The sun was setting on the Attic plain, turning the boughs of the poplars and plane trees on either side of the narrow road a pale gold. The light fell on the groves of olive trees and harvested cornfields, colouring the withered corn plants the same honey shade as the retsina I had drunk with Monsieur Casanova. All around us, the land of Greece glowed with swallowed light. My large body felt light, as if I, too, was being transformed. Even Monsieur Casanova's face looked youthful and happy.

And then, darkness fell. There is no twilight in this beautiful land, I am learning. A mile or two along the lonely road, we came upon a house by some plane trees. Monsieur Papoutsis shouted to our driver who stopped the carriage, and without so much as a glance at us, he and Monsieur Gennaro climbed down with the driver and disappeared into the house.

"Is the road safe from robbers?" I asked.

But Monsieur Casanova was fast asleep in his seat, and so I sat with Finette in my lap, looking out at the ridge of low mountains whose bumpy hilltops glowed with a soft amethyst light. Athens lay somewhere in that direction. I felt alone in this rough place, and I cursed myself for having set off on this wild journey. Who in Athens, I thought, will know America? Perhaps even the name will only draw puzzled stares.

In a while, and just as the moon peered over the top of the farthest hill, Monsieurs Gennaro and Papoutsis stumbled back out, talking noisily and clapping one another on the back. They clambered on board, urging the horses to a trot, which woke Monsieur Casanova from his nap.

"Manolis and Domenico have been sampling the mysteries of the east," he whispered.

But when I looked puzzled, he did not explain. I told him I was thirsty and he poured me a glass of ouzo. No one thought to bring along food or water so I made do with the smelly liquorice-flavoured drink.

For about an hour, our carriage rattled along the country road, barrelling through the towering trees whose trunks and branches could be clearly seen now because the full moon was high in the sky. I began to feel unwell and felt greatly relieved when we caught tiny glints of light moving like fireflies on the craggy silhouette of a hill rising up out of a huge, dark plain. Monsieur Casanova said these lights were Athenians carrying lanterns in their hands. On the top of the moonlit hill, I recognized the bone-white columns of the Parthenon. And through the roof of this glorious antiquity soared the spindle of a minaret.

"Oh, Venus, you who are known here by the name Aphrodite, bless this place," Monsieur Casanova whispered, and crossed himself. My new friend is Catholic but he sees God differently from most Papists. In one breath, he speaks of the Supreme Being as his mistress, and in the next, he throws in womanly Providence for good measure. To Monsieur Casanova, it seems all great powers are feminine.

We passed through cornfields whose silvery stalks glittered in the moonlight and came to the city wall that Monsieur

Casanova said had been built to keep out pirates. By its gate sat a turbaned man, his feet swaddled in rags.

"What's wrong with his feet?" I whispered, as the guard swung open the gate.

"*Bastinado.*" Monsieur Casanova hissed the word. "Beating a man's feet is a common punishment in these parts."

Athenians filled the evening streets, many of them carrying the lanterns we had seen from a distance. As we turned down a dirty lane, I felt my stomach churning. Elevated gutters ran along its sides, spilling out foul-smelling sewage. I made out half-starved dogs in the shadows of a Christian church that stood beside a small mosque. As we rattled by, the dogs barked and howled at us, until the whole village rang with their cries. So this backwater is Athens, I thought. I am disappointed.

*June 30, 1797*

*Dear Isaac,*

*My health is better, my friend, than it has been in months. We arrived yesterday in Athens—only four days from Corfu under a hot, cloudless sky. Sadly, my friendly overtures to the Mussulmano family were misunderstood by the father. I will not go into it here, Isaac, except to say that providing the customs official with baksheesh saved the Mussulmano's wife and child.*

*Thanks to my reputation as a man of letters, our guide was able to find us lodgings at the home of the widow Mavromatis. The name means black eyes, but hers are a cornflower blue—the legacy of a Venetian ancestor.*

*As we unpacked, she brought out letters from English guests who had stayed with her that year and asked if I would write to* them and offer cheaper rates upon their return. My hostess was surprised when I explained that English is a language I have yet to master. (Please excuse the blotches, old friend. The widow secured the ink from her son who says he makes it himself from Aleppo galls grown near Smyrna, along with sulphate of iron, water, gum Arabic and verdigris—if I understood his Greek. He keeps this primitive concoction in a wooden keg for months before he strains it into one of the little bottles sitting before me. As I write, I am careful not to touch it with my fingers in case the green goo burns my skin.)

We have our own suite of rooms opening onto a pretty court-yard with five or six large lemon trees; my room has a writing desk—apparently a gift from the French consul—and several chairs, a rarity in Athens whose inhabitants still practise the habit of floor sitting.

The night is as close and warm as the day, so some hours after we arrived, I went out to a small bathing shed in the court-yard, looking for a jug of water to wet my sheets—the method you taught me for keeping cool on hot nights so many years ago. I stepped inside the shed. The wall of the partition separating the sexes is designed for beings smaller than myself and I could see easily across the barrier into the women's area. I looked there out of curiosity and spotted a head of auburn hair. A moment later, the lovely coppery head swung up, and I was staring into the frightened eyes of the Puritan girl.

She stared back horrified and then bowed her head.

"Monsieur Casanova," she sobbed. "Help me! I am inebriated."

"Jacob."

"Yes—Jacob." I heard her retch miserably.

"I will look after you, dear girl."

The confined quarters in which we are lodged have had the happy result that I am on better terms with Miss Adams. Of course, she is not a true Puritan although she exhibits a charming interest in self-improvement. Those joyless folk were, after all, her ancestors.

I bade her sit and tenderly bathed her forehead with a wet cloth, and when she could walk with some steadiness, I took her to my room. For all her brave boasts about not needing a protector, my young companion is still an innocent. After I settled her on my couch, I lay wearily upon my own bed. In minutes, my limbs were damp again with perspiration, and, for the first time in many months, I experienced the full breadth of myself. My head, my heels and my hands, each of my limbs equidistant from the next, like the five-pointed star that is Leonardo's splendid sketch of a man. This is the genius of Greece. It gives us mortals back our bodies, and reminds us that the base of all metaphysics lies in the physical. No wonder Philhellenes the world over offer up thanks to the cloud-free skies of Greece.

I slept under the widow's late husband's bedclothes on a straw mattress stretched across two trestles, and I was as comfortable as if I was lying in the Doge's Palace. And in the morning had the pleasure of watching the widow's daughter sweep the dust with her hand broom into a large crack in the floor seemingly designed for that purpose.

And now, dear friend, it is time to turn to a copy of Ad Helviam by Seneca. I intend to prove to Miss Adams that her beloved Seneca scoffs at the notion of Platonic forms. If I have learned anything in this lifetime, Isaac, it is this— one should never try to realize the ideal, but find the ideal in the real.

Yours,
Jacob

On the bus to Athens, Luce reread Casanova's phrase, "find the ideal in the real." Was he talking about the need to appreciate daily experience, or the dangers of idealizing those you love? She carefully put down the photocopy so she wouldn't waken Lee sleeping in the next seat. Luce had never heard of Casanova visiting Athens. In the eighteenth century, the Ottoman Empire had extended to Athens and much of the eastern Mediterranean, although its power had started to decline long before Asked For Adams began her travels. She found it exciting to think of him in this part of the world. If only his letters were easier to read! There were black spaces on a few of the photocopies indicating the places where the dark "green goo," as he put it, had eaten through the paper. In graduate school, she had written a paper about the old recipes for ink made from homey ingredients such as lamp black and pine resin. She felt sympathy for Casanova, who had run out of his gold ink from Venice and was obliged to turn to a local Athenian brew. History bristles with stories of wars and battles, she decided, and ignores such crucial tools for human improvement as a dependable ink that doesn't destroy the paper it's written on.

June 30, 1797

Last night, very late, I awoke to the sounds of moaning. At first, I thought I was delirious from fatigue and insect bites, and then I understood the noise was coming from myself. Across the moonlit room, a corpse-like figure lay beneath a mosquito curtain.

"Jacob?" I whispered, still uncertain about using his name. At the sound of my voice, Finette leapt onto my stomach and licked my face.

"Come here, Finette! That's a good girl!" The corpse-like figure shook off a layer of bedclothes and I beheld Jacob Casanova in a long undershirt. A rope of reddish-grey hair hung down beneath his nightcap. I have never seen him without his wigs, and indeed, wig bags of all shapes and sizes lay on the writing desk by his bed. I stood up and the room whirled about me. I fixed my eyes on the desk in an attempt to steady myself. The desk was as fine as any in Mr. Franklin's formal house in Passy. It was large and curved, with a bronze lip at its edges to prevent papers sliding onto the floor, and he had placed his journal with its packet of scraps and letters on the veneered surface. But it was no use. The room still spun wildly. I sat down quickly and he turned away from me. As he bent over his plate chest, I noticed that his nightshirt was hitched up at the back. I tried not to stare at his pale haunches glowing in the moonlight. Despite his age, Jacob Casanova's buttocks are manly and firm.

"You drank too much ouzo, Miss Adams," he said, pulling down his nightshirt and handing me a goblet of water. "If you feel well enough, I can accompany you to your room. I will be no danger to you."

"You have not harmed me before so there is no reason to think you will do so now."

He laughed. "Miss Adams, you have an empirical habit of mind, like my friend Monsieur Voltaire. You would get along with him, whereas I had difficulty doing so."

"You and he did not agree?" I was making conversation to hide my nervousness.

"Voltaire argued that we must be free of superstition. But superstition is linked to faith. And faiths of all kinds—both big and small—are how we understand the mysteries of our lives."

"I have faith in you, monsieur," I said.

"And that, Miss Adams, is possibly the very place you should not put faith. I am, as you can see"—he tugged the greying rope on his shoulder—"less than I appear."

"That is no reason not to trust you."

"Dear girl, I am honoured. But do not depend too greatly on Giacomo Casanova." He seated himself next to me and I could feel my heart battering my ribs.

"Do you ever worry what Aimée will look like now?" I asked. "Perhaps—perhaps she has grown fat."

He startled me with a laugh. "What does it matter, when I am not as I was? Every part of me is crumbling. Look!"

He lifted his hand so I could see his fingers clutching a small ball. For the first time, I realized the knuckles on his thumb and forefinger were badly swollen.

"Rheumatism. See! I loosen my hand every day with Finette's toy."

I could not answer him. The truth was I felt greatly excited to be alone with Jacob Casanova.

I do not know when it happened. Perhaps when his hand fell glancingly across my chest, grazing my skin with a touch like a Massachusetts sea breeze. I shuddered, thinking of the twinkling glints of light the sun makes on the great Atlantic. And my lower regions rang like a wind chime, reverberating with delicious sensations that echoed one upon another in a chaos of feeling I lacked the skill to orchestrate.

He drew back, staring.

"Miss Adams, did I bring you happiness?"

I was still quivering with the after-effects of pleasure and could only nod yes.

"Ah, then I am still good for something," he murmured.

"Shall I continue with these old warriors?" He held up his hands, smiling.

I shook my head. "I wish to think about what has happened."

"Of course! You will need to test and verify, will you not, Asked For *Philosophe*?" He smiled. "May I call you Asked For now that we are better acquainted?"

"You may," I said.

I retired to my room. What do Jacob Casanova and I mean to each other? It is as if he is all things to me and none. I feel I know him as intimately as I know anyone and yet I do not know him at all. I am never certain how much to believe him, or in what light to take the tenderness I feel for him.

First Inquiry for the Day: Why is my body not My Good Friend when it can ring with joy?

Fruitful Thought Never to Be Forgotten: Jacob Casanova belongs to the woman who has borne him a son.


How extraordinary that the graze of a touch could have such power! And how lucky Asked For was to have had her first sexual experience with the legendary Venetian who would certainly have known far more about love than a farm boy like Francis Gooch. Luce winced at the thought of her own first experience. All that clumsy fumbling.

The bus began to slow down, and in the seat next to her, Lee stirred sleepily.

"Are we in Athens?" Lee sat up and looked out the window of the bus. They were entering a suburb and the lights were harsh after the darkness of the Greek countryside.

"Looks like it," Luce said.

Twenty minutes later, at the bus stop in Athens, Lee found them a taxi and soon it was speeding through the dark streets of the Plaka. And now, without warning, it swerved up on the sidewalk of a gloomy lane and came to a sudden stop in front of a stained marble façade. Above a door, the words "Hotel Athena" glittered faintly in gold lettering. There were no lights in the old stone houses along the lane. For all Luce knew, she'd stepped back into the time of Asked For Adams and Jacob Casanova. Clutching the cat's carrying case, she followed Lee into the lobby and over to the front desk where an old man in wire spectacles sat reading a newspaper. Surely Lee could have done better than this, Luce thought. In the dim pool of fluorescent light, the marble of a time-worn floor shone like the dusty yellow of old teeth.

"That thief tried to overcharge us." With the tilt of her head, Lee indicated their cab driver. He had slipped in behind them and was watching CNN in the lobby with a group of unshaven old men. When the cabby heard Lee's comment, he whispered to the old men who bent their heads to listen. They nodded, spinning beaded bracelets and turning to stare at Luce.

Exclaiming in phlegmy exasperation, the elderly clerk pointed to the men in the lobby and shrugged. Then he opened his palms, raised his eyes to the ceiling and slowly, very slowly, reached into a cubbyhole in a dusty cupboard and handed Lee two ancient brass keys. She hurried Luce through the shadowy lounge, and Luce did her best to keep up, stealing a backward glance at the strange old men who returned her stare with their own curious, assessing looks. They entered an ancient elevator and Lee pressed the button for the eighth floor. But before the door of the antique lift closed, the cabby put out a hand to stop it.

"Is the girl wishing company?" he asked. As Lee pushed his hand away from the door, his bracelet seemed to make a disapproving clacking. "And the lady? Is the lady wishing company?" he called through the grates.

On the eighth floor, Lee unlocked the door of a small room.

"I'll take this room," she said. "There's another downstairs—it should be cooler." She threw herself into a chair. "I can see you're going to attract a lot of attention."

"I didn't mean to—"

"Oh, don't take it personally. He's just being Greek. And so is this horrible creature!" She kicked angrily at something near her foot, and Luce saw a giant cockroach scuttle behind the chair.

"Go downstairs and tell them we want our rooms fumigated."

Leaving Lee to fend off the creature, Luce avoided the old lift and clattered back down the endless flights of stairs. It was obvious Lee was an old hand in Greece, she thought. Getting off the ferry in Patras, Lee had given the captain a bottle of Metaxa and he had allowed Luce to pass unchallenged through customs with the cat in the carrying case, while he and Lee chatted in affable tones about the drop in tourists that spring. But if Lee knew so much about Athens, why had she chosen a dump like the Athena? In the lobby the cabby was still watching CNN with the old men. When he saw Luce, he said something in Greek and the men laughed.

"We have cockroaches in our room," Luce stammered, uncertain if the elderly clerk would understand. He tinkled a bell on his desk, and a red-eyed boy shuffled out of a dark region behind the television.

The old clerk acknowledged the boy with a little half-wave of his palm. "May I present Mr. Exterminator?"

"You want your room sprayed?" The boy yawned.

"What kind of pesticide will you use?" Luce asked. She added nervously, "We may have to move to another hotel."

"I am sorry," the old clerk said. "It is late. The hotels in Athens are fully booked. But—if you like . . ." He nodded doubtfully towards the phone.

Luce and the boy found Lee drinking a glass of wine at the window, the tall blue shutters open wide. She was smiling up at a Disney-like spectacle on a cliff above their hotel, its fabled columns glowing acid pink.

"The sound and light show at the Acropolis is on every night," Lee said. "Isn't it glorious?" She toasted the sight. At that moment, the boy spotted the cat on the floor by Lee's chair patting the cockroach as if it was a toy.

"You can't have that filthy *gata* in our hotel!" the boy cried. Lee spoke to him in Greek and he waited stonily while she fished around in her purse for a bribe. He deposited a can of Raid on the dresser and left without another word.

"I'd forgotten how relaxed I feel in Greece. Would you like some retsina?" Lee asked, her startling big, light blue eyes soft with happiness. She held up a golden bottle and smiled at Luce.

A mysterious shift seemed to have taken place in the older woman since Luce had gone downstairs. Lee stood hatless by the open window, her head a wild landscape of black curls, her cheeks flushed. Luce noticed that her own face felt hot. For the first time, she was aware that the room was airless even though the occasional breeze caused the skinny white curtain to flap listlessly. There was no sign of an air conditioner.

"I'm not fond of Greek wine," Luce said, remembering Casanova's remark about pine resin.

"You'll end up liking Greece, Luce. Everyone does."

"I'm not everyone, am I?"

"What did you say?"

"I said I'm not everyone."

Lee sighed as Luce moved to the door. "Haven't you forgotten your little exterminator?" She bent down and pulled Venus out from under the bed. Then she opened the door of the carrying case in one quick, nimble movement, and the cat succumbed, feet first, into his plastic prison. "I think we should re-christen him Aphrodite." She picked up the case and handed it to Luce. "We're in Athens now."

"Aphrodite?" Luce asked.

"I'll take that as an affirmative. *Calo iypno*. It means have a good rest."

Luce's room was on the ground, seven floors below. It was identical in every spare, utilitarian detail to Lee's room except that it was half the size and looked into a dirty cement courtyard instead of up at the Acropolis. Lee had taken the best room, she thought irritably. Hearing her mother's stories about Greece, she'd pictured an idyllic land where lucky travellers lazed about under olive trees, sipping fine Attic wines. Well, she'd imagined wrong: the Athena offered all the comforts of an army barracks.

Locking the door, she let the cat out of his case, and he began to hop about anxiously on his three legs, meowing up at her. Luce patted his head, and then she, too, began looking around anxiously. Finally, she noticed the dead potted plant in the small courtyard outside. She picked up Aphrodite and set him on her windowsill. He seemed to understand; in seconds, he was out the window and scratching in the dirt of the plant holder. A moment later, he hopped back into the bedroom and began to eat the tuna she'd scraped out of a can onto a magazine she'd found by the bed. Then he settled down on the short, narrow bed, and she stretched out beside him.

July 2, 1797

I stayed in my room this morning to contemplate my circumstances. Jacob, as he insists I call him, gave me a friendly wave this morning as he set out with Monsieur Gennaro. I am confused by soft, new feelings. It is as if I dreamt our encounter, and perhaps that is the truth of it. I barely heard a word of my Greek lesson this morning from Stavroula, the Mavromatises' half-grown daughter. If one has studied Hellenic Greek, it is possible to make out the local dialect. Still, I find it difficult, and Stavroula was patient with my awkward noise. I was glad when our lesson was done, and I could return to my daydreams.

Under a tree dripping lemons as big as fists, I sat and pictured Jacob as he was with me the other night. Did his hand linger on my cheek while I lay in my ouzo stupor? Or on my breast? As I allowed my thoughts to drift I became aware of someone playing a mandolin. I stood up and peered around the corner of the house and saw Jacob seated on a rush-bottomed chair, singing a Venetian aria in the little courtyard.

I did not call out to him.

He began to play a lively, pre-revolutionary tune I had heard before in Paris, and when he was done, he put down his instrument and danced the *forlana*, which Francis and I had learned so clumsily in Venice. His arms raised gracefully, his legs in his satin breeches folding and unfolding, he smiled and bowed to an imaginary partner. So it is with my companion, I thought. I watch him as one watches an incoming storm that leaves the viewer uplifted and uneasy.

I was not the only one watching him. Stavroula stood in the courtyard door. He beckoned her over, and I realized he had been dancing for her all along. She accepted his hand shyly and he bowed, like an elegant heron extending its long-necked head to a fledgling. Stavroula lifted her skirts and pranced in front of him and Jacob motioned with his hand for her to lift her skirt higher and this she did, spinning and lifting her skirt until even I could see the plump cleft between her legs. Then, suddenly, he was on his knees before my Greek tutor, kissing her bare toes in a sprightly fashion while declaiming in Italian. Giggling and shrieking, Stavroula ran out of the courtyard, and I stole away, ashamed and excited by what I had seen.

First Inquiry of the Day: What has shocked me more? Jacob Casanova's admiration of a girl's beauty or my own greedy need to see what would happen?

Lesson Learned: It is not my curiosity but what it yields that is hard to accept.


*July 6, 1797*

*Dear Isaac,*

*I intend to spend the rest of my life in this antique land. The Arcadian sunlight makes every man feel like a god! Yes, here, I can breathe without fear. And I have the company of Asked For Adams, whose capacity to appreciate beauty rivals my own.*

*Yesterday morning I took her with me to a tailor. I appreciate the leave-taking sum you bestowed on me, but there is a practical need for my new expenses. It is fiercely hot, and my clothes are* unsuitable. My favourite lilac vest and suit, my sulphur-yellow drugget, my garters with the gold brass buttons over rolled-up silk stockings are not for a climate such as this.

I found our tailor on the outskirts of town, near the Temple of Jupiter. When he had finished taking our measurements, he invited us to lunch. As I began to make excuses, Asked For accepted the man's offer. In Athens, it is usual for servants to sit down for coffee with their betters, and on the street, rich and poor Greeks greet one another like old friends. Asked For admires this custom of theirs, while my opinion of the rascals is mixed. The Greeks cheat any foreigner they can—and this I understand. I have never turned down the opportunity to take advantage of a fool myself.

Perhaps one needs to grow up in the backwoods, Isaac, to be comfortable in the Ancient World.

In any event, the tailor served us a democratic meal of tiny brown fish known as merides, and eggplant baked in his own homemade cheese. To fayito ton theon—the man called his peasant fare—the food of the gods. And I did not quibble with him.

I itemize the following purchases for your amusement: (1) two baggy pairs of pantaloons; (2) three cotton shirts resembling a woman's chemise with baggy sleeves; (3) a large embroidered shawl known as a "zone," which is wrapped in layers around the waist and used by many rich gentlemen for the storing of purses and documents—the wealthier the merchant, the bulkier his zone, so they say here; (4) a pair of blue satin slippers and five pairs of short socks; (5) a vest and a jacket of silk in mazarine blue, bordered with gold lace, and one of the immense felt caps called a calpac that are worn by the Greeks instead of turbans. Aside from their hats, you would be astonished at how difficult it is to tell the Greeks from the Mussulmani. Even the Greek women wear veils in public and slip them to the side of their faces only when no Mussulmano is present.

Meanwhile, Asked For purchased several new walking dresses. I bought her a pair of pantaloons and a man's blouse, pointing out that it is easier to go about in the heat wearing the clothes of a Turk. How she blushed when I whispered that such a wardrobe is the best way to excite the imagination of a man like myself. Then, Isaac, the look on our tailor's face when she reappeared in the trousers I had bought for her. I laughed heartily. But he accepted the spirit of my gift and gave Asked For a calpac that sat like a crown on her auburn hair. Her beauty is bringing us attention, although she is as fierce as a barnyard rooster when admired.

Returning home, she attacked a group of local herdsmen, Isaac. The courage of New World women! We were walking back across a sandy field by the temple to Jupiter when we heard heartrending cries. A flock of baby lambs had been penned inside a shed on the dusty grounds while a crowd of Greeks were noisily intoning some ancient encomium. The ewes stood outside the shed bleating pitifully and this noise made their babies cry more loudly. The Greeks paid no attention although clearly they were the cause of the animals' misery. Without warning, my pretty hoyden strode past me and threw open the shed door. A wavy river of woolly heads surged around her pantaloons. The men turned on her angrily, and Finette raced barking into the dusty clouds of wool as the little things ran baw-baawing to their mothers. I called out to Asked For to shut the gate. Did she listen to me, Giacomo Casanova, a scholar of the world and its ways? No. She hurled one of the men to the ground. And when the fellow realized his attacker was a woman, his face took on the Stygian shade of local egg-plants. I strode to her defence, and one of the knaves drove his

head into my stomach. I fell backwards, carrying him on
my chest.

I wished at that moment I was dressed as Tante Flora and
not Giacomo Casanova.

"Sir!" I cried when I could get my breath. "Be a gentleman
and get off me!"

The man shrieked noises into my ear, and I felt a sharp object
press my ribs. Then, with a frightened intake of breath, he suddenly lifted himself off me and I saw two horses galloping
towards us, one rider brandishing a whip. It was our new
friends, Domenico Gennaro and Manolis Papoutsis.

"She fights like a man!" Domenico said, nudging me with his
riding crop as I staggered to my feet and patted the dust from my
new clothes. The shepherds had taken to their heels, and Asked For
appeared unhurt. "Do you think she could best you in a struggle?"

I laughed. "Why, Dom, I am sure of it! What were these
Greeks doing here?"

"They are shepherds," Manolis explained. "They hoped the
bleating of their flocks would move the heart of Zeus."

"They were praying for rain?"

"There have been public prayers for nine days," Manolis said.
"The drought is very bad."

After our battle with the shepherds, I escorted Asked For to
our lodgings and then set out with Dom to see the dervishes in
the Tower of the Winds. In its hall, we found a man beating a
kettledrum while the Mussulmani spun slowly about in long
white skirts, one palm to the heavens, as graceful as women. The
sublime picture quieted my heart.

There is a quality to this land that pushes one's emotions to
the extreme. Even Asked For is obliged to put aside her stoical
view and embrace her feelings while I, born of the floorboards
like many a Venetian, know these lessons well.

*Ah, the lively daughter of my hostess, the widow Mavromatis, has arrived with my morning chocolate. I have run out of time, old friend. I will finish this another day and see if she can help an old man sweeten his morning mood . . .*

*Yours in friendship,*
*Jacob Casanova*

*Postscript*

*Isaac, how I wished for you today! I have been amusing Domenico Gennaro with tales of our days spying for the Council. My new friend makes sketches for a Neapolitan named Roberto Gambello who is paying him a stipend to record the glory of the ancients. I spent yesterday wandering with him through the ruins.*

*While Dom sketched, I told him of my report on the ballet depicting the life of General Coriolanus. I explained how I had described the ballet as an allegorical criticism of the Venetian Senate and its sumptuary laws, particularly its restrictions on the clothing of women. (I said not a word to him about the help you gave me on its wording.) He laughed a great deal over my heartless denunciation of those exquisite dancers and said that art is never mere entertainment. He claims it invariably serves the views of the governing class. I have believed that too, in my time, yet I shudder to think how I went on about the ballet's corrupting influence, as if I were no older than the Puritan girl.*

July 8, 1797

Independence Day came and went without my noticing. It was too hot to think. The heat grows worse by the day and today we have all kept to our rooms. Even Jacob, who likes the sun, said he was suffering. By evening, it had cooled enough for us to take a late supper of squid cooked in their own juices, along with a bowl of lightly oiled cucumbers and tomatoes. When I retired to my room, I found a note on my pillow: "Dear Asked For Philosophe: Read this little book if you wish to round out your education. Jacob."

The book was *Thérèse Philosophe*, a French anti-clerical attack written before their revolution. Some years ago, I noticed the novel on a bookshelf in Benjamin Franklin's house in Passy. I read several pages before Father caught me. He hid it away with a smile, saying I must wait and learn about love from my husband.

The novel tells the story of an abbé who instructs a girl, Thérèse, in the art of mutual pleasuring. As long as there is no harm to the social order, the abbé believes pleasure benefits both the sexes. It is also his claim that because the body of a woman is a smaller version of a man's, she too can experience joy in lovemaking. This is the philosophy Jacob Casanova praised in Piraeus. I mulled over his book and then repaired to bed to test it for myself. That is, I repeatedly pressed the throbbing region of my female parts and soon fell asleep in happy exhaustion.

~

Upstairs in her room, Lee had put away her retsina and was searching wearily in her suitcase for Kitty's essay on Minoan Crete. She had to pull herself together and finish preparing for her lecture at the British consulate. After all, the lecture fee was paying her travel expenses.

But Lordy, it had been a long, tiring ride from Patras. She and Kitty had always wanted to sail to Greece and her guidebook said it would be a leisurely way to go, conveniently overlooking the tedium of the bus trip at the end of the day. Well, it was obvious that Luce held the long ferry ride against her. And the hotel too. What a moment earlier when Luce had said she didn't like Greece! Who would have thought someone as soft-spoken as Luce could sound fierce? A spark of Kitty flaring up in the girl.

She hoped Luce had been given a good room. She should have explained that she and Kitty had always stayed at the Athena, that they had loved its run-down charm. So many of the new Athens hotels were ugly imitations of North American chains. She felt too weary now to check on the girl's accommodation. Not that one hotel room differed much from another. The Greek word for hotel was *xenothohio* meaning a container for strangers—and that was an appropriate description of the Athena.

Ah, well, tomorrow they were lunching with her friend, the tour guide Christine Harmon, who had organized Kitty's tribute. Christine's earth-mother charm would put Luce at ease.

Lee found Kitty's essay and settled it on her lap:

### Minoan Crete: A Peace-Loving Matrilineal Society, or a Culture Based on Blood Rituals and Human Sacrifice?

### by Dr. K.A. Adams

In 1992, I received research funds to go to Crete for eight months to work on a site near Archanes. Before I start, I want to point out that I am white, English-speaking and Canadian. My parents were Christians, and as a child I attended Anglican Sunday schools, but I write here as a member of the Goddess Religion.

In academic circles it was now a convention to declare one's bias, Lee thought. But how typical of Kitty that she would use it before anyone else. Kitty's openness had been a wonder. If she had learned anything from her lover it was the need to be receptive to the world. She supposed this quality was what had partly drawn her to Kitty. That, and the way Kitty rarely became discouraged. Kitty loved the Acropolis from the first moment while she, Lee, had been disheartened by the depictions of war on the classical landmark—Athena, in the Acropolis museum, with her snake, and her cruel, smiling mouth, beating back the giants; frenzied horsemen on terrified horses; a mother weeping over her fallen son, and men and boys leading wide-eyed animals to a sacrifice.

It had taken her a while to learn to see it in all its astonishing glory. If Kitty were here with her now, she would be encouraging her to work on her speech. She tried to refocus.

The site in Crete known as Anemospilia is located on a small hill facing north to the sea, about fourteen kilometres from the palace of Knossos. I had been invited to help investigate the findings of the Sakellarakis team (a husband and wife) who argue that their discovery of a body in the ruins of the temple at Anemospilia proved that the peaceful Minoans practised human sacrifice.

First, some background: The English archaeologist Arthur Evans coined the term *Minoan* from King Minos mentioned in *The Iliad*. It was Evans who, at the turn of the century, carried out the first major excavations at Knossos, along with a partial reconstruction of the palace.

A wealthy Englishman, steeped in Greek history, Evans came to Knossos expecting to find a political kingdom run by men, and that is what he believed he had found. His faith was in "the glory that was Greece and the grandeur that was Rome"—Byron's phrase. Evans believed Knossos was ruled by a king although he was impressed by palace frescoes that showed women playing a prominent role in sports and religious processions.

Modern archaeologists have been slow to respond to twentieth-century feminism and its fresh interpretation of Knossos. Many within the academic establishment have criticized the findings of the late Marija Gimbutas, who argued that the Minoans were part of a Neolithic group she called "the old Europeans," and that they, like other Neolithic peoples, worshipped a goddess of regeneration. Her carefully mapped research has been largely ignored.

The reaction of Kitty's colleagues was frustrating but predictable enough, Lee thought. It hadn't stopped Kitty. No matter how hard she had tried to dissuade her from such debates, her lover never gave up defending Gimbutas to her colleagues who dismissed the work of the late Lithuanian archaeologist as a science fiction fantasy about prehistoric goddesses.

In 1978, Gimbutas's beliefs about Minoan culture were challenged by a team of Greek archaeologists who announced they had found evidence of human sacrifice at a Minoan site near Archanes. The skeletal remains of four bodies were discovered by the Sakellarakis team in a temple site at Anemospilia. Three of them, a woman and two men, were thought to have died in an earthquake. The woman was found lying face down; one of the men was face up, his arms protectively raised in "the boxer position" common to earthquake victims attempting to ward off oncoming blows; and the other found face down in the hallway of the temple. It was the fourth body that led to the Sakellarakis team's claim that human sacrifice was practised at Anemospilia. This victim, a male whose age was pinpointed at twenty-eight, was found lying on his side on a small raised platform (which the Sakellarakis team call an altar), his left leg bent so far back that his heel appeared to touch his thigh, leading John Sakellarakis to conclude that his feet had been bound behind him.

A knife was found near the chest of this victim, and the bones on the part of his skeleton touching the ground were white. John Sakellarakis conjectured that this meant the blood had left the body before the quake occurred.

During my stay in Anemospilia, I examined the artifacts excavated by the Sakellarakis team and concluded that we do not have definitive proof that this site was a temple. (1) It is smaller than most Minoan temples and the pattern of three small rooms is atypical. (2) There is no evidence that the small raised area on which the alleged sacrificial victim was found is an altar. Most Minoan altars were made of wood, and wood disintegrates, while this raised area consisted of stones. (3) The alleged sacrificial knife is larger than most knives used by the Minoans and is, in all likelihood, a spear. This is suggested by the two vertical slots located about two-thirds down the length of the blade from its tip. And rather than being placed next to the victim's body, as the Sakellarakis team suggests, this instrument could have fallen onto the victim's body during the quake. (4) Contact with the earth could have kept the bones white by protecting them from full impact of the fire that followed the earthquake. To argue as Sakellarakis and his team do that the blood had been drained from the body during the sacrifice is a doubtful proposition.

To sum up, no one has found conclusive evidence of human sacrifice in Anemospilia or anywhere else in Crete. Gimbutas and other archaeologists have interpreted the designs on Minoan artifacts as evidence that Minoan palaces, far from being sites of sacrifice, were cult centres administered by women priests and used for the celebration of the rituals connected to the harvest. It is possible that some human sacrifice may have been performed at the end of the late Palace period as a way of warding off earthquakes. Yet it would be foolish to construct the culture of the Minoans as resembling the warlike society of for example the Mycenaeans. It is more likely that it was based on the beliefs that shaped the Neolithic society of Catal Huyuk in Turkey, which James Mellaart excavated in the early 1960s. Mellaart claimed that the evidence showed there had been no warfare at Catal Huyuk for over 1,500 years.

This, then, is my conclusion: that unless new findings are uncovered in Anemospilia, Minoan culture remains a possible model of a prosperous, artistic society that did not rely on warfare to further its agendas and did not regularly practise human sacrifice. Archaeologists who oppose this theory may be objecting for reasons of ideological bias. To believe more humane cultures existed in the past is a gentle heresy, but it is a heresy nonetheless.

Setting aside Kitty's essay, Lee rose and poured herself a fresh glass of retsina. She could never be as eloquent as Kitty, she thought sadly. Or as good. She was the jealous one who had let Kitty down, and Kitty hadn't stopped believing in her. But it was too late for regrets. She gulped the wine and stood at the window frowning up at the Acropolis. Well, she wasn't trying to change the minds of traditional archaeologists. Her audience of English expats would be more easygoing, and hungry for news from an English-speaking lecturer. Still they would want her to stick to the premise: Was there a blood sacrifice or not in Minoan Crete? That's what they'd want to know. It was the same old tiresome focus on violence.

The next morning, Luce awoke early. She fed the cat a tin of tuna and put the drops in his eyes. The antibiotic seemed to make him drowsy and he was soon asleep on her pillow. She left the window to the light well strategically open and set out to explore the Plaka. Leaving the hotel, Luce began making a list of the city's disagreeable features: First, the hotel washroom which doubled as a shower stall and displayed a tacked-up sign in English ordering her to deposit used toilet paper in the waste basket. It seemed as if the plumbing hadn't changed since Asked For visited Athens. And then the smoggy, yellow light—the pollution in Athens was worse, far worse, than in North American cities; the shaggy-haired men who called to her to eat in their outdoor tavernas; the churning tourist warren of the Plaka, with its shop windows displaying huge glass eyes to ward off evil spirits along with racks of postcards featuring malicious centaurs gleefully clutching their huge, tulip-shaped penises.

Walking up a high, noisy road by the Acropolis, Luce realized she had taken a wrong turn. She had strayed farther than she intended from the cramped lanes of the Plaka. Puzzled, she stopped at an espresso bar to get her bearings. She reached into her knapsack for her map of Athens and by mistake, pulled out the manuscript with Arabic writing in its acid-free folder. She had packed it in her knapsack that morning, intending to study it in some quiet, protected place. She would soon be coming to the end of Asked For's journal, and she was curious to see if she could find a connecting thread to the mysterious document. She set it on the table and brought out her map. Satisfied that she knew where she was, she fished again in her pack for the photocopy.

At the other tables, men and women were reading newspapers and chatting to one another in Greek. At the table next to her, an older woman in a tight-fitting jersey sat alone, a guidebook on her lap, glancing about the room as if she was waiting for someone. She turned to look as a blue-shirted Greek boy shot by on a motor scooter. Luce watched the woman gaze after him as the noise of his machine dwindled into a mosquito-like wail.

What do women that age long for, she wondered—husbands, divorced or dead? Or lovers gone? Or possibilities never considered? Do they resent it that men's eyes don't seek them out but follow the young girls instead, while their hearts long to be with the boys who float like bright butterflies down an Athens street, shirt sleeves flapping in the breeze, their scooters roaring out a sooty trail behind them? Or is it their younger selves they miss?

She turned to the next entry by Asked For Adams.


July 12, 1797

I put out a plate of bread to catch a husband.

To amuse myself, yesterday I went with Stavroula to the shrine to Aphrodite on the Acropolis. She told me that the young girls of Athens leave offerings there when the moon is new, hoping the goddess will catch them "a pretty young husband." It was not as hot, and I followed my little tutor up through the ruins of the old Greek agora. We stopped by the temple of Theseus, a novel sight in the midst of a cornfield, until she grew impatient and ran off to join a troop of older girls going up to the Acropolis. I lingered, awestruck, thinking of the ancients who trod there long before the first Adams set foot in the New World.

When we fell in step again, Stavroula whispered that the other girls came from rich families, and that it is not usual for Athenian women to go about in public unaccompanied by a chaperon. Certainly, this troop of beauties seemed happy to be on their own. They talked loudly in self-assured voices and, like the Venetian Macaronis, jingled and tinkled prettily because their necks and arms were covered with strings of gold coins.

The girls directed astonished looks at my Paris walking dress whose Grecian banding had been inspired by their dresses. The two embroidered bands—on their hips and beneath their breasts—gave them the appearance of having a double waist. I am certain I looked as odd to them. It was a queer sensation to meet exemplars of fashion in a cornfield.

The girls and I left the old marketplace and traversed a path winding above the whitewashed huts of Athens. From the path, it was possible to look down on the courtyards of the ramshackle houses whose walls are made of mud and pieces of marble from the ruins.

It was cooler up here. A fringe of shrubbery hugged the Acropolis and doves flew in and out of this tangle of greenery. On either side of the path, poppies and mimosa bobbed their heads among the blond grasses.

Finally, high on the northwest side of the craggy hill, we came to a small shrine carved in the rock. Standing at a polite distance, Stavroula and I watched the girls set their plates on the grotto ledge. Some girls added salt and honey to their dainty offerings of bread. When they left, we went up to the ledge ourselves and Stavroula gave me a conspiratorial smile as she took one of their plates and tossed its contents away. Then she made her own ritual, using her mother's bread. I did the same, feeling hot and uncomfortable.

The breeze had dropped, and the heavy, still air pressed on our skin. I stared longingly at the Aegean in the distance, glistening in sheets of turquoise and dark blue. The sun's position told me it was the mythic hour in this land—the hour just before the sun vanishes, when all things shine golden in the pale light. I heard a sudden rustle in the bushes, and flocks of crows flew up above our heads, cawing noisily. Startled, I spun about and there, shimmering in the hazy air, I saw the torso of a male figure glistening like a plant wet with dew. The apparition was unclothed, and its male instrument stood up large and imposing.

I thought of what Jacob said about the beauty of our physical selves. As I stared, a fierce, hot wind blew up the slope of the Acropolis, making my sleeves flap and my hair stream back from my face. The wild gust filled me with exultation, but the next thing I knew the wind had dropped and all was still and sultry as before. Father's moral peevishness lingers in me, and I turned away from the hallucination telling myself the heat had affected my senses. I said not a word to Stavroula and began to hurry down the slope. She called after me, but I did not wait. The path was wider on this part of the slope. I heard voices nearby, and saw a white horse tethered to a fig tree. And on the grass beside it someone had left behind a single high-heeled shoe. I left the path and pushing aside the branches found myself in a small grove. Behind a large, pale rock, Jacob lay as if dead. For a terrible moment, I thought of Father abed in Venice. I ran towards my friend, panting from fear.

"Wake up! Please! Are you sleeping?"

Drowsily, he opened his eyes. When he saw who it was, he gave me a delighted smile.

"Dear girl! Is something wrong?"

I could not help myself: in my excitement, I began to describe my vision, and he listened thoughtfully. While I talked, Monsieur Gennaro came walking out of the bushes, shouldering his telescope. Monsieur Papoutsis followed, holding an umbrella above the painter's head.

"Dom! Come here!" Jacob called out before I could stop him. "Asked For has seen the Apollo Belvedere!"

I did not see the Apollo Belvedere. I know this from having viewed the god's likeness with Father in the Vatican museum. The statue of the young Apollo wears a fig leaf with serrated edges like the leaves of Quincy maples. And aside from the frozen waves of marble on its head, the Vatican statue lacks bodily hair. I saw something else, and my vision displeased Monsieur Gennaro.

"Her vision lacks the calm grandeur of the ancients," he said. "It is a crude pagan thing."

"Ah, but Asked For is opening up to the beauty of the world, Dom," Jacob said. "It doesn't matter whether her apparition was pagan, surely?"

Our painter friend grew surly at this, and his eyes followed me, as we returned to our lodgings, in a way I found humiliating.

First Inquiry of the Day: What is the meaning of my vision?

Lesson Learned: If there is a lesson to be learned from seeing a naked god on the slopes of the Acropolis, I do not know it, and neither does Monsieur Gennaro. But I cannot help thinking that if this pagan god turned his back to me I would see that he had buttocks like Jacob Casanova.

The espresso bar grew noisy and Luce finished her coffee and left, eager to get away from the gregarious Athenians. She consulted her map again and headed for the temple of Zeus where Asked For had fought with the Greek shepherds, wearing the Turkish pants that Jacob Casanova had bought for her. Her guidebook said it was built by the Roman emperor Hadrian. She walked down a large hill, and sure enough, its huge marble columns were towering beyond a sidewalk cluttered with stalls of fresh-cut flowers and ticket sellers whose lottery coupons fluttered from spikes as long as medieval lances. She crossed the thoroughfare and in minutes found herself inside the temple grounds, hardly more than a dusty field lined with crumbling stone walls half hidden by bits of greenery. It was quiet despite the nearby traffic and it felt good to be away from the racket of Athens. She drank greedily from her bottled water and stared at the Corinthian columns rising up to the delicate acanthus leaves on their crowns.

She grew aware of someone waving at her across the temple grounds. A dark-haired man wearing sunglasses and a bright yellow-and-black Walkman.

She shook her head, warning him away. Earlier that morning, the old men in the lobby had pestered her, calling out in Greek and offering her their cigarettes. Lee had pooh-poohed the men and their "gentle Mediterranean hustle" and assured her that the incidence of assault was still low in Greece. But she was growing weary of approaches and she turned to go, just as the man strode over. A dog, a Samoyed puppy, followed, its snowy fur glittering in the hot sun. He looked close to her age, perhaps in his late twenties. He held out her file with the Arabic manuscript.

"This belongs to you, *neh*?" he said, using the Greek word for yes although he spoke English fluently. "I was in the bar and saw you leave it behind."

"Oh, my God! I don't remember doing that!"

"It's from an old book, isn't it?" He smoothed down a wing of black hair but it sprang back the moment he removed his hand. The effect was one of suppressed energy, as if an interior force was making its way out despite him.

"Yes. And I wish I could read it, only I don't understand Arabic."

"I glanced at some pages. It's not Arabic. It's in old Turkish writing."

"Are you Turkish?" Luce asked.

"I am Greek. My family lived in Turkey."

"Oh," she said. "Can you read it?"

"It's too complicated for me, but I have a friend who reads such things. My name is Theodore Stavridis. And you are—?"

"Luce Adams."

"Where are you staying? I could give you his address."

"At the Athena," she said, and instantly regretted her openness. "I must be getting back." Glancing at her watch she realized she had to meet Lee at the hotel for breakfast. "I'm late."

A dog barked and they turned to see his Samoyed disappear into a thicket by one of the old walls. There was a flash of white followed by the noise of frenzied yelping. The Samoyed puppy appeared to have treed an animal. He smiled.

"She is following her instincts." As he hurried after his dog, he called, "*Ciao*, Luce! We'll talk later."

Outside the temple grounds, Luce hailed a cab to take her back to the hotel. Lee was in the lobby, talking to the old porter with a plastic bag in her hands.

"I was just leaving this for you. I thought Aphrodite might like to sample the local fare," Lee said.

"Thank you." She took the tins gratefully and put them in her purse.

"You're welcome. Remember we're meeting your mother's friend Christine Harmon and her husband, Julian, for lunch. I'm going to the Blegen Library first to check a few of my facts for my speech tomorrow night. Would you like to come? They have some of your mother's work."

"I'd rather continue exploring Athens, if it's all right with you."

"Of course it's all right with me. Do you want a coffee?"

Before Luce could object, the waiter appeared with a tray, and she was obliged to accept a cup of instant Nescafé—the awful muck that passed for coffee at the Athena.

Upstairs in her room, Luce fed Aphrodite a tin of the local cat food and gave him another round of drops. Then she climbed up through the car-free streets and alleys of the upper Plaka to the northwest side of the Acropolis to find the grotto where Asked For had experienced her vision. Behind Luce sprawled the city of Athens and all its suburbs—a vast, smoky white bowl of low-rise apartments and houses that from this height resembled jumbled boulders recklessly scattered by some god—perhaps Asked For's pagan Apollo. It was still too early in the day for the infamous *nefos*—only a few smoky wisps of smog hovered over the Attic plain. A light north wind was blowing yesterday's polluted air out to the sea and she had a breathtakingly clear view of the tiny, gravel-sprinkled terraces below.

She turned a corner onto a narrow dirt path running alongside a wire fence and realized she was standing at the foot of the bulky limestone crag of the Acropolis. Tourists usually approached it from the opposite direction but Lee had told her this way up the hill was quicker and she seemed to have found the right path. It led past clusters of whitewashed houses and then into a small, fragrant pine wood where a young man lay sleeping on a wooden bench. On the back were carved the English words: "Live as you want."

She tiptoed past him, smiling. Farther down the slope, the tourist stalls were selling ice cream and Loutraki, a local brand of bottled water. Despite the north wind, the sun felt fierce overhead, and she stopped to sit for a moment on the grass.

From her knapsack, she brought out a photocopy of a small sketch that had been inserted into the journal. Its artist, possibly Casanova or the painter Domenico Gennaro, had drawn Asked For skilfully. In the sketch, a young woman with a strong-featured English face stood in pantaloons and a loose-flowing Turkish shirt. A large cap lay in the grass near her feet. Do I resemble her? Luce wondered. Her hand strayed to her cropped hair. The journal suggested they were similar in height and broad-shouldered slenderness, but her own eyes were pale grey, and Casanova had said the eyes of Asked For Adams were the same light green as the Adriatic.

She put the sketch away and moved on along the path up the hill. Suddenly she let out a little whoop. Yes, surely Asked For would have stood right where she was standing now. From here she could look down on a maze of houses and courtyards, like the ones Asked For had described in her journal. Only, the houses looked sturdier than the mud huts propped up with marble from the ruins that Asked For had described.

She was aware of the warmth of the sun on her face and the smell of the pine woods mingled with something sharp and peppery, perhaps wild oregano. For a moment, she felt as if Asked For Adams was standing next to her, and she waited, half-daring the pagan Apollo to appear. But Luce saw only Athens spread out before her, and the glistening Aegean.

Why did she feel disappointed? She lived in a different age. She started back down the Acropolis path with a sense of loss for all that lay beyond her reach. She was to meet Lee and her mother's British friend, Christine Harmon, at the Platanos, a taverna in the Plaka. Lee had shown her where it was on the guide map, and Luce had been surprised to discover that the old section of Athens was no bigger than a village. And that, she thought, was exactly what Athens had been in the time of Asked For Adams.

She hurried down the path through a meadow, perhaps the same meadow in which Asked For had found Casanova asleep. And then past the sidewalk cafés on Adrianou where young men and women lingered over iced coffee in the heat-swollen afternoon, listening to the mournful sounds of Rembetika.

Near the Temple of the Winds, around a bend in a lane, she came upon people eating at tables placed in the shade of several large azalea trees. She spotted Lee sitting next to a small birdlike woman and a rosy-cheeked man who was smoking in the ferocious Athenian manner.

The trio rose to greet her, the man quickly snubbing out his cigarette. "This is Christine, Luce." Lee smiled. "And this is her husband, Julian Harmon, the process philosopher."

Lee's nickname made Luce think of processed cheese, as if Julian were a fast-food version of the real thing.

"I knew your mother," he said, shaking Luce's hand. "Unlike Lee, she saw merit in my views."

"Now Julian, Lee's bark is worse than her bite," Christine said, extending her tiny hand to Luce. "I am honoured to meet a new Minoan sister," she added, bobbing her head gracefully in a gesture that reminded Luce of swallows dipping and swooping.

"Thank you," Luce murmured. She lowered her eyes to avoid the look of curiosity on the Englishwoman's face. Minoan sister was a term Kitty had used to describe the women who shared her beliefs about ancient Crete. Luce didn't believe in a lost golden age, whether it was the ancient Greeks or the Minoans. She wasn't sure she even believed in the possibility of human improvement.

Giving Luce a conspiratorial smile, Christine took off her floppy sun hat, exposing a bowl-shaped nimbus of silver hair. They all sat down and Julian poured them glasses of golden wine.

"We miss your mother's enthusiasm, Luce," Christine said.

"I miss Kitty too," Julian added. "She believed there was a bond between Alfred Whitehead's school of philosophy and hers. As I'm sure you know."

"Oh, I don't actually share my mother's beliefs."

"What did you say, Luce?" Christine asked.

"I don't really understand process philosophy," Luce said, raising her voice.

"Dear child, then I will tell you." Julian smiled. "In the past, male theologians have made a number of grave mistakes—"

"You can say that again," Lee nodded.

"Quite, thank you, Lee. Where was I? Yes, I was saying that Christian theology emphasized a fatherly medieval image of God—and that God was perfect and unchanging. But for us, Luce, God, like nature, is in a state of becoming."

"Yes, as Julian says, we are all in process, Luce." Christine bobbed her head.

"Is Julian finished?" Lee said. "I've spent my life listening to men make speeches and I don't want to do it on my holiday."

Neither Julian nor Christine seemed bothered by the sarcastic tone in Lee's voice. They smiled at Luce.

"Let's discuss our trip to Crete," Christine said. "You know the tribute is going to be better attended than I expected— over forty participants."

Luce didn't know why Christine would be startled by the prospect of a crowd; it was an old story as far as her mother was concerned. Kitty had always been surrounded by adoring fans.

Christine explained that they would spend part of their time in Crete visiting the Minoan shrines that her mother had written about. At the tribute in the cave, each person would say a few words about Kitty and leave an object that symbolized his or her feelings for her on the ancient Minoan altar. "Despite the numbers, we will try to keep the tribute simple," Christine said. "Kitty hated pompousness, didn't she, Luce?"

Luce smiled weakly.

When the food arrived, she found she wasn't hungry. She picked at her *moussaka*, eyeing her mother's friends as they talked. It unsettled her to think of Julian and Christine knowing Kitty so well. She noticed Lee was not saying much either, though she was eating her usual lunch for two: stuffed green peppers, fried squid, and lamb with lemon sauce. But it wasn't until their coffees arrived that Lee pushed back from the table and gave them all a friendly smile.

"Well, now that we have your attention, Lee, let's talk about Gaby," Christine said. "I'm afraid she won't be able to join us. But she wants you to come to Zaros. She sent you this." Christine handed Lee a postcard.

"I'd like to go to Zaros," Luce said.

"There isn't time," Lee objected, fanning herself with the postcard.

"Oh, Lee. It's where Kitty died. And it's not far from Herakleion. Why don't you take Luce to see Gaby? It will do you both good."

Lee didn't reply.

"Who is Gaby?" Luce asked.

When Lee didn't answer Christine cleared her throat and turned again to Luce. "Gaby was an old friend of Kitty's, dear. Are you coming to Aegina this evening? The temple there was built on the sanctuary to the great goddess."

"If it's okay, I'd like to stay by myself in Athens today." Luce stood up, knocking her head into a branch of thick, pink azalea blossoms.

Lee and Julian stared at Luce, and across the table, Christine made a disappointed noise. "You don't want to go with us to Aegina? It was important to your mother."

Luce glanced at Lee, hesitating.

"Didn't I tell you, old girl, that the young are not interested in your message?" Julian said.

"Many times, Julian," Christine sighed. "Even so . . ."

"I'll stay with Luce," Lee said. "It's too hot for the ferry to Aegina anyway."

"No, please go, Lee," Luce said. "I'm fine on my own."

"Oh, balls! I want a nap," Lee said. "Leave me under a tree somewhere while you go exploring."

Luce waited for Lee to pay their bill, feeling like someone plagued by a suitor who barges ahead, ignoring the polite little signs that say "go away, leave me alone!" The two women set off together, moving slowly for Lee's sake. As they walked through the Plaka, Lee exchanged pleasantries in Greek with the shopkeepers who beckoned from doorways garlanded with handbags and leather sandals. But soon she lapsed into silence. Lee seemed tired, and Luce guessed that the morning spent in the library researching Kitty's work had been hard on her.

Lee took her to the old agora where they stopped to rest. Inside its park-like grounds, Lee stretched out in the shade and Luce seated herself a few yards away on a half-sunken wall. She pulled out the copy of the journal. It was so peaceful in the wild, overgrown meadow she might have been in the country. Pines grew thickly around her, and doves fluttered and cooed in the branches above her head. In no time, Lee was fast asleep, her Birkenstocks sticking out from under the diaphanous fabric of her sun wear like the half-shod hooves of a weary draft horse.

July 15, 1797

Hardly a day passes when we don't visit some antiquity whose ruins lie in unexpected places. It is common, for instance, to come across ancient blocks of marble strewn in a laneway or meadow, and fragments of statues are regularly dug up for use in the construction of new buildings.

Like Jacob, I am interested in the Greek temples, so we were both surprised and pleased when Monsieur Gennaro asked us to join him on a sketching party to the Acropolis.

I was glad Father was not with me to see his beloved Parthenon. Everywhere we looked, the decay was severe. A small Mahometan chapel has been built near the entrance to the old temple while a mosque rises out of its ruins. Monsieur Papoutsis tells me that the Christians converted the Parthenon into a church; the Venetians blew up part of it when they shelled Athens; and now the Turks have made it a military garrison. We strolled in silent horror. Many of the Parthenon's statues are missing or broken, the doors of the mosque have been chewed by animals, perhaps rats, and goats graze inside the Erechtheion whose floor is piled with cannon balls. A battery with ancient-looking cannons perches on the cliff just below.

We found an ill-kept garden within the ruins—growing a small patch of flat broad beans and one withered tomato plant. And under a yellowing grape arbour, the single spot of shade, the military governor sat smoking a flexible pipe, the wooden base of which was decorated with yellow jewels. He gave us watery tea, fed our cakes to his rough-looking children and drank down Monsieur Gennaro's wine with barely a word spoken.

It was a sorry occasion, and Jacob excused us from the unhappy tea party and said we wanted to finish our sightseeing. We passed two veiled women who stood on the ramparts shouting cheerfully down at the people on the street below and pointing up at a dark, towering cloud. The sightless eyes of the caryatids holding up the Erechtheion's roof gazed out across the olive groves and cornfields growing peacefully on the plain.

"They carry a heavy burden," I said.

"Ah, but the caryatids are fulfilling their duty, Asked For. Isn't this what your beloved Seneca said we must do?"

"Yes, I was taught to be self-sacrificing." I thought of how I had ignored Father's wish for me and left Francis behind. "Jacob?"

"What is it, Asked For Philosophe?"

"Have you heard from Aimée? When does she expect you to arrive in Constantinople?"

He turned to look at me and slowly shook his head.

"Then perhaps something unfortunate has happened."

"I have another interpretation, dear girl. What if fate is giving us this time to enjoy one another, away from the cares of the world? Dom has asked me to visit his friend's country house near Sounion. I would be sad to go without you."

He could see that I was flattered, and whispered that I should take him to the little grotto where I had seen my vision. I led him down the path through the vines to the northwestern side of the Acropolis. As always, I felt overjoyed to have him to myself. Although there is much to commend in the hard work of those who raise you, the greatest gratitude must go to those who accept and cherish you for who you are. This love does not come from duty but from the deepest place in the heart.

There were no plates on the ledge by the grotto but the view of the Aegean beyond the mud huts below was as beautiful as before.

"Jacob?" I said. "I have thought about your offer."

"Do you mean my suggestion that we enjoy ourselves?"

"Yes." I stepped close to him and breathed in the fragrant scent of rosewater. "This is my answer."

"Have you had enough time to test and verify, Asked For Philosophe?" Jacob held me at arm's length, laughing softly. I laid my hand against his cheek.

"Do not tease me, Jacob."

"Ah, dear girl!"

He let out a low groan, pulled me close, and we began kissing urgently, my lips and cheeks wet with what I took for my tears. I drew away to look up at Jacob and that is when I noticed the dark cloud, like a woman's woollen skirt, spread across the length of the sky. There was a clap of thunder and it began to rain harder in windy gusts. We broke from our kiss and ran for shelter.

First Inquiry of the Day: Why have I never seen men's beauty?

Lesson Learned: I have feared the power of men too much to see them. So today, as I write, I rejoice in the beauty of men. The strong stalks of their necks, bullish or slim; the delicacy of shaven cheeks, the sweet, heartfelt line between ear and collarbone. Yes, I am astonished by the wonder of men in all shapes and sizes, whether they are bald-headed or thick-haired, aged or sapling-young, by their well-shaped wrists and long, supple arms, by their thighs and the trunks of their bodies, moving so purposefully towards what draws them.

Today, even Manolis, with his knitted zone shawl, or the shepherds who pass us in the lanes, with their bare calves and slippers, are pleasing.

Luce found herself holding her breath in astonishment. Asked For's entry was the most exciting one she'd read so far. But low wailing cries were breaking her concentration. It penetrated the sound of the doves cooing in the pines overhead. Was it an animal? The noise persisted. She stood up quietly so she wouldn't wake Lee and headed towards the Temple of Theseus, whose marble pillars were visible through the pines. In a little clearing, a dark-haired man was digging in the earth.

It was the same young man she'd met near the Temple of Zeus earlier in the morning. Who would have thought it possible to run into the same person twice in Athens? Casanova had left out the magic of coincidence in his travel principles, she thought. Travellers were like migrating birds who, soaring free from the ties of home, possess the ability to see the synchronous patterns that shape experience.

As she watched, the young man threw down his shovel. He wiped his eyes with the back of his hand, and she realized he was weeping. He stooped to pick up a bundle and began carrying it carefully towards the hole. Not wanting to intrude, she stepped back into the bushes, but the movement drew his attention. He wheeled about, staring at her in alarm. There was no doubt about it: it was Theodore, the young man who had found the manuscript with the old Turkish writing.

He smiled sadly at her, holding his bundle close.

"I thought you were the police," he said. He tilted his head towards the hole. "A car hit my dog. This morning, after I saw you. So I brought her to the place she loved. Our footsteps are here. Heeonati's and mine." He looked around the clearing. "When it is your time, it is your time."

"I'm very sorry," Luce said. "Can I do something?"

He gestured towards the puppy's toys lying on the sand. Luce picked up the rawhide bone and the bright blue spongy ball and waited as he lowered the pathetic bundle into the makeshift grave. Then she handed over the toys and he placed them on the dead Samoyed puppy. Bowing his head, he knelt by the grave, letting handfuls of sandy earth run through his fingers. He was murmuring gently, soft sounds like an adult speaking to a child.

Luce knelt beside him, her own eyes filling with tears. "It is terrible to lose a pet." Theodore sat back on his heels, turning to look at her, half crouched on the ground beside him.

"It is not right. You are a stranger."

"No, no," Luce said. "I am glad to help you. Your puppy was very beautiful." She handed him a Kleenex, and nodding gratefully, he wiped the dirt from his fingers.

"Thank you for the kindness of your soul." He rose to his feet and Luce rose with him. Then he picked up his shovel and finished filling in the dog's grave.

"Can I buy you a coffee?" he said when he was done.

"That would be nice. But I have to tell my friend," Luce replied.

She woke Lee and together they walked back to find him. He had composed himself while she was gone and now he sat smoking on a bench beside the path, the Temple of Theseus glinting in the sun behind his head. It struck her that he resembled the billboard advertisements for cigarettes she saw everywhere in Athens—there was nothing bland or politically correct about the men in the Greek ads for Karelia Lights: they smoked hungrily, staring lasciviously at indifferent women in filmy white dresses.

"Theodore," Luce said. "This is my—my friend, Lee Pronski."

"*Yiasou*, Lee."

"Dr. Pronski." Lee shook his proffered hand. "You live in Athens?" she asked.

"I work for Dolphin Travel. Are you from America, Dr. Pronski?"

"I lived in Brooklyn as a child," Lee said.

"So I was right about the accent. In my business, I have to know these things."

"Well, I wouldn't be so cocky if I were you. I spent years in Toronto." Ignoring his startled face, Lee took Luce aside. "He seems harmless enough," she whispered. "Although Lord knows what he was doing with a Samoyed in a place like Athens. The heat must have been hard on his dog."

"He's the man who returned my old manuscripts," Luce said. How did her mother put up with Lee, she wondered. Did nothing touch her?

Turning back to Theodore, Lee said, "Well, I guess we can have a coffee with you."

"Lee, I think—" She wanted to tell Lee she preferred to go on her own, but the young man interrupted.

"I'll get my car. The two of you, wait here, please. *Endaxi?*" He picked up his shovel and left before Luce could change Lee's mind.

In minutes, it seemed, the trio was off in Theodore's small Volkswagen, hurtling down the Possidonos, the wide boulevard skirting the sea, passing the car dealerships and lighting shops and huge billboards of men and women drinking Metaxa brandy.

"Will you get another dog?" Luce asked. She was frowning at the back of Lee's head. Her mother's lover was sitting where she had hoped to place herself, in the front seat by Theodore.

"Not today—next year maybe. If I can find one as beautiful as Heeonati." He half turned his head, looking back at her in the rear-view mirror.

"Some Greeks I know would put their dead dog in the garbage," Lee said, raising her voice to be heard over the traffic.

Theodore made no reply. They passed a saddle-shaped amphitheatre, then block after block of concrete apartments whose flower-bright balconies were shaded by tiger-striped awnings. They sped past warehouses and waterfront ferry offices and market stalls selling fish and tomatoes and barrels of olives, hurtling through Piraeus until they stopped finally at a taverna on a little hill overlooking the harbour. At the edge of the road, across from the taverna, Luce saw empty tables set with cutlery and checkered cloths. The tables had no protection from the fumes of cars and their location required the waiter to dodge the traffic to reach his customers. "*Yiasou,*" Theodore said to the waiter, who grinned as he set down a litre of homemade retsina in front of them. They drank thirstily and she found that it didn't taste like turpentine. She looked out over the harbour crowded with Greek ferries and huge white cruise liners. On the wharf, backpackers, bent double under knapsacks, were running in all directions as if they were already late for their journeys.

A small dark-haired woman appeared bearing a plate of *anthikolokithia*, fried zucchini flowers, the first of the season. Next to it, she set down a dish of tzatziki and a huge bowl of *horiatiki salata*. Thick, bright slabs of feta lay across the cucumbers and tomatoes like tiny biblical tablets commanding enjoyment. Lee spoke to her in Greek and she returned to the kitchen without answering.

"My mother is nervous with strangers," Theodore said, shaking his head.

"That was your mother?" Luce asked.

"My mother is . . . is very shy if my friends know she is a cook. She comes from a good family in Istanbul. We lost everything after my father died—and so . . ." He gestured towards the kitchen.

"How hard for her!" Luce said.

"Where do you live?" Lee asked.

"My mother and I—we live in an apartment near Constitution Square."

"You live with your mother?" Luce smiled.

"Of course. And your mother, Luce? Where is she?"

"My mother is dead."

"My condolences. Was she a good woman?"

"She was a well-known archaeologist." As she repeated the pat description that might have come from her mother's resumé, Luce realized she was speaking in the false, singsongy voice she always used when asked about Kitty.

"Luce's mother wrote about the Minoan culture in Crete," Lee added.

"Kriti? Your mother liked Kriti? She was a smart woman. I know! Like mother, like daughter!" He lifted his glass towards Luce, nodding appreciatively, and Luce was aware of her face reddening.

"To Luce's mother and to—Heeonati, my little snow girl."

They drank, lifting their glasses to one another. The retsina was doing its work and an unexpected image came to Luce of herself and Theodore alone in her hotel room. They were making sweaty, athletic love, Theodore shuddering with pleasure above her.

"Luce is an archivist," Lee said. "I've always thought her choice of profession was based on something she and her mother had in common."

"What's that?" Luce asked.

"A belief in posterity." Lee helped herself to another glass of retsina. "Archivists and archaeologists are keepers of the collective memory. But so far you don't share her love of Greece."

"You don't like Greece, Luce?" Theodore asked.

"I like—Greek food."

"For me, food is serious." He gestured at the platter of *merides*, the small brown fish fried in batter, the small spinach pies called *chortopitakia*, and oily green *dolmades*. "So eat!"

"Is it like a religion for you?" Luce said, thinking of Asked For Adams, who had included the pleasures of the table in her list of faiths.

"*Endaxi*, Luce. And I believe in nature, like the ancient Greeks." Theodore waved a hand towards the sea. "And the poet Cavafy. Yes, for me it is Cavafy who is sacred . . . 'And now what shall become of us, without any barbarians?'" His tone was undercut with an emotion Luce couldn't identify.

"'These people were a kind of solution,'" Lee said, quoting the next line of Cavafy's verse.

"So you know the poem." Theodore's voice was low and embarrassed, and his eyes moved from Lee to Luce, as if bracing himself for their reaction. "It's not always easy to be a fan of poetry in Greece," he said unexpectedly, "even if it's the birthplace of poetry. But tell us what you believe in, Dr. Pronski."

"Like you, Theodore, I believe in nature. And the healing powers of the sacred feminine."

"Interesting, *neh*? And the Holy Spirit?"

"Why separate the two? You men are the ones who divide the spiritual from the physical realm."

"Yes, in some ways it is not sensible to think like this. And does masculinity have equal value, Dr. Pronski?"

"The sacred masculine is not my field, Theodore. My concern is to right the balance in religious doctrine. We need church liturgies that include women." Lee's lecturing tone made Luce uncomfortable. She wished she could change the subject; Lee was ruining their afternoon.

"Ah, so that's all it is? Righting the balance!" Luce said icily.

"Is that a problem for you?"

Luce turned to Theodore. "Like my mother, Lee believes in a female deity. My mother was a spokeswoman for the goddess movement," she added.

"Correction," Lee said. "Your mother didn't believe in the goddess except as a metaphor for the feminine spirit. Of course, she approved of the Gaia hypothesis, that the earth is a living being. And she believed the early peoples in Europe revered an earth mother figure. But she was too influenced by our culture of scientific materialism to believe in a deity. And so am I. Have you read Clifford Geertz?" Lee reached for the platter of pale brown fish as both Theodore and Luce shook their heads.

"Let me see if I can get the quote right. Yes, I have it now. Geertz said that religion creates unique motivations in people . . . by clothing our perceptions in such an aura of fact that our feelings seem real."

"Whatever," Luce said in her whispery voice.

"And you, Luce? What do you believe?" Theodore looked at her inquiringly.

"I don't believe in religion. Or in any fairy tale about women being better treated in prehistory. I think people like my mother make up stories about a golden age to satisfy their psychological needs." She glanced at Lee who met her glance impassively and then gazed off at the Aegean. "What we need is the resolve to create a better future," she added.

Theodore nodded solemnly and ordered another round of retsina. The sun was low in the sky, but the Aegean was a light blue, broken in the distance by humps of large, pale brown islands. In the harbour below, where Jacob Casanova once caused problems for the Muslim wife, neon advertisements had sprung up out of the dusk: Shell, Nike, 7UP and Karelia Light. It was only half past seven, still early for dinner in Athens, and they had no appointments to keep or phones to answer, nothing to do except stare at the sea.

On the drive back to their hotel, Athens shrieked with honking cars and wild soccer fans waving little white flags. Motorbikes roared past, their riders screaming into the windows of the car. Unimpressed, Theodore drove on, politely pointing out Athenian landmarks: the floodlit government buildings on Constitution Square, the Telfrique on Mount Lycabettos, the Olympian Temple of Zeus again, now shadowy and mysterious behind the roar of night traffic, and the Acropolis, a ghostly vision of spindle-like columns floating above the thousands of apartment blocks glistening with lights across the Attic plain. Luce stared up at it, remembering Asked For's first glimpse of the ruin sprouting a minaret and the dome of a mosque. It must have been a startling sight in eighteenth-century Athens.

Luce found the cat waiting anxiously in their hotel room. He rubbed up against her calf, meowing softly, and she quickly fed him another can of Lee's cat food. "I'm sorry—I didn't expect to be gone so long," she murmured as he gulped down his food. When he jumped out into the light well so he could do his business, she fished out the phone number Theodore had scribbled down for her. The hotel clerk dialed Theodore's number and a woman with a gruff voice answered, "*Neh*?"

"I want to thank you for the wonderful meal!" Luce burst out. The woman shouted angrily at a person in the background and hung up. Was she the same woman who had cooked their meal in the taverna? Luce remembered that Theodore's mother didn't speak English, and probably didn't know who she was. She would try again in the morning.

Lonely and frustrated, she laid out the contents of her knapsack on the bed. She found the pendulum kit. Why not try it again? she thought. She closed her eyes, holding the pendulum between her thumb and forefinger. "Can you hear me?" she murmured. The pendulum swung in slow, satisfying circles. "May I ask a question tonight?" Once again, the pendulum swung in circular arcs. But when she asked, "Is Theodore attracted to me?" the pendulum swung quickly back and forth, signifying no. Feeling slightly foolish, she brought out the fan-shaped chart of pentagrams arranged under the words Yes, No and Maybe. This time, she held the pendulum over the chart, hoping the answer would be more satisfying if she followed the kit's instructions to the letter.

"Purge the pendulum with hyssop, and it will be clean," she said, reading from the instructions. "Wash it, and it will be whiter than snow."

What was hyssop? Wasn't it the biblical herb sprinkled in old Hebrew rituals? Odd to think she was borrowing from the Bible. She felt pagan, crude, a true child of her mother. Nevertheless, she washed the pendulum, dipping it in a glass of water, and dried it with a Kleenex. Then she began again.

"Am I travelling with a woman named Lee Pronski?" she asked the pendulum.

It swung between her fingers in slow circles.

"Am I in Greece?" Luce asked. Once again, the pendulum swung lazily, around and around. But when she asked, "Is Theodore attracted to me?" the pendulum swung back and forth, and this time the arcs of its swing were larger than before. She sighed and put the pendulum back in its case.

What was it that Asked For said about the beauty of men? She rose from the desk and picked up the journal, flipping to the entry she wanted: "The strong stalks of their necks, bullish or slim; the delicacy of shaven cheeks, the sweet, heartfelt line between ear and collarbone . . ."

Asked For could have been describing the line of Theodore's jaw, she thought.

Seven floors up, Lee Pronski emerged from her washroom feeling martyred and cross. She was clad in fresh underwear under her black kimono and three bulky wads of sanitary napkins whose adhesive underpinnings chafed the tender skin of her thighs. All afternoon she had felt a sensation of doom, as if she were a helpless sea creature buffeted by tidal currents on the primordial ocean floor, and she had found herself thinking that the trip with Luce was a mistake. Ordinarily, she would recognize the gloomy mood—its doleful note foretold the onset of her period. Annoying that after all these years she could still be fooled by a few spiking hormones. And what a ridiculous, humiliating business earlier in the day to find herself obliged—at her age—to stuff her pants with the bark-like toilet paper supplied in Greek washrooms. Lordy, it was a nuisance, the nervous checking of trousers when no one was watching. She hadn't been prepared—it had only been ten days since the horror of the last one. Perimenopause, a harbinger of "the change," and the perils of its gory flooding.

It had wearied her trying to explain her beliefs to the two young people, although Theodore had sounded sympathetic. Interesting that he had appeared to think they might laugh at him for his love of poetry. For surely his quoting of Cavafy was a signal. She was surprised that anyone his age still read the dead poet. Cavafy had been a favourite with her generation, and she knew that the term "a follower of Cavafy" was sometimes used as a code word among older Greeks for homosexual. She wondered if Luce understood that Theodore was gay. The girl had been making big cow eyes at him as if she hadn't noticed.

And Luce had been overtly hostile. It would have hurt Kitty to hear Luce dismiss her views.

Perhaps she no longer knew how to appeal to young people. If Kitty had gone to the taverna with Theodore and Luce, she would have known how to talk to them. *Oh, my dear*, she thought, *please help me. I am floundering.*

Turning from the window, Lee opened her purse and extracted the letter from Kitty that had been written the year they fell in love. She often reread it when she felt discouraged because it conjured up her memory of the Raki festival in Crete, when they visited a still not far from the water-bottling plant in Zaros. They had sat with the men on wooden chairs with raffia seats, eating baked potatoes and drinking *raki*. When one of the men passed a pomegranate to Kitty, she had rested the arch of her foot on Lee's stout knee and whispered, "There's no turning back now." Lee knew Kitty had been referring to Persephone who was obliged to spend half the year underground with Hades for eating the seeds of the pomegranate plant. After they said good night to the others, she had taken Kitty into the woods by the trout stream and told her that she loved her.

She unfolded Kitty's letter reverently.

My darling Lee,

How can I ever thank you for our wonderful days in Crete? My hunch is that women on Christine's tour claim it has changed their lives but then go back to their usual routines. In my case, I know the impact will be lasting. Yesterday, I told the dean I intended to retire because I needed more quiet time to think. "With Lee," I very nearly added. I didn't mention my plan to join you in Crete. I will talk to Luce about it first. I hope she will take the news well and be happy for my sake. She has always been a very understanding child. Still, she's lived with me all her life, and it will be an immense change for her.

I've told my friends about you, without going into my experience in the Skoteino cave. One needs to be there to understand it, I imagine. And how can I do justice to the emotions I felt when the women called out the names of their female ancestors? There it was: the link to our lineage and the truth that society hides from us—that women's bodies are the foundation on which human culture rests. All those mothers, going back in time farther than we can remember, nurturing the spark of life.

And thank you, dear one, for not teasing me after
I confided that a little voice in the cave whispered that I
should stay close to the earth. I knew it was telling me
how to spend the years I have left. A great stillness over-
came me. What is the promise of eternity next to the gift
of physical existence?

So you have my word: I intend to be less frenetic. It
will be easy to slow down in your company because, like
the Cretans, you take so much joy in the rhythms of daily
life. Do you remember the farm-women on our trip to the
old Turkish steam bath on that godforsaken mountain
road? At first they looked like ugly penguins soaking in
the near scalding water, the coarse red skin of their faces
and arms clashing with the milky white of their sagging
bellies and breasts. And yet, when I looked again, I saw
their bodies as they are—not flawless or deformed, but
alive and human. That's a vision I wish to keep with me.

Much love,
Kitty

P.S. I've just found a poet I like, Erin Moure. When challenged about my views, I intend to quote this verse of
hers: "If they accuse me of mysticism, all right, I'm guilty.
I'm a mystic. Now do you feel better? But it's only an act
of the body. My soul is simple and doesn't think at all."

Her hand still holding the letter, she sank heavily down on her
bed and stretched out on its uncomfortable mattress. She wanted
to be good to Luce and make amends for the problems she had
caused Kitty in the last months of their lives together. Lord
knows, she was doing her best, but the girl wasn't having it.

~

That night, Luce dreamt about her mother. In the dream, her pale-haired mother stood at the top of the Aereopagos, holding up silvery hands in benediction to the masses of her followers streaming down the moonlit hillside of the Acropolis. Then her mother floated off towards the horizon, twinkling with a cold, rare light. As the dream faded, Luce felt a heavy sensation between her breasts, as if her heart had turned into a stone.

The heavy weight shifted and began to emit sharp little whining noises. She opened her eyes slowly. The cat was sitting on her chest, gazing down at her, one paw lifted to prod her back to life. He looked different in the moonlight filtering in from the light well, and she realized her antibiotics had cleared up his left eye so he actually resembled a Siamese now. Sleepily, she spooned out the rest of his can and watched him toss back his food in large gulps as if he were choking. Satisfied, he climbed back onto the bed and watched Luce, who had started up her iBook. She opened her saved e-mails, looking for her mother's message about Crete.

Kitty's tone was more conciliatory than she remembered.

Dear Luce: When you were small, you punished anyone who hurt you by withdrawing, and this is what you are doing to me. Well, I won't give up on you and you must not give up on me. I have so much to share. Only I need you to listen.

The Minoans knew something we've lost, and I want you to have it. Will you come with me when we go the next time to Crete?

There it was: the generous offer that Luce had refused. When Lee had asked her to come to Crete, she had told herself that this time she would honour her mother and accept. She needed to go, too—not just because she wanted to pay an overdue homage but to see for herself the mountain road near the town of Zaros where her mother had died. She had read all the news reports about her mother's car losing control after swerving to avoid a truck carrying a load of tiles; it was an accident, she knew that, although there'd been hushed talk at her mother's funeral about Constantine Skedi, the young Albanian who drove the car and died with her mother. He was reputed to have a juvenile record for breaking and entering, but Lee had told her that Constantine was her mother's friend.

It was foolish to imagine she could have stopped the accident from happening. Still, if she had been with her mother during her last autumn in Crete, if she had gone when Kitty had wanted to go, maybe her mother wouldn't have died.

As a child, she had liked looking after her mother, and it was her special task, her mother told her, to run the house. But after the frightening rise in terrorist incidents, when Kitty was off travelling with Lee, her urge to protect her mother had grown until it sometimes felt uncontrollable, a huge, leaping yearning that reached out to Kitty like an anxious hand. Wanting, she thought sadly, to keep her peripatetic mother close and safe. She had been too proud to tell Kitty how she felt.

If only the trip was going smoothly, but travelling with Lee was difficult. Lee didn't want to go back to Zaros—claiming there was no time was only an excuse—and Lee seemed to think she should chaperon her as if she was a girl and not a woman who was almost thirty. Well, she *would* go to Zaros. She would see with her own eyes where the car carrying her fearless, magnificent mother had vanished from the earth. Just let Lee try and stop her.

She extracted her small cloth bag from her travel pack and removed its contents: her mother's compact of golden powder and tube of lipstick called Brazilian Samba. Sitting on the bed, with slow, upward strokes like the ones Kitty had used in front of the mirror, she rubbed her face with the sweet-smelling sponge, trying to brush a layer of her mother's skin cells onto her cheeks. When her face was thoroughly dusted with golden powder, she applied the dark brown lipstick, drawing it slightly above the tip of her upper lip, the way her mother liked to wear it.

Then she lay down on the bed beside the cat who pressed himself against her thigh and begun his rattling purr.

"I'm glad you're here, Venus. Or are you Aphrodite?"

The cat purred more loudly, as if he wanted to reassure her. Meanwhile, outside her hotel, life in the streets of Athens seemed felled by the same ominous melancholy. The Athenians had gone home from their bars and tavernas. It was long after midnight. The light show at the Acropolis was over and the old landmark stood in shadows under the dark void of the sky. What was it Asked For Adams had said about losing her father? That life is as absolute as death.

The next morning, Luce phoned and found Theodore Stavridis at home. She was surprised at her nerve, and told herself that she was calling to ask him about his friend who translated old Turkish. His voice sounded gruff but friendly, and Luce was glad he had answered instead of his mother. She suggested they meet for lunch. He named a place but she could tell from the change in his tone that he didn't want to see her. She asked if something was wrong and he didn't answer. She heard him inhale deeply and realized he was smoking.

"Luce?"

"Yes, Theodore."

"I am—I am a man who likes men. Can you hear me, Luce?"

"Yes, I heard you."

"*Neh*, it is hard because I like women very much. But as friends."

"I understand. I'm going to hang up now."

"No, Luce, wait! My friend, the translator, Ender Mecid—he is coming to Athens and wants to see your old Turkish writing."

"I'll talk to you another time. Goodbye."

She hung up. So the oracle had given her the right answer about Theodore after all, she thought despondently. She had used the pendulum because it was associated with her mother but she accepted its advice only when it told her what she wanted to hear—she had not been credulous enough to take its bad forecasts seriously. She supposed this was sane. She didn't believe in mystical divination, or any other godly power in the universe. She was just aesthetically delighted and soothed by the kit's lyrical advice, its pretty tasselled bag and fan-shaped chart. And if Lee was right about her mother keeping her empirical views, perhaps Kitty's interest in the kit had been mostly aesthetic too.

She stuffed the pendulum back in her knapsack, taking out her iBook. Mulling over the trip to Crete, she realized she still hadn't decided what she wanted to say at her mother's tribute. It was only a few days away and it was impossible to find the right words. She opened the file labelled "Kitty's Memorial" and reread her notes:

How can I possibly sum up what I feel about my mother?
I'm a grown woman and I still can't even see her as a person.

When I was small, I thought she was the most perfect
human being I had ever met. She was so kind and brave and
I wanted to keep her from harm's way . . . then she neglected
me and ran off with Lee Pronski. Isn't it strange the way
your mother can hurt you but you refuse to believe it? You
just keep on idealizing her, as if the childhood picture of her
love that you carry around in your mind is stronger than
the reality of the woman who acts and speaks in the world.

These were her true feelings about her mother, but she could
never admit how she felt to Kitty's friends, especially not Lee.

~

That evening, Luce took a cab to the British consulate to hear
Lee give her lecture on Minoan Crete. When she arrived,
Christine and Julian were in the foyer talking to an older,
dark-skinned woman and a plump girl with a shaved head.
Next to the girl stood a woman whose body resembled one of
the rotund goddesses Luce used to see on her mother's tables
and desks. The girl, who looked as if she could be the plump
woman's daughter, was carrying a copy of her mother's *An
Archaeologist Looks at Prehistory.*

"Luce! We're over here!" Christine waved.

Luce walked over. The women gathered around her as if
they wanted to touch her clothes.

"You're her daughter, aren't you?" the girl with the shaved
head asked. "Christine told us who you were."

"She's Kitty's daughter all right. I can see it in her eyes and
chin." The plump woman smiled. "I'm Jan, and this is my
daughter, Toby. Kitty and I met in high school. We got re-
acquainted on one of Christine's tours."

"I didn't know that," Luce said.

Keeping her eyes lowered, she followed Jan and Toby into the consulate and found a seat at the back of its library. British and Greek flags hung limply from a wall in the airless room. The people waiting to hear Lee were a mix of her mother's friends and English expats there to attend the monthly lecture.

In the front row, applause broke out as Lee walked to the front and sat down heavily at a table strewn with microphones, her Borsalino tilted at a combative angle.

Julian Harmon stepped up to the podium. "It's good to see so many familiar faces," he said into the microphone, "because tonight I am honoured to introduce my old friend Dr. Lee Pronski, who will talk to us about Dr. Kitty Adams and her views of Minoan Crete."

At the mention of Dr. Adams, a few rowdy cheers broke out. Julian motioned for silence, smiling approvingly.

"Will everyone quieten down, please? The daughter of Dr. Adams is here with us tonight, and we're very proud to welcome her into our midst. Are you there, Luce? Will you stand up and say a few words?"

Luce rose to her feet. The applause was loud and she saw people all around her swivelling in their seats, craning their necks to see Kitty's daughter. She stared blankly across the room at Julian. Then she turned and ran out of the consulate.

PART THREE

# A Gentle Heresy

The taxi let Luce out on a dusty road near an olive grove, somewhere in the northeast foothills of Crete. There was no human habitation that she could see, but the driver pointed up the hill, past trees hung with nets that he said would catch the ripening olives in the fall. The women had gone in there, he told her. Then he drove off before she could ask him to help her decipher the map that Lee had left at the hotel in Herakleion. She'd caught a spring cold and slept in that morning, and Lee and the other women had gone off without her, leaving a note asking her to join them for a picnic lunch in Kitty's favourite olive grove.

She started up the road that wound its way in ridiculous loops around the olive grove. Underfoot, the ground was sandy and massed with little stones that bumped out and caught the arch of her sandalled foot at unexpected angles.

The sloping hills and valleys played back her sense of isolation. She felt disoriented by the wildness of the place; if only Crete looked more civilized, she thought forlornly. The last few days in Athens had passed in a blur—of apologies for her panicky flight from the consulate and of self-recrimination for her naïveté in misjudging Theodore. But in the end she and Theodore had talked amicably again. He had phoned unexpectedly to give Luce the e-mail address of his friend in Istanbul, and then had surprised Luce by offering to take Aphrodite while she was in Crete. She'd agreed, because she knew it would be hard on the cat to take him with her. She had watched sadly as Theodore drove away over the cobbles of Apollonos Street while a caged Aphrodite yowled at her from the front seat of the Volkswagen.

The hot noon sun was making her feel feverish. She saw no sign of the women. Looking for shade, she noticed a wide stone beneath a large, spreading tree; some olive nets lay bunched across the stone. She moved them and sat down to rest. There was still no sign of anyone and though she strained to listen she couldn't hear much over the racket of cicadas which seemed to grow louder as she concentrated. At least now she could see that the olive grove ended about a mile away in a low-lying mountain range she hadn't noticed from the cab. Its rounded peaks shimmered in the heat, a row of dusty green humps.

She heard a shout. A group of hikers was walking over the brow of a hill to her left. They had on veiled sun hats and light-coloured clothes, and some wore what looked like garlands of vegetables hung around their necks. From where she sat, they resembled a family of beekeepers searching for an apiary.

Two women walked behind the others. The heavier woman was plodding along in diaphanous sun wear, swinging her arms like a bandmaster. Luce had no difficulty recognizing the stagy drapery of Lee's sun hat and the birdlike figure of Christine Harmon. As they came closer, she spotted Julian Harmon with the mother and daughter from the consulate, Jan and Toby. She rose to her feet and waved.

"Is that you, Luce?" Julian yelled.

"It's me!" she called.

Christine cheered, and the group walked over. There were over forty now, not counting Christine. They had met up with the rest of the group at the hotel the day before and Luce was struggling to remember their names. Julian was the only man; he wore a long-sleeved white shirt over denim pants and an old straw hat, while the women were dressed in baggy clothes and thick-tongued Nikes. Bulging Loutraki bottles dangled from their waists or shoulders. And it *was* vegetables she'd seen hanging from their necks, necklaces of garlic bulbs and onions. The faces of several of the older women looked slightly woebegone, and for the first time it struck Luce that the women who came to her mother's talks often seemed to be asking you to care for them in some frightening, unspecified way. She wondered if her mother had felt this way.

"Look, everyone! She's found the *kernos* stone!" Christine cried.

"Beginner's luck, Luce." Lee smiled.

"Luce, the Minoans worshipped a harvest goddess who was their version of the Great Earth Mother," Christine said. "And we are very glad you are here with us today because your mother wrote about this very altar. We've been looking for it all morning."

Luce stared curiously at the stone she'd been sitting on. It was a flat, circular grey slab, ringed with small holes along the edge.

"How's your cold this morning?" Lee asked, as Christine rounded up the group.

"The heat seems to be making it worse," Luce whispered.

"All right, everyone, let's begin," Christine said. "You know the words . . . 'The earth is our sister,'" she prompted.

"'We love her daily grace,'" the group responded.

Luce watched as they made a circle around the stone and joined hands; some of the women began pulling apart their vegetable garlands and filling the holes in the stone with cloves of garlic and onions.

"'The earth is a circle . . . She is healing us,'" Christine said, grasping the hands of Luce and Lee who stood on either side of the tour leader. The group repeated, "'We are a circle . . . We are healing you.'"

"And now repeat after me, everyone," Christine said, lifting Luce's and Lee's hands high into the air. "'Merry meet and merry greet, and merry part—and merry meet again. Blessed be.'"

Holding up their clasped hands, the group repeated the refrain. It reminded Luce of a nursery rhyme. Then they dropped hands and, talking and laughing, headed back down the hill, taking a new route through the trees. Luce ambled along behind. Did her mother come to Crete to play-act schoolgirl games? Surely not, she told herself. She hoped the noisy group wasn't visible from the road. She didn't want anyone to see her with this band of dotty middle-aged tourists pretending to understand a civilization that wasn't their own.

The road led to a grassy meadow where a lunch had been spread out on tables set up under a huge olive tree. Luce recognized some of the dishes Theodore had introduced to her in Piraeus, the crusty brown red mullet, *barbounia*, and the welcoming bowls of *horiatiki salata*. There were also new discoveries, plates of tiny Cretan olives, along with the sour local bread that needed to be moistened in water.

Two men stood by the table, opening bottles of yellow wine. They were short and thickset, with high cheekbones and sloping foreheads; the pair could have been father and son, their resemblance was so strong. The younger man had tied his reddish-brown hair back in a ponytail and he was dressed neatly in a plaid jacket, jeans and Kodiak boots. The fillings in the older man's teeth shone in the sunlight as he talked and laughed with his young companion. His hair, a bunching mass of dark grey curls, made him resemble a woodland satyr with curling horns growing out of his forehead. He wore a grass-stained mechanic's suit, with the words "Andreas. Shell Service" in gold thread on the breast pocket.

When they heard female voices, the two men turned and stared frankly at Luce.

Andreas limped over to her in his floppy sandals. She noticed that one of his ankles was bound with a dirty tensor bandage. "Motorbike, eh, shorty?" he said, pointing to his foot. "Engine burn Andreas!" He made a jubilant, roaring noise, grasping at a pair of imaginary handlebars. "I call you 'shorty.' No problem, eh?" Andreas said.

Luce looked helplessly at Lee, who was walking over to her with Christine.

"Of course Luce minds, Andreas. Behave yourself now. Luce is Kitty's daughter." Christine beckoned to the other man, and he came towards them with big springy steps.

"Luce, Yannis Vatakis is our local guide. And this is his uncle, Andreas, who knows the caves around here better than anyone."

"*Ela*, Christine!" Yannis wagged his finger at the older guide. "If anyone make Andreas-*kamaki* good boy, it you."

Andreas turned to Luce, pinching together his finger and thumb, measuring something infinitesimally tiny. "Yannis, my nephew. Too small for you, eh?"

Yannis spoke in a low voice to his uncle, who growled back an indecipherable answer that sounded like a curse.

"Stop that, you two," Christine said. "Yannis, this is Kitty's daughter."

"I know Kitty," Yannis said, his dark eyes lingering on Luce's face.

Before she could respond, Christine interjected, "Luce, Yannis lost his friend, Constantine, in the accident that killed your mother."

"Oh, I'm sorry," Luce said.

"We all are," Christine replied.

"You didn't tell me *he* was coming," Lee said, nodding at Yannis.

"I do apologize, Lee," said Christine, and it seemed to Luce that she was straining to speak gently. "I must have forgotten. But, yes, Yannis and Andreas are helping us." She turned away towards the others, calling, "Lunch is served, everyone. Eat well because this afternoon we are going to the Skoteino cave."

Luce smiled shyly at Yannis who had retreated from their group and stood smoking under a large olive tree. He smiled back, his cheeks forming sunburnt hollows as he sucked on his cigarette. If he had known Constantine, perhaps he would help her find a way to Zaros, she thought.

Luce sat in the shade of one of the olive trees. The picnic lunch of simple, country food was over and on the other side of the meadow her mother's entourage now lay about in small groups, chatting or sunbathing. She had chosen a spot as far away from them as she could manage, but a group of older women had come over and settled themselves under a nearby tree. From where she sat, the plump drooping forms of the white-haired women looked like burst milkweed pods, leaking the silvery fluff of their seed pods. It startled her that these women didn't care about their appearance; they lazed about on the grass, carefree, oblivious to the way their T-shirts and shorts exposed their breasts and the meaty slabs of their thighs. She knew she was being cruel—she had youth on her side—but she didn't mean them harm. She thought of her own looks as a temporary loan—like an overdue library book that would one day be recalled.

Ignoring Luce, the older women began to tell each other their life stories and Luce realized, with a little lift of her heart, that she finally had a moment to herself. Reaching into her knapsack, she brought out the pictorial guide to Crete that Lee had bought for her at Knossos. Three days had gone by since her rush from the consulate, and none of the women, not even Lee, had asked for an explanation. They had all been tactfully sympathetic, and even Lee had seemed determined to avoid the subject.

She stared curiously at the guidebook's photographs of Minoan artifacts—clay rattles, cylindrical seals made of lapis lazuli, an ivory fly, and a gold signet ring depicting a woman and a griffin—all relics of the artistic, exuberant culture that had meant so much to her mother. She could see how Kitty would be entranced by their beauty, as Lee obviously still was. She paused at a picture of a statue of a Minoan snake goddess whose fierce black eyes seemed to shine with ecstatic fervour. Or was it cruelty?

Setting the guidebook on her lap, she glanced again around the meadow. Lee was nowhere to be seen and the rest of the group were asleep or resting. She retrieved Asked For's journal from her knapsack and placed it discreetly inside the guide to Crete. She wanted Casanova all to herself.

July 20, 1797

I find myself delighting in my sensuality. Jacob has been my ravisher, and I his—our parts so intermeshed that, between us, we each possess breasts, wombs and manly steeds. I love the feel of Jacob's sun-browned skin, not dry and papery, the way I imagined an old man's skin would be, but soft and surprisingly pliant. And Jacob's manhood is as thick and long as the morels I once found under the maple trees of Quincy. As a girl, I would turn them over in my hand, marvelling. Clearly, men are the princes of the vegetable kingdom.

Our days by the seashore in Sounion pass quickly.

Yesterday Jacob and I took an evening stroll to escape Domenico and his friend, our host, Fotis Stamatapoulos. The sea air was warm and the place so quiet we could hear the bees in the sage bushes. Soon we found ourselves on a path to the beach. There was no one to see us so I untied my hair and walked barefoot, thinking of the Quincy shore with its distant views of Boston. I began to gather treasures from the sea, as I had as a child. I found sprigs of sage, the briny shells of dead snails and clams, and strands of kelp, even the dead carcass of a crab, which are called lobsters here. Jacob began to play at my game, finding finely polished black stones that shine like eyes. As we rounded a bend in the shore, we came upon a small fishing village.

Still barefoot, my hair long about my shoulders, I followed Jacob past a group of young fishermen who sat on the sand mending nets. Jacob asked them where we could buy food, and they pointed at the first house near a small wharf. As we walked on, I heard them whisper and I felt the involuntary shudder a large being like myself experiences when the eyes of men fall unfavourably upon you. How I wish sometimes to be quick as the wind, or invisible like a grain of sand, and not this long-limbed, lumbering creature.

Outside the first house, Jacob called out and soon an old woman in a long black shawl came towards us, slowly navigating across the rocks. We told her that we would pay for any food she could give us. She could hardly answer us for giggling. After she left, Jacob whispered that she thought I was with child because he had asked her to bring so many dishes.

This information captured my tongue and for a few moments I could not look at him. The woman brought a salad of olives and tomatoes and a platter of squid fried in flour. I was hungry and ate with gusto while Jacob watched, smiling. When I finished the squid, he called for lamb and potatoes, and then he cut off the finest slices of the shank and fed them to me. I gave in gladly to his ministering, knowing that the woman and her family were watching us. We must have made a picturesque sight.

It was still very humid, although the sun had finished setting over the sea. Wispy clouds streaked the horizon's edge like crimson laurel wreaths. It was so pleasant to be with Jacob, gazing at the Aegean, that at first I did not mind the mosquitoes. Yet, by and by, their nasty work began to torment me, and I told Jacob I was going to go into the sea.

"You can swim?" he asked.

I laughed. "And you?"

"No," he said gruffly.

"Then I will teach you!"

In moments, my outer garments were off and I stood on the rock closest to shore, beckoning to Jacob to join me. When he shook his head, I dived in and swam far out.

It was now very dark. On the shore, torches had been lit near the taverna so the young men could fix their nets.

Jacob called once or twice but I did not come in. I swam under the waves, emerging a great distance away where I knew he would not look. When his cries grew louder, I swam back towards the spit. There I saw the young fishermen half stumbling over the rocks with their torches. Jacob was on his feet, waving his arms.

"Come in now! Asked For, I beg you!"

On the shore, the young fishermen surrounded him, the light from their torches shining on their faces.

"The fishermen will see me," I called.

"They will not harm you!" he called back.

I paddled in and hauled myself to my feet, wearing only my thin tunic. There was a loud murmuring among the young men but the look of pleasure on Jacob's face reassured me. Then each man took off his cap and held it, face up, in a gesture of homage.

"They say you are Aphrodite," Jacob smiled.

"They are very kind," I replied. I realized that the awe I saw on their faces was genuine. And for the first time I found myself able to accept admiration as it was given to me.

Solemnly, one by one, the fishermen filed off the rocky spit. Jacob wrapped me in the large tablecloth and we stood, our arms entwined, looking out over the dark sea. I was too happy to speak and wished that the slow, swelling feeling of peace and quiet joy would always be with me.

When I grew chilled, we walked to the little house where he had found us lodgings for the night. Upstairs, we undressed, kissing tenderly. Then, after emptying my skirt of its trinkets from the seashore, I led Jacob to the narrow bed.

In the small, shadowy room, with the waves lapping below our window, I took off Jacob's wig with its braided plaits and combed out the long rope of his greying hair. Laughing softly, I dressed his head with the strands of kelp and clamshells I had found on the shore. Next, I took a handful of his black shiny stones and placed two in his ears. Then I placed the crab's skeleton on his belly button and hid five of the smoothest pebbles along the sides of his groin where the skin is palest. With a trembling hand, I touched the largest stone to the tip of his instrument and it lazily swung upward. Jacob's eyes flew open and he smiled.

"Darling girl," he said. "I am weak with shame over the joy I feel when you give me pleasure."

"Do not feel ashamed," I whispered. "Nothing satisfies me more."

It is true: each time I make love to Jacob I rescue him from death. And by the time our lovemaking is done, Jacob is younger than I am. We have proof enough in the new black hairs growing on his face and chest.

July 22, 1797

Fotis Stamatapoulos took us to his mother's village in the hills behind Sounion, because Monsieur Gennaro said he wanted to paint a country scene. We rode for hours on donkeys, seated on uncomfortable wooden saddles, following a narrow stony path that gradually circled its way higher and higher up to a pine-clad ridge. The air was sweet with resin, and the heat the most severe since Athens. Fortunately, Fotis took it upon himself to make the rest of us comfortable. He is a portly Greek who dabs himself frequently with a lemon-scented handkerchief. I believe he feels the heat more than the rest of us.

We lunched on figs and small stuffed birds and drank a refreshing yogurt drink to cool our throats. To stay cool, I hid my hair under my *calpac* and dressed in the blouse and pantaloons Jacob purchased for me in Athens. The men laughed and joked that I had become like a brother to them.

For the first time in many days, I thought of Father with his stern, plump face, lying under the sand of a Venetian beach. How he wished I had been born a son, and not a large, willful daughter.

The village of Fotis's mother was a farming hamlet with whitewashed houses. We rode in as the men of the village were having their tea. Jacob found it amusing when they mistook me for a man, even though I did not try to fool them. Fotis told us that my size makes it easy for me to confuse his countrymen who do not expect to meet women outside the home, let alone a woman as tall as myself. And certainly, in the village, there was not a female face to be seen. Emboldened by my disguise, I left Jacob and the men to enjoy themselves and set out to find the women. I discovered them in the fields, hoeing the ground in bright jackets and billowing skirts, their faces as round as water-smoothed stones. They turned away when I smiled at them, and I realized they were frightened of me in my man's clothing. It gave me a lonely feeling.

This evening, I am writing in these pages while sitting with Jacob and the men of the village, watching *ghazals*, as they are called, from a small travelling fair. Rapturous music floats in the air, and the dancers slide their heads like snakes from side to side, their arms rippling like wind in the grasses. They do not seem to grow hot or perspire.

As we sit in the deepening shadows, a large woman comes forward, clothed in gold coins which hang in tiers from her neck. Even her mammoth hips are sheathed in belts of coins. Clapping tiny gold cymbals above her head, she insinuates herself hip-first into the circle of dancers. Now the fat woman's hands flutter about her head; she touches her forehead and her breasts. And then, pivoting with an upraised hip, she offers her body in generous supplication. The men peer lasciviously at her and she utters high little shrieking sounds in her throat, animal-like in intensity. Jacob is watching her with fascination. It seems a bee or some other insect is trapped in her garments. She peers down through her blouse, shaking and bobbing. And suddenly the blouse is on the ground and the fat woman stands before us clad in large pantaloons and a second blouse. The men laugh. She begins again to turn and pivot, her face twisted in mock distress. She flicks the material of her blouse in and out so her gold coins clatter and ring, and I am frightened she will remove her clothing. I have never seen such a fat woman.

She lies on the ground and allows one of the village men to place two water glasses on the curve of her enormous belly. Then she wiggles her stomach so the half-full water glasses clink together musically. A virtuoso feat! The men grow mad with pleasure. They throw sweets and flowers at the large dancer, and Jacob is laughing and clapping. She has won him over and I am glad. We have both felt gloomy lately, knowing our time here is coming to an end.

Lesson Learned: There is no body too large or too fat for the pleasures of the dance.

"Did I tell you your mother tilted her head just like that when she was concentrating?"

Luce glanced up to see Lee standing before her. Behind Lee, the guides were clearing the food tables and putting empty retsina bottles into packing crates.

"Yes, you told me that in Venice."

"I've never met anyone who concentrated so intensely. It was as if she pulled down a blind."

"My mother could be . . . distracted." Luce closed the guidebook so Lee wouldn't see the copy of the journal hidden inside.

"Your mother had a difficult time understanding that she mattered to others. I don't know why. It was as if she couldn't see herself."

"My mother couldn't see herself?"

"Well, God knows, it's hard for any of us to see who we really are, isn't it?"

"Yes, I think so," Luce said, startled by the reminder of how Lee had loved and accepted her mother.

"May I sit down for a minute?" Luce nodded, and Lee lowered herself carefully onto the grass.

"Kitty would have liked the idea of you being here, don't you think?" Lee asked. Luce felt a twitch of dread. Even though she knew she was stalling, and not only that, trying to deny the sad afternoon that lay ahead, the last thing she wanted was to talk over family matters with Lee. She had only a few more entries to go and she had hoped to finish before they had to leave for the cave near Skoteino.

"She was always sorry to leave you behind, you know. You could have come with us any time. She said she asked you."

"I had to do my university courses."

"Oh yes, that's right. But I wondered . . . did you—did you disapprove of us?"

"Well, I didn't feel totally comfortable with—you know."
Luce shrugged angrily.

"No."

"With her being far away—in a place where I couldn't look
out for things."

"You felt responsible for Kitty?"

"If she'd stayed in Canada she wouldn't have died."

"Luce, no! Any of us can be in the wrong place at the wrong
moment. We can't control the world's chaos."

"We can. If we try."

"Everyone dies, Luce. You will find a way to make peace
with this—I know you will. Do you know what you are going
to say this afternoon?"

"I think so. But I don't have an object that symbolizes my
feelings for her."

"I wouldn't worry about it. Most of us are bringing something from Greece because Kitty loved it here. You'll see.
Things will go smoothly today." There, Lee thought. She had
said her words of maternal comfort. But now the girl was
looking at her as if something more was expected.

"Lee, can I ask you something?"

"Fire away."

"Why don't you want to go to Zaros?"

"Who said I don't want to go?"

"You keep finding excuses."

"Fair enough. Well, you're right. I don't go in for morbid
experiences. Seeing the places Kitty loved is more important
to me."

They sat for a moment in silence, Luce's head bowed, her
chest moving rapidly up and down. Finally, Lee heaved herself to her feet and lumbered off to join Christine, who stood
talking to Andreas. And when she was sure the other woman

wasn't coming back, Luce opened up the guidebook to the user copy, her face stubbornly turned away from the group in the meadow.

*July 23, 1797*

*Dear Isaac,*

*How sad I was yesterday, old friend. My dear companion has asked me if we should go on to Constantinople to find Aimée. I want to stay in Greece where she and I can find a home for ourselves and love each other well. There is so little time left to me.*

*And so this morning, I awoke from unhappy dreams. The worst were of my mother as she was when I was a boy. "Her son of the floorboards," as she called me. Naturally, my brothers and sisters took her to mean that I was conceived in the hull of a gondola, but already I knew enough to deduce that I was the result of a lagoon rendezvous with Grimaldi and not the son of the wretched man I called Father, who died agonizingly of an ear abscess. My conception in a boat left me with my lifelong craving for crayfish.*

*In my first dream I was a boy hardly into breeches, standing with my grandmother on a balcony above the Piazza San Marco as a magnificent parade swept by. At the head of the parade, I saw my mother in a gold mask and a padded wig so high it stood half as tall as myself. My mother was costumed as Diana, the mistress of the hunt. In her hand, she held a golden bow as bright as the sun. I cried out to this heartless, dazzling creature who stood flirting with the masked actor beside her.*

*"Zanetta! Speak to your child!" my grandmother called.*

*My mother turned my way, smiling and parting the opening*

*of her gown so I saw the ripe swell of her breasts. Then she began to laugh and point.*

*"Look at my bambino!" she shouted. "The bird has risen!"*

*I stared down in horror. L'uccellino si è alzato! I had burst out of my breeches. I hid my face in my grandmother's skirt while the crowd laughed.*

*The second dream was so vivid, I wondered if it was a memory revisiting me. I dreamt that my mother's lover, Michele Grimaldi, had anchored his craft in the rushes by the witch's house in Murano so they would be well hidden from the village. She had coaxed him into bringing me along and he agreed on condition that she kept me out of sight. Of course, I disobeyed her, and from behind a curtain I watched as he removed her extravagant bonnet with the wax fruit and butterflies; skilfully unbuttoned her brocade gown and then her zenda whose black lacy pleats fluttered in the breeze. I was jealous of him in his handsome bag wig and drawers, his waistcoat open to display the fine quality of his undershirt. Tenderly, he sheltered my mother with his bulk so the sea winds wouldn't dimple her young body. "Zanetta, why should you feel a chill?" he whispered, and when she was naked, he fed her a little crayfish and several glasses of prosecco. After she finished these delicacies, she excited him by sitting on the stern, legs akimbo, releasing water over the side of the craft . . .*

*I could not help myself. I burst out of the cabin, giggling, and the two of them stared at me in shock.*

*"Look, Zanetta," Michele Grimaldi said. "The boy loves you as much as I do!"*

*He pointed at the tent I was making of my trousers, and I wept with shame while my mother laughed.*

*Why do we cry out for our mothers at the moment of our death, Isaac? Because we need her still, and while we may travel*

*to the end of our lives before we know this truth, as a boy, I
already knew it well.*

Yours,
Jacob Casanova

Luce noticed that some of the women were packing up
their things. She knew that she should do the same. She put
away the photocopy and walked over towards the women lining
up to get on the bus. Only Toby and Jan were still lounging
under the olive trees. Julian was shouting for them to come.
Andreas had slipped into the driver's seat and was already
starting the engine.

That afternoon, the tour bus climbed a hill and stopped near
the small whitewashed church of Agia Paraskevi, which had
been built above a Minoan shrine. Waves of green hills rolled
away from the church towards the same pointed mountains
Luce had seen from the olive grove.

Her mother's entourage filed out of the bus, talking in
excited, boisterous voices. She trailed after them. She had
never been inside a cave and the prospect was daunting. She
had not realized until now that she was frightened of going
below ground.

Around her, the women began putting on their "cave
clothes"—what they called the closed-toe shoes and the pants
that they pulled on over their shorts and sundresses. Yannis
had politely absented himself, but Andreas stayed on to watch,
playfully hiding his eyes behind his fingers as if the women
were stripping to the buff.

Luce turned her back on Andreas and pulled on thick
denim jeans and a sweatshirt over her light summer clothes.

She had no idea how far down they were going. She'd over-heard Andreas joke that it was hundreds of feet and the group would have to climb down a vertical drop, but she didn't know whether to believe him.

"Are we all here?" Christine clapped her hands and the group stopped talking and nodded.

"Andreas and Yannis are joining us today for the tribute," Christine said, turning to smile at the two guides. "As some of you know, Andreas has been guiding people down this cave for most of his life."

"Yannis and me—we cave men!" Andreas said, and Christine waited politely while the group laughed.

"The guides will help any of you who need assistance," Christine said. "Ready, Andreas?"

Andreas nodded and started down the narrow road, walk-ing with his sloppy, shuffling gait. Yannis strode quickly after him and the group followed. The opening to the cave lay halfway down the hill, directly below the church. The two guides halted at the entrance and pointed solemnly at a formal stone staircase leading into the cave under a high, arched opening. Lee whispered to Luce that the black lime-stone rocks above the entrance had been darkened by bon-fires built during the annual celebration of festivals for the Virgin Mary.

The line of women followed Christine down the stairs, some of them carrying little clay figures of Minoan snake goddesses they had bought in a shop near Knossos. On the fourth step, Luce stopped. Perspiration, thick, almost creamy like hand lotion, was trickling down between her shoulder blades, and there was an uncomfortable moist sensation at the back of her neck. She remembered that she had left her bottled water on the bus. She stared at the stream of women moving past her, wondering what to do. Then she spotted Lee, already far below, looking up at her.

"Keep moving, Luce," Lee called up. "It's a long way to the bottom."

She began to walk slowly downward, fighting the impulse to go back. This was not what she had come to Crete for—to be enacting goddess rituals with older women. But she couldn't run away like she did in Athens, she told herself.

On either side of the passageway, the rocks were sweating like ripe cheese. Up ahead a flashlight was illuminating a large grotto where some stragglers like herself stood gazing up at the cave wall, murmuring admiringly. Huge stalagmites rose up out of the darkness like gigantic folds of wet drapery. When Luce looked closely, she realized they had been created by other formations growing down from the cave ceiling. The group moved on and she lurched after them, trying to keep her arms from touching the moist walls of the passageway. She felt as though she were threading her way through slick intestines.

About fifty yards ahead, Luce heard someone yelp in surprise. "Damn it, turn that thing off! Do you want to blind me?"

Julian was on his knees in front of an impenetrable rock wall, his glistening, sweaty face lit up by a flashlight. The flashlight dimmed and Julian's back and shoulders melted into the rock. The group appeared to be crawling through an opening in the rock face. Was that what she was expected to do? She wanted to turn back, but the floor of the cave felt slippery and treacherous. She carefully bent down and touched it. Her hand came back greasy with wet clay. She took a step backwards, shuddering, and fell hard on her rear end.

"Are you all right, Luce?" Christine called. She saw the dim outline of a woman in the shadows. "Shall I send up one of the guides to help you?"

"No. Please go ahead." She sat on the damp clay, looking apprehensively at the place where Julian had vanished. Now one of the white-haired women disappeared into the rock and then another followed. She didn't want to follow them into the bowels of the earth; she would wait until the last one went through and then she would crawl back up to the cave opening. Without warning, someone extinguished the last flashlight and now the world of the cave lay in darkness. She could no longer see the tendrils of sunshine floating down from the cave's mouth. She had no flashlight, not even a book of matches to light her way back.

Someone shouted from below. A woman had made it to the bottom of the cave. Luce heard another shout and a volley of chattering voices rose up from the depths of the cave. She closed her eyes, and a series of images appeared— as if on a film loop—of angry Greek villagers sealing off the mouth of their cave. *Left without light for the rest of time. The goddess women.*

"Psst! Look there! The gods knew how to laugh, eh?"

A torch lit up a small owl carved in a niche on the cave wall barely an arm's length away, and Andreas loomed in front of Luce, the light spilling ghoulishly across his bearded face. "You fear, eh, *kopela*?"

Luce bowed her head. She felt as if the moist air of the cave was choking her. When she looked up, Andreas was farther down the path, and Yannis stood before her.

"I help you!" He grasped her arm and she staggered to her feet. Her head was throbbing.

"I'm all right." She pulled herself free and started down a few more steps, nearly slipping again on the mud. She felt a weird numbness around her mouth. She ignored the sensation and barely glanced at Andreas waiting by the hole in the cave wall.

Closing her eyes, she hunkered down and crawled through. What else could she do? It was too late to go back now.

She was through to the other side. Andreas and Yannis were close behind; Luce could smell male sweat and the rich scent of cologne. Somewhere below, the weaving shafts of flashlights lit up the glistening stalactites dripping down from the limestone cave overhead. It was a sobering vision, she thought wonderingly. The voices of the women sounded far away, as if they were lost somewhere in the basement of a derelict building.

A beam from a flashlight picked up her Nikes and one of Yannis's Kodiak boots; they were standing on a ledge hardly wide enough for their feet.

"I take care of you, don't worry," he whispered.

Luce couldn't help herself. "I want to go back!"

"Luce!" Christine called up from below. "Let the guides help you. You're not in a good position to turn around."

"If you don't move, I kiss you!" Andreas said.

She heard Yannis speaking angrily to his uncle in Greek. She ignored the two men and began to edge cautiously across the ledge. "I can't get enough air!" she croaked. She cowered against the wall rising up behind the ledge, breathing in panicky gulps.

Nearby, she heard Yannis and Andreas shouting in Greek, and then Christine's voice reverberated again in the darkness. "Luce, put your head in Yannis's jacket and breathe slowly. You're hyperventilating. It's not dangerous."

Yannis handed her his jacket, and she did as she was told, burying her face in the coarse-grained fabric. Slowly, her breath began returning to normal. "I'm all right now," she said in a small voice.

Yannis took back the jacket and stood at the edge of the ledge, his arms touching the cave wall to form a protective bridge separating Luce from the open space beyond the ledge.

"*Ela*, Luce," he called to her. "Come."

Shivering with fear and humiliation, she inched forward, ducking her head under his arms and trying not to look down.

"That's it, Luce—one step at a time," Lee called up.

"You okay," Yannis said. He tapped her backside with his flashlight and made a shooing gesture towards the passageway sloping down to the floor of the cave where the rest of the group sat waiting. Her breath coming again in regular bursts, she began to crawl down the path on her hands and knees. Her mother's friends clapped as she reached the bottom of the cave.

"Good for you, Luce," Christine called out.

She was in a large oval space, perhaps fifty feet wide, with a high ceiling. A cluster of pumpkin-coloured fairy lights had been placed near a huge white stalagmite, ringed like a giant icicle with dripping calcite. The group were seated in a circle around the natural formation, and Luce guessed from their serious faces that it was meant to be a representation of the Great Minoan Earth Mother.

"We are here today to honour Kitty Adams," Christine began. "There will be some moments when the flashlights are turned off. If anyone becomes frightened, don't hesitate to ask me to bring back the light."

"Blessed be," someone murmured, and several voices answered, "Blessed be."

"Lee, why don't you start?" Christine said.

A flashlight illuminated the face of her mother's companion standing directly across the circle from Luce. Lee looked foreign and strange—a handsome figure whose head might have been carved from the limestone of the cave.

"I'm offering water to The Great Earth Mother of Crete in honour of my companion. If I'd been more generous, she might still be here," Lee said in an unfamiliar, remorseful tone. Luce heard the noise of liquid hitting the earth. The little jewellery-draped icons on the altar gleamed wetly. "Without water, the human race would perish. Without Kitty, I am without water."

Luce was taken aback by the pain in Lee's voice, and by her admission that she was not faring well without Kitty. Across from her, she heard Lee blow her nose, and stared sympathetically in the other woman's direction, but she could no longer see Lee in the gloomy flickers of light.

"Blessed be," a chorus of voices said. Luce thought of the Anglican services her aunt Beatrice had taken her to as a child. She remembered people standing up and sitting down again, murmuring repetitive refrains, just like her mother's friends today. For a moment, she felt comforted.

Christine said, "Julian? Can we hear from you?"

"I am leaving a Cretan jar of honey because I found Kitty's company sweet," Julian said, his voice ragged. "I'm not a Minoan sister, but a chap like me can still appreciate Kitty's work . . ." His words trailed off and Luce realized he was deeply affected. After a moment, he resumed: "So I have chosen to say the words of the American poet Walt Whitman . . . 'I bequeath myself to the dirt to grow from the grass I love. If you want me again, look for me under your boot soles.'"

"Thank you, Julian," Christine said.

In the wavering light of the candles, Luce glimpsed Julian rise to his feet and place a jar by the plump Neolithic goddesses on the altar. When he was back in his seat, Christine rose and poured wine over the small figures. "First water and then wine to the goddess Vritomartis and to Skoteini, the dark one who lives in the cave. And now, in honour of Kitty, I am going to call out the names of my female ancestors. And I want each of you to do the same. Start with your own mothers and grandmothers and then go back as far as you can.

"I am Christine, daughter of Jane, daughter of Martha," Christine began.

Through a trance of sadness, Luce heard voices calling out in Greek and English, and the women's names seemed to float above her in the damp air of the cave. "I am Luce," she whispered, ". . . daughter of Kitty, granddaughter of Pauline." Around her, the voices were melting into the rock walls of the cave in quavering echoes.

As the last voice faded away, Christine spoke:

"Luce, do you want to say something about your mother?"

She began to cough. Her body shook in chest-rattling bursts. In the gloom, someone slipped an arm around her shoulders and she heard a voice whisper, "Luce, drink this." An object, warm and rubbery, was thrust into her hands.

"Do you want to say something?" Lee whispered.

"Yes." Luce drank gratefully from the bottled water and she brought out the scrap of paper on which she had written down the words of Jacob Casanova. She balled up the paper in her fist. She couldn't read in the dim light.

"I . . . I am trying to remember a quote from a journal that belonged to my great-great-great aunt—well, I don't know how many greats she was." Luce heard gentle laughter. She waited a moment, then continued. "'Why do we cry out for our mothers at the moment of our death?'" she said softly. "'Because we need them still, and we may travel to the end of our lives before we know this truth.'"

There was silence. Austere and total. Then Christine whispered, "Light and darkness."

"Light and darkness," the group whispered back. Someone lit a candle and slowly, one by one, the flashlights were turned on again, their beams glowing like amber wands in the still air of the cave.

As Luce stumbled out of the cave, leaning on the shoulder of Lee Pronski, she stared in awe at the billowing folds of green foothills around the little church of Agia Paraskevi. The afternoon sun was still spilling its honeyed light on the Aegean landscape that seemed to bear no relationship to the strange, forgotten Minoan landscape underground. My God, she thought, it's beautiful, the earth is beautiful.

"It's a relief to be back above ground, isn't it," Lee said.

"Thanks for helping me. I panicked. I'm sorry."

"No, I'm sorry. It was too hard. I should have realized that before. Here, let's rest. I have something to say to you."

Luce let Lee lead her to the little Orthodox church and they sat down on the bench by its door.

"Did your ancestor write the words you spoke?" Lee asked as they sat down.

"No, it was Casanova."

"Really? Well, it was a good choice. Now, Luce, I need to know something."

"Yes?"

"Do you still want to go to Zaros?"

Luce nodded.

"Then you should go. I'm going to talk to Christine. She and Yannis will find a way to get you there."

"Aren't you coming?"

"No. Gaby and I had a falling out. I will tell you about it another time."

"Thank you, I'd like to see where my mother died."

"We agree then. Good." Lee rose, sober-faced and magisterial, and Luce followed, her young face bright with relief.

On the other side of the road, a long line of women were filing into the bus.

It was early evening as Luce watched the backlit shadows of the speeding motorcycle on the roadside cliff. Christine had talked to Yannis and he had arranged for his friend Achilles Tridafilakis to drive her to Zaros. And now she was doing what she swore she'd never do, riding for hours on a motorbike without a helmet. Under her legs, Achilles's bike jumped forward in steady bursts of power as vignettes of nineteenth-century village life rushed by: isolated farms without electricity, and pretty lighted villages where men lounged in cafés and women and girls sat on front stoops shelling peas.

By the time Achilles's bike drove up the hill into Zaros, the sun was setting behind the Psiloritis mountains. It wasn't hard to find news of Gaby. Everyone knew who she was. Her home was a few miles from the old monastery, up one of the mountain passes.

Still, it felt like hours to Luce before Achilles found the house with the nineteenth-century Turkish numbers still above the door. It stood back from the road, a homely white-washed building with a cornflower-blue door, an icon of peasant life replicated in the tourist postcards of the Aegean. In the yard, a tethered goat cropped the grass near a small grove of almond trees. When it heard the bike, it lifted its shaggy head expectantly. Luce said goodbye to Achilles and stood for a moment on the road, getting up her nerve. As the roar of the bike faded, she became aware of sheep bells. In moments, she was trapped in a stream of dusty, woolly animals whose bells chimed prettily in different octaves. She stared down timidly at the giant cloud of fleece. A shepherd called to his dog circling behind them and the sheep scattered and flowed together again, the tinkling of their bells only intensifying her sense of aloneness. For a moment, she faltered.

Then the sheep moved on, freeing her, and she walked into the yard with her graceful, loping stride and knocked on the blue door. She heard the noise of a bolt being drawn, and a panel fell open. Behind an iron grille, a burly arm appeared, and a stocky, round-faced woman stood before her adjusting her hairnet, her mouth full of bobby pins.

"*Neh?*" the woman said.

"Gaby," Luce said softly. "It's me, Luce. Kitty's daughter."

"Kitty? You Luce?"

Luce nodded shyly. The door opened and the round-faced woman pulled Luce into her arms, pinching her cheek and shouting Greek words of welcome.

"You come! Good. I expect you, Luce."

Luce let Gaby lead her into a small sitting room furnished with a stiff Victorian sofa and chairs. She knew she was in the right house. A large framed photograph of Kitty and a young man hung on the wall by a small stove. Luce stared in amazement at her mother smiling up at the proud-looking young man with fierce black eyes. She realized the young man was Constantine Skedi, and she was struck by the protective expression on his face as he smiled down at her mother. It reminded her of her own feelings about Kitty. Had her height made her think of herself as her little mother's protector, she wondered. Or was it some childlike quality in her mother that drew this protectiveness out of those close to her?

"You like my boy? *Poli oraio*, eh?"

Luce nodded gravely. In the last few days, she had picked up enough Greek words to understand.

"Yes, he's very handsome, Gaby."

Luce sat up and reached for the pitcher of water that Gaby had left for her on the bedside table next to a vase of wildflowers and a large *bleh mati*, one of the good luck charms in the shape of a glass eye that she had seen for sale in the tourist shops of Athens. Gaby had given her the *bleh mati* on the first night, explaining in her broken English—gringlish, as Gaby jokingly called it—that Cretan mothers sometimes pinned the blue eye on their children's clothes to protect them.

Luce filled a glass of water and drank it down. She'd experienced a beautiful dream just moments before waking. In the dream, she was standing at a *vaporetto* stop in Venice, watching her mother and Lee chug away from her in an airport *motoscafo*. The doll-sized figures of the two women at the stern of the launch were as plump and round as the Willendorf Venus. And their smiling faces were partially hidden under gigantic eighteenth-century hats decked with roses and toy sailing ships with brightly coloured flags flying from their mastheads. The two women were waving and calling to Luce, their faces alight with happiness, and Luce had felt her anger at her mother drain away.

Kitty had been happy before she died, Luce thought as she rolled out of bed and began to dress for the morning. And her mother's life with Lee had been good, even brave and inspiring.

Since the afternoon in the Skoteino cave two days before, she had been thinking about her refusal to acknowledge her mother's courage. Had she been so unsure of herself that she resented her mother's power and success? Or was it something less obvious? That her mother no longer needed her? Yes, perhaps. For all the years of her childhood, she had believed that it was her strength that sustained her mother after Luce's father abandoned them. Certainly, she had helped her mother, she knew that. But it was a child's dream to think that someone as purposeful and talented as Kitty couldn't survive on her own.

She paused by the window to admire the view of the mountains. It was a lovely morning in Crete. She turned towards the dresser where she had stacked her guidebooks next to the copy of the journal and the manuscript with Turkish writing. She picked up the travel diary and opened it to the final entries.

*July 30, 1797*

*Dear Girl,*

*I am writing to you because it is sometimes better to set down the words on paper so the reader can digest their meaning. I did not want to leave you last night and go with the other men to the party for our host, Fotis Stamatapoulos. As you know, it was a private masquerade for gentlemen, and I could not bring you. Dom claims Fotis is a powerful man in Greece and I would do well not to offend him. (Dom and his politics—he works hard to please the influential citizens here.) So I toasted Fotis's health in gloomy spirits. I was concerned with you and how you would be feeling left on your own.*

*Asked For, I do not understand the uncivilized habits of these wealthy Greek merchants who dress up and converse with other men. It is not the Venetian way. So you can imagine my delight when I returned to my room and found your note saying you had a surprise for me. Piece by piece, I removed my costume and stood before the long mirror that a sea captain had given our host in lieu, I am told, of payment for a debt. How you fool yourself, Giacomo, I told myself as I beheld the wreckage in the glass—the teeth no longer white, the stooped shoulders, the sway-backed loins where the scurze about my manhood grows tipped with frost.*

*As I stood surveying the old creature in the mirror, you stole into my room. And my surprise was complete. How beautiful you* looked, darling girl, dressed like Aimée in the portrait on my watch chain. I could not have been more astonished. And I could not have been more moved by the generosity of your play-acting. And then how seriously you listened when I told you I was too old for you.

"'Giacomo, my love will make you young,'" you said, cleverly quoting Aimée's own phrase from her letter. "'What is love except the force that defies death?'" you murmured. "'Our happiness will stop the ticking of the clocks.'"

"Aimée," I groaned, playing at your little game, "will you tell Asked For it is her that I love?"

You must understand my distress, dear girl, when you stopped your play-acting and began to sob. You said our love is wrong and that you must deliver me to Aimée who is the mother of my child.

"My soul," I said, taking you in my arms and sliding my tongue into the hollow spot between your collarbones—for what else could I do but try to comfort you? "That was long ago, dear girl. Do not let your sense of duty spoil our chance for happiness."

Asked For, it is you I love. Your beauty has given me back to myself, and once again I feel the giddy sense of release all men like to dwell in—to know that what has lain dormant and hidden is becoming free.

As I write, you sleep peacefully in the bed beside me. The wind blows the white curtains of this simple room in and out and the golden light of Homer blazes upon the crash of waves below. And now I put down my quill and weep at the thought of us parting. To have given up hope of finding happiness, Asked For, and then to have jouissance bestowed so generously—once again. I love, I love. I appeal to you and the Fates of Greece— stay by my side always.

Jacob

August 1, 1797

I write this on a hillside near Sounion. The men have gone
off to sketch the spot where the father of Theseus threw
himself from the cliff when his thoughtless son forgot to
raise the victory sails. Some time ago, I watched Jacob and
Domenico disappear down the narrow, sandy road to the
top of the cliff. Manolis ran back and forth between them,
holding up the sun umbrella. And now I sit, my journal on
my knee, and stare at the Aegean. I am sad that we are
going on to Constantinople. But there is no other plan for
us. Jacob wrote to Aimée, promising to rescue her from a
life she does not want, and she is the mother of his son. For
that reason alone he must go. When I tell Jacob that he
must do the honourable thing, he shakes his head and
groans. Then he grows thoughtful and asks if going to
Constantinople is what I desire.

I say yes, because I have no right to hold him back and
yet I want to shout to all of Greece that I want Jacob for
myself.

Neither he nor I know what to do about our circumstances, and this morning Manolis took us to the witch of
Sounion to ask about our future.

I will describe our meeting to see if I can understand
her words:

Manolis led us through the tall grass of a meadow overlooking the Aegean. It was a difficult walk. Several times
Domenico bumped against my shoulder, or came up
beside me to offer sweets. I ignored him. Eventually we
stopped at a marble column that lay on its side in the
grass. A handful of peas lay sprinkled across a coloured rag
placed on the marble.

"Stand back, Asked For! It's the Devil's goods!" Manolis cried. It was all I could do not to laugh. What foolishness! Manolis is as superstitious as a child. We walked to a nearby shepherd's hut, where a girl holding a baby stood cooking before a fire.

The girl was no more a witch than I am.

When she greeted me, I smiled and touched her baby's cheek, and she shocked me by spitting in the child's face.

"Miss Adams, the Greeks believe showing a child favour brings the evil eye," Domenico said. "Although it is hard to believe that a woman of such beauty could have the evil eye." And he gave me a horrible, leering smile. Jacob did not see the incident. He was too busy questioning the witch about our fortunes. The girl spoke to Manolis and disappeared into her hut. A moment later, she reappeared with a handful of the same dried peas I had seen on the marble column. She threw them on the ground and began to speak rapidly to Jacob in Greek.

Someone is calling my name. Domenico, I think. Here he comes up the hill, puffing as usual, and grinning as if he has a treat in store for me.

Luce had come to the end of the journal. There was nothing left to read except what might be in the manuscript of old Turkish writing, and for now it was impenetrable. She felt as if she had lost Asked For to the sea winds of Crete, which had blown away everything that once anchored her to the earth. What if she never learned what happened to Asked For Adams that eighteenth-century afternoon? She had to find a way to decipher the old Turkish manuscript. She gently lifted it up and opened its tea-brown leather cover. Inside, on its margin-less pages, she saw the dense flawless symbols that made her think of flocks of seabirds flying towards her. A *fonds d'archives* depended on the archivist's ability to find a thread of connection, but she wouldn't be able to find a connecting thread if she couldn't read the old document.

How disappointing that Asked For's journal ended abruptly. But why should her ancestor have something up her sleeve? Asked For had written her entries over two hundred years before, not knowing if anyone would ever read her journal.

She had to face the possibility that she would never know what had happened to Asked For. And yet perhaps help would come her way. Yesterday evening, Theodore had phoned her at Gaby's to say his friend, Ender Mecid, was hoping she would stop in Istanbul on her way home because he wanted to see the old Turkish manuscript. Theodore had added that Aphrodite was happily chasing mice at his mother's taverna. Should she go to Istanbul? After the phone call, Luce had consulted the pendulum and it had swung in wide, clockwise circles, signifying yes.

She packed the document carefully away in her knapsack. She could hear Gaby in the kitchen below, chopping vegetables. They had spent two days enjoying each other's company. The first night Gaby had received her warmly, plying her with mountain tea and a large portion of *nostimi vounisia pestrofa*, a sweet-tasting mountain trout; they had moved on to a jug of homemade retsina and small glasses of *raki* when the meal was done. Together they had sat on Gaby's stiff-backed horsehair sofa and looked at photo albums of her mother and Lee with Gaby. Gaby sat close to Luce, patting her arm and shoulder and smiling when Luce had tried out her pidgin Greek.

Downstairs, Luce found Gaby rolling out sheets of pastry dough on the kitchen table. She smelled the scent of mint, and on the stove, onions and what looked like dandelions were simmering in golden oil. Gaby turned when she heard Luce and gestured at the stove.

"We have *chortopitakia* for lunch, eh, Luce? Then you and I, we work in garden."

Gaby took Luce's arm before she could protest and drew her over to a table. She gestured to the vegetables spread out before them: wild carrots, *stafilinkaki*; corn poppies, *koutsoundades*; milkworts, *galatsides*; saw thistles, *tsochi*; wild fennel, *maratha*; and baby leeks, *prasakia*. She handed Luce a small knife and with a series of hand gestures made it clear that she wanted her to chop the bunches of wild carrots and fennel.

Luce was the first to see the van drive up to the gate as she and Gaby sat on the front stoop, snipping off the tips of beans and dropping them into a pot. She rose while Gaby struggled to her feet, puffing noisily, in anger or pain, Luce wasn't sure. Out on the road, Lee was climbing out of the front seat of the van. She spoke to Yannis, who drove off, and walked into the yard. By the stoop, she took off her Borsalino and began to fan herself with it, looking up glumly at Gaby and Luce. Around the little house, cicadas sang their jubilant heat song.

"Why you no come before?" Gaby said.

"I left you a message," Lee said, frowning. "I was tied up with Kitty's tribute."

"Bah! You bad girl. You forget Gaby." Gaby picked up the pot of beans and struck it emphatically against the wooden table on the stoop.

Luce thought Lee was going to yell at Gaby. Instead Lee hung her head like a scolded child.

"Yes, that's right. I'm an old fool, Gaby."

In an instant Gaby was off the porch. She walked over to Lee and put her hands on either side of the woman's face and pulled her head down to kiss her brow.

"You not fool. I know that. Come. We make party, drink raki."

Gaby linked her arm with Lee's, and the two smiling women walked over to join Luce.

At the window of the room she and Kitty had shared whenever they had visited Gaby, Lee stood watching Luce picking tomatoes in Gaby's garden. The girl moved with a touching purposefulness, combining the androgynous quality bestowed by her height with her feminine gracefulness. Lee felt surprised by the tenderness of her feelings. Lordy, how could parents bear to watch their children grow up? She had never given herself the chance to experience such painful confusion. Helping Luce find a safe passage into adulthood had been Kitty's concern—not hers. Once she had watched a mother starling throw a fledgling out of its nest. The mother had brought worms all day to the baby, waiting for it to learn how to fly. Overnight the baby starling died. Lee had found its remains pressed into the earth, killed by the cold, or a neighbourhood cat. The death of the fledgling had upset her. I suppose I have discounted maternal love, she thought, without realizing it can be a metaphor for the affection we feel for anyone close to us.

Below her window, she heard Gaby call out to Luce and, as she peered forward, she saw the woman's foreshortened figure under the grape arbour, waving at the girl. And Luce came hurrying over, walking without her little forward stoop. Well, the girl was learning her strength, she decided. She watched Luce nod gravely as she bent down to hear what Gaby was telling her.

*Get on with it. You owe it to the girl. She's never done anything to harm you.*

Lee turned away from the window and picked up the letter she'd started that morning:

Dear Luce,

    I think I owe you my account of your mother's death. Constantine Skedi entered our lives the year Christine had extended the tour to Zaros. Its mountain resort is a good midway point for a rest. The tour always stayed at the small hotel near the water mill, the one with the terrace where you feel close to the stars and wake up breathing the cool mountain air because the Psiloritis are the highest range in Crete. Your mother met Constantine in the village one afternoon. Christine had asked her to keep an eye open while we were there for a second bus driver. Constantine offered his services and drove her back to our hotel where he was coldly received by Andreas, who announced that he didn't socialize with a *palioalvanos*. (That's an insulting Greek word for a damn Albanian, Luce.) Constantine just turned on his heel and left.

    Your mother insisted that Andreas go down to the village the next day and find him and bring him back. And that is what Andreas did. Constantine was living over a taverna then, with his mother, Gaby, and his brother. His father was Albanian and had come to Crete as a deckhand on one of the ferries. When that ferry line had gone out of business, he decided to stay and live among the mountain people of Crete. He soon met and married Gaby. Constantine told us that Cretans see all Albanians as peasants and marriage between Greeks and Albanians is frowned upon.

    So Constantine came the next night for dinner and told us his story and your mother forced Andreas to accept him. And the next year, he worked on Christine's tour as a guide, and Gaby came to work at the hotel in Zaros. In those days, we saw a lot of Gaby and we became fond of her.

All was resolved, you might think. Except for my jealousy. Maybe it came from my own profligate history of love affairs, but I coveted your mother's attention fiercely. I even suspected Christine of trying to steal her from me although I knew rationally that this was a ridiculous worry since Christine is a loyal friend who has stayed in love with Julian.

When your mother spent time with Constantine, I felt heartbroken. The fact that he was clever and good-natured, and skilled with his hands and that everyone who knew him came to love him only made things worse. He was naturally grateful to your mother who changed his life when she made Andreas and Christine hire him. (We didn't know about his record for breaking and entering in Athens; this all came out after the accident and it must have made the bestowal of her favour miraculous to him.)

He was constantly bringing her things: flowers, wild marjoram for the mountain tea she favoured, small beaded purses and hats to go with the colourful outfits she liked to wear, and she would kiss him thank you on the cheek as I watched. I came to dread our descents into Skoteino. He would hover by her side, helping her through to the lowest level, his hand finding an excuse to touch her arm or shoulder.

I began suspecting your mother of encouraging him. I dreamt of her abandoning me and running off with him. If I had it to do over, I would have spoken to your mother in a way that she could understand, and we would have settled the matter between us. But I was proud and I

began to accuse her of things she had never done, knowing she had never done them, knowing I was no better
than the jealous Cretan husbands we saw in the villages
who project their guilty consciences onto their wives.

We stopped staying with Gaby, and I forbade your
mother to speak to Gaby and Constantine, and with
Yannis who knew them both, claiming her interest in
Gaby's son was undermining our relationship. Kitty
refused at first, but when she saw how serious I was, she
complied. Then I talked Christine out of using
Constantine as a guide and your mother wept from
embarrassment and shock but she did nothing.

The next year, he came to find her in Zaros. It was the
night she died. He knew our arrival date from the hotel
clerk, and he waited on the terrace until I had gone up to
our room. Kitty had stayed behind to help Christine pay
some bills and he found her in the hotel office and begged
her to let him come back. He had trouble finding work
after he was fired as a guide. Albanians are good enough
to hire as labourers, but in some Cretan villages they are
considered troublemakers. Constantine asked your mother
to go for a drive and talk about his situation. She went,
leaving me a note. They drove off together and they died
together and I thought that was the end of my happiness.

I was wrong about her intentions. I don't think that she
slept with him, but she loved him. I'm sure of that. I am
starting to see that your mother loved Constantine like a
son. Knowing you has helped me understand her feelings.

I realize your mother might have gone off on that drive
and died even if I hadn't made it difficult for her to talk
freely to Constantine. Could be I'm just a lapsed Catholic
in need of absolution Luce, but I want you to understand

what happened. Your mother never deliberately wanted to harm you when she went away with me to Greece for the last years of her life. We were blind and selfish in our love. We neglected you. I see that now. But sometimes it is unbearable to notice that we are hurting those close to us. And if that person looks as if she is doing all right on her own, it's easier to overlook the fact that we aren't paying attention.

With good wishes,
Lee

Luce finished Lee's letter in the old olive-press behind Gaby's house. No one used it now, and the rusting treads of the machinery were thick with cobwebs and dust. Outside, the sun had set, and shadows were falling in the musty interior of the building. From where she sat by the door, catching the last of the daylight, she could hear birds in the nearby almond trees. And somewhere close by, an angry bee was banging against the glass of a window. It must have flown in with her.

She had gone to the abandoned press to read because she guessed that Lee had something important to tell her about Kitty. She had seen it in the other woman's face when she gave her the letter at supper. So now she understood the reason for Lee's remorse in the cave. And Lee had confirmed that Kitty neglected her. It stung to hear the truth from the mouth of another person. Well, Lee also said that Kitty had loved her. She knew she did, she always had, even when Luce thought her mother expected too much of her.

She opened the door of the press and the bee buzzed out with her. She took a long breath and gazed about the small valley around Gaby's house. Summer had come although it was still only June; the fields of dry grasses, already brown from the heat, were glowing the colour of old brass in the fading light. She wondered if her mother had stood where she was standing on such an evening in early summer. It was too late to know. They had missed the chance to enjoy Crete together. Clutching the letter, she set off to find Lee.

She discovered her sitting on the terrace, making notes. An array of goddess icons stood on the table next to a tray of *mezes*. Luce hesitated, touched by the sight of Lee's bulk next to the small, delicate objects: the round, squatting snake goddess of Ierapetra, Crete; the tall poppy goddess of Minoan Crete with a crown of poppies, her palms facing outward in a benediction; and a porcelain replica of a praying Virgin Mary. There, in miniature, were Kitty's gods, arguably objects of worship and admiration. And here sat the life-sized figure of her mother's companion whose body must feel like an unwieldy suitcase to its owner.

"Well, did you read it?"

"Yes. I . . ." Luce felt herself start to choke.

"I know you were angry with me for taking your mother away."

"I'm not angry now."

"Balls."

Luce tried not to smile as she lowered herself onto the bench beside the other woman. She had a feeling Lee enjoyed using the word.

"Lee, you don't have to be so tough on yourself. My mother's accident——it just was. It wasn't your fault. And it wasn't mine either."

Lee nodded sadly and for a moment they sat together in silence in the summer twilight. Luce noticed the dejected look on the older woman's face.

"I guess that doesn't help much, does it. Is something else wrong?" Luce asked.

"When I want help, I'll ask. All right?"

"Okay, Lee," she said, trying not to smile. Here was someone as uncomfortable with accepting help as she was.

"Good. I was just thinking I'll be sad when our trip is over."

"But we'll see each other when we go home, won't we?"

The anxiety in Luce's voice gave Lee an experience of pleasure so sharp that she felt a momentary shame, like a child who has been given a present greater than she believes she deserves. Her face softened into a smile, and she nodded, yes.

The next morning, the two women set out to find the gorge where Kitty had died. Gaby reminded Lee that it lay to the west of her house about half a mile up the dusty road winding by a small lake. Despite the heat, they went on foot, toiling past cratered fields of brittle, sunburnt grass to find the hairpin turn where Kitty's car had gone off the road. The sound of Lee's breathing worried Luce. The older woman was trudging gamely alongside, but she looked hot and uncomfortable in her baggy, sun-proof garments. Luce walked slowly, feigning interest in the wildflowers on the dusty hillside. She would miss Lee when she left Crete. She had decided to go to Istanbul. Gaby had phoned the airlines and changed her ticket. *Just when I decide I like Greece, I find myself leaving,* she thought wryly. Well, she was discovering that this was how she moved in the world. She said no first and then waited to see how she really felt. She had always needed more time than her mother to understand her own reactions. Halfway up the steep bluff, they stopped to take stock. Ahead lay two nearly identical turns in the road; each one looked down on an equally steep hillside.

Then Luce spotted the little roadside shrine. Gaby and some of her friends had placed the *eklisaki* by the road. The shrine resembled a mailbox made of metal and glass. Mounted on metal legs, it stood in an arid spot tucked away behind a rock. Nothing was growing there but a few dried-out bushes. Luce wished she knew their names. Except for the shrine, the spot was hardly worth a second look.

They walked over and opened its door and together they peered inside. Luce saw a small oil lamp placed next to a photograph of Kitty Adams and Constantine Skedi.

"*Yiate psiethis*, for the light of her soul," Lee murmured as she lit the wick of the small lamp. She stepped back and lightly touched Luce's shoulder.

Luce reached in and placed the small blue-eyed charm that Gaby had given her by the burning lamp. "Mother, wherever you are," she whispered, "Lee and I wish you peace."

PART FOUR

*the City of Convergences*

I t was twilight when the taxi dropped Luce at the Arasta Hotel in Istanbul. She registered at the desk, then set off up the hill to the moneychangers' shops on the street by the Blue Mosque and Santa Sophia. The northern blue of the sky lent an eerie solemnity to the majesty of the old buildings. Swallows floated on air currents above her head and a pale filament of jet stream was stretched pink and radiant from the immense dome of the Blue Mosque to one of its slender minarets. She stood gazing at the swelling shapes of the mosques, unaware that her appearance was creating a sensation with the passersby in the street who were turning to stare. The Cretan sun had turned her skin the colour of dark honey and lightened her hair so that she no longer resembled the pale, timid archivist who had come into Venice in a water taxi with Lee Pronski.

She noticed a tall young man with a striking Levantine face stop to gaze at her. Then, as if he felt he'd been impolite, he turned away and she watched him head in the direction of her hotel. On the doorstep, he turned and looked for her again before stepping into the Arasta.

A group of loitering men with dark eyes and soft, musical voices were commenting on her hair and clothes.

"What country are you from?" one of the loiterers called to Luce. She tried to ignore him, but he jumped in front of her holding up a badly worn briefcase. She realized he hoped to impress her with his badge of Western commerce.

"No, no—no!" she said firmly.

The man bowed sadly. "You are from the country of no, no, and I am from the country of yes, yes."

Luce stifled a laugh, and continued on up the hill, her movements quick and graceful as she threaded her way through the ogling throng. She imagined the withering comment that Lee would have directed at the loiterer. The country of *no, no*—indeed. She wasn't looking to meet anyone, and it was a good feeling. To her surprise, she felt comfortable travelling by herself, although there had been a bomb scare in the Athens airport when she left. As police with machine guns inspected her luggage, she'd panicked and considered booking a flight back to Toronto that night. Then she'd calmed down and flew on to Istanbul, thinking of Asked For Adams and the hazards she had faced in Athens—and Istanbul, too, if her ancestor had made it that far. It had always been dangerous to travel, she told herself, and the list of harrowing perils grew or dwindled, depending on your destination. But even more than its dangers, she supposed travel and the prospect of chaos in other places had gone against her sense of order. Until she read the old journal, she had resented the sense of possibility that travel represented and its freedom which had captivated her mother and transformed her beyond recognition.

She changed her euros into Turkish lire and walked over to the Blue Mosque. She paused and peered through one of its huge windows. Inside, partly concealed by metallic bars, she saw a huge, majestic room, where hundreds of men lay face down before a robed imam intoning a prayer into a microphone. She stared in fascination at the prostrate men, searching for signs of female worshippers, since she'd heard that women worshipped at the back and sides of mosques, segregated from the men just as they were at Orthodox Jewish synagogues. How did Aimée Dubucq de Rivery survive in such a world, she wondered—or had the Catholic idea of Christian humility prepared her for submission to Islam? In her convent, the young Aimée would have certainly learned about submission to both God and husband.

Luce wondered what Aimée would have thought of Asked For Adams' belief that only the humane and reverent way you practised a faith mattered, not the slavish following of a doctrine. Perhaps Aimée would have agreed.

Back at the Arasta, she discovered a note waiting for her at the hotel desk.

Dear Ms. Adams,

Theodore told me you are staying at the Arasta and I'm writing to offer my services. I will come by tomorrow at 11 a.m. to examine the old document. Please call me if this time isn't suitable.

He had left a phone number and a name, Ender Mecid.

Mr. Mecid doesn't waste time, she thought. She wondered if he would be like the manuscript librarian from Bulgaria whom she'd met at a conference in Toronto, an excessively polite man who smoked a pipe, had messy, longish grey hair and a little notebook in which he'd scribbled his favourite poems. From time to time, he would pull it out and recite her a poem. Well, she would put up with any number of bores if they could translate her manuscript.

In her room, she phoned Lee in Crete and told her she had arrived safely after the bomb scare in Athens.

"It's frightening to come back into modern life after the experience of the ancient world with its wisdom," Lee said.

"I guess there's nothing we can do to ward off the unexpected. The Minoans lived in fear of earthquakes, didn't they?"

"Good for you, Luce. Statistically the chances of getting blown up are the same as winning the lottery."

Then, with a little catch in her voice, Lee told Luce how much she missed her. She had gone with Christine to Archanes on the north shore of Crete and found that the museum that had once exhibited the bones of the allegedly sacrificed Minoan was closed. But they hadn't been too disappointed—they'd laughed about it and spent the day at the taverna instead, she said. She was going back to Brooklyn in the morning.

It struck Luce after she put the phone down that Lee had always been reassuring her about one thing or another in the early days of their trip, but she hadn't understood that the other woman's concern was genuine. She began to unpack, surprised to find herself feeling grateful for the trip and just a little nostalgic. She retrieved Lee's gift from their first morning in Venice from under a pile of tank tops and placed it on her dresser top, noticing for the first time the two heads above its pairs of pebble-sized breasts. She hung up her clothes, and when that chore was done, she brought out the blue notebook she had purchased that morning in a Herakleion supermarket. She hadn't used a diary since high school. "Tuesday, June 28. I arrive in Istanbul and find myself missing Lee's unflappable manner," she wrote on its first page. "Lee doesn't lean on me the way my mother did. I suppose that was one of the things Kitty enjoyed about her. She could turn to Lee for strength while the world sucked on hers. Well, Lee and I have decided to like each other and that's a relief."

She paused and looked over at the double-headed figure on her dresser. Then she added: "First Inquiry of the Day: What is the most common sight in the world? Lesson Learned: Two female heads side by side. The image is as old as time."

Pleased with herself, she crawled into bed.

Luce's hotel was in Sultanahmet, the old European section of Istanbul. She opened her curtains to the morning light and saw a street of worn clapboard houses with unscreened verandas piled high with old lumber and broken furniture. Her room was directly opposite a crumbling apartment building whose windows were shrouded with grey curtains. The building and the wooden houses alongside it were screened by a line of tall plane trees that grew like bushy weeds, blocking out the sun. Her room that morning felt humid and gloomy which must have been why her small washing from the night before had stayed damp.

She climbed a high, spiralling staircase up to the roof terrace for breakfast. The terrace overlooked the Sea of Marmara, glowing grey-blue in the morning mist. Luce gazed at it in awe, moved by the hypnotic morning stillness and the delicate fan-shaped wakes of the freighters.

"Just like New York City, isn't it, madame?"

She turned to see the clerk who had checked her in the night before and whose name, according to the tag pinned to his jacket, was Aziz gesturing at the hilly shores strewn with a colourful bricolage of offices and apartment buildings. Behind Aziz, a waitress carried platters of pale yellow cheese, tomatoes, olives and fresh, sweet-smelling bread to the other guests on the terrace. Was Istanbul like New York? The atmosphere felt more northern than she'd expected—perhaps slightly Russian. And the breeze was cooler than Crete, although that wasn't saying much. A slight metallic odour drifted across the terrace.

"Do you put lead in the gas here?" she asked, and he nodded.

"Cars come, factories come, so progress equals pollution." Aziz shook his head mournfully as he led her to a table. When she had seated herself, he asked if she would like him to take her to Topkapi Palace.

"You will need a guide. The men in Istanbul are bad, very bad! You must be protected."

"I think I can manage on my own," she said, thinking it was a good thing that Lee hadn't come with her. The constant pestering of female tourists would have made Lee irate.

"No, no!" Aziz said. "You don't know Istanbul. You need a man at your side."

"But you have a job to do at the hotel," she protested.

"Today I am sick with cold, too sick to work. So I can take you to Topkapi. You cannot go there without man," he said.

Luce heard someone laugh good-naturedly.

"Ah, come now, my friend—chivalry is a protection racket," said a male voice speaking in an East Coast accent. She turned and saw a tall young man standing behind her. His handsome face behind a pair of oversized black glasses was thin and refined. Despite his unmistakably American voice, he looked Turkish to Luce or possibly Israeli. Ignoring Aziz, he asked, "I hope I have the right person? Luce Adams? I was told I would find you up here. My name is Ender Mecid."

"You're Theodore's friend?" Luce said, rising to her feet.

"Yes, he and I were boys here in Istanbul. I live in Boston now." Ender Mecid spoke Turkish to Aziz who glowered up at him.

"I told him you and I would like some tea," he explained as Aziz hurried sullenly into the kitchen. "And to stop bothering you."

They stood looking at one another uncertainly. There was so much to tell him, she wasn't sure where to begin.

Ender picked up the old leather-bound manuscript that Luce had fetched from her room and ran his hand along the strange, incised indentations on its leather cover. They had moved to a table under the branches of a large plane tree, so that he could examine the document without the sun falling on its pages. He flipped through it once slowly; then he lapsed into a thoughtful silence.

"So what do you think? Can you translate it for me?" She tried to keep herself from sounding impatient.

"Yes, I think so. It's written in the Ottoman language, the basis of modern Turkish. And like most old Turkish texts, it starts here." He opened the document at the back and pointed to an inscription. She stared at the roiling curlicues and loops.

"The script is Naskh, whose flowing lines are said to evoke a walk in the country . . ."

"How lovely!" She smiled and he nodded.

"Naskh is the script that's often used to transcribe the Koran. And it notes here that the author is an Ottoman scribe writing to his sultan, Selim III. The scribe's name is Sari, an Ottoman word for a fair-haired person, and look, this is interesting—his father's name was George Campbell. We've got a Scottish, or half-Scottish, Ottoman bureaucrat here, from the looks of things. And there's mention of a foreign woman. Someone called Asked For? The last name is Adams."

"That's her," Luce said excitedly. "She's my ancestor."

"How fascinating! Do you want me to try doing the first few pages for you now? It will be rough, but it will give you some idea of what we have on our hands."

"I do. Oh, yes!"

"Professor Mecid at your service. Only now you must wait." Ender gave her a mock-ironic bow. Then he pulled a notepad from his pocket and began to scribble a few words. She sat quietly, reading her guidebook so she wouldn't disturb him. From time to time, she glanced up to make sure he was holding the manuscript by the edge of the pages so he wouldn't leave fingerprints on the paper. There was no need to worry. He only touched the document in order to turn a page and he was absorbed now in his work, mouthing words to himself and then scribbling intently.

Aziz was setting the tables for lunch when Ender looked up and nodded at Luce.

"I have done a few pages. It's hard going sometimes." A nervous, frowning look passed across his face. "I used to translate more quickly. But you know . . ." He gave Luce a sheepish glance. "My Ph.D. interfered."

"Please don't apologize." She smiled back, startled by the concentration of his gaze. "Take all the time you need."

"Yes. I may need a few days to do this. I don't want to give you a careless translation, you understand."

"I do. But can you tell me what you have done so far?" He nodded and then began to read with such a grave look of anticipation that she had to turn slightly away so he wouldn't notice how excited she was by his interest in the manuscript.

Warrior for the Faith, Custodian of the Sacred Relics, Protector of the Pilgrimage, Servitor of the Two Holy Cities and Caliph, I, Sari Mustafa, son of Mustafa the Scotsman, am a mere scribe, yet it brings Your servant great happiness to acknowledge your request concerning the American-born Giaour, Miss Asked For Adams, and her travelling companion, the Chevalier de Seingalt, cited for treason in a letter by Kabasakal Edib Efendi.

As I write, I have before me the foolish and dangerous words of my enemy, and although Kabasakal Edib Efendi does not mention Miss Adams by name, I respectfully suggest his phrase "self-admitted sensualists" refers only to her companion. The Chevalier de Seingalt, as he made himself known, exhibits certain Giaour characteristics of a pleasure-loving sort, while Miss Adams possesses a steadfast character even if she engages in the pursuit of freedoms unbecoming to women.

As Your Majesty knows, the actions of foreign women do not reflect on us the same moral obligations as do those of our own women, but to answer your question, "Will the Giaour Asked For Adams give ammunition to my enemies opposing reforms after the Frankish model?" I willingly submit the following report analyzing the danger Miss Adams represents to Your Imperial Court, along with my final recommendation that I trust will please Your Majesty whose superior understanding is second to no servant of God the Almighty.

The meeting of your brother Prince Mahmud with the Giaour, Asked For Adams, took place in Salonica three moons before the Holy Month of Ramadan in the year 1212 of the Hijrah of the Prophet. Miss Adams came down the gangplank of the sailing ship in a man's clothes, so at first, Your Majesty, we did not realize the tall youth was a foreign woman. The youth, who was wearing a turban that resembled a loose-fitting sack, had a bandaged hand

and was carrying a small dog. An old European gentleman followed her, brandishing a tasselled walking stick at anyone who stood in the way.

As they walked among the unbelievers, the Giaour's dog disappeared yapping into the crowds. When she ran after the little dog, her turban blew off and out fell her long, auburn hair. Prince Mahmud and I were both impressed by the sight she made with her great height and long, womanly tresses. After assessing the circumstances, the young prince set off to help Miss Adams, his heart overflowing with curiosity over the beauty of a woman who travels as freely as a man in our lands.

He found her little dog trapped by the hounds of Salonica who, like the dogs of Constantinople, are wont to surround the animals that venture into their territory. Some say our dogs do it to protect the newcomer and lead it home. Others say our dogs trap the newcomer to kill it. But that afternoon on the wharf, Prince Mahmud gave the dogs of Salonica no chance to show their hospitable nature and snatched her pet from its tribunal of curs. When he presented it to Miss Adams, she was greatly pleased, and she and the aged gentleman invited us to sup with them that evening.

I saw no harm in the prince accepting their invitation, Your Majesty. In order not to attract attention to ourselves, we were travelling in the garb of commoners, thus, to her mind, Prince Mahmud was only a Muslim boy returning with his tutor from his studies in calligraphy at the school in Belgrade, and possessing a welcome knowledge of French. And my own fluency in English was most welcome. If I may humbly say, Miss Adams laughed merrily at my Scottish brogue. And thanks be to God Almighty, I, too, was happy to meet someone who could speak English.

As one with hair the colour of fire (the heritage of our redheaded chief whose bright hair lives on through his descendants), I was only too glad to explain how different the fate of my father, born George Campbell in South Uist, Scotland, would have been if Baron de Tott hadn't interceded on his behalf and brought him to the gracious Sultan, Abdul Hamid, May He Rest in Peace. (My father's head would have ended on a spike at the Tower of London, or in a lifetime of indentured work in the Colonies—of this I can be sure.)

Then she told us their tale while the Chevalier de Seingalt listened. He appeared tired and bewildered by their difficult circumstances. Nevertheless, he hung on her every word and she seemed equally fond of him, glancing his way lovingly as she described their rough sea voyage to Greece, and how on a hillside in Greece a man she assumed to be a friend, Domenico Gennaro Efendi, threatened her with the knife he used to cut canvas murals because she rejected his advances. As Your Majesty may guess, the way she defended herself greatly increased the young prince's respect.

"I demand an inspection of your weapon," he said, using the democratic *"tu"* of the French Revolution to impress her. I whispered to Mahmud that he might offend our companions with his princely manner. But there was no reason to worry, O Glorious Master. The Giaour responded warmly, using the same intimate *"tu"* as Mahmud.

*"Comme tu veux,"* she said, pulling a pistol from her pantaloons, and folded down the little bayonet on the pistol barrel. She handed it to the young prince. It is a dainty lady's weapon with a tiny panoply of flags and a

brass panel engraved with the flag of her homeland and the maker's name, W.M. Howell of London. Mahmud made Miss Adams go over each detail of the shooting again and again, his eyes glittering, and if it please Your Majesty, I will briefly recount the incident here.

After the man threatened Miss Adams, she shouted for help but the wind took her cries. She fled through the tall grasses, her steps on the crumbling clay sending up plumes of dust, and hearing the sound of his ragged panting drawing close. Caught in a gully and with nowhere to turn to save herself, Your Majesty, she was obliged to take out her father's gun and shoot her attacker in the foot.

The next morning she and the old gentleman fled Athens, because the man she injured threatened to pursue her in the courts. It is a sad story. The Giaour explained that a soothsayer had told them that morning that their happiness would not last the day. The aging gentleman noted that misfortune often befalls us after our happiest hour.

Ender stopped reading. "That's as far as I could get in the translation. If I continue, I may make many mistakes. But if you have time later this evening, I will leave more pages for you at your hotel."

"I am very grateful to you," Luce nodded. He stood up smiling, then bent down and slowly traced his finger along the incised decorations on the leather cover of the document.

"It's amazing, Luce. These pictorial motifs are more commonly found on mystical writings. My guess is that these designs indicate a shared interest in Sufism on the part of our scribe and his sultan. Perhaps they had a personal relationship, which would have been unlikely then but not impossible. Selim III was a man interested in European ways and reform—as his question to the scribe indicates."

She peered at the dark brown cover. Its leather, she guessed, must have once been light brown. Ender turned the document over so they were looking at the design on its back.

"This is both a picture of a man's face *and* a symbolic representation of the Prophet Mohammed and his family."

"I didn't think Islam allowed the making of images."

"The Koran doesn't explicitly forbid it. I will explain it to you later when I have more time."

"Ender, I'm beginning to understand that I was lucky to find you. Thank you."

He gave her a quick, sardonic smile. "You don't know how good it is to hear you say that. I'm afraid very few of our historians know much about calligraphy. It continues to be the black hole in Islamic art history."

"Is that your field of study?"

"Not exactly. I will tell you more soon, but I have an appointment now, I'm afraid." He shook her hand and left, the manuscript with the old Turkish writing carefully tucked inside the folder that she had provided. She watched him descend the stairs. Then she moved to the edge of the terrace and looked for him in the street below. She spotted the tall figure striding under the plane trees, realizing for the first time that she had seen him the day before when he delivered her note to the hotel. She watched until he was lost in the crowd of sightseers heading up to Topkapi Palace.

Later that evening, when she returned from treating herself to a steam bath up a side street by the Santa Sophia, she found a large envelope with more translated pages waiting for her. As she began to riffle through them, an envelope fell to the floor. It contained a note from Ender:

Dear Luce,

From what I can tell, your document looks authentic. There is the date, the eighteenth day of November 1797. And the seal of the library at Topkapi Palace has the date of 1811. And the signature of "Mahmud II"—the Prince Mahmud of the document, and the half-brother of Selim who followed him to the throne. The second date suggests that Mahmud may have decided to move the document to the palace library when he became the sultan. You'll have to have this checked out with someone more knowledgeable than myself, but I'm convinced. Will you have lunch with me tomorrow?

Ender

She let out a whoop. Unless Ender was mistaken, the document appeared to be genuine. And she would gladly go to lunch the next day. She wondered if her delight in the invitation suggested she had more than a professional interest, but she didn't want anything to interfere with the translation of the old manuscript. And anyway, he had two strikes against him as far as she was concerned: his height and his looks. She wasn't usually drawn to very tall men whose size felt like a physical command ordering you to take them seriously. And she didn't trust handsome men with flawless, even features— too often they reminded her of the unanimated faces of dolls.

She stretched out on her bed and turned to the newly translated pages.

The gun Miss Adams used to shoot her attacker gave her a painful powder burn. Indeed, that evening, she still had a tiny piece of pistol wad embedded in her right palm. I was able to extract it with my penknife. As Your Majesty might expect, the way she defended herself greatly increased Mahmud's respect. And since his own mother, the Most Illustrious Nakshidil Sultan, is of the French race, and with Your own interest in the wider world as an example, perhaps it is natural that the prince is curious about foreign women.

When she explained that she had kept a faithful account of her travels but that her wounded hand made writing in her journal impossible for a few months, Mahmud suggested that I do this task for Miss Adams, to record her travels in our own country. She declined his offer, but kindly asked if I would demonstrate my skill in calligraphy. And so, of course, I obliged my prince, as I am wont to do. Crouching on the floor, I allowed my hand to fly across the notepad on my knee. I had not used my pens for two days because we had been travelling home by coach from Belgrade, and it is difficult to write under such conditions. If I may humbly say, Your Majesty, Miss Adams and the old gentleman were delighted by my brush strokes.

The Chevalier de Seingalt considered my sketch of the dervish with a human face (Your Majesty's favourite), and said he thought that the Qur'an forbids the representation of images. So I pointed out to my companions that they will not find unfavourable references in the Qur'an to the making of figures. And furthermore, I argued that the Prophet's wife was allowed to make "a cushion or two" out of a curtain decorated with images. The old gentleman muttered a dismissive phrase about "Mussulmani non-sense." As I will explain in my final recommendation, the Chevalier de Seingalt does not look upon our ways with the same interest as Miss Adams.

Not one to be defeated, I drew the four letters of God and showed him how cleverly the vertical strokes evoke the fingers of the human hand. And if I may humbly say, the old gentleman lost his tongue when I said it was his Western vanity that led him to think the Qur'an forbids image-making. Giaours believe the making of animate images is more natural than other forms of art, and so ignorantly conclude that there must be a decree against image-making if the people of Islam prefer composing abstractions.

Greatly excited, I went on to describe the learning of Islam, and how our mosques and libraries made manu-scripts available to the people long before the Giaours invented their printing press.

~

She awoke an hour later to hear the wails of the muezzins calling out the evening prayer from the minarets of Sultanahmet. The pages of Ender's translation were still in her hand. Sitting up sleepily, it struck her that Asked For Adams and Jacob Casanova would have heard these same sounds if they had managed to finish their journey and find Aimée Dubucq de Rivery. Her guidebook noted that contemporary muezzins used electronic megaphones, but the piercing voices she heard in the darkness must have sounded much the same to her ancestor. Soon the modern sound-and-light show would be starting at the Blue Mosque, and the neighbour-hood dogs would begin to bark at the loud, disembodied male voices. She was becoming accustomed to the evening sounds of the old world, she thought as she turned back to Ender's translation.

The winds were very high that week in Salonica, and not expected to abate since this is the season of the *meltem*. The northerly wind meant a rough voyage so travelling overland was the best plan for us. Before we set out, Miss Adams accepted my help with her disguise—it was clear from what I saw in Salonica that she had not the slightest idea how to keep a turban on her head, so obeying my instructions, she wrapped her hair around the headpiece that serves as the turban's anchor. Then she fashioned a moustache out of her own curls and pasted it on with gum arabic. The neat appearance of her turban along with the false moustache gave her the look of a tall youth smirking at his elders.

God the Almighty gave me the wisdom to tell our innkeepers and other travellers that she had been born dumb. And if I may humbly say, she was grateful for my ingenuity, Your Majesty, although she at first found the turban warm.

We were riding across the plain of Filibe when the bandits struck. The alluvial plain is so pleasant with its fields of tobacco and cherry orchards that we had been lulled into forgetting all prospect of danger. The thieves came at daybreak while we slept, and disarmed us swiftly.

Alas, we were travelling without bodyguards. As Your Majesty knows, the young prince often goes about as a commoner, so he can learn the ways of the people who will one day be his subjects. It is a practice his mother taught him. The thieves were too ignorant to see through Miss Adams' disguise although they found the pistol in her travelling chest, and took the scimitar belonging to myself. The old gentleman had no weapons on him. And it was easy for them to ascertain that Mahmud had been born into a good family in Constantinople, although, Praise God the Almighty, they failed to guess how truly exalted is his rank. Their plan was to hold him ransom and extract a handsome sum from his family, and for this nefarious purpose they kept him separate from us. It was all I could do not to lose heart. Still, if I may humbly add, there have been enough brigands in Your Majesty's Court to keep my wits sharp. To that end, I told the thieves Mahmud was my nephew, and that his family would send them the ransom monies in Constantinople if I went to his father with their request.

Some days after our capture, janissaries were sighted in the distance, and the thieves hurried us out of the foothills up into the mountains. It was a hard march. The thieves rode horses and made us go on foot. Meanwhile, the weather had changed, bringing high winds and rain, and at night the ground by our fire was wet and infested with ticks. Mahmud was still kept apart from us, taking his yogurt and broth on the other side of the fire, and unhappily the thieves stopped me from giving him my ration.

In the mountains, the Chevalier de Seingalt came down with fever. Every day he grew weaker, until we had to carry the old gentleman in a hammock held together by long poles, his dog running alongside him. It was touching to see the care Miss Adams lavished on him, feeding him herself and wiping his brow when his fever was high. I believe her friendship with the old gentleman is dear to her, although such a friendship cannot last long.

I made a habit of sitting with the thieves when they took *keyif*. They had never met a Muslim like myself, and they delighted in my freckles and red beard, never losing an opportunity to call me "the Fair-Haired One." I did my best to accommodate their questions. As a boy, I was deeply impressed by my father's flexible nature, and if I may humbly say, the acorn does not fall far from the tree. Soon the thieves began to share their opium with me around their evening bonfires, which I made a pretence of smoking, while Miss Adams and the old gentleman sat at a distance.

Praise God, they were simple farmers who had taken to robbing travellers because a drought had ruined their poppy crop. They blamed their luck on Bendis the Destroyer, an ancestral goddess who plays cruelly with the fates of men. I asked polite questions about this deity whose cult is known in the back hills of Thrace, and once they had fallen into a trancelike state by the evening campfire, the thieves would talk willingly about her.

It seems Bendis has been worshipped by the people in that region long before Mohammed, and this faith is practised secretly so as not to arouse the ire of the mullahs. They described Bendis as dual in nature: she is the mistress of stones, forests, springs and healing waters, and the crone of the waning moon, whose savage powers can bring a man to his knees. They told me strange tales of Roman times when men cut off their genitals in order to appease Bendis, and their faces broke into relieved smiles when they said such sacrifice was no longer demanded.

Soon after, we descended into a magnificent pine valley and made camp at the foot of a cliff. Above us, in the rocky edifice, was a large cave from which flowed a mountain spring. The thieves believed the cliff was haunted by the goddess Bendis, and pointed out the ledge, where in times of trouble Bendis was said to appear and offer help to mortals in need. The thieves were greatly excited and said that if I dug in the earth at the foot of the cliff below the cave I would find strange pagan idols left by her worshippers.

To prove it, the chief amongst the thieves, by the name of Kemal, showed me a clay figure he had found in the ground. An embellished triangle on the antiquity signified its female nature.

That night, Kemal built a huge bonfire and scattered its ashes over the small figure. Soon everyone fell asleep, but I was unable to close my eyes because, Praise God Almighty, an idea had been born that would lead to the deliverance of Mahmud, along with myself and my two Frankish friends.

~

Luce was helping Ender prepare lunch. His apartment was in the old district of Sultanahmet in one of the wooden houses she had noticed from her hotel. He had set a table for two on the balcony. It was cleaner than the cluttered verandas she had seen from the terrace of the hotel but simply decorated with a picnic table and a few old plastic lawn chairs. Ender explained that the apartment belonged to his uncle who had gone to his summer house in the Princes' Islands and given him the run of the place so Ender could research the history of art under the Ottomans. Part of his research touched on the practice of calligraphy.

"Casanova's opinions about the scribe's 'Mussulmani nonsense' is typical of Orientalist stereotypes," Ender said, frowning. "You know, the barbaric Turk, that sort of attitude? Or else Western travellers exoticize the Ottomans just as they do the rest of the East. And yes, it's a pet peeve of mine, so ignore me at your peril."

Luce laughed as she sliced up tomatoes. "I promise not to act like an ignorant Westerner. I'd be too terrified!"

He gave her a bemused look from behind his oversized glasses and it struck her that his glasses sat on the bridge of his nose like an afterthought, or perhaps an apology. She wondered if he wore glasses defensively the way men who wore beards often wanted to be perceived as more manly. Perhaps he needed or wanted those large, strange-looking spectacles to defuse the impact of his attractive appearance.

"But why would Asked For Adams be accused of treason? An American woman wouldn't pose much of a threat to the Ottoman court, would she?"

"Foreigners like Baron de Tott helped to train a new corps of engineers and artillery for Selim's father and the work continued under Selim III. That's probably why he rescued the Scotsman from death or imprisonment after Bonnie Prince Charlie's rebellion and brought him to Turkey. De Tott reorganized the gun foundry and taught new European mathematics. But there was fierce resistance from the janissaries to learning new techniques."

"Did Selim welcome Western influence?"

"On some parts of Ottoman life, yes. In 1808, Selim was murdered at Topkapi Palace. Mahmud—the scribe's young prince—continued the reforms."

"And how does Asked For figure in this?"

"Who knows what talk there would have been about a man like Casanova in Istanbul? His subtlety and intelligence would have been appreciated but his liberal way of thinking would have raised eyebrows in the Sultan's court, perhaps providing the enemies of Western reform with another reason to cause trouble. But we don't know that yet, do we? I've only just started translating the scribe's letter."

Ender motioned to the table set with a wooden basket over-flowing with the stuffed flatbread called *gozleme*, a hunk of *beyaz peynin*, the white cheese that looked like feta to Luce, and a platter of dry meatballs, *kuru k'ofte*, nestled next to slices of fat red *domates*.

"Shall we eat?" They sat down to the modest lunch they had prepared together.

~

On the third morning in the hills, I saw my chance to save us from the thieves. It came about, if I may humbly say, because Kemal had taken a liking to me and admired the say-ings I copied from the Holy Book for him and his wife. The thieves, by now, had grown lazy and unconcerned, believing we could not find our way out of the hills without their help.

So Kemal was agreeable when I asked him to show me the secret path to the ledge, and once we were out of sight he let down his guard and warned me that the food supply was dwindling and that his companions spoke about shoot-ing us so they could return to their homes before the win-ter set in. Perhaps because I am less than thirty years of age, Your Majesty, I was unable to imagine my own death. If I may humbly say, the end of a man in the middle of his life is a crime in the eyes of God the Almighty—like the sun setting at midday.

In addition, I lived in daily torment because we broke camp often to avoid detection and our constant movement

kept me from the tasks whose sacred nature is well loved
by Your Majesty. With each hour that passed, I grew more
aware of the nimbleness leaving my fingers. At night, I
dreamt that Your Majesty had replaced me with my enemy,
Kabasakal Edib Efendi, who rides through my dreams like
a stalking horse, ever ready to take for himself the favours
you bestow, O Glorious Master.

I have not forgotten how he slyly copied my tale of
"The Scribe's Honeymoon" and offered it as his after
Your Majesty asked us to provide stories during the
long, rainy weeks last winter. Then my enemy left out
the delicate ending I'd provided, foolishly imagining it
would evoke Your Imperial Anger. Does Your Majesty
recall the tale? One night, around the campfire, while
Miss Adams slept, I recited the tale in its entirety to
the Chevalier de Seingalt who was delighted by the
charm of its ending, which I humbly include here for
Your Imperial Pleasure:

I accepted the little invitation that she offered me and
began to introduce my reed into her ink pot when she cried:
"One-third, that is already too much. Don't you see that its
inner parts have not taken on the imprint before?" It was
too late. The head of my instrument was inclined at an
angle, the ink flowed, and my sentiments found their
satisfaction.

There are very few who understand the soul of a scribe,
and I count Your Majesty among them. Our essence is
this—if we do not copy God's words, we do not live.

Ender put down his notepad because Luce was laughing.

"I'm sorry, Ender. The scribe—it's the same old male pre-occupation with size!"

"It *is* a quaint and humorous tale," Ender agreed. "Not to mention the scribe's evident lack of interest in his partner's satisfaction. Ah, that reminds me. I had almost forgotten." Ender rose and disappeared into his uncle's apartment. He returned a moment later carrying a little enamelled wooden box.

"It's a scribe's pen-box. I found it this morning on my uncle's desk. He likes to collect old things. And this was in the pen-case," he said, handing her a postcard. "My uncle must have put it there to show what the man who used such a box looked like."

The card depicted a scribe seated on the floor of a disorderly room, making brush strokes in a book on his knee. She was touched by the scribe's fastidious appearance and the delicate way he held his reed pen.

"You see how serious he remains in the midst of chaos? I thought of our scribe's confession—if he does not copy God's words, he does not live!"

"Yes, he looks like he takes his job and his faith very seriously." She set down the card and opened the little pen-case, gently extracting a reed from its innards. The reed pen felt brittle to the touch of her fingers. She quickly put it back. Heaven knows how old it is, she thought. "What did the scribes make their ink from?"

"Out of lampblack usually. And this makes me remember another fascinating thing. The architect of Süleyman the First designed his mosque so air currents brought the soot from all the oil lamps in the building to a special room. The currents deposited the soot on the wall of this room so his subjects could come and scrape it off to use in the making of ink."

"Are you serious Ender?"

"I'll take you there one of these days and show you the room. Believe it or not, Luce, they knew a few good tricks back then."

"You're making fun of me." She was quiet for a moment. "Are you religious?"

"I grew up a Muslim but I do not practise any faith. I avoid religious doctrine—as much as possible." He waved dismissively. "It is the cause of too many troubles in the world."

"But you have a faith, Ender. Everyone does. I suppose mine is a belief in the importance of keeping records," she added, remembering Lee's comment in Athens that, like her mother, she believed in posterity.

"Then my hobby of studying Ottoman calligraphy is my faith. Let me tell you a story that will explain the way writing is seen in Islam. Once, an Islamic scholar found a boy sitting on an oil can manufactured in England.

"'Get up,' the scribe told the boy. 'There are words on the side of the can.'

"'This is infidel writing,' the boy said, pointing to the English words.

"'There are Muslim people and infidel people,' the scribe replied. 'But all writing is equally holy.'"

"I like your story," she said softly.

He gazed at her so warmly that she dropped her eyes, pretending to be absorbed in his uncle's enamelled box.

"Good. And now allow me to read you the next section of the letter." He grinned as he picked up his notepad. "Our scribe is a surprising fellow."

I digress from my purpose, Your Majesty. I was recalling the night when I spoke with the Chevalier about my plan for our escape. We whispered about it to one another after the thieves had slipped into their opium dreams. He is a man it seems of imagination and talent, who has escaped from a few tight corners in his time. He undertook to convince Miss Adams that there was no other course open to us.

I do not know if Your Majesty has heard the story of Bendis. But as the thieves danced about their fire, a figure appeared on a rocky ledge and, as a result of my cunning, our captors were able to behold the goddess.

One by one the idolatrous thieves climbed the steps on the cliff and knelt before her. When it came time for Mahmud's guard to take his turn, he pulled Mahmud along with him, thinking that if he did not, the young prince might try to use this opportunity to escape. Mistakenly believing I was in awe of their despicable ways, they allowed me, too, to climb up the steps carved into the cliff face, with my hands bound and my head bowed. As we approached the ledge, the moon passed behind a cloud, and we were in darkness. Cursing softly, Mahmud's guard lit a small torch and pushed the young prince forward. We beheld a naked figure, tall, with arms as well muscled as our palace guards. Yet the idol of the thieves was feminine in all aspects, with ruby lips and eyes the same glorious turquoise as the Bosphorus on summer days. And then the goddess cried out to the awestruck thieves that their poppies would grow again if they freed their prisoners.

Overcome, Mahmud took a step backwards, extinguishing his guard's torch, and nearly fell from the ledge. As he cried out, a hand grasped his arm, and the idol whispered his name. When the torch was relit and we looked again, she had vanished. The young prince was deeply troubled and confused by what he had seen, until I told him it was the hand of God Almighty gripping his through the hand of the pagan goddess of Thrace.

I have not told Mahmud the true identity of the Thracian goddess, Your Majesty. But I humbly urge Your Majesty not to overlook the bravery of the Giaour who grasped the prince's hand in the presence of the thieves. She did not know Mahmud would be among her worshippers, and if I may humbly say, even with the benefit of my coaching, it was terrifying for her to stand unclothed in the moonlight.

The next day, we awoke to find our guns and horses restored to us, and the thieves gone. They left us boiled rice and a map with crude instructions on how to reach Xanthi at the eastern end of the plain.

~

Evening was falling in Istanbul. Luce and Ender were finishing supper at a little fish restaurant in Kumkapi, facing a small square.

"So it seems your ancestor saved the young sultan-to-be," Ender said.

"Or the scribe made up the story to impress the sultan. After all, he wasn't just a scribe, was he? He invented erotic tales to please Selim."

"You may be right. Ah, look at the sunset, Luce. Isn't it wonderful?"

In the dying light the spires of minarets gleamed in every direction like magic flutes designed by a wizard to delight and fascinate. She didn't exclaim on the beauty of the city in case Ender decided she was an impressionable Western tourist exoticizing the East.

They had spent part of the afternoon "Bosphorising," as he called it. They had walked down the hill from his uncle's apartment in Sultanahmet and taken a bus to Yeniköy. Then they wandered through the streets near the famous river, stopping to watch the freighters and public ferries gliding up and down the strait. It was warm by the water and an iridescent sheen of light played on the narrow wooden mansions lining the opposite shore.

Now, in the restaurant, Ender pulled out the translation and put the finishing touches on a new section of the scribe's letter. He had left the document at his uncle's apartment, but he wasn't satisfied with his reconstruction of some of the scribe's flowery sentences. She felt a thrill of pleasure at the sight of him sitting across the table, his eyes, under the thick black brows, bright with interest, his hand moving with slow, careful strokes across the paper. As he worked, the breeze from the Bosphorus ruffled his hair.

Finally, he put down his pen, apologizing for taking so long, and she teased him for being a perfectionist. He told her how he had become interested in calligraphy as a small boy, how an elderly man who knew his father had been a scribe, and how he and Theodore Stavridis used to go to the old man's house and watch him make his flawless, sweeping strokes with an old reed pen. He had been fascinated with the man's tales of medieval calligraphers like Shaikh Hamdullah, who died in 1520. After his death, Ender said, other scribes would bury their reed pens for a period of time near Shaikh Hamdullah's tomb, hoping the aura of the great calligrapher would be passed on to them through these pens. "If I lived then, maybe I would have been a scribe too. It was an honourable profession."

"How do you do make a living?" She realized she had been too taken up with his translation of her document to ask him.

"I'm an art historian, only this summer I'm working as a copy editor at a publishing house here." Ender smiled. "The pay is poor but it gives me time to work on my history of art under the Ottomans. And you?"

"I work at an archives in Toronto."

"You? An archivist? How romantic!" His smile deepened. "Of course, I don't precisely know what an archivist does . . ."

"Librarians store books and archivists preserve evidence . . . old documents and so forth." She was aware of sounding a little pompous. "I guess I don't look like who I am."

He laughed and they turned to look at the Bosphorus where a fishing boat was vanishing into shimmers of golden light. The sun had set, and above the hilly, wooded shore on the Asian side of the Bosphorus, she noticed a large evening cloud assembling itself into the shape of a man's head. She picked out a fan-shaped hat and a frock coat. It was the silhouette of a perfect eighteenth-century gentleman.

"Ender! It's him, it's Casanova!" she whispered, pointing. Too late. As he turned to look, the cloud broke into fragments across the evening sky. The way our lives change is mysterious, she thought as she watched the wisps of cloud drifting above the hills on the opposite shore. The process is often slow and gentle, like a symphony shifting into another movement. At first, we are oblivious as it carries us along into the next phase of our lives. Then gradually, we grow aware of how it is sweeping us up into the momentum we started ourselves.

"Are you far away, Luce?" Ender asked.

"Not so far." She smiled. He nodded and picked up his notepad. In his deep, quiet voice, he began to read from his translation.

After twenty-four hours, we came to the old military road through the mountains that leads to Edirne, finally reaching the beautiful gardens and country houses that surround this city. I am tempted to tell of our adventures along the way, the new mosque and public clock Your Majesty commissioned in the square at D.; the strange sight at R. of Christians and Jews entering the mosque together, proving the habits of village life are sometimes stronger than religious differences; and the nuisance of having to rescue the old gentleman's dog at the fair in U., where Russian furs are sold in abundance.

Your Majesty already knows about our problems with the officers of the customs house on the road outside Pera, and how angry I was when they held us up on the pretext of examining our luggage, falsely claiming that I had forgotten to obtain a *tezkire* in Constantinople when I set out for Belgrade with the young prince. Their impudence was an insult. I was pleased to learn that they were dealt with swiftly. And I accepted with humble gratitude Your Majesty's gracious suggestion that we should not enter the city in open triumph. Your Majesty is wise to see that public knowledge of Mahmud's kidnapping could weaken the faith of Your subjects in the Sublime Porte.

Even so, as Your oarsmen rowed us across the Bosphorus, I was not prepared for the sight of four golden Montgolfier balloons soaring up over our heads and floating off down the Bosphorus like dazzling Imperial suns. We were all overjoyed by the demonstration of Your Majesty's power. But the old gentleman grew increasingly sad the closer we came to Constantinople, for reasons which will soon become clear.

As Your Majesty knows, Giacomo Casanova did not accompany us to Topkapi Palace. He was weary from our journey, and indeed, he still seemed unwell. I found him rooms in Stamboul in a *konak* near the Imperial Gate. There he and Miss Adams rejoiced in the majesty of the Blue Mosque and Santa Sophia whose domes rise out of the earth like the swelling chests of giant war-birds. They were delighted by the peaceful beauty of the Sea of Marmara, its waters lightly wrinkled by the passage of eight-oar caiques and fishing vessels.

Alas, there had been a fire in the neighbourhood the day before—one of the old wooden places went up like a tinderbox—and the acrid smell of burning still lingered. If I may humbly say, the late summer rain that God the Almighty sent to douse the blaze had, at the same time, muddied the roads up the hill named after Your glorious ancestor, Sultan Ahmet, whose abode is Heaven, may God's mercy be upon him. The axles of our coach wheels continually ran aground, and each time it floundered in the mud, barking neighbourhood dogs surrounded us, driving the old gentleman's terrier into a frenzy.

But when the Imperial Gate loomed in sight, these small nuisances vanished, Your Majesty. We settled the old gentleman in his lodgings, and there he gave Miss Adams a letter to deliver to Nakshidil Sultan.

But as we turned to go, he surprised me by begging her to stay instead.

"Dearest," she replied, "I have resigned myself to our circumstances. Aimée is expecting your help. I set out to help you find her and I cannot intervene now."

Giacomo Casanova sank onto a divan, his head in his hands.

"Dear Jacob," she said. "You have given me so much. When we met, you taught me what *you* believed—that love is your *first* faith. But Aimée is your destination and it is your responsibility to help her. As for me, I have come to realize that my faith is travel. I intend to go around the world twice before I die."

"Ah, the pupil has outgrown the master!" He rose, with tears on his cheeks. He held her to him and bade her farewell. I saw that she was fighting back tears. There was no reason that I could see for the old gentleman's misery since they were about to attain the purpose of their journey together.

Why do I bother with an account of a personal matter like the old gentleman's tears, Your Majesty? So that you will understand that while Mahmud's homecoming was a celebration for you, it was a sad occasion for the Chevalier de Seingalt. And I will return to this matter in a moment.

Miss Adams was startled when I explained that as a woman she could not go with me to witness Your happy reunion with Mahmud. If I may humbly say, she later thanked me for my descriptions of the Imperial Gate which she said were as good as seeing it with her own eyes—Your Majesty's dazzling carpets, the wall emblazoned with Your Majesty's jewels and the lines of turbaned courtiers stretching out in impressive stillness, their eyes averted in deference.

She listened, wide-eyed, to my description of the viziers in the freshest spring green, the chamberlains aglow in scarlet, the ulema and mullahs, adamantine in purple and the deepest of blues. She was especially pleased when I mentioned the French engineers, distinguished by their bare heads and *carmagnoles*.

Naturally, I could not go with Miss Adams into the Seraglio to deliver the letter to Nakshidil Sultan. I had arranged for her to go on her own. When I explained that Nakshidil means "beautiful picture embroidered on the heart," she smiled sweetly. With the deepest piety, and with no wish to seem disrespectful of the garden of Your Majesty's happiness, I later encouraged Miss Adams to describe her impressions of Your Imperial Palace and the Seraglio. She exclaimed at everything with a wondering heart—the monumental elegance of Your Majesty's Tower of Justice and the airy grace of Your Pavilions overlooking the Golden Horn. She was delighted to find gardens as well tended as those in the Garden of Paradise. Then she was escorted into the Seraglio by one of the black eunuchs who had been selected to take her to the apartments of Nakshidil Sultan.

~

Luce was sitting by herself on a public bench near the Hagia Sophia. The dome of the old Byzantine basilica rose like the shell of an overgrown pink turtle above the glistening waterways of Istanbul. The building had been converted into a mosque after Istanbul fell to the Turks in 1453, and Luce had read in her guidebook how a famous Ottoman architect had solved the problems of its fragile dome by shoring up the sides of the building with buttresses. But it wasn't the history of Istanbul that occupied her thoughts. She had spent the morning worrying about the fate of Asked For Adams. After breakfast, she found a note from Ender, suggesting they meet at Topkapi Palace at noon.

The translation he had given her had stopped just before Asked For Adams was about to meet Casanova's lost love, but

Luce suspected him of having held something back. What was he afraid of telling her? She was sure by now that Jacob Casanova had loved her ancestor, and there was no danger that he would choose Aimée. Yet Ender had given her a strange smile when she asked if he was drawing out his translation to prolong the story's suspense. She didn't know him well, but what she had seen of his nature made her suspect he might be protecting her.

She saw him coming now, sauntering unchallenged through the gauntlet of loiterers near the taxi stand. She rose to her feet and called his name and he came hurrying up the hill towards her, grinning. Together they went through the Bab-i Hümayun, the Imperial Gate of Topkapi Palace. Inside its grounds, she saw rose gardens and closely cropped lawns shaded by plane and fir trees that grew next to spiky cactus and myrtle bushes. Aside from the delicate peaks of the palace towers, she and Ender could have been in a well-tended monastery somewhere in Switzerland. If Athens with its smoggy golden light was like a large Mediterranean town, Istanbul was a leafy European city on a spectacular sea-river. Except that in the palace's imperial heart had lain the great harem. The Ottomans adopted the practice of polygamy that they'd adopted from the Arab nomads they had conquered.

Ender touched her arm and pointed out a tall stone arch with a panel of golden Islamic script above the entranceway they were about to pass through.

"The Seraglio," he said solemnly. They joined the tourists moving through its door like eddying fish in a current, past the high, dark halls with iron grilles and tall wood-panelled cupboards.

They followed a tour group into the Sultan's apartment and stood by a huge screened window where Luce imagined

Mahmud must have watched his mother Aimée and other harem women bathing in the pool below. According to the guide, the Sultan would select a new partner during a visit to his mother's apartment. If he liked the girl serving their tea, he would give her the symbolic handkerchief. She was surprised to see that the lavishly tiled bathroom of the Sultan's mother was adjacent to the bathroom of her son, the Sultan. The harem, she mused, with its numerous women, camouflaged a semi-erotic dependency between mother and son.

"What are you thinking about?" Ender whispered.

"Aimée—I am imagining her living here."

"Don't forget, to be a slave in the harem wasn't equivalent to slavery in the States," Ender replied. "These women and their servants were treated as dependants, not inferiors."

"The wives were sequestered. That sounds like the fate of an inferior to me."

"Yes, perhaps. It was never good to be a woman in earlier times."

"My mother would have said it was better in Neolithic times." Luce smiled.

They left the harem's maze of shadowy tiled rooms and crossed the lawn to inspect the Treasury Pavilion. In the upper gallery, they found a portrait of Selim III, the sultan to whom the scribe had been writing. Selim looked kind, with droopy, sleepy eyes and a narrow nose. Selim's murderers, Ender told her, were renegade janissaries who didn't like Selim's attempts to reform the army with French military practices. Nearby hung the portrait of Mahmud, Aimée's son. Ender whispered that Mahmud didn't resemble Selim, perhaps because they had different mothers in the harem. The painting showed a man with large, intelligent eyes and a small, angry mouth partly hidden by a dark beard.

"He looks as if he spent his reign dealing with frustrations," Luce said.

"Maybe so. Mahmud fought to change the dress code to the fez and the frock coat," Ender replied. "But he was more successful with introducing Western reforms than Selim."

Out in the courtyard, they found a quiet bench in the shade, away from the bustle of the palace.

"You've finished the scribe's letter, haven't you?" she asked. He nodded.

"Why didn't you tell me?"

"It was not the right time. I wanted to prepare you. I mean, Luce, I didn't know how to prepare you—so I waited to see if an idea would come to me."

"You're warning me, aren't you, that I shouldn't expect a happy ending?"

He said nothing. He took some pages out of his knapsack and handed them over. She began to read with a certain hesitation.

In the private apartment of Nakshidil Sultan, Miss Adams saw plump *bergères* thick with pale satin cushions and giant mirrors in swagged golden frames and pretty satin-wood tables, on whose surfaces rested sweetly scented bowls of potpourri.

Miss Adams lost her tongue as Nakshidil Sultan came into the apartment, a vision of Imperial loveliness in a silk gown embroidered with emeralds and ruby-red carnations. When Nakshidil moved, her wheat-coloured hair glittered with the light of tiny diamonds. Wordlessly, Miss Adams handed her the old gentleman's letter and then she waited.

Nakshidil Sultan handed the letter back to Miss Adams with a shake of her head.

"There is some mistake," Nakshidil Sultan said. "It is not addressed to me."

When Miss Adams read it, she began to sob brokenly. I dutifully submit my translation of the old gentleman's baroque French.

*My darling Asked For,*

*By the time you read this, I will be on a coach to Edirne, Finette on my lap and Tante Flora's wig on my head to keep the autumn chill from my bones. And you will know everything, dear girl. By that, I mean it is you I love—and that I have adored you from the first moment I experienced your kindness on the public barge sailing into Venice.*

*Do not be sad, my soul. It was not my intention to arouse longings I cannot fulfill. Yet it is our longings that provide us with the text of our lives and lead us to the faiths we need to enact our destinies. And our paradox is this: the true art is not to satisfy our longings but to learn how to cherish them.*

*Aimée's letters, which first won me your sympathy, were made up of words I borrowed to please you from the letters of all the women I have loved and who loved me in return. Darling girl, with you I have felt more contented than ever before. I am certain I never will feel as contented again.*

*In a few hours, the coach will come and I will return to Bohemia and complete the history of my life. Many times, I thought of telling you the truth about Aimée Dubucq de Rivery, and knowing your kind nature, I was certain you would forgive me. But I cannot ask you to join an old crustacean when life and travel calls you. Know that I will never forget you, and that I salute you, Asked For Philosophe.*

*And so, you and I have come to the end of our journey together. I have spoken to our new friend who will look after you in Constantinople when I am gone. I have given him enough monies to see you safely to America or wherever your heart might direct—these are held in trust by him for your use.*

*My hope is that you will travel more easily through the world than I, Giacomo Casanova, who fled across Europe and Asia, seeking love and pleasure and resting nowhere for long. Wherever you alight, Asked For, may home await you. And may your adventures inspire a thousand faiths, large and small.*

*Your loving Jacob*

Miss Adams was greatly upset when she returned to our lodgings. I am not certain she heard me when I told her that I had promised the Chevalier de Seingalt that I would take her into my home if troubles befell him. And naturally, I had not had the slightest warning I would be called upon so soon to make good my words.

The poor woman lost her faculty of speech and did not talk to my wife or me for three days. She would turn her head away when Aisha approached her with food, and to my knowledge she did not eat. Instead she left the house and went for walks by the shore of the Bosphorus, not caring whether rain fell or the sun shone. Aisha was finally able to entreat her to join us at the table with bowls of sweet-smelling soup.

That said, Your Majesty, it pleases my wife to have another grown woman about. Our three young sons and two young daughters are now attempting words and discovering language. And Aisha often complains that my work as your Imperial scribe leaves her with no adult company, and she frequently catches herself babbling in a child's tongue.

And now I come to my final recommendation, but first I wish to point out that Nakshidil Sultan told Asked For Adams that she did once meet the old gentleman. When she was a girl, she recalled meeting a tall, bewigged gentleman by the name of the Chevalier de Seingalt near Nantes walking his dog in the garden. He tipped his hat and made a friendly remark to her about the swans on the grounds. Nakshidil Sultan also recalled leaving behind a small portrait of herself near P——— in Martinique. It seems the old gentleman claimed the portrait as his own and wrote the love letters under the name Nakshidil Sultan to mislead Miss Adams. It is indeed a curious story, and I do not know as I approach my final summing-up the exact nature of Miss Adams' relationship with the old gentleman. Clearly, it involved deep affection on both parts.

All that remains is for Your Majesty to accept my recommendation that Miss Adams reside under my supervision where she will be out of reach of scheming courtiers until such time as she is ready to leave. She is a dependable woman who has shown herself courageous and trustworthy with the young prince, and he has repaid her with his respect and friendship. The old gentleman, by contrast, turns out to be a practised dissembler, although Miss Adams defends him and sees good in him still.

She is pleased by the prospect of living with my family in our home. Yesterday she and my wife enjoyed *keyif* in our garden by the Bosphorus, and Miss Adams was pleased to learn that my wife speaks a little English, although Aisha must work harder to perfect her grammar.

And now I come to the moment when I must offer thanksgiving for the overflowing generosity of Your Imperial Self. The execution of my duties on Your behalf is reward enough, although I trust that Your Majesty, in Your Superior Wisdom, will allow Miss Adams to reside in my home so that I may enjoy the pleasures of speaking my father's tongue with my house guest. O Glorious Master, such conversations are precious interludes that help to bring my dear old father back to life.

This was written by the Poor, the Wretched, the Neediest of God's Mercy, the scribe Mustafa known as Sari, Son of Mustafa the Scotsman, May he rest in peace and may God forgive our sins and draw a veil over our mistakes! Amen! Completed in Konstantiniye, the capital, in the year 1212 of the Hijrah of the Prophet.

Luce put down Ender's translation of the scribe's letter and gazed with a stricken face at the Golden Horn. It was past noon, and the harbour was jammed with freighters and tourist boats bearing sightseers.

"It's so sad," she whispered.

"He's Casanova—he has to keep moving."

"But he didn't, Ender. He went back to a castle in Bohemia and spent his last days there as a librarian for a count who mistreated him."

"Well, then, perhaps his pride wouldn't let him be a burden on someone so young. His bad health in Thrace must have been humiliating for him."

"He was protecting Asked For from his old age? Is that what you mean?"

"Perhaps. I had my suspicions about those letters from Aimée Dubucq de Rivery. I have been reading the copy of the old journal you loaned me and I found some of Aimée's grammatical constructions awkward. For instance, she sometimes left off the article that French grammar requires. In Italian, you don't need to use 'the' so frequently."

"I suppose I made allowances for the French because it was written in the eighteenth century."

"Yes, I agree, the errors are subtle. But I was struck by a phrase in Aimée's last letter to Casanova: 'You are the man the most important of *all* the men.' Obviously, I thought to myself, Aimée has made a grammatical error and forgotten the comma after 'you are the man.' Otherwise why would she say such a thing? She was shut away from the world in the harem, and yet the sentence suggested she had other lovers."

"I don't understand. Why would Casanova put in an extra 'the'? Are you saying that he intended to leave it out?"

"My hunch is that he knew his tic so he put in an extra 'the' to compensate and still ended up writing French like an Italian. There are certain native tendencies we all acquire while learning a language and most of us carry those tendencies to the grave," Ender said smiling. "Even Casanova."

"That's clever of you. But I feel unsatisfied. I don't know what happened to her after she stayed in Istanbul."

"Perhaps there are more documents. They may turn up yet."

He reached over and gently encircled her wrist with his hand. She felt him hesitate as if he expected her to jerk free, and she surprised herself by letting her hand rest in the warmth of his fingers. She heard him take a little breath, and when she looked up, he was watching her with unusual seriousness.

"Maybe so," she said doubtfully.

The following afternoon, Luce awoke from a nap on the beach to feel the heat of several hard little weights on her back. She was lying on the stretch of shore in front of Ender's uncle's summer house on the Princes' Islands. She had started to write in her journal and fallen asleep. She stirred drowsily. There were tiny pulsing sensations of warmth running up and down her spine. She opened her eyes and another soft little weight, radiant with heat, touched the nape of her neck below her swim-damp hair.

"Don't move," a voice whispered. "I haven't finished."

She obeyed, thinking she was in a dream. Then she looked sideways and saw Ender's face.

"I'm going to sit up," she whispered.

He made a reproachful sound. "You can't move. You are a sea creature I've pinned to the sand."

She laughed as the last smooth, hot weight settled on her skin, now tingling from the stones and the electric brush of his fingers.

"All right. Tell me what I should do."

"You must tell me if you are involved with anyone." He lay down next to her on the sand and stared into her eyes. Luce found herself flushing with embarrassment. Out here under the fiendish afternoon sun, with the noise of the surf in her ears, and the small stones a delicately balanced weight on her back, she felt exposed. She held his eyes beneath that single, unbroken eyebrow.

"No. I prefer my own company."

He laughed.

"And you?" She raised her head and several of the small, hot stones slid onto the sand with dull little plops. "How do I know you aren't married?"

He sat up, frowning and sucking on an arm of his sunglasses, and for a moment she thought she had insulted him.

"I was engaged to someone. It ended last year. I couldn't please her." He sighed. "She accused me of being too serious. I tried to change her mind." Ender rose to his feet, the humour draining from his face. He began to brush the wet sand from his bathing suit. He looked so frustrated and unhappy that Luce rose to her feet too and touched his arm reassuringly.

"Maybe she didn't really think that. Maybe she was just afraid of being close."

"Ah, Luce. Why must you leave when I am just getting to understand you? Can't you stay on?"

"I wish I could. But my job starts again in two days."

He took her hand, shaking his head ruefully.

"You must come back, then, and together we will find out what happened to your ancestor here."

"I'll come back, Ender. I promise."

"Luce," he said, "I would like very much to believe you."

They began to walk hand in hand up the shore towards his uncle's house, their shadows stretching ahead of them on the sand in long spidery patterns.

# PART FIVE

# In Her Own Backyard

L uce was sitting in her mother's study, her study now. It overlooked the garden where the grandson of Aaron Adams had once raised sheep and tended a small orchard of pear and apple trees. Only a few fruit trees remained, and plots of phlox and blushing sedum flowered along a meandering stone path. Timothy, Aaron's grandson, had sold most of the farmland late in his life to build a summer cottage on the St. Lawrence River. But he had left his family the handsome Victorian farmhouse and garden, an island of countryside deep in the heart of the Toronto's maple-shaded Annex.

From the large picture window of her mother's study, she could see Aphrodite asleep on the table she had set for lunch under the pear tree. The goblets made of thin old Canadian glass, the silver cutlery that went back to Timothy's time, and the festive touch of the bright blue napkins. The "Sexy Fig Salad" (she had found the name in a newspaper recipe) draped with slices of prosciutto and buffalo mozzarella and a sprinkling of shredded basil waited in the kitchen along with dessert, a platter of homemade yogurt and raspberry sauce.

She had finished her preparations and Lee wasn't due for another hour at least. She walked over to the pine bookshelf on the north wall of the study. On the top shelf, her mother's collection of goddess icons sat along with the two-headed figure that Lee had purchased for her in Venice. She ran her fingers lightly along the shelves that held some of her mother's books, including *The Collected Essays of Dr. K.A. Adams*—Lee had helped Luce find a publisher for it the year before and written an introduction.

Had she put all the treasures she wanted Lee to see on the study table? She didn't want to leave anything out. Lee had been as excited as she was about the news that a scholarly journal, *North American Feminist Studies,* had agreed to publish her own article on the family documents. A copy-edited draft of "An Archivist Looks at Her Family Papers" sat on her mother's roll-top desk next to her travel diary about her trip to Istanbul. She picked up her diary and flipped through it quickly. Its pages were mostly empty. She hadn't proved to be much of a journal keeper; she knew from her work at the Miller that most journals tend to record only the unhappy moments. She put down her travel diary and picked up the copy-edited draft of her scholarly article. Although she had been through most of it the night before, she hadn't yet double-checked the preface:

> I would like to acknowledge the help of Lee Pronski who suggested *North American Feminist Studies* as a possible publisher. In addition, I wish to thank the art historian Ender Mecid, whose knowledge of Ottoman calligraphy was indispensable to my understanding of the old texts.
>
> The journal containing the "Dubucq-Casanova" letters has been authenticated by Harvard authority Charles Smith. The authenticity of the scribe's letter was more

recently confirmed by the well-known American calligrapher Ahmed Tabaa.

Aimée Dubucq de Rivery's remarkable story was well known even in its time. Many romantic novels have since been written about her and so perhaps it is no surprise that Casanova was attracted to her plight and made her the central figure in his forged letters.

Readers of the "Dubucq-Casanova" letters should note that they contain a number of Orientalist stereotypes typical of eighteenth- and nineteenth-century accounts by Western travellers in Turkey and the Balkans. I have listed some of the more offensive stereotypes for readers who may be unfamiliar with Ottoman chronicles:

No primary Ottoman sources offer evidence of Muslim women being stuffed into sacks and stoned, as described in the Adams manuscript. The common Ottoman punishments were strangling and beheading although an example of a woman being stoned to death for adultery has been related by one of the more credible Ottoman historians.

"Zak," the name given to the Muslim husband in the Adams manuscript, is not a Turkish name. Some Orientalist fiction published in France during the eighteenth century consistently gives non-existent, pseudo-Oriental names starting with the letter Z to its characters. Apparently this was viewed as exotic. Readers will find a great deal of imaginary and/or incorrect naming in Orientalist literature. The term "Arabic libraries" in one of the Dubucq-Casanova letters is likewise misguided. A large number of Western books were on the shelves in the library of Selim III. Furthermore, there is a Western tendency to use Arabic as an all-purpose adjective to indicate half a dozen languages including Persian and Ottoman

Turkish when it correctly refers to only one. Arabic is the language of civic and religious law. The effect is similar to an American using the adjective "Latin" to describe all the books in the European languages in the Library of Congress, although Orientalism, with all its faults, has created an enormous corpus of highly scholarly work on Islamic literatures.

*L.K. Adams lives in Toronto and was recently appointed assistant archivist at Miller Archives and Rare Books. The scribe's letter was translated by Ender Mecid, Ph.D., the author of* A History of Art in the Ottoman Empire. *Dr. Mecid is currently a guest lecturer at Marmara University in Istanbul.*

Luce placed her article back on her mother's desk next to a box belonging to Timothy Adams. In the box lay letters from Asked For Adams and Count Waldstein. *My Life with the Ottomans,* a small hardcover book that Ender had found in Istanbul sat nearby. He'd sent it on with a great deal of excitement because it contained a reference to her ancestor, Asked For Adams. She opened it to the note that still lay between the pages. "Dear Luce, I hoard my memories of you the way others keep money in the bank," he had written. She removed the note and gently closed the book again.

She surveyed her arrangement. She had made a kind of exhibit, she realized, for Lee's benefit. The archivist doing what she knows best—arranging a *fonds d'archives* in a satisfying order for the reader.

She looked up from her daydreaming. The doorbell was tinkling. She ran flying down the long panelled hallway to greet Lee Pronski.

After they had finished their lunch of fleshy black figs and the 1991 Meursault that Luce had bought for Lee, she led her friend into her mother's study and picked up the Ottoman memoir from her mother's desk.

"This is for you." She handed Lee the book. "And I want you to read it now."

"The afternoon is almost gone and you want me to read something?"

"Yes. I want to share it with you. Ender sent me a memoir about a woman who was a maid of honour to the princesses in the Ottoman harem. She was the granddaughter of the scribe who knew my ancestor. Are you interested now?"

"Get on with it, Luce."

"The memoir was published abroad. In 1889. It mentions a particular friend of her grandmother's. And it's worth noting that the name of her grandmother's friend was a Miss A.F. Adams. Shall I read you an excerpt?"

Lee nodded and Luce began to read the page flagged with a bookmark:

On April 20, 1846, my grandmother, Aisha, buried her American friend, Miss A.F. Adams, in the small Christian cemetery near a favourite picnic spot across from the Sweet Waters of Asia. Miss Adams' tombstone stands higher than the rest and is crowned with a large stone garland of acanthus leaves. She was like a second mother to us and loved by all my brothers and sisters. Most foreigners are determined to preach and convert but Miss Adams came to discover and revere. For that, she will be greatly missed.

Her funeral was a difficult occasion. The death of Miss Adams from malarial fever was unexpected. She had been planning a journey back to America to see her family and

towards that end she had already sent on a few of her posses-
sions. I helped her pack, and placed in the trunk some of her
journals, including the letter by my grandfather to his sultan,
Selim III, which my grandmother found after his death some
years ago and had given to her. It was precious to her, I know.
Many of her travel-writing journals had been lost in a spring
flood, despite our attempts to save them.

After my grandfather's death, Miss Adams' income had
been a boon to our family. For many years, she made a living
writing for the British newspapers, using a male pseudonym.
We were all overjoyed when her journey across the Black Sea
in a Montgolfier balloon was reviewed in an edition of a
London literary journal featuring twelve women travel writers.
I recall Miss Adams telling my grandmother that she first sub-
mitted her article as A. Adams with a note that she was "a stu-
dent of the East." She was delighted to discover that the publication welcomed contributions from literary gentlewomen.


Luce put down the Ottoman memoir. Aphrodite had
climbed on to Lee's lap and she stroked him as she gazed out
at the garden whose drowsy September fragrance was drifting
in through the study window. Luce recognized the stern
expression. It signalled that Lee was absorbed by her
thoughts.

"So your ancestor made herself a new life in Istanbul?"

"Yes. As a travel writer," Luce said. "It seems she found a
family who loved her, too."

Lee picked up her Borsalino that lay discarded beside her
chair, and the cat jumped off her lap. She fingered her hat
thoughtfully. It was a new fedora, serpent brown with chocolate banding. "I wish we knew how she felt about Casanova."

"Oh, but I do know. And I can prove it to you."

"What's that?"

"Just wait." Luce picked up the wooden box belonging to Timothy Adams. She was aware of pausing dramatically to arouse Lee's curiosity. "I have Asked For's response to Casanova's last letter to her. My aunt found several more letters hidden in some of my great-great-great-grandfather's things. These wooden boxes were given to Canadian senators on their appointment. The boxes were usually filled with paper, pens, nibs, even a porcelain block on which to doodle—"

"Luce, why did you wait to tell me? Have I told you that you can be really infuriating?"

"Yes, many times. But listen, please. Asked For tried to write to Casanova, only he died in 1798 before her letter reached him. Timothy Adams put Asked For's letter to Casanova in this box. My aunt says he must not have known what to do with it. The letter must have just been more embarrassing evidence of a relationship outside marriage that wasn't considered proper in Victorian times. But I'd like to think he thought about Asked For and wondered what he should do."

"Get on with it, Luce."

"It's what I've been waiting to do." She opened the box and took out the letter.


*October 19, 1800*

*Dear Jacob,*

*I have been too angry to write since you left Constantinople three years ago. How I hated you for going to such lengths to fool me. And for your foolish belief that you needed to deceive me in order to*

*arouse my interest. But you must understand that I hated myself
too. I began suspecting you had forged the letters from Aimée when
we were travelling through Thrace. You muttered things in your
feverish state that led me to this conclusion. When you recovered, I
waited for you to confide what you had done and I promised myself
I would forgive you. When you did not tell me about your forgeries, I
punished you by insisting that we journey on to find Aimée. Pride,
Father always said, is an Adams failing. Had I not concealed my
knowledge, our path might have been different.*

*Enough time has gone by for me to have a deeper understand-
ing of our love for each other. And I have made a new life for
myself in this extraordinary city. I am sorry now that I did not
come out and say what I felt because I no longer believe you
meant to hurt me. It is true that I was naive, but perhaps I
needed you to deceive me. How else could I throw off the yoke of
a domestic future with Francis? I realize now that you wanted
me to live without the burden of an older person to nurse. You
were wrong. Let me join you in Dux and you will see for yourself
how gladly I shoulder such a burden.*

*Your Asked For*

"She knew," Luce said. "She knew he had deceived her. And
she wanted to punish him. I think I can understand. I used to
think there was something pathetic about people who allow
their hearts to be broken."

"We are always afraid of being played for a fool," Lee said.

"At least she created a new life in a foreign city. But wait—
there is one more thing: a reply to her letter from Count
Waldstein," Luce said.

*December 6, 1800*

*Dear Asked For Adams,*
   *The Chevalier de Seingalt died two years ago from an infection. His death occurred a few days before a visit from the chemist, Isaac Bey, who arrived too late with his herbs and medicines and the crayfish he loved. Monsieur Bey thought you would like to know how happy you had made the Chevalier de Seingalt at the end of his life. So he asked me to send on the letters written to him by the Chevalier during your journey together.*

*Count Waldstein*

"Well, what do you think, Lee? Do you still dislike Casanova?"

"Who said I disliked him? He was a creature of Venice, the city that spawned him. He wasn't able to moor himself to anyone. But he knew how to enjoy life. I admire him for that. And for his appreciation of—"

"Of women?" Luce was smiling wryly.

"You are your mother's child, aren't you? You go straight to the point. I suppose you know what happened to Casanova after he left Asked For in Istanbul?"

"It's in an essay by Arthur Symons. You know him? He's the Victorian scholar who discovered the two missing chapters from Casanova's published memoirs."

Lee shook her head.

"Yes, Symons discovered chapters four and five from the final volume. Of course, I hoped he would have found a letter that referred to Asked For Adams. But he makes no mention of Casanova's visit to Venice at the end of his life. He does refer to Finette, Casanova's dog. When I read this, I felt as if I could reach out and touch Jacob Casanova."

"Is Symons a reliable biographer?"

"Yes. He visited Count Waldstein's castle a hundred years after Casanova's death. He found the missing chapters of the memoirs in one of the six cardboard cases full of Casanova's manuscripts and letters in the library where Casanova worked. It was on the ground floor with some twenty-five thousand volumes and an engraved portrait of Casanova on the wall."

"I can see that you've done your research. I should expect that by now from you, shouldn't I?"

Luce smiled at her. "That's enough about Casanova. I have a special dessert waiting, one I don't think you've ever tried before."

# Epilogue

Luce Adams
The Miller Archives and Special Collections
131 Huron Street
Toronto

March 15, 2005

Dear Luce:

    Thank you for your invitation to go with you and
Ender to research Asked For's travels around the Black
Sea. How curious to remember that his translation of the
scribe's document was what first brought you together. It
seems like a long time ago now.

    I wish I could go with you. None of us can live without
the occasional wild journey that tells us what we're made
from, can we? But my summer course finishes in August and
until then Lynn-Anne and I are content teaching and reading. Every afternoon, we walk to the ocean to watch the fishing boats come in. I've told her that you work in an important archives up in Canada and sift through your old documents wearing a white lab coat. Do you still use it? The last
time I visited I thought it made you look like a pastry chef.

Love,<br>Lee

P.S. I researched the scribe's description of Bendis, the
goddess of the thieves. As far as I know, Bendis has no
relationship to Aphrodite although Bendis was associated
with Artemis. As Mistress of the Wild Beasts, she would
have taken the form of a bird, possibly a raptor. I will
check Farnell's *The Cults of the Greek States* and send a
note to Ender if I find anything.

Lee Pronski
22 Homecrest Avenue
Sheepshead Bay, Brooklyn, New York
11235

April 2, 2005

Dearest Lee,

Do you realize I am writing you on Casanova's birthday, "blackening paper," as he would put it? I am in the Reading Room, the last place you might expect to find someone on an early spring evening. How hard it is to believe that in a few days Ender and I will be thousands of miles from this gracious library with its rosy Persian carpet and six storeys of old books and folios. Only moments ago, one of the regulars stopped reading and smiled at me, the pool of light from his study lamp warming his bearded face. I smiled back and he returned to his reading, murmuring the words out loud to himself. My assistant affectionately calls him the Hummer although he is a professor of history and has a dignified Anglo-Saxon name. I try to be stern with professors (no slur intended, Lee). But tonight I am too full of anticipation to chide him even though professors frequently break our rules, licking the pages or making notes with messy ballpoint pens instead of using the pencils we provide.

They believe tenure gives them the right to leave yellow Post-it notes on our archival material no matter how many times I point out that the Miller has some of the oldest books and manuscripts in the world. One comes across strange behaviour here. It's the concentrated atmosphere. On some days, this place feels like an enormous bedroom where people sit reading and not speaking, as if they are having sex without touching.

Yes, I still wear a white coat along with a pair of cotton gloves if I'm looking at one of the Shakespearean folios. I trust you still have your fedora. It was very striking. I thought you'd be interested to know that I have donated the original journal of Asked For Adams and the scribe's letter to the Miller and I keep the old documents in a special room in the stacks where a humidity gauge is fixed at forty percent. (A change from the way I used to lug them around in Venice, isn't it?) Casanova's letters will be given to a reputable auction house on our return. The Sansovinian has had them long enough.

If anything happens to me, you will know where to find the family papers. Not that I expect things to go wrong. Ender and I are both disappointed you and your new friend can't come with us. His course secretary has found us a roomy old house in the hills outside Istanbul. It has four bedrooms, more than enough for the two of you if you change your mind.

It's only a matter of days before we are on our way.

I just thought of Casanova again. He once wrote that all he needed to be happy was a library. He would have liked the notion of the Miller as a bedroom, wouldn't he?

Love,<br>Luce

P.S. I just took another look at the travel principles of Jacob Casanova. They hold up very well but I think they are summed up nicely in his wish for Asked For Adams.

*Wherever you alight, may home await you.*

ACKNOWLEDGEMENTS

I would like to thank the late Jack Crean who first recommended Casanova's memoir about escaping from the Leads; Carol Christ for introducing me to Minoan Crete and for writing *Odyssey with the Goddess: A Spiritual Quest in Crete*; Alberto Manguel for taking me to Venice; Judith Keenan for making my novel the subject of the first BookShort; my beloved editor Louise Dennys who was there from the beginning; Kendall Anderson for her first-rate editorial acumen; Bernice Eisenstein, Chris Doda and Noelle Zitzer for crucial editorial suggestions in the early stages; the extraordinary agents Bruce Westwood, Hilary McMahon, Nicole Winstanley, Derek Johns, Kim Witherspoon and Alexis Hurley for finding the right publisher; Toronto archaeologist Mima Kapches for showing me the similarity between novelists and archaeologists; Patrick Crean and Samantha Haywood for loving support; Karen Rinaldi for her honesty and insights; writer Lynne Suo for the magic of her farm; Tricia Postle and Patricia Hluchy for their time and Sumach Press for its hospitality; Johanna Stuckey for being a special reader and for writing *An Introduction to Feminist Theology in*

*Judaism, Christianity, Islam and Feminist Goddess Worship*; Russell Smith and Joy von Tiedemann for help with the young photographer; Natalee Caple for her insights on her generation; Domenico Pietropaulo for his work on Casanova's grammatical tics; Karen Connelly for sharing the isolation of novel writing and for her understanding of Greece; Vicki Poulakakis, James Papoutsis, Gale Zoe Garnett and Stavroula Logethettis for help with the Greek language, and Francesco D'Angelo for her understanding of Italian; the archivists Sean Smith, Suzanne Dubeau, Luba Frastacky and Richard Landon for unstinting support; Deirdre Molina and Janine Laporte at Knopf Canada for their help in the thirteenth hour; John Knechtel and Diana Bryden for research; professor Amila Buturovic for leading me to Irvin Schick; and Irvin Schick (author of *Writing the Body in Islam*) for his astonishing erudition, help and insights into Western travellers in the Ottoman Empire.

Hundreds of books helped to make *What Casanova Told Me*. I am particularly indebted to *No Place for a Lady: Tales of Adventurous Women Travelers* by Barbara Hodgson; *Venice* by Jan Morris; *Sheep's Vigil by a Fervent Person* by Erin Moure; *Minotaur: Sir Arthur Evans and the Archaeology of the Minoan Myth* by Joseph Alexander MacGillivray; *The Imperial Harem of the Sultans* by Leyla Hanimefendi; *The Travels of Theophile Gauthier* by F.C. De Sumichrast; *Night Letters* by Robert Dessaix; *The Man Who Really Loved Women* by Lydia Flem; *Abigail Adams: Witness to a Revolution* by Natalie Bober; *The Language of the Goddess* by Marija Gimbutas; *Casanova at Dux* by Arthur Symons; and of course, *History of My Life, Vols. 1 to 12* by Giacomo Casanova, Chevalier De Seingalt.

Susan Swan's critically acclaimed fiction has been published in twenty countries. Her novel, *The Wives of Bath*, was a finalist for the U.K.'s Guardian Award and Ontario's Trillium Award, and was made into the feature film *Lost and Delirious*, which was shown in thirty-two countries. *What Casanova Told Me* was a finalist for the Commonwealth Writers' Prize (Canada and Caribbean Region). It was a *Globe and Mail* Best Book; a *Calgary Herald* Top 10; a *Now* (Toronto) Top 10; and a *Sun Times* (Owen Sound) Top 10; and Asked For Adams was named one of *Maclean's* magazines Top 5 characters.

Swan shares a Puritan background with her heroine Asked For Adams. A branch of Swan's family immigrated to America in 1635. They settled on farmland near Boston, then moved on to Connecticut. Two centuries later some of the family immigrated to Canada.

Swan lives in Toronto and is an associate professor of Humanities at York University.

Please visit Swan's website at www.susanswanonline.com.